ALSO BY NED BEAUMAN

Boxer, Beetle

The Teleportation Accident

Glow

MADNESS

IS BETTER THAN

DEFEAT

MADNESS

IS BETTER THAN

DEFEAT

WITHDRAWN

Ned Beauman

Alfred A. Knopf · New York · 2018

THIS IS A BORZOI BOOK
PUBLISHED BY ALFRED A. KNOPF

Copyright © 2017 by Ned Beauman

All rights reserved. Published in the United States by Alfred A. Knopf, a division of Penguin Random House LLC, New York. Originally published in Great Britain by Sceptre, an imprint of Hodder & Stoughton, a Hachette UK company, London, in 2017.

www.aaknopf.com

Knopf, Borzoi Books, and the colophon are registered trademarks of Penguin Random House LLC.

Quote from *Heart of Darkness* appears courtesy of the Estate of Orson Welles. Represented exclusively by Reeder Brand Management.

Library of Congress Cataloging-in-Publication Data
Names: Beauman, Ned, author.
Title: Madness is better than defeat / by Ned Beauman.
Description: First United States edition. | New York : Alfred A. Knopf, 2018. | "This is a Borzoi Book." | "Originally published in Great Britain by Sceptre, an imprint of Hodder & Stoughton, a Hachette UK company, London, in 2017."
Identifiers: LCCN 2017024820 (print) | LCCN 2017027794 (ebook) | ISBN 9780385352994 (hardcover) | ISBN 9780385353007 (ebook)
Subjects: | BISAC: FICTION / Literary. | FICTION / Psychological.
Classification: LCC PR6102.E225 (ebook) | LCC PR6102.E225 M33 2018 (print) | DC 823/.92—dc23
LC record available at https://lccn.loc.gov/2017024820

Jacket design by Tyler Comrie

Manufactured in the United States of America
First United States Edition

PART ONE

Madness is better than defeat. Down the river is the light of reason.

(From Orson Welles's screenplay for an unproduced adaptation of Heart of Darkness, *1939)*

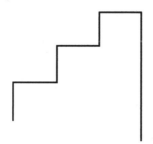

SPRINGFIELD, VIRGINIA—1959

The tribunal will not reconvene until I've had a chance to consider all the available evidence in my case. That is my right as an American and as an officer of the Central Intelligence Agency. If the testimony I've submitted is true, then the proof may be somewhere in that warehouse, and therefore I must be allowed to look for it. My persecutors pretend to regard this rule as an inconvenience, because without it they'd be permitted to empty the warehouse tomorrow to make more room for stolen Politburo cigar stubs or whatever else they want to archive out here in Virginia. But really it delights them. There's no easy way to take a measure of "all the available evidence in my case," but I estimate it at about three hundred million feet, an alchemical prodigy of urine and rock salt and Mayan armor, glossy bales decomposing into nitric frass. To pick through it all with proper care, building a chronology and a concordance, is the work of decades. And I don't have decades.

This is how I know. During the failed Cuban War of Independence in 1868, a wealthy Spanish family called the Azpeteguias, who owned sugar plantations near the Valle de Viñales, were besieged inside their villa by their own farmers. They died of yellow fever, all sixteen of them, before they could be relieved by the army. It was decided to send the bodies to Havana for burial to ensure they wouldn't be desecrated by the locals. But the farmers ambushed the caravan in the hills, prying open the coffins and tipping the bodies into the dust. In 1953, when I was still working for the agency in Cuba, I did a significant favor for a friend of mine in Pinar del Río and afterward he gave me a bottle of rum that had been aged in a barrel made from staves of Azpeteguia coffin wood.

I have about twelve ounces left. It's what's called a diagnostic liquor. According to folk medicine, the long aftertaste is the most volatile fraction of the rum escaping out of your mouth as tinted vapor after it's already washed through your guts. You taste yourself on it. There are some old bourbons with the same property. When I first opened it, back when I was in good health, Azpeteguia *añejo* was the most exquisite rum I'd ever sipped, but now I can taste poison at the end of every mouthful, a bile so rank and doomy your standard pre-vomit is like maple syrup in comparison. One of these days I'll have a doctor palpate my liver just to make it official, but I know perfectly well what he'll tell me. Between my stomach and my lungs sits a wedge of black gristle. Instead of a functioning organ I have only a ruin, a sinkhole, a blocked sewer.

I'm forty-three years old. Alcoholism runs in the Zonulet family and it's going to kill me even younger than it killed my father. I will die long before I finish preparing my defense. Early on, I asked if I could have an assistant to help me hack through this jungle, but they said they wouldn't give security clearance to anyone but me. They've fucked me and they know it. Really, there is no need for the tribunal to reconvene, because a life sentence has already been handed down, in the most elegant possible fashion, with nothing so clattering or banal as a verdict spoken aloud. I am my own jailer, in the prison of my inalienable rights. They know I never wanted anything more to do with that temple, and now I'll be trapped for the remainder of my life among its ribbons of silver drool.

From the very beginning I've given the same testimony. I did everything I could to prevent what happened in Honduras, but the forces arrayed against me were too powerful (and some of those same forces are now discreetly overseeing my prosecution). The censure I'm threatened with is not proportionate to the rules I may have bent or broken in pursuit of entirely valid aims, nor to my peripheral culpability in a sequence of events that for the most part were far beyond my control. I'm a fallible human being, and I regret the mistakes I made, but with a sound mind and a clear conscience I can avow that I was acting in the best interests of my country. I know dozens of guys back in Foggy Bottom who've done much, much worse and suffered nothing but commiserations on their bad luck.

I spent a decade with CIA, and three years with the Office of Strategic Services before that, and what do I have to show for it? Just one friend, Winch McKellar, my only ally in the whole crew. He's back from Jakarta now, but he can't do anything to help. Sometimes I'm tempted to go to *The Washington Post* and tell them everything I know about Branch 9, and sometimes I'm tempted to burn the warehouse to the ground with myself inside, but what keeps me from either variety of self-immolation is that the proof I'm looking for, the proof that would vindicate the testimony I submitted to the tribunal, is somewhere on those shelves. In theory, I might find it tomorrow. That is, at least, mathematically possible.

In any case, if I do die before I hit the jackpot, I want it to be there in the warehouse. They'll wonder where the smell is coming from until they notice my body draped across a steel roof truss like a pair of sneakers tossed over a telephone line. No one will be able to figure out how I got up there and they'll have to fish me down with a crane.

So every night I stay there until ten or eleven o'clock at night with my flatbed editor and my notebooks. Then I peel off my gloves, say goodbye to the guard, and stop at the diner on the way home for a hamburger that tastes like scorched oakum. Back at my apartment, I don't sleep much, so I'm never sure how to pass the time. But now I have a hobby. *Tap tap tap tappety tap.*

This is going to be a tell-all. But the only person who's ever likely to read it is the junior from the Office of Security who, after my death, will be assigned to examine my papers and prepare a detailed report on their contents. Presumably, that whelp is going to wonder how I seem to know so much about what happened to people I've never met in places I've never been.

A great deal of what's done at the agency is textual analysis of some kind—often, in its methods, verging on literary criticism or scriptural exegesis—and one of the guys who helped train us in OSS was the Yale ethnologist Newton Mathers. He spent years studying the oral traditions of the Amazon, which are of inconstant usefulness if you're looking for solid historical fact, and he taught us always to look for what he called "the stench of truth." A stench is a stench because it's too complex and microbial and surprising to be merely an odor. Created things have odors. Natural things have stenches.

Since the whelp from the Office of Security will already have been told that before my death I submitted an absolutely cockamamie testimony to the tribunal, he may assume this memoir is just an elaboration of that fantasy. But if he judges that it's detailed and consistent and lifelike enough to exude the stench of truth, and he knows I didn't have some treasure chest of surveillance reports and wiretap transcripts to draw from, he'll be looking for an explanation. Is it really possible that, from only the data I had available to me in the warehouse, I inferred the rest of the universe? That, from just a few clues, I filled out the measureless crossword?

In our first week with him, Old Man Mathers gave us Leibniz to read. "Let us suppose that someone jots down a quantity of points helter-skelter upon a sheet of paper," Leibniz writes in his *Discourse on Metaphysics*. "Now I say that it is possible to find a geometrical line, whose concept shall be uniform and constant, in accordance with a certain formula, which will pass through all of those points, and in the same order in which the hand jotted them down. When the formula is very complex, that which conforms to it passes for irregular. But God does nothing out of order." Even the jotting isn't truly helter-skelter. Everything happens for its own opaque reasons. Consequently, if you have enough of the points to deduce the formula that determines them, you can in turn deduce all the other points you don't already have.

If it sounds like I'm stretching Leibniz a little far, recall that he goes even further himself. "When we consider carefully the connection of things," he writes, "we can say that from all time in a man's soul there are vestiges of everything that has happened to him and marks of everything that will happen to him and even traces of everything that happens in the universe." In other words, you can deduce every formula from just one point. Maybe it will take a few days' interrogation for that point to break, but it will spill its guts eventually.

Yet that isn't how I did it. I didn't discover the formula. I didn't read the traces in one point or extrapolate from many, like a diligent intelligence analyst. I used a much cruder method, almost a cheat. I went to the aleph, the point from which all other points are visible. I crawled inside that temple in Honduras and I saw everything at once. If you asked the director of *Hearts in Darkness,* the most ill-starred movie in Hollywood history, he'd assure you that the gods talked to me in there. I maintain that the explanation is mycological. What the whelp will conclude, I don't know. He'll be my obituarist, my executor, and my grave robber all rolled into one, so perhaps in the long run his opinion is the only one that counts.

When he sees the cinder block of typescript on my desk and real-izes he's going to have to crawl through the whole thing, perhaps he'll feel the same way I did when the guard flipped on the halide lamps my first day at the warehouse: I cannot possibly get through all this. That would be fine by me. I'm past the point of cultivating a readership, which I had to do not only as a crime reporter with the *New York Evening Mirror* but also as a case officer of the CIA. I remember a supervisor of mine once rejected my account of a brawl I'd witnessed among some communists in Paris because it was "too Hemingway." The reference was a little out of date but along the right lines. The agency generates millions of pages of documents a year, much of that in the form of first-person narratives, and although the internal literature of the agency may never have had its Modernist or its Beat period, it's absurd to suppose that a bunch of neophiliac college-educated guys at their typewriters would be totally unaf-fected by what's going on out there at the publishing houses that in some cases they're secretly funding. I asked my supervisor what style I should write the report in, and he shouted back, "You don't write in any style at all, Zonulet, you just damned well put down what happened!" Obviously after that I couldn't write another word for about a month.

This time, though, I don't have to worry about critics. So I won't agonize about where to begin. I'm going to begin twenty-one years ago, in 1938, on 49th Street in Manhattan, with a bet.

⚬

The terms of this bet declared that for every ten seconds under sixty seconds it took the diver to wrestle the octopus out of the tank, Elias Coehorn Jr. would lose a hundred dollars, and for every ten seconds over sixty seconds, he'd win the same increment. The diver that night was a Chelsea longshoreman who could break your nose so badly with one right hook that a doctor would have to tweezer the cartilage out through your nostrils, and he'd never been known to take more than a minute and a half to humble an octopus. Once or twice he'd even flipped the beast out of the tank almost the instant the bell rang with the nonchalance of a teenage swimming pool attendant retrieving a deflated flotation aid. "The first thing you have to learn," he'd been heard to say, "is that you can't put a crotch hold on a fucker with eight crotches."

Although Coehorn had stamped on his own wristwatch back at his friend Irma's apartment to emphasize some rhetorical point that could not now be recalled, he estimated that it was some time after midnight on Saturday, which meant he'd been up for at least thirty-six hours, and his own consciousness floated in a tank of champagne, gin, cocaine, hashish, Benzedrine, and sewing machine oil. Despite all that, he didn't need a slide rule to tell him that those odds weren't in his favor. And yet he'd taken the bet anyway, because he believed this particular octopus wouldn't give up so easily. Earlier, as he'd stood there with Irma admiring the noble bulge of its purple cranium, she'd pointed out that this captive Martian had only seven intact limbs. Petticoat rags of intertentacular membrane trailed from the stump of the eighth. This octopus already knew what it felt like to fight for its life.

"Hey," someone said to Coehorn, "anybody ever tell you you look just that singer, uh . . . what's his name?"

Coehorn rolled his eyes at Irma. "Frank Parker?"

"Yeah!"

"Only about half a million times."

The impresario who organized these weekend sprees in the basement library of the derelict New York headquarters of the Bering Strait Railroad Association of North America had never bothered to clear out the rotting atlases from the bookshelves, and the sulfides in the blue inks had begun to give the dead oceans within an appropriately algal reek. Tonight the whole venue was so alarmingly crowded that if you wanted to provoke a morbid giggle from your date you could point at the precarious candelabras and make a reference to the recent West Side abattoir fire that had turned the Hudson into bouillon for a day. I was on my way to 49th Street myself, because I was hoping to run down a source of mine in the Boilermakers' Union case I was looking into for the *New York Evening Mirror,* but I wouldn't arrive at the basement for another few minutes. As I've explained, this memoir is going to describe a number of events that I didn't see with my own eyes but learned about some years later when I went inside the temple.

The hubbub diminished a little as the diver got to the top of the stepladder beside the tank. The thin straps of his black swimming costume did such a tenuous job of containing his pectorals that they brought to mind a burlesque dancer's lingerie. After taking a bow he turned back toward the tank and bent his knees in readiness like a marble Kratos on a plinth. "Good Lord, look at him," said Irma appreciatively. Coehorn himself found ostentatious sexual characteristics—in physique, dress, or behavior—to be unattractive in both males and females. Having sampled everything under the sun, he now felt that his ideal concubine would be a wiry hermaphrodite, equipped for any configuration, groomed and tailored so exquisitely as to transcend sex. He tried to get the octopus's attention, hoping to communicate his warm wishes, but too many different refractive media were interposed. Then, as the bell rang and the diver made his short dive, Coehorn felt a hand on his arm. He turned.

"I didn't know you were a gambler, Mr. Parker."

If you found this creature scampering around your kitchen one night you'd telephone for a fumigator, and although there was an oily familiarity to his manner, Coehorn was certain they'd never met before.

"Yes, I'm banned from the Saratoga track, so I have to come here instead," he replied sardonically. Two in a row. Sometimes he found himself resenting Frank Parker as deeply as if the crooner had adopted the resemblance as a willful mode of bullying. Parker was an Italian Jew who'd changed his name, whereas Coehorn didn't have a drop of Jewish blood. Plus Parker was at least five years older. The most insulting episode of all was when he was approached by a scout from a celebrity impersonators' agency called Seeing Double! who told him that he could probably get some occasional work if he were willing to pay for his own singing lessons.

"I ain't had the pleasure of your acquaintance, ma'am," said the ratty man, turning to Irma, "but I hope you'll allow me to say that the two of you make a very eye-catching couple."

"We aren't together," said Coehorn.

"Oh, I'm sorry. Well, in any case . . ." He stuck out his hand. "Leland Trimble. *New York Evening Mirror.*" He really seemed to have convinced himself that Coehorn was Frank Parker. Coehorn was about to tell him to go to hell when he saw Irma turn pale.

Not more than thirty seconds had passed since the splash, but he was astonished, in a woozy sort of way, by what he saw when he turned back to the tank. The octopus seemed to be riding the diver piggyback, with its beak nuzzling between his shoulder blades. Two of its tentacles were suctioned to the glass wall of the tank for leverage; two more had the diver's wrists trussed behind his back; a fifth tentacle was a long way down the diver's throat; and a sixth, though concealed by the seat of the swimming costume, seemed to be equally deep in the diver's rectum.

The notion of an octopus getting the drop on a wrestler was as laughable as the notion of a greased piglet at a county fair trampling the farmhands trying to catch it, but on the other hand this could hardly have been a deliberate strategy on the diver's part, and the diver's bulging eyes were enough to assure Coehorn that he'd been correct in his earlier evaluation of the octopus's vigor. Apart from a few chattering girls at the opposite end of the basement who probably didn't even know there was a fight going on, an uneasy silence had fallen over the crowd. By the time the clock showed sixty seconds, you could tell from the kicking of the diver's legs that his current ambition was not so much to unknot himself from the rapine harness as it was simply to get up to the surface of the water where he might have a chance of breathing through his nose. But the octopus wouldn't even let him do that. He should have been able to hold his breath without any trouble for at least three, maybe three and a half minutes, but perhaps the shock of enclosing about a foot of mollusk at each end, like reverse food poisoning, had prematurely loosed a few pints of air. Coehorn wondered how that would feel. He'd had dicks in his mouth and his ass at the same time before but, fortunately or unfortunately, none of them had been prehensile.

"Which way did you bet, Mr. Parker?" said Trimble.

"Long," said Coehorn.

"Same here! You know, the rules say the clock keeps running until either the diver or the octopus is out of the tank. So, technically, if he croaks in there, they got to keep paying until somebody dredges one of them out. We've got a home run on our hands. Unless they argue that he's not in the tank any more because he's already in heaven, but I don't think they could get away with that."

"You don't mean he could actually die?" said Irma.

"I don't see why not," said Coehorn.

"Isn't anyone going to do anything?"

"Like what?"

"Smash the glass and get him out."

"What about the octopus? It's only defending itself."

"You can fill up a sink for it in the men's room," said Irma.

"This waistcoat is lacewing silk and my tailor specifically told me not to get so much as a drop of water on it."

"For heaven's sake, Elias, if I have to watch that man die I won't be able to sleep for a year!"

Coehorn could never say no to Irma, who was very sensitive. Also, this would make a good anecdote. "Well, all right." He rolled up both sleeves, knowing there was a particular phrase you always said in this kind of situation. Then he remembered it. "Stand back, everyone."

"Hey, hey, hold on just a second, Mr. Parker," said Trimble. "How much are you up?"

Coehorn looked at the clock. He was now up three hundred dollars. If he made five hundred dollars tonight, which would only take another seventeen seconds, he could hand it straight over to Irma to reimburse her for the money she'd lost on the paintings he'd taken it upon himself to entrust to that "charming" "White Russian" "gallerist" while she was away in the desert, which would be a wonderful gesture. Surely she would prefer that to this capricious intervention in the life of a stranger, and if there was a choice of problems to solve, Coehorn always preferred to solve the one he could solve neatly with money. Admittedly, he wasn't sure that in good conscience he was allowed to put off saving the diver's life for another seventeen seconds. But perhaps he was allowed to put off making the decision about whether he was allowed to put off saving the diver's life for another seventeen seconds for another seventeen seconds. That is, for another sixteen seconds. Fifteen seconds.

"Elias!" shrieked Irma.

By now the seventh tentacle of the octopus had blindfolded the diver, who was still wriggling like a bad escape artist but looked as if he was beginning to slacken. Shuffling from foot to foot, Coehorn willed the time to go faster. When he glanced at the spectators behind him he found them as detached as masturbators. Deciding that Irma was right and he'd rather find her last hundred dollars somewhere else than wait another nine seconds, he reached for the metal stepladder so he could smash the tank with it.

But just as he was hoisting it unsteadily over his head, four hands yanked at his shoulders and the stepladder crashed back to the stone floor.

At first he assumed that some other gamblers who'd bet long on the octopus were trying to keep him from curtailing their prize. But then, instead of the punch in the nose he'd been expecting, he felt himself being dragged backward through the crowd.

Twisting left and right, he saw that his new escorts were two men in black serge suits, built like sasquatches, even more muscular than the diver. Coehorn owed a lot of people money but he was careful about the lenders he used—nothing more harrowing had ever resulted from his delinquency than a chocolate box full of dead cockroaches in the mail—so there was almost no chance that these were thugs here to collect. "Irma, stop them!"

But Irma was now struggling to lift the stepladder herself, and the other spectators were still too entranced by the floor show to notice Coehorn's abduction. "Whoever you're looking for, I can guarantee it's not me!" It wasn't until he was at the stairwell that he came up with another guess about what might have happened. "Now, listen, I'm not Frank Parker! Do you hear me? I don't know what he's done, but I'm not him! I just look like him. If he was younger." He craned his neck for one last look at the diver, but Irma and the tank were already out of sight.

I'd just arrived at the building, and at the top of the stairs I had to press myself up against the wall to let the three men past. The recent craze among midtown filing clerks for a new chewing tobacco that was supposed to whiten your teeth had turned the sidewalks here piebald. Outside, Coehorn found 49th Street painfully bright. "Good grief, is it Sunday morning already?" he asked, squinting. That's the only part of this I saw with my own eyes.

For the first time one of the sasquatches spoke. "Monday morning."

"Oh," said Coehorn.

Without loosening their grips, they marched him to a Buick limousine parked at the corner. Waiting in the front seat was a chauffeur and on the back seat a steel bucket. Coehorn got in, moved the bucket from the seat to the floor, and sat down with a sasquatch on either side of him. "We won't need this," he said, "I'm not going to puke. I never puke." As the chauffeur started the engine, the sasquatch on Coehorn's left took from his trouser pocket what looked like an asthmatic's nebulizer. "What's that?" said Coehorn. The sasquatch jammed the nozzle of the nebulizer up Coehorn's nose and gave the bulb three brisk clenches.

Coehorn felt as if he'd been shot in the frontal lobe with a bullet made of mustard powder and static charge. Turquoise flares went off in his eyes and he got a strange cramp at the base of his tongue. Then he felt the remains of his last meal stampeding out of him. He bent over the bucket and puked so hard he thought he was going to punch through the bottom. When he'd finished, the sasquatch on his right handed him a silk handkerchief and a glass ampule of lavender water, so Coehorn gargled and wiped his mouth before dropping both the handkerchief and the empty bottle into his dregs. The sasquatch cranked down the tinted side window, dropped the bucket into the road, and cranked the window back up before Coehorn could get any idea of which direction they were headed.

That was when Coehorn realized he wasn't swacked any more. Careful introspection didn't turn up the slightest blush of champagne, gin, cocaine, hashish, Benzedrine, or sewing machine oil. He had no hangover. And he didn't even particularly want a cigarette. His head hadn't felt so clear since he was about sixteen. The tank had been smashed, and now he lay there in a puddle with nothing between him and the grasping fingers of the world. As a child, Coehorn had been a drooping orchid—bilious and photophobic, deeply in love with his bed and his dog, so late to puberty you might have taken him for a castrato—until the day he got drunk for the first time and discovered he could be as gallant as anyone else for as long as he forgot that he wasn't. "What did you just give me?" he mumbled. The sasquatches didn't answer. Deglazed by this horrible new clarity, Elias Coehorn Jr. now found himself able to deduce his real destination without any trouble. The sasquatches didn't think he was Frank Parker. They knew exactly who he was.

They were taking him to see his father.

By the late 1930s, Elias Coehorn Sr. was an almost mythological figure in New York life, a frost giant or skyscraper khan, honored in the persecution fantasies of more raving Bowery bums than anyone else in the country. And he was not the type whose aura dissipates the first time you meet him in person. Quite the opposite. In 1934, during my very first week working at the *Mirror,* I went to interview an albino from Mott Haven who had managed to convince a lot of people that God was in the habit of schmoozing with him directly. God, he reported, had plenty to say about the dismal future of the United States under a socialist president. We'd scheduled the interview over the telephone, but when I arrived at his apartment he was no longer interested. "I'm going to see Elias Coehorn this afternoon," he said, meaning Elias Coehorn Sr. "He told me I couldn't talk to the press in the meantime." Elias Coehorn Sr., in addition to being one of the wealthiest men in New York, was an avid collector of Christian visionaries, and the albino was understandably giddy because this had the potential to be a very lucrative engagement. When I got back to the office, however, Beverly Pomutz, my editor, called me a "fucking witless mealworm" for taking no for an answer. So the next morning I returned to Mott Haven without an appointment, and I found a husk of the guy I'd met the previous day. He was curled up under a blanket like an invalid. "Coehorn saw right through me," he said. "He knew right away I was making it up. The way he looked at me . . . It was so fucking scary." "So scary it almost turned your hair black?" I joked, facetiously. But the "albino" missed the joke. "No, actually, it won't grow out black for another few weeks." He confessed that he paled himself with bleach, rice powder, and eye drops. "Coehorn saw that right away too. I don't know how. Nobody else ever guessed."

I never met Elias Coehorn Sr. in person myself (although I believe I later came very close—only a matter of inches between us). But everyone I knew who did, whether they wanted to admit it or not, felt like they'd barely escaped with their souls. Even Elias Coehorn Jr., who'd had a lifetime to get used to his father, and made a policy of regarding him with utter derision, had to steel himself as he was ushered into his father's office on the thirty-second floor of the Pine Street headquarters of the Eastern Aggregate Company.

There was no chair on the near side of the titanic mahogany desk, so he asked for one. Phibbs, his father's private secretary, started to say that he'd be happy to fetch one from the vestibule, but he was interrupted: "My son will stand and listen."

Coehorn Sr.'s thin face was framed, as ever, by bushy white sideburns and an upturned detachable collar; he'd permanentized his style four decades ago, around the same time he'd permanentized his diction, ridding it of the last traces of the Pennsylvania workingman's accent that would once have betrayed his origins on the outskirts of Hershey.

He'd started his first business making pard liquor in a shack at the age of fourteen. Pard liquor, in the 1880s, was still produced by sawing up any available dead horse that wasn't worth tanning for leather, stuffing the meat into a barrel along with plenty of sorghum jelly and caustic potash, and flipping the barrel twice a day for a week before straining out the resultant brown goo, which local butchers liked to mix with wood chips to ensure a slow and steady burn when they were smoking hams or congealing blood sausage. The work was not pleasant, especially in summer. But because there was so little demand for pard liquor outside certain Dutch hamlets in southeastern Pennsylvania, nobody on this side of the Atlantic had ever bothered to start producing it on a large scale, so even a lone entrepreneur with no initial capital using pre-industrial methods was able to stay competitive.

One winter, a butcher sifted from a bucket of Mr. Coehorn's pard liquor an engraved wedding ring belonging to a Hershey schoolmistress who'd recently vanished without a trace. Dark conclusions were drawn, and Mr. Coehorn might have been torn apart by a mob if that same afternoon the schoolmistress's body hadn't been discovered in the woods, intact apart from a few fingers most likely chewed off at some earlier juncture by one of the raccoons with which the boy made a thrifty practice of bulking out his horse barrels. That incident spurred his decision to leave Hershey for Manhattan, where his career began in earnest. (He didn't entirely forswear the pard liquor trade, however: forty-seven years later, within one of Eastern Aggregate's dozens of subsidiaries, there was still a division manufacturing a comparable product, which was nowadays used as an additive in luxury women's cosmetics.)

"There was no need for a kidnapping, Father," said Elias Coehorn Jr. "You could simply have called." He preferred not to concede that he'd been at all rattled.

"I did call."

"We have placed many, many telephone calls to a variety of residences and establishments with which you have been associated, Master Coehorn, but with no results." Phibbs had found infant fame as what the newspapers now called a "medical miracle": he had been an ectopic pregnancy, developing outside the womb, and could not have survived but for a nearby fibroid tumor on the outer wall of the uterus that had soaked him generously in the blood it embezzled. His chinless head lolled on his long neck like a boxer's punching ball.

"Yes, well, my friends know never to take messages. What's so urgent?" Before this Coehorn hadn't spoken to his father for over a year, and he had come to feel like a migraine patient who goes for so long without an attack that he begins to wonder if he's cured.

"I am never sure exactly how much willful or pretended ignorance I am to assume on your part," said his father. "But you must be aware, I suppose, that there exists a body called the Coehorn Missionary Foundation."

"Am I to be presented as an exemplar of why their attention is urgently needed back here in New York?" Coehorn had always found his father's naive schoolhouse Christianity, and in particular his obsession with latter-day Saint Francises who claimed to be in touch with God, to be his most mockable quality—and his most incongruous, too, given the rigor he applied to every other section of his life.

"In Spanish Honduras, the foundation operates a mission station in the northeast, near a town named San Esteban at the edge of the jungle, bringing the Lord's word to the river traders and the native Pozkito people. Eight days ago, they received an unexpected visit from two Frenchmen, begging for water and medical aid. They were the only survivors of a party of nine archaeologists who had ventured deep into the jungle. They were both feverish and one still had a three-foot arrow through his forearm. But they reported that they had found a temple. The settlement at Copán has long been assumed to be the easternmost of the major Mayan ruins, but this one was apparently almost two hundred miles further east, and its design was at variance with any such precedent."

When he heard "Mayan ruins," a picture came into Coehorn's mind of the sort of limestone ziggurat with fourfold symmetry he'd seen in *Life;* but the small balsa-wood model that Phibbs set down on the desk was not quite like that, because instead of four stepped sides it had two stepped sides and two sheer vertical sides, like a pair of stepladders pushed together end to end to make a podium. When Coehorn picked the model up, it fell apart into two pieces. He could hardly be blamed for its shoddy construction, but his father nevertheless gave him a look he knew well from childhood.

Those looks. Sometimes, when you got a glimpse of the ice caves behind Elias Coehorn Sr.'s countenance, it was hard to believe he'd ever been able to father an heir: you'd expect any woman who submitted to an injection of his animal fluids to be frozen solid from the cervix outward.

Nevertheless, Ada Coehorn had managed to survive the procedure—only to fall from one of Braeswood's turrets the winter of her son's sixth birthday in 1918. From the staircase of old dictionaries she'd built to get up to the high window (W–Z; R–S, T–V; J–L, M–O, P–Q; A–B, C–D, E–F, G–I) the police had concluded she'd been trying to free a moth that had got trapped between the sashes, but for a long time Coehorn had assumed, as anyone would in the circumstances, that in fact his father had murdered her. When he was fifteen, however, and he had the idea of bribing his Latin tutor to go to the Glen Cove courthouse and transcribe a copy of the coroner's report, he discovered to his surprise and displeasure that it would be very hard for any reasonable person to dispute its verdict that neither his father nor his father's butler could possibly have had anything to do with the death. For a second time, thirty-six years after the schoolmistress in Hershey, his father was grudgingly acquitted of murder, grudgingly because it would have fit so much better if he had done it.

"I trust you won't be too obtuse to appreciate the magnitude of this discovery," Coehorn Sr. continued after Phibbs had retrieved the halves of the model, "but at any rate, the salient point for our purposes is that nobody else knows about it yet. The missionaries wouldn't have permitted the Frenchmen to leave the mission station even if they had been medically capable of doing so. The details were transmitted by cipher, and the sketches the Frenchmen drew were presented upside down to the wirephoto operator in La Ceiba as plans for a new gold mine."

"What does any of this have to do with me?" said Coehorn.

"I want this temple. You are going to fetch it for me. Preparations have already begun for an expedition to Spanish Honduras. A crew of native laborers will disassemble the temple, after which it will be carried out of the jungle stone by stone, loaded aboard a number of ships, brought to New York, repaired of its long neglect, and reassembled on the grounds of Braeswood where the north firefly pavilion currently stands. You will be in command of this entire endeavor."

Coehorn smiled. "I'm about as likely to bring you back a basket of roc eggs from the Cape of Good Hope."

"You are twenty-six years old, boy. I don't have to tell you again what I had already accomplished by the time I was your age. I have allowed you to waste all these years in your circus of jockers and dope addicts in the expectation that you would tire of such divagations of your own accord. But that has not happened. Enough is enough. Perhaps you were expecting that one day I would offer you the vice presidency of the radio division or some other puerile sinecure. But instead you are going to do some real work for a few weeks."

"If the French archaeologists were delirious, how do you know these ruins are even real?"

"Their account of the temple was specific and plausible. This is not the architecture of delirium. I can assure you that, unlike the Frenchmen, you will be in no physical peril as long as you are not too careless."

In the past, a direct order from his father would have been like a tentacle around Coehorn's throat, but these days he felt more confident. "I'm afraid I have a prior engagement forever so I'll have to decline. A pleasure to see you, Father, as always."

"You will do as I say or the money stops."

"That's not much of a threat, because you never give me any money as it is. I've learned to manage perfectly well on my own."

"Actually," said Phibbs, "over the last twelve months your father has deposited nearly twenty thousand dollars in your bank account."

Coehorn smiled and shook his head. "No, that is certainly not the case."

"Yes, sir, it is," said Phibbs.

"But it can't be, because I'm skinned out all the time." Sometimes they let him make a withdrawal and sometimes they didn't but he never bothered to check the balance on the account.

"Whether or not you admit the existence of your allowance, you will have no more of it to spend."

"There's a trust. Mother made sure of it. I know what I'm owed. I'll sue."

"You are owed nothing. No lawyer will represent you. However: this is the last condition I shall ever set. For all I care you can convert to Kropotkinism afterward, or bigamize with a couple of Eskimo women. Get this temple for me and on your return your trust will be fully vested six years early."

"If I don't go, who will do it?"

"I'll send Phibbs."

That was hateful to Coehorn, the thought of Phibbs going to the tropics in his place, because a direct substitution would imply that he was on a level with this sniveling chamberlain. More likely than not, however, his father had already resigned himself to such a swap. More likely than not, most of his father's plans had been drawn up with Phibbs in mind on the reasonable assumption that Coehorn would say no. More likely than not, if his father had been there to watch the farce with the octopus, it would only have confirmed his belief that his son was no good for anything. Since Coehorn wouldn't allow himself to get caught up in the sort of dreary Freudian determinism that he found it so easy to identify in the emotional lives of his friends, he tried to see the instinctive appeal of proving his father wrong here as no better than a dog begging at the table. But he couldn't ignore his father's threat to take his money away, to smash the only tank that really mattered. He remembered how many of his acquaintances from his one and a half semesters at Harvard had disappeared from sight after the Crash, not all at once that fall but one by one in the years that followed, like a disease from the mainland spreading gradually across an archipelago. Now here was one more dose of Black Tuesday. If he had no money to spend, his New York friends would drop him, and he wouldn't blame them because he'd done the same to others many times. He tried to form a mental image of the jungle, but the best he could do was the Brooklyn Botanical Garden. As it happened, on a recent Sunday afternoon there he had overheard a girl say, "Isn't that Frank Parker?" "No," replied her companion, "no, I think it's that Rockefeller kid." Coehorn was grudgingly willing to admit his resemblance to Frank Parker, but he looked nothing whatsoever like any of the squinty-eyed Rockefeller brothers. There among the peonies he could feel his identity dissolving. But out in Spanish Honduras none of these names would yet mean anything at all. Not even the name Elias Coehorn Sr.

"Well?" said his father.

⚭

In Hollywood there was a slang term, "bumps," for the strivers who came from all over the country believing they had a future in the movie business, a word derived from the stories of young actresses who got so desperate they threw themselves in front of studio limousines in the hopes of getting noticed by the powerful men in the back seats. In the land of the bumps, almost everybody dreamed of receiving a telegram like the one Jervis Whelt held in his hands. And almost everybody would have dismissed it as a belated April Fools prank if they had actually received it. *See me at home noon tomorrow Arnold Spindler,* read the telegram in its entirety.

As the founder-chairman of Kingdom Pictures, Spindler was second only to Jack Warner at the highest echelon of the movie business. "Home," in this context, was his Bel Air estate, and he did not often invite guests there. He was famous, in fact, as a recluse and a paranoiac, ever since a near-fatal accident in 1929. An enthusiastic futurist in those days, he was not content merely to bang the drum for sound film and Technicolor, but had gone so far as to hire a team of aeronautical engineers to design and build an experimental non-rigid thermal airship that could be used to take aerial shots from static vantages at low altitudes with almost no engine noise. Instead of using a test pilot for its first flight over the Owens Valley, he went up himself in the cameraman's gondola. But the airship's envelope failed, and it crashed into a ridge. Spindler, who barely survived, needed a series of marathon operations to repair his fractured skull. Since then he had seldom been seen in public and conducted most of his business by telephone or by proxy. There were rumors, of course, that Spindler's brains had gone bad, like ham in an unsealed can— that Kingdom now had an addled king, and if there had been only a mild commercial and artistic decline at the studio over the last nine years it was because his deputies made all the decisions. And there were contrary rumors that Spindler was as astute as ever and the injuries had merely given his eyes a painful sensitivity to light. No hard evidence was available either way.

So even a director at the top of his field might have been surprised to receive a personal summons from Arnold Spindler. And Jervis Whelt wasn't a director at the top of his field: he was a director at the bottom of somebody else's. That other field was education. He taught two evening classes, in directing and screenwriting, in a windowless classroom at the Hancock Park Technical High School, whose daytime occupants had access to such an impressive array of etching, carving, and engraving tools that they never had to resort to fountain pens to advance their project of ornamenting every visible surface with a stupendous tapestry of indelible genitalia. Although he was still only twenty years old, he lectured with full confidence. He had never been involved in the making of a movie, but he understood how movies worked, really understood it, deep in the marrow of his intellect where philosophers kept their law of excluded middle and physicists their principle of least action. That was how he had invented the Whelt Rule, which he gave, reverently, a paragraph to itself whenever he wrote it down.

In any successful story, the action must intensify in a series of five or six regular increments, reach its highest level before giving way to a thrilling interval of weightlessness or flight, and then return safely to the status quo.

Every hit movie he had ever seen followed the Whelt Rule, and he believed that all the great screenwriters and directors must already be aware of it on some level without necessarily being able to identify or articulate it. When one of his students had complained that the Whelt Rule was so self-evident as to be virtually tautologous, or words to that effect, Whelt had responded by asking her why, in that case, the theaters were always so clogged with flops that broke it. Thousands of writer-bumps came to Hollywood every year thinking they could make it up as they went along, but Whelt knew that you couldn't get anywhere in life without rules, unbreakable rules, as many rules as you could find, to be hoarded as a form of wealth.

Consequently, he felt no disbelief or even surprise that the chairman of Kingdom Pictures should wish to see him. Most likely Spindler meant to bribe or threaten him into suppressing the Whelt Rule. Spindler prospered so exorbitantly from business as usual that he wouldn't want to allow Whelt to revolutionize how movies were made with the clarity of his new thinking.

Whelt had no intention of muting his gospel. However, just because he was about to make a bitter enemy, that didn't mean he would break his rule about arriving for every important appointment at least an hour and if possible two hours early. Since, in his experience, people often responded with confusion or even mild hostility to such precautions, perhaps because it reminded them of how recklessly they lived their own lives, he had parked his car at the foot of the hill, out of sight of the estate, and was now sitting in the front seat performing his usual exercises. After reading and partially memorizing an entry from the slightly water-damaged two-volume encyclopedia he kept in his car, he would invent three separate movie plots involving the subject of the entry, each obedient to the Whelt Rule (easy enough for "Circuit Court," less so for "Circulation of Sap"), and mark them down in the special notation he'd invented with which any conceivable story line could be reduced to a short sequence of graphemes. Once he'd done this for five entries he would try to guess to the nearest ten seconds how much time had passed since he last looked at his watch, before checking to find out the actual figure. And while all this went on he was squeezing a volleyball over and over again between his thighs. In two hours he could make greater improvements to his general knowledge, narrative imagination, mental chronometry, and adductor strength than the average person made in a whole year, and he was planning to develop a fifth simultaneous exercise in the near future. However, all this took a lot of concentration, so he didn't notice the blond woman trying to pass him in her car until she'd gotten out, walked over, and tapped on his side window.

"Excuse me, I can't get by," she said after Whelt rolled the window down. "Could you possibly move your car?"

"Are you visiting the Spindler mansion?"

"Yes."

"Did you get a special telegram from him, like I did?"

"No."

"You won't be able to see him without an appointment," Whelt said. "He's a famous recluse. Don't you know that?"

"I do know that. Listen, is there any way you could take me inside with you? Say I'm your stenographer or something?" She was pretty enough for a supporting role in a movie, Whelt thought, with limber, calligraphic eyebrows.

"Why would I do that?"

"Yes, I guess that is a reasonable question."

"If you really want to see Mr. Spindler, I hope you get to see Mr. Spindler, but I don't think I can help you."

"All right, well, will you at least move your car so I can drive up there?"

In fact, it was almost time now for Whelt's meeting, so he put his encyclopedia and volleyball to one side and drove up the hill himself. The woman followed in her car. At the head of the driveway, a guard looked over the telegram and asked if she was with him, and he said no. Once he was through the gates, he got out of the car and shielded his eyes to take in the view across the palmy basin. Off to the east, like a weeping sore on the flank of the sky, hung one of the hot-air balloons that had been dropping pink cotton "cherry blossoms" over Hollywood Boulevard as part of a promotional campaign for a new historical romance about the Convention of Kanagawa.

There was no one waiting for him on the portico, so after a moment Whelt cautiously pushed open one of the tall front doors. He had braced himself for the grandeur of the entrance hall, crystal chandeliers spuming from a ceiling on which frescoed cherubs aimed hand-cranked kinos at nymphs concealing their modesty with wreaths of 35mm film, an imperial staircase switchbacking up to a gallery overlooking the foyer. But he found himself instead in a disused warehouse that had been conquered by gigantic spiders.

Or at least that was what it resembled at first. The space was gloomy, unpartitioned, and strung from wall to wall and floor to ceiling with a random trapeze of crisscrossing strands like what you see when you pull a fresh wad of chewing gum from the sole of your shoe. Examining the nearest white strand, he discovered it was composed of some sort of heavy, raw-edged canvas, as if torn in long strips from a tent or a sail—indeed, an encampment of tents or a flotilla of sails, since there were thousands upon thousands of feet of it here—and that it was tied down at this end on a metal hook hammered into the marble floor. Stitched into the canvas at intervals along its length were tiny harness bells that jingled with any movement of the strand, like a dummy in a pickpocketing academy. Whelt thought of old Jerome, the ash-colored tomcat who lived in the orphanage where he'd grown up. After Jerome had hunted down every last mouse on the grounds, he'd started killing songbirds and leaving their remains under beds, so he'd been fitted with a bell on his collar to scare off his prey. Astonishingly, within a few months, Jerome had learned how to glide along like a dolly shot, the thimble of noise under his chin brimming but never spilling, and he was killing just as many songbirds as before. No human could be so dexterous, so although Whelt couldn't see more than a few yards in any direction through the musical rigging, his movements would be audible to anyone nearby. He was starting to feel pretty spooked.

"Hello?" he called out. Listening hard for a reply, he heard only a distant tintinnabulation. Someone else was here.

He wanted to turn and leave. But instead he pressed forward through the strands, ducking and hopping and occasionally tripping. Further into the jungle, it got so dark that he decided to strike a match.

"Thank you for coming to see me, Mr. Whelt."

The matchbook fell from his hand and he whirled round, but he couldn't make anyone out. "Mr. Spindler?"

"That's right," said the voice.

"It's a very great privilege to meet you, sir." Whelt was trying to marshal the advice he'd learned from a correspondence course he'd been taking called "The Road to Prosperity," specifically Lesson 3: Dazzle an Important Man the First Time You Meet Him, but something about these particular circumstances made it difficult.

"Do you know why you're here?"

"Uh, is it because of the Whelt Rule?"

"Yes, Mr. Whelt, it is."

He'd rehearsed this line: "Sir, I won't be bought," he said. His host did not immediately reply. Then Whelt remembered he was alone in a web in the dark. "Well, uh, that is, I *might* be bought . . ."

"Please relax, young man. This chamber is designed to ensure my safety, not to intimidate my visitors. May I ask, have you read a fictional novel called *Hearts in Darkness* by Q. Bertram Lee?"

"No." Whelt made a mental note that from now on he would read three novels a day so that when he was next in this situation he would certainly be able to answer yes. Lots of people used that expression, "mental note," but Whelt's mental notebook had the tangibility and permanence of a physical object.

"Kingdom Pictures is making a motion picture out of *Hearts in Darkness*," said Spindler, who had a voice of such chocolate-malt warmth that somehow it made Whelt feel almost safe here. "But there isn't a single director under contract with Kingdom who has any new ideas at all. So I decided to look around for a young buck. I heard about your Whelt Rule, and I thought to myself, This boy already understands more about motion pictures than most directors ever will. Anyone can frame a shot, but not just anyone can tell a story. Mr. Whelt, I want you to direct *Hearts in Darkness* for me. Understand?"

Whelt didn't know what else to say but, "Yes, Mr. Spindler."

"The picture ought to sit somewhere between *It Happened One Night* and *Too Hot to Handle.* Let me explain the scenario. There's a rich gadabout lad named Coutts who isn't interested in anything but champagne and roulette and dancing the Half Doodle with popsies. To straighten him out his father decides to send him along on a Harvard University archaeological expedition to an old Mayan temple in the jungle. The months pass and word comes back that in fact what Coutts has done is set up a nightclub there at the temple and it's now the most fashionable spot in the Torrid Zone for anyone who can find it. Coutts's father pays for an expedition to bring the boy home but they don't come back either because they're having such a fine time at the frolic pad. Meanwhile, Coutts's sister Marla wants to get married, but there's an old tradition in their family that it's always the brother, not the father, who gives away the bride, otherwise the marriage is certain to smash up in short order. So the sister and her fiancé decide to go up the river themselves to fetch Coutts for the wedding. The trouble is, there's only one explorer experienced enough to get them safely past the natives, and that happens to be Marla's ex-fiancé, who's a somewhat more dashing personality than her current one. Et cetera, et cetera. I'm sure you can fill in the rest for yourself. One of my script editors asked Lee where he got the idea, and he said it all happened to a friend of his.

"Now, when we made *Congo Cavalcade,* it was on a sound stage. We didn't even think about shooting it on location. But then the fellows who made *The New Adventures of Tarzan* in '34 really did take themselves off to Guatemala, because they didn't have a studio of their own in Hollywood, and the public loved it. I say that's the future and in twenty years I've never been wrong about that sort of thing. The trouble is, after *Tarzan,* the Guatemalans thought they'd struck gold, and now they want money for the use of their ruins. But there's a place we can go in Spanish Honduras. It's spectacular and it's only just been discovered and it won't cost us a dime. Don't ask me how I know about it. We'll throw everything together in a whistle and you'll leave in two weeks. Understand?"

Once again Whelt gathered his courage, which already had that crumpled quality of courage that's been gathered too many times in a row. "But does *Hearts in Darkness* follow the Whelt Rule?" he said.

"Pardon me?"

"Mr. Spindler, there's nothing I want to do in the world more than direct a picture. But if I can't direct a picture that follows the Whelt Rule, I don't want to direct a picture at all. Frankly, this offer of yours is the greatest opportunity I've ever had in my life. That's why I don't want to let you down. But when a scenario doesn't follow the Whelt Rule, there's nothing that you or I or anyone could do to prevent it from flopping. So I can't agree to direct your picture unless I know that the action intensifies in a series of five or six regular increments, reaches its highest level before giving way to a thrilling interval of weightlessness or flight, and then returns safely to the status quo."

"Listen, Whelt, I respect your Rule. That's why I brought you here. If you don't like the ending, you can change it. Any other misgivings?"

Whelt was telling himself that he shouldn't be startled by what was happening here, because almost every time he went to the movies he felt one hundred percent sure that he could have done a better job than the director, and for Spindler to have recognized these talents was an instance of exactly the sort of perspicacity that you would expect to find in the second-richest studio boss in Hollywood. But however unruffled Whelt might originally have felt about the telegram, he could not now shake the niggling feeling that, for all his confidence in his Rule, it was quite hard to imagine any truly sane and rational businessman handing over responsibility for a four- or five-hundred-thousand-dollar movie on that basis alone. He felt the sort of doubtful pride you would feel if your son had just been put in charge of the navy at age seven. Could this be right? "No misgivings at all, sir."

"Good. Tomorrow morning at eight you'll report to the Kingdom

Pictures lot on Formosa Avenue. They'll be expecting you. Now, when you see your pals at the taproom tonight, what are you going to tell them about me?"

Whelt never drank liquor and did not have any pals. "Uh, I don't know, Mr. Spindler, what would you like me to tell them?"

"Are you going to tell them that I'm cracked? That I'm unfit for human company? That I've converted a perfectly good mansion into a carnival spook house?"

"No, Mr. Spindler!"

"No?"

"I mean . . . yes? Should I say all that? I can say all that."

"You can say what you like. Already so much hogwash in the stockpot that nothing else you put in there could possibly affect the taste. But I want you to understand that there is a reason for the interior scheme of this house. There are many who wish me dead. Even within my own company. That's the natural consequence of my position. And there is no bodyguard alive who I trust as much as a bell on a string. Understand?"

"Right. I understand."

"But I can tell you're still skeptical."

"No, sir, I'm not at all."

"I can tell that you are. I want you to look me in the eye." Those last few words came from just behind Whelt's ear.

He turned, his heart gonging in his chest. Spindler must have been as nimble as Jerome the cat, because he hadn't rung a single bell on his approach. Beside every article about Spindler they printed the last confirmed photo ever taken of him, from the *Congo Cavalcade* premiere a year or so after his accident. But that photo was in profile, so you couldn't have seen that his eyes didn't line up any more, the right eye socket having slipped about a quarter of an inch down his face and tilted over toward the nose, a permanent Cubist squint. His long tongue twitched around in his mouth even when he wasn't speaking, and his breath smelled like cask-ripened foot bandages. For some reason he wore a loose boiler suit made from the same material as the stuffing of his mansion. "Here I am, boy," Spindler said. "Now that we've stood face-to-face, we shall be on more straightforward terms. We shall get the real measure of each other."

"Yes, Mr. Spindler."

"Very well. Time for you to go."

As Whelt, relieved, began to back away, he stepped in the wrong place, lost his balance, and toppled over backward. But before his head hit the floor, another strand caught his shoulders, and he found himself reclining as if in a hammock.

For the first time he saw that twenty or thirty feet above him, visible mostly by its corner glimmerings, some sort of long metal cabin was nestled like a tree house in the canopy. He wondered if it might be a Union Pacific dining car. But then he understood the truth. This was the gondola.

Spindler had made a nest from the carcass of the airship that almost ended him. The vessel's envelope had been a heavy cotton varnished not only with iron oxide but also with the same cellulose acetate butyrate that was being introduced as a safer replacement for nitrates in photographic emulsions. That filmy hide had been reused as the basic material of Spindler's hermitage: the hand-stitched boiler suit he wore, and the bell ropes that supposedly kept him safe. Perhaps he even slept up there in the gondola, Whelt thought, although he'd have to be agile to make the climb.

When Whelt righted himself he found that his new boss had gone. He was in such a hurry to leave that the network pealed left and right as he pushed his way through. But near the front doors he realized that there were a thousand questions he was an idiot not to have asked. Turning, he shouted, "Mr. Spindler, do you have any, uh, advice on how to make a movie?"

"Just keep it simple, Whelt." The voice didn't seem to come from anywhere in particular. "Introduce all the principal characters in the first scene, and whatever you do, don't try to be clever. Remember that. Keep it simple."

Outside, the sunlight threw its arms around Whelt as if they hadn't seen each other in years. Driving past the gates, he found that the blond woman was leaning on the hood of her car smoking a cigarette, and this time it was he who couldn't get past. It must have been obvious that he needed her to give way, but she didn't, so he put on the handbrake and got out.

"So is he crazy like they say?" she said.

"No."

"Is that what they told you to say?"

"Nobody told me to say anything."

"Nobody told you to say anything and nobody swore you to secrecy either?"

"He said I could say whatever I wanted to whomever I wanted."

"Gosh, now I feel churlish for assuming that just because a guy goes into hiding he might have something to hide. How do you rate my chances of getting an interview if I wait for the rest of the day?"

"You're a reporter?"

"My name's Meredith Vansaska and I'm from the *New York Evening Mirror.* Do you think he'll talk to me?"

"No."

"He absolutely won't?"

Whelt shook his head.

"No, I thought not," Vansaska said. "Listen, would you answer some questions if I bought you a sandwich? I don't know what sort of money you make so I don't know if a sandwich is a big inducement but you're the first person I've met out here who has spoken to Spindler in the last five years and will admit to it."

Normally Whelt would have declined, because lunch with a stranger was nowhere on his schedule for the day and he did not care to squander his afternoons socializing with females. But he was hungry and he had something to celebrate. "All right," he said.

ᘓ

When a Cambridge undergraduate named Joan Burlingame took a train through the English countryside to visit her former tutor, about a week after the events I've just described, she was so nervous that she brought with her, like a protective amulet, a copy of *Folklore of the Tucanoan-Speaking Peoples.* This was the masterwork of ethnology that had made Dr. Sidney Bridewall's name when he was only twenty-nine. She felt that if it were fresh in her mind and heavy in her handbag she might in some occult way be able to establish a connection with the courteous young Dr. Bridewall of the early 1920s, who was not nearly as daunting a character as the one she was about to visit. That morning, just after breakfast, a porter had come to her room at Newnham to tell her that she was wanted in the lodge to take a telephone call from America, his tone of voice suggesting that this was an act of inexcusable pretension on her part, as if she'd arranged for the delivery of a sapphirine pianola.

"Hello?" said the voice on the other end of the line, barely audible over the gale of interference. "Who's this?"

"This is Miss Joan Burlingame." The porter stood there watching her as if to ensure that the extremely important young lady was satisfied with her extremely important telephone call. "May I ask to whom I am—"

"This is Elias Coehorn Jr.. I want to know if you have any idea where to find this elusive Dr. Bridewall. I've spoken to about a hundred people and all they could tell me was that a girl named Burlingame sometimes comes to pick up his mail. Is that right?"

"Yes, but I haven't seen him in quite a while." Although Dr. Bridewall had lost his positions at nearly all of the professional associations to which he had once belonged, he still received frequent invitations from various smaller bodies—the Winchester College Ethnography Club, the Amateur Archaeological Society of Southern Rhodesia, the Boston Conventicle for Ladies' Edification—who hadn't yet heard the news of his disgrace, asking him to deliver a lecture or contribute an article to a newsletter. There was no point referring them to Notcote Hall, because even if Dr. Bridewall had received the letters he would have ignored them. Burlingame felt guilty for replying to the letters on her former tutor's behalf, since he'd never given her permission to do so, but she also would have felt guilty for stopping, since each unanswered invitation was one more avoidable mar to his reputation. In other words, whatever she did, she felt she was doing the wrong thing, which was a familiar condition from every single other area of her existence. Well, she thought, "it can't be helped"—putting mental quotation marks, as always, around any phrase that had established itself in her mind because her mother used it so often at home: "it can't be helped," "it can't be helped," "it just can't be helped," as if life's tribulations were a succession of dying animals being wheeled through a veterinary surgery.

"If you don't see him, Miss Joan Burlingame, then why do you pick up his mail?" asked Coehorn. When she didn't answer straightaway, he said, "All right, never mind that. Where is he?"

"He isn't at the university any more. He lives near a village called Notcote."

"Does he have a telephone?"

"No, but I can give you the address if you like."

"There isn't time for me to write. Is this place Notcote far from wherever you are?"

"Not far, no."

"Can you take him a message? I'm going on an expedition to the jungle in Spanish Honduras. Pozkito country, around the Río Patuca, about fifty miles inland from the Caribbean Sea, although we'll approach from the other direction. I understand that the natives around there are chummy with Bridewall. I want him to come along as our guide and liaison. We leave at the beginning of next month. He'll be extremely well paid—limitless resources—the Eastern Aggregate Company's backing us. In fact, I specifically want you to use that phrase: 'limitless resources.' All he has to do is get himself to a telephone and call me collect at Audobon 281 so we can make the rest of the arrangements. Audobon 281. That's New York, obviously. Have you got all that?"

Burlingame realized too late that the words "not far" had been construed to mean a stroll across the fens rather than a round-trip train journey that would take up a whole afternoon she could not spare. She wished she could make a clarification but it didn't seem right to mention it because Coehorn might have thought she was shirking her responsibilities or even hinting she wanted some kind of compensation. "Yes, I've got all that," she said. "Thank you very much, Mr. Coehorn." If she went to Notcote she'd be lucky to finish her translation of Montejo's *Las Curiosidades de Yucatán* before two in the morning. Well, she thought unhappily, "it can't be helped."

Among Burlingame's younger cousins were several members of that irritating category of child who insists on showing you its entire collection of pipe stems or seashells or cigarette cards whenever you come over for tea. In much the same way, the view out of the window of the 13:38 from Cambridge would apparently not be satisfied until it had methodically exhibited every living cow.

So that afternoon there was not much to distract her from *Folklore of the Tucanoan-Speaking Peoples,* even though she already knew the contents well. The quality of the scholarship was utterly invigorating—the patience and thoroughness with which Dr. Bridewall, extending the methodology of Antti Aarne's *Verzeichnis der Märchentypen (Motif-Index of Folk-Literature),* seemed at first to be working within the confines of Newton Mathers's earlier work on the subject, but by the end had cracked that work open like a mere plaster mold, revealing the lustrous form of a more visionary understanding—and by the time the train got into Notcote, Burlingame felt as if she had established an affectionate bond with Dr. Bridewall's diligent and gentlemanly younger self.

This was of no help, however, when she was greeted at the front door of grand old Notcote Hall by Lady Alice, eldest daughter of the late Earl of Notcote, naked but for a skirt of bark and a necklace of flowers.

"Oh, I'm frightfully, frightfully sorry!" Burlingame said, turning away and bringing her hand up to her eye as a blinder.

"For what?" said Lady Alice.

Upon his return from an expedition to the jungles of Spanish Honduras in 1935, Dr. Bridewall had canceled all his obligations at the Department of Archaeology and Anthropology in favor of traveling to fourteen different lecture halls across England to deliver a slide presentation entitled "What I Learned from the Pozkito People." The natives of that region, he announced, were the happiest, wisest, sincerest people in the world. They had no gods, no kings, no wars, no private property, and, above all, no rules of sexual conduct. They spent most of their waking hours having strenuous inter-course with one another, often in trios or quartets, pausing only to pluck fruit from the trees or scoop fish from the stream. They used a safe and reliable form of natural contraceptive that they made from sap. Within a few weeks of his arrival, they had come to accept Dr. Bridewall as one of their own, and he had come back to England only because he believed it was his duty to alert his countrymen to what they were missing. Once a devout Anglican, from now on he would be living as the Pozkitos did, and he invited men and women from any walk of life to join him, subject to an interview to deter-mine that they were not merely journalists or sensation seekers. At several of these lectures Dr. Bridewall was shouted down by an out-raged audience, and at Dudley Opera House he was taken into cus-tody by the police. Then, as a result of the scandal, he was invited to dinner at the London residence of young Lady Alice, who liked to surround herself with decorative iconoclasts, and not long after that he was installed in Notcote Hall alongside all three of the late Earl of Notcote's daughters. Society pals of Lady Alice were understood to travel regularly to Notcote to find out what they, too, could learn from the Pozkito people. Her closest male relative, a botanist older cousin, was in northern Australia waiting for the Queensland udum-bara to bloom and so could not intervene in the situation except by a series of unanswered postcards.

"I'm here, er . . ." Any two normal people in this situation, thought Burlingame, would instinctively conspire in the pretense that perhaps Lady Alice had been getting dressed after an early bath when somehow she mistook the doorbell for a fire alarm.

"You're here for Dr. Bridewall?"

"Yes," said Burlingame, relieved. She felt rude for talking to Lady Alice without looking at her but she also would have felt rude for looking at her.

Lady Alice shouted behind her into the house. "Sidney, get out from under Gwyneth and come into the hall—a girl's arrived." She turned back to Burlingame. "How long are you expecting to be with us? I see you haven't any luggage. Sometimes that means people only expect to stay the afternoon and sometimes it means they expect never to leave. I'm afraid that isn't very probable unless we all take a special shine to you."

"No," said Burlingame hastily, "I'm not . . ." I'm not one of you, she wanted to say.

"My dear, you won't last very long around these parts if you can't so much as bring yourself to contemplate a pair of charleys."

When you wished to defy someone who had just spoken to you like that, did you turn round and look her in the eye or did you literally turn round and look her in the areolae? The latter did not seem possible to Burlingame, who found even the company of the marble nudes in the Fitzwilliam almost too mortifying to bear.

But at that moment her former tutor appeared behind Lady Alice. He, too, wore only a kilt of bark and a necklace of flowers, and his face was as flushed and moist as an exposed gland. "Miss Burlingame!" he exclaimed between deep breaths. "What an unexpected pleasure!" This time, Burlingame was almost able to convince herself that perhaps while Lady Alice had been taking her early bath Bridewall had coincidentally been chasing a thief who ran off with his pajamas, since her only inkling of how a man might behave following sexual congress came from that Latin proverb, sometimes attributed to Galen, about how "all animals are sad after . . . ," so if he really had just got "out from under Gwyneth" she would have expected him to be grave and soft-spoken like a witness to a hunting accident. Still, she knew that this was not the Dr. Sidney Bridewall of *Folklore of the Tucanoan-Speaking Peoples* and that somewhere under that bark skirt there must nestle a malign procreative instrument. "My goodness, Alice, why haven't you invited her in?" he said.

"Er, no, I won't come in," said Burlingame, taking an involuntary step back. Her fear of appearing ill-mannered had marched her toward a lot of unpleasant places in her life. The doorstep of Notcote Hall was the latest. If she could possibly help it, a Pozkito orgy would not be the next.

"Why on earth not?"

"I have a message, that's all."

"From the university?" Since leaving Cambridge he had let his graying hair curl down to his shoulders.

"No." She cleared her throat. "Mr. Elias Coehorn Jr. of New York wishes you to accompany him on an expedition to the jungles of Spanish Honduras, around the Río Patuca, about fifty miles inland from the Caribbean Sea. He needs a liaison to the natives."

Lady Alice stroked Bridewall's arm. "Oh, Sidney, isn't that wonderful?"

All that excess blood had abruptly drained from Bridewall's face. "Around the Río Patuca, fifty miles inland from the Caribbean Sea?"

"That's what he said."

"But there's nothing to see there. Absolutely nothing. No reason to go. Much better not to go."

"Except for the locals!" said Lady Alice. "You're always saying you'd be so thrilled to go back to the jungle if you could only find the funds."

"Yes, well, that's exactly the rub. He probably thinks he can do it for the price of a trip to the Riviera. I get requests like this ceaselessly."

Burlingame was in a better position than anyone to know that in fact he did not. "He says he has limitless resources. He has the backing of the Eastern Aggregate Company."

"Oh, I think Daddy had some of their stocks," said Lady Alice. "Sidney, you must go! They'll be so pleased to see you! All the old faces from last time. Like a school reunion."

"But I don't know anything about this man's credentials."

"If he's paying for you to go back to the jungle it doesn't matter if he's a circus pony with a tie on."

"You don't really expect me to leave you and your sister here on your own?"

"What's come over you, Sidney? Of course you can leave us here on our own."

Burlingame was asking herself similar questions. Why would Bridewall be so reluctant? Then he turned back to her. "You will go," he said.

"Pardon me?"

"Nothing is more incumbent upon the old than to know when they should get out of the way and relinquish to younger successors the honors they can no longer earn and the duties they can no longer perform. I know Central America is your chosen field. When I was not much older than you I went to Burma and I made my name there. You were always a fine student and you deserve the opportunity to do the same."

"But you're not old," said Lady Alice. "You're not even fifty."

Bridewall ignored her. "You can tell Mr. Coehorn that you have my full confidence. He may have wanted me but what he is getting is one better."

"Sidney, I hardly think she'll flourish among the natives. Look how terrified she is of a few inches of flesh."

"My decision is made. You are my official delegate to the Pozkitos. You will either have to tell Mr. Coehorn that you are going or you will have to tell him that no one is going."

"But I haven't even finished my tripos," said Burlingame. Of course, this was just one of a dozen reasons why Bridewall's proposal was ludicrous. Another was that she could never make her own name as Bridewall had once made his—not only because she was a woman, but also because, as he said, she had chosen the classical civilizations of Central America as her specialism, a choice she now half-regretted. The Yanks were working with such piranha speed down there that by the time she was qualified enough to try to attach herself to one of the rare British expeditions to the region everything would already be mapped and sketched and translated and there would be nothing left but gristle. Whenever Burlingame had twinges of personal ambition she ignored them, but even if she'd been genuinely determined to make a contribution as momentous as *Folklore of the Tucanoan-Speaking Peoples,* she would never have the opportunity. The best she could hope for was a career of pedantically crosshatching other people's discoveries in long books no one would read, a prospect that gave her a pleasant feeling of rightness and security, like the smell of her attic bedroom at home.

Bridewall changed tack. "Look here, Joan, why don't you come in and we'll talk it over properly?" He smiled and licked his lips. "Once you've got a taste of what life is like at Notcote Hall you might be very keen to experience its tropical precedent for yourself."

That was when Lady Gwyneth appeared in the doorway between her sister and Bridewall. "Who's this?" she asked in a rather child-like voice. She was completely nude, heavy-lidded, shining from head to toe like one of those Titian portraits with forty layers of glaze, and yet it was the strand of auburn hair pasted with sweat to her freckled cheekbone that stole all of Burlingame's attention, because it seemed to sum up the general impossibility in a world such as this of forbidding from clinging what ought not to cling, of forbidding from moistening what ought not to moisten. She wondered how often Notcote Hall's pipes must get blocked by some new and unfamiliar secretion that one of the inhabitants had discovered deep inside his or her corrupted body. Burlingame took one last look at Lady Gwyneth before she nodded goodbye to Dr. Bridewall, turned around, and walked as fast as she could away from Notcote Hall.

Because of the expression she knew he would fix her with, she couldn't ask the Newnham porter to help her place a collect call to New York, so when she got back to Cambridge she went straight to the Glengarry Hotel, which had a public telephone inside a booth. The operator took nearly half an hour to connect her with Audobon 281 and she didn't have *Folklore of the Tucanoan-Speaking Peoples* to pass the time because she'd deliberately left it behind on the train.

"You woke me," said Coehorn. "I was up until five making calls, like a bookie. What time is it there? Michaelmas? Widdershins? Some other English time?"

"I'm sorry I woke you." This was sincere. Burlingame hated to wake up sleeping people even when they'd specifically asked her to. Like spiders or babies there was something almost hostile about their fragility.

"Did you see Bridewall?"

"Yes."

"Is he going to come to Honduras with me?"

"No."

"This isn't a telegram, Miss Joan Burlingame, you're not being charged by the word. Tell me what happened."

"He said he'd rather that I went in his place. But that's impossible, of course." She forced a dead little giggle just to emphasize how much like a joke she found the suggestion. "I wish I could give you better news."

"He didn't want to go? You have to go back and tell him about the temple. That will hook him."

She couldn't go back. "What temple?"

"This is top secret, but they've found a spectacular ruin out there in the northeastern jungle, somewhere between San Esteban and the coast. That's where we're going."

"I'm afraid you must have been misinformed, Mr. Coehorn," said Burlingame. "There are no such settlements east of Copán. Dr. Bridewall assured me that there is nothing at all to see in that part of the rain forest." In fact, one of the objectives of his fateful trip to Spanish Honduras had been to develop a theory to explain why the Mayans hadn't pressed their empire any further.

"Yes, so everybody thought. But this new joint has been found. And it looks different from all the other temples."

Burlingame felt suddenly short of breath. "How much scientific work has been done on it so far?"

"Practically none," said Coehorn. "We'll be the first major expedition to go and so far we don't even have an archaeologist. Listen, what do you mean that Bridewall would rather you went in his place? Are you a Mayanist too? You say the fellow trusts you—well, I'm very pressed for time so that's good enough for me. What do you say, Miss Joan Burlingame? If you want the job, you're hired." For a moment there was nothing on the line but a bluster of static. "Hello? Are you still there? Hello?"

☙

Beverly Pomutz, my old editor at the *New-York Evening Mirror,* hadn't taken a single day off except for Sundays and Christmas Day in the twenty-nine years that elapsed between his honeymoon and his recent heart attack. After he came back to work following the second of those crises, he declared that he'd learned what it felt like to die—not when his coronary artery squinched shut and he fell to the floor of the wire room, but rather when he had to spend an entire week in a hospital bed quarantined by doctor's orders from telephones, telegrams, radios, and newspapers, including his own. As is the case for many men of his age, it took a big scare to make him realize that he might have only a few years left on this earth and it was time to stop neglecting the parts of his life that really mattered to him. So he resolved to start going into the office on Sundays and Christmas Day, too.

But this was not an easy arrangement to negotiate with his wife, who'd wanted him to step down from the job entirely, and that was how he ended up coming to work every day with a small tan Pomeranian on a leash. Although Pomutz's doctor had found that ten minutes spent stroking a small dog would reduce a patient's blood pressure, the primary purpose of this ball of fluff was that it had been trained to bark a warning whenever it heard raised voices, and also, like a tamper-proof alarm, to bark whenever Pomutz was out of its sight. The bark took its pitch from the emergency brake of a subway train and was unendurable for more than a few seconds at a time. It was supposed to remind Pomutz to stay calm when his wife couldn't be present to pat his shoulder. He named the dog Scofield after the publisher of the *Mirror.*

By early afternoon on his first day back, Pomutz had dealt with enough urgent business among his senior staff that he now felt like finding out from his junior reporters what else he'd missed during his convalescence. Standing at the door of his office, he called out, "Miss Vansaska, Mr. Zonulet, Mr. Trimble—get in here," perhaps at random or perhaps because the three of us didn't look as if we were working hard enough.

"First order of business," said Pomutz when we were seated. "Mr. Trimble, can you tell me what the fuck is wrong with Mr. Busby?"

"I don't know what to say, boss." Gul Busby, the *Mirror*'s gossip columnist, almost never bothered to come into the office, but Leland Trimble, his assistant, was expected to garrison himself here in case he was needed at short notice. Since the day he was hired, Trimble had been transparent in his desire to steal Busby's job, but so far his plans had come to nothing, partly because Busby was known as one of the best in the business and partly because Trimble had a way of alienating his own sources. Recently, however, Busby had become more and more erratic. At first, there was just something off about his columns that you couldn't quite articulate, a feeling in the prose like a pinched nerve. But over the last week or so, it had got far worse: although he still wrote about New York celebrities, he now seemed to be ignoring their romances and rivalries in favor of describing, for instance, the appearance of the veins of Gertrude Niesen's arm as she raised a glass of Pernod to her mouth, or the asymmetrical lacing of Joe DiMaggio's sneakers when he was seen getting into a cab near Yankee Stadium, all written in flat, declarative sentences bleached clean of the colorful Broadway slang for which he was known. Because Busby had a long-standing agreement with the paper that only Pomutz himself was allowed to edit his work, during Pomutz's absence these columns had been printed intact, and there had already been a number of vexed letters from readers.

"Has the man had a fucking nervous breakdown?" said Pomutz. At his feet, Scofield issued a verbal warning. The animal did have three black dots to serve as a face, but in a competition to give a convincing visual impression of sentience it would have fallen well below a Halloween pumpkin and perhaps about level with the headlights and grille of an idling taxi. "Have we got a fucking abulic on our hands?" the editor added in a lower voice. "Did you talk to him?"

"He says he's got 'misgivings' about the column as he's been writing it up until now," said Trimble.

Vansaska noticed that Trimble was wearing a new silver tie clip. She knew he only bought jewelry for himself when he had a big gambling windfall. There was no one at the *Mirror* whom she disliked more than this human tophus. On her first day here she had made the mistake of going for a slice of apple pie with him after work because he seemed friendly and he promised to tell her how the office really worked. What he meant by that, it turned out, was an objective account of whom she ought to screw. If she screwed the city editor everybody would hear about it, if she screwed the deputy city editor everybody would hear about it, she couldn't screw Pomutz because he never cheated on his wife, there was no point screwing a guy like me because I didn't have any influence, and so forth, but if she screwed Trimble himself, she could not only count on his mentorship, which was her best chance of quick advancement, but also on his absolute discretion. "There's nobody like a blab man for keeping a secret," he said to her. "That's what they call a paradox." She waited to feel a sticky hand on her knee, but instead he just sat back, apparently waiting for her to act on the irrepressible gratitude she would no doubt feel for his kind offer.

So she informed him that she was engaged to be married, that she wouldn't so much as graze his dick with a boat hook if he could make her the editor of the *Herald-Tribune* starting tomorrow, that there were about three and a half million men in New York she'd sooner fuck than him and dozens more arriving with every hour that the Dixie Bus Center was in operation. She said all that calmly, but when he just gave her a big complacent smile in response, she wanted to scream at him that by voicing her refusal she had not entered into an implicit ongoing negotiation. He was a five-star creep. All the same, she saw him as unthreatening in the final analysis. He would never have the strength of character to do anything really monstrous.

"Misgivings?" said Pomutz.

"He says he's 'come to feel it's intolerably disingenuous to present anthropic experience as if it can be reduced to these discrete, predictable narratives,'" explained Trimble. "He says he's not sure he 'even believe[s] in distinct human personalities any more.' He says the world is 'a slip-slop of complex, fractile interdependencies and the only thing of which you can be truly certain is the immediate reality of physical objects moving through space.' He says 'mere sentiment is no longer of any interest to [him].' I'm just quoting direct here, boss. He was using a lot of ten-dollar words so I hope I've remembered everything right."

"Is he negotiating for more money?"

"I don't think so."

"So you're telling me we are lumbered with a fucking gossip columnist who isn't interested in 'mere sentiment'!" said Pomutz, shouting the last two words, so that Scofield started barking self-righteously. Vansaska winced and covered her ears. Pomutz took a slow breath and looked down at him. "All right, point taken, you cunt-licker." Scofield quietened. "Has he got anything for tomorrow's paper?"

"He says he's got a lot to write about the pattern of the water droplets in the basin after Jimmy Dorsey washed his hands in the bathroom of the Lollipop last night."

"Christ."

"Come on, boss. Let me take over. Busby lost his way months ago. It just wasn't showing til now."

"Absolutely not."

"Busby's a good man," I said. That's the syntax I'm going to use here—"I said"—even though my personal recollection of that day has faded so much in the wash that I might as well be writing about some other guy entirely. After all, this was over twenty years ago. But the odd thing is that, because of what happened to me when I went inside the temple, I remember with almost perfect clarity what Vansaska was thinking. So, at best, I can report how I looked to her observant eye: most of the time I seemed to her ostentatiously languid, slumped in my chair, except for the variable section of me that was just the opposite at any given time—tapping my foot, picking at a hangnail, clicking my tongue—as if a minor nervous disorder were touring my body. And she thought I wore my hat indoors too often. I was only twenty-two years old then.

"Just give me a week's probation," said Trimble.

"No," said Pomutz. "You'll spend a week introducing yourself as our gossip columnist. But the gossip columnist is an ambassador for the paper. And you make people feel uncomfortable."

"A day at a time, then. Let me write tomorrow's column."

"The fact that you happen to be the only half-qualified blab man occupying my field of vision right at this moment shouldn't be sufficient reason for me to agree, but I'm obliged to admit that it is. You take it straight to me when you finish, though. And you'll pull stories from everyone in the newsroom. I want quality."

"I got enough to fill it by myself."

"Hot cockles?" said Pomutz. This was his word for scoops, a strange Anglicism that he'd picked up nobody knew where.

"Sure. Number one, I ran into Frank Parker last week."

"Who?"

"The singer. He had a nice piece of ass with him—pardon my francophonics, Miss Vansaska," added Trimble, as if anyone who'd worked for Pomutz for more than five seconds could possibly object to profanity. "He told me he was banned from the racetrack. Then a couple of zbyszkos pulled him out of the place. They must have been mob guys coming to collect. He was hollering but nobody did anything."

"That wasn't Frank Parker," I said.

"Huh?"

"I was there when they dragged him out. Frank Parker wasn't in that basement. It was just a fellow who looked like him. The Coehorn boy, I think."

"I introduced myself, all right?" said Trimble. "I recognized him because I've seen him sing before. We had a conversation. It was Frank Parker."

I turned to our editor. "Bev, I'm telling you it wasn't."

"Let me note in passing that there should never be any need for two of my reporters to be at the same nightclub at the same time, unless each of them is only doing half his job," said Pomutz. "Did you actually talk to him, Mr. Zonulet?"

"No. Trimble and I were there on unrelated business."

"Boss, this is too good not to use," said Trimble. "Frank Parker's got this soap-sud mummy's-boy image and here he is getting dragged out of an octopus-wrestling match because of gambling debts. Besides, half the stuff we put in that column is just hearsay, but this time I was right there watching it."

"It's a few days old?"

"Yeah, because Busby ain't been taking anything I've been giving him. But it's still fresh. None of the other papers have used it."

"Okay, write it up and I'll look it over. Next: back to Mr. Zonulet. This cop who's taken up the current fashion for losing your fucking mind all of a sudden even if you're a grown man with a job to do."

Pomutz was referring to the case of Joseph Cybulski, a young police officer in Red Hook, Brooklyn. On Friday, Cybulski had vanished during a watch, and the next morning he was found wandering around Red Hook Park, shirtless, chest hair matted with vomit, mumbling nonsensically. According to the dispatcher at the station, there had been reports of noises coming from inside an old deconsecrated church on the waterfront that had been boarded up ever since the roof collapsed during an unlicensed taxi dance, and Cybulski had gone down there to sweep the place for vagrants. Considering that, back in '35, Cybulski had needed only a recitation of the Lord's Prayer to gird himself against the sight of five dismembered bodies in the back of a truck he'd stopped at a junction—I'd interviewed him about that case myself—then whatever he found in that church must have been pretty fearsome to send him out babbling into the night like that.

Or, I suggested, "maybe he just had some bad oysters. Bev, I still don't think there's much of a story here. I promise you my time is better spent on the Boilermakers' Union case. There's a week of front pages there if I can crack it open."

"You have strong reasons to believe that?"

"Yes."

"You've been doing a little more work on it?" Pomutz said casually.

"A little. As it happens, the reason I was down at the Bering Strait Railroad Association basement, where I saw a guy who definitely wasn't Frank Parker, was because I was running down a source . . ." As I tailed off, Vansaska couldn't help wincing at my mistake.

Pomutz slammed both of his palms on the top of his desk as he rose from his chair. "You are on the Cybulski story! You are not on the Boilermakers' Union story!"

Scofield starting yipping.

"Boss—"

"Everything you tell me about the Boilermakers' Union story reconfirms for me that it's a dead end and I've told you that half a dozen times, so what the fuck you think you're doing wasting your time and my money on a snipe hunt that at this point can only really be described as a recreational activity because it sure as hell isn't your fucking job . . ."

Vansaska didn't know anyone but Pomutz who could yell such long sentences. Yipping even louder, the Pomeranian jumped up and down as if someone were dangling food just out of its reach.

"Boss—"

"The reason I am able to accord my reporters such an exceptional degree of autonomy is because they do what I fucking tell them! That's how things work around here! You know that! You are on the fucking Cybulski story!" Then he looked at Scofield and his hands clenched into talons. "I hate you more than anything on earth," he said in a conversational tone, "and I wish your own mother had eaten you when you were still a puppy." The animal subsided. "Now, Miss Vansaska," said Pomutz, turning to her. "When did you get back from the Land of Sunshine and Wealth?"

"Friday night." She had felt such dread on the last leg of the train journey from Los Angeles that a derailment would have come as a miraculous reprieve. In the west it had been easy enough to forget about the engagement ring that she'd sequestered in her toiletries bag. But speeding back into New York felt like entering a black basalt prison dressed up in peonies and crinoline and ivory card stock. As she got into a cab outside Penn Station she saw an old man with a placard warning pretty imprecisely that the last judgment was "on its way," and she wanted to inform him that in fact it was there on the calendar in four months and twenty-two days. Wedding bells, how sweet the music!

The cab started uptown and she slipped the engagement ring back on her finger, realizing that no matter how briskening she had found Hollywood, she still wasn't up to breaking Bryce's heart—not to mention both their parents' and her brother's, since her family had looked forward to the two of them getting married ever since they'd played together as children. A few nights before she left she had deliberately started a quarrel with him about whether she would keep her newspaper job after the wedding, but even that didn't rile her enough to make it easy. Usually she was the opposite of sentimental, but in this case she felt like a slaughterhouse foreman who couldn't bring himself to stamp on a wounded fledgling. She hated herself for every moment that she couldn't do it and she hated herself even more for how she was treating her handsome fiancé in the meantime. Her toes curled whenever she thought of how lovingly he'd told her that it made no difference to him that he was a virgin and she wasn't. He didn't have any moralistic objection to sex before marriage, he'd said, stroking her hand, but personally he'd never felt willing to do anything with a girl that later in life she might come to regret. She wished that just once he could stop being so warm and generous and upstanding and devoted. What a joy it would be to arrive unexpectedly at his house one day and find him in the kitchen jerking off into a stolen polio brace.

"So: is Arnold Spindler crazy?" said Pomutz. "And on the evidence of this meeting, do you agree with me that our publisher might as well change the name of this newspaper to the *New York Dementia Chronicle*? Two questions for you."

"Everybody in Hollywood says Spindler's crazy," she said. "They say he's too much of a crack-up to run his own studio. They say his deputies have been making all the decisions for years. But in fact Spindler's still in command."

"You talked to him?"

"I talked to a source." When you met a man in those circumstances then of course you knew you'd never see him again. That was part of the point. And yet she'd hardly stopped thinking about Jervis Whelt, the aspiring director, since the afternoon in the motor hotel. Like her fiancé, he'd never been with a woman before. He wasn't a homosexual, he told her, he just kept to a rigorous schedule and he didn't understand the purpose of nonreproductive intercourse. Staring up at the ceiling fan that shooed away her cigarette smoke,

Vansaska had asked him why, in that case, he'd let her seduce him at the diner, and he claimed it had occurred to him that one day he might have to write or shoot a scene in which a couple were implied to have just finished making love and he wouldn't want to embarrass himself by his inexperience. Indeed, she'd noticed that during the act even his body had seemed computational in its small shifts and adjustments, as if he'd been determined that by the end of his first venture he'd have taught himself how to pleasure a woman as efficiently as anybody in California. But when she had asked if he understood the purpose of nonreproductive intercourse any better now, he had blushed a little, so she could tell he wasn't quite as bloodless as he put on. If she wasn't already certain that she had no maternal instincts whatsoever, she might have accused herself of feeling a suppressed impulse to take care of him. Certainly, this boy was a change from the French banker she'd been sleeping with back in New York, with whom her increasingly bruising encounters seemed to be underwritten by nothing but mutual distaste. From some angles Whelt could almost have been a precocious nine-year-old. Yet she'd found that she could talk to him more easily than any of her friends, more easily than the analyst her parents had sent her to, a hell of a lot more easily than her fiancé. Bryce, who'd known her for twenty years, was still so convinced of her sunny disposition that whenever he caught her looking less than sunny he would insist that "it [wasn't] like [her] to be glum!" But Whelt didn't even seem surprised when she talked to him about the black basalt prison, about sometimes feeling as if she belonged in a psychiatric hospital. Somehow, in his equable, alien way, he seemed to understand.

"Miss Vansaska, maybe 'everybody' in Hollywood agrees that Mr. Spindler is a King Ludwig," said Pomutz. "But Kingdom Pictures continues to operate on the premise that its chairman is its chairman. Hundreds of people go to work there every day on that premise. That premise has a lot on its side already. If a source tells you a legally capable person is also a factually capable person, that's not a hot cockle. What else have you got?"

"Spindler's still in command, but he's definitely half crazy."

"This is your source again?"

"Yes. He'd just come out of a meeting with Spindler at his estate."

"He'll go on the record?"

"No."

"So we have a source anonymously refuting—no, *refining* a rumor that most of our readers never heard in the first place. Jesus Christ," said Pomutz, still trying to muffle himself for the sake of the dog. "Do you have anything whatsoever?"

"Kingdom Pictures is rushing a comedy into production with a first-time director. They're shooting it on location at a temple in the jungle like *The New Adventures of Tarzan.*"

Pomutz gave up trying to muffle himself. "I pay for you to sun yourself in California for a week because you promise to get me something juicy about Arnold Spindler," he roared, "and you come back with nothing to show for it but an item I could have read in a fucking press release?"

The truth was that Vansaska had worked harder on the Kingdom Pictures story than on anything else she'd ever covered. She'd called on dozens of people in Hollywood and spent days waiting outside Spindler's estate. The mystery still gnawed at her. But she was finding it impossible to compose a defense, so she was relieved when Pomutz switched his attention to Scofield. He picked up the barking dog, carried it over to the open window, and held it out over Fifth Avenue. "If you don't shut up, I will drop you!" He rotated the irritant. "Do you see that, you little shit-heel? You will burst down there on the sidewalk like a fucking five-pound rambutan!" To its credit, the dog continued to bark as if it were more than willing to give up its life in the line of duty.

"Hey, Bev, there's no need for that," I said.

A vein stood out so far from Pomutz's temple that it looked as if you could have plucked it out in one motion like a shrimp's. "Yes, there is."

"Bev, just settle him down on the desk and I'll show you what I do when I'm trying to interview somebody and there's a baby crying nearby." Pomutz grudgingly withdrew the animal from the window and did as I said. Fixing a big smile on my face, I got up and walked over to the desk. "Oh, what a beautiful little muffin you have here! I just love babies. Can I say hello?"

"Uh, sure," said Pomutz, who hadn't realized he had also been cast in this scene.

"Is it a boy or a girl?"

"I never actually bothered to check."

I took from an inner pocket an object resembling a miniature bicycle horn. "Do you like shiny things, little muffin? Do you?" Sticking the toy right in the dog's face, I beeped it a couple of times. Scofield's eyelids fluttered and then it went limp.

There was a short silence as everyone stared at the dog. I put the horn back in my pocket. "What the fuck did you do?" said Pomutz.

"I gave it a spritz of benzoic oxymorphone."

"Is it dead?"

"I don't go around killing babies. I just put them to sleep for a half hour. A lot of people, if there's a baby getting on their nerves, they'll never relax and open up."

"Well, you're back in my good books, Mr. Zonulet," Pomutz said as he dropped Scofield without ceremony into the wastepaper basket beside his desk. "Although if it starts to snore . . ." But the animal only turned over noiselessly in its sleep, swaddling itself like a genuine baby in the crumpled sandwich wrapper that had broken its fall. Pomutz sat down. "You, on the other hand, are not in my good books," he said to Vansaska. "You are in my bad books. You are in the books so bad the fucking Vatican won't even ban them because it doesn't want the pope to get wind they exist. Where is this picture being shot?"

"Spanish Honduras."

Pomutz leaned back in his chair. "You know, my old buddy Hal Denny spent some time in the jungle during the uprising in Nicaragua. He said he'd never been in a place that seemed so indifferent to human endeavor, and then he stopped himself and he said, 'Nah, that's not right, it's only half the time that it seems indifferent to you, the other half of the time it seems like it passionately fucking hates you.' He said he wouldn't go back to the jungle if they paid him ten million dollars. Miss Vansaska, guess where you're going?"

"I don't understand."

"You're going to tag along with this picture. They're sure to take you if we offer. They'll want the advance publicity."

"But what's the story?" I said.

"They're shooting a movie out in the jungle with a first-time director. The story is when the whole fucking thing falls apart and they come home empty-handed just like you did. In the meantime, you can get some gossip for our starving column."

Vansaska knew this was meant as a punishment, and it was a blatantly disproportionate one, arising from Pomutz's compounded displeasure with all three departments in this meeting. But in fact she was so happy she could hardly stop herself from beaming. She'd longed to visit the jungle ever since she was eight years old and her father had sent her to take piano lessons.

In the apartment below her piano teacher's, there was a childless old woman who happened to die during that first dissonant summer of lessons, and when the old woman's nephews arrived to see about the body they found that she'd filled the apartment with dozens and dozens of spider plants and dumb canes and aroid palms, so many that one could hardly move around inside. While the nephews made preparations for the funeral, they instructed one of their sons to start clearing out the apartment. What the entrepreneurial seventeen-year-old did instead was charge the neighborhood kids a nickel each for admission to the "jungle."

The radiators were turned up high, and back in the kitchen four big pots of water were boiling on the stove, so you could feel the jowls of humidity in the air as soon as you walked inside. Under your feet the floorboards were gritted with a thin layer of loose soil and dry mulch. The potted plants had been arranged into an avenue leading from the front door, so you had to push the foliage aside with every step. For some reason that year every fruit and vegetable stall in New York was selling mealy Mexican guavas, and either they attracted drosophila faster than any other fruit or they already had eggs in their skins when they were sold, because a bag on a sideboard would populate a room within twenty-four hours, so the corners of the apartment had been heaped with them. The winks

of nervous blue in your peripheral vision were the single live butterfly the grandnephew had employed along with the fruit flies, and
there were also a few budgerigars chirping in a cage somewhere out
of sight. Even with the windows closed, you could hear the rum-
ble of the elevated train outside, but it might have been a distant
pachyderm. As you got about halfway into the living room, a pulley
squeaked and then something pounced from the ceiling. This was
a taxidermied jaguar cub that thumped to the ground and then lay
there on its side staring up at you with empty eye sockets, a rope
trailing from its left hind leg, the black fur on its flanks worn away
in patches like an old rug. And while you were still recovering from
the scare, a witch doctor appeared out of nowhere.

The grandnephew wore a ghoul mask painted with red stripes and
a bearskin rug that he'd pinned into a sort of toga, and he pranced
and gibbered for a minute before giving you a taste of roasted crocodile, which was pork rind dyed green with food coloring. Then he
shook your hand and escorted you out of the apartment. Several
of the other kids apparently asked for their nickels back, but not
Vansaska. The amateur jungle stayed with her for years. She had so
many questions about it. Why would the grandnephew have gone
to such trouble when it couldn't possibly have been worth his while
financially? Where had he found the stuffed jaguar cub and the live
butterfly? Was the jungle supposed to be located in Africa or South
America or Asia or at some impossible tripoint like the Rock of the
Three Kingdoms? Why did he think crocodile meat would be green
all the way through? And how long had the apartment been like
that before the neighbors intervened? Long enough for the imitation
to become real, for the jungle to legitimate its exclave, as the birds
laid eggs and moss ate the wallpaper and the floorboards warped
up like revenant trees? When Bryce took her on a date to see *Congo
Cavalcade* she loved it because the unconvincing sound-stage sets
made her feel as if she were right back in the Upper West Side version. Several times in the motel room in Westwood she'd told Whelt
how jealous she was that he'd get to see the wilds for himself. Now
Pomutz was telling her that she would have the same adventure.
For at least a few more weeks she'd be far from Bryce, far from her

father, far from New York, far from everything—but close to that awkward, long-lashed boy.

Nevertheless, she knew that she ought to look chastened in case her editor thought he hadn't made his point. So she said, "All right, boss," and stared at the floor. The meeting soon came to a close, and afterward we all agreed that Pomutz had been in an unusually pleasant mood today.

❧

"They'll have to cut the narration at the start of the script, won't they?"

"Why?"

"All this stuff about the jungle."

"It's straight from the book."

"I know that."

"It gives a literary feel."

"A literary feel? Have you read it? 'Implacable, impenetrable, imperial—half a million acres of darkness and disease—a sheer wall against which men have hurled themselves since the time of Cortez the Killer—the mighty Honduran jungle . . .' Do people really need to hear this? Do they really have to hear that it's hotter than hell and the vines make you trip and the fish swim up your piss-hole?"

"Does it actually say the fish swim up your piss—?"

"In the narration? No."

"We should use that. 'The mighty Honduran jungle, where fish swim up your piss-hole.'"

"Now that I come to think of it, that might be the Amazon. About which this whole place is nursing an inferiority complex. 'Half a million acres,' like that's supposed to be a lot. In any case, every man, woman, and child in America saw *Congo Cavalcade. Too Hot to Handle. The New Adventures of Tarzan.*"

"Nobody saw *The New Adventures of Tarzan.*"

"Okay, but the point being, they've seen hundreds of these movies. The older ones probably still remember Teddy Roosevelt going to look for the River of Doubt. They know the jungle's a nasty place. We don't have to tell them again."

"First of all, folks never tire of being reminded that the jungle is a nasty place. It renews their appreciation for the air conditioning in the theater. Second, you can't just rely on allusion to previous movies to do the work you don't want to do yourself. We have to establish that the jungle is a nasty place in *Hearts in Darkness*. Just because the jungle's a nasty place in *Congo Cavalcade,* that doesn't mean it's a nasty place in *Hearts in Darkness*, because *Congo Cavalcade* is not a part of our movie."

"But it's the same jungle!"

"It's a new jungle every time. The world of our movie doesn't exist until the instant the first reel starts. Nothing carries over. The opening narration is Genesis. Every poisonous fern is still dewy with vernix."

"So we have to treat the audience as if they have amnesia? We have to narrate every last thing? 'The mighty hat, a fabric covering for the head with a horizontal brim.' "

"People have seen hats for themselves. They haven't seen the Río Patuca for themselves."

"Neither has Q. Bertram Lee! The narration is a writer who's never been to the jungle explaining to everybody else what the jungle is like. What the hell is the point of that?"

"What about you, Mr. Trimble? I assume you're a moviegoer. What do you think?"

Trimble looked up. He'd been watching the tucuxi dolphins twirling in the wake of the boat up ahead like overheated kids in the spray from a street corner hydrant, their skins the mottled pink of a dog's hairless belly.

Assuming they were keeping to schedule, by now they must be almost at the site. One of the men out on the upper deck was the first assistant director and the other was the second assistant director, but he wasn't sure which was which. "Don't you Hollywood guys have test screenings to settle this kind of thing?" he said.

The day after the gossip column of the *New York Evening Mirror* had led with Trimble's item about Frank Parker getting kidnapped from an octopus-wrestling match by a couple of mafia zbyszkos, Trimble had taken a phone call from a contact who tended bar at the

Goldilocks warning him that he ought to get out of town in a hurry. Apparently, Parker had been unhappy about the harm the item had done to his reputation as a nice Christian boy. In fact, he'd been so unhappy about the harm the item had done to his reputation as a nice Christian boy that he'd sworn to tie Trimble over a rocking horse and fuck him up the ass with a condenser microphone, which was how he always dealt with people the first time they crossed him. Trimble had been threatened with violence before, of course, but usually you could either find a favor to offer as reparations or just lie low for a while. Parker was different. The singer of "Wherever You Are, Sweetheart, I'll Find You"—currently at number 12 in the *Billboard*'s chart of sheet music sales in the United States—was not given to exaggeration. And his manager was said to be twice as bad. Trimble told his Goldilocks contact to spread the world that the item had been Busby's fault, but he doubted the ploy would work because he'd already bragged to too many people that he was writing the whole column now.

That same afternoon, in the *Mirror* offices, he'd overheard Vansaska on the telephone making the arrangements for her trip. Kingdom Pictures had chartered a vessel to take the *Hearts in Darkness* cast and crew from Los Angeles down the west coast of Mexico and then through the Panama Canal in a loop back up toward Spanish Honduras, so Vansaska booked a cabin on a passenger steamship that would sail from New York via Havana to La Ceiba in time for her to rendezvous with the filmmakers and travel with them into the jungle. She also booked a taxi service to take her to the harbor on the morning of her departure. And that was how Trimble played his prank. He hurried down to the pay phone across the street and placed a call to the same taxi service Vansaska used. After he got the chief dispatcher on the line, he explained that his sister Meredith believed she was running away from her family to a secret enchanted temple in the tropics, where she was going to become either a movie star or an intrepid lady reporter (she never seemed to be able to make up her mind). And it was important that she should be humored at every step or else she'd start trying to prize off her own fingernails again, which was why he'd allowed her to use the telephone just now. But in fact she needed to be taken straight to the Creedmor State Hospital for psychiatric treatment.

Early the next morning, just to make sure, Trimble took the subway to the Upper West Side, and when the taxi pulled up outside Vansaska's building a few minutes before seven, he walked over and knocked on the window. He explained that he would be following at a safe distance in his own car, ready to take charge of his sister and pay the driver when they arrived, but Meredith was certain to try to jump out when she realized she wasn't en route to the secret enchanted temple, so under no circumstances should the driver stop the car before they got to the hospital. After that, Trimble carried on to the harbor, where he talked his way without difficulty on to the SS *Alterity*, and although he had no idea if Vansaska had really been delivered to the asylum, she certainly didn't turn up in time to eject him from her cabin. In the telegram he later sent Pomutz from Havana, he explained that he'd hoped to surprise his cherished colleague with a friendly send-off at the pier, but when he realized she must have been delayed, he took the initiative for the sake of the *Mirror*. There wasn't another steamship to La Ceiba for three days afterward, and by that point there would have been no hope of catching up with the *Hearts in Darkness* expedition.

Trimble knew that in the long run Vansaska wouldn't mind about the prank. Back when he was growing up in Gowanus—back when no one would have believed that within a few years he would earn his keep mingling with the ritzies on the Great White Way—he had three teenage cousins, all of them a little simple, who despite close supervision managed to get pregnant so often that their stepfather was rumored to keep an abortionist on retainer. After a while Trimble learned to recognize the change in complexion before the girls even knew themselves. During that editorial meeting on Pomutz's first day back, he was almost sure he'd seen it on Vansaska. The "mighty jungle" was no place for a woman in pup.

One theory on the ship was that déjà vu was spreading through the Pozkitos by some sort of hysterical contagion. That was why the locals kept asking about "the other Americans" who'd just passed through. Who the hell were they? How could there be "other Americans" out here? When Trimble himself was called upon to speculate, he pointed out that once in a while a slipup at the *Mirror* would allow prophecy into the gossip column when it published detailed eyewitness reports of parties that hadn't actually taken place yet. Maybe the Kingdom Pictures expedition had been outpaced by echoes of themselves. Reports that they were about to come down the river had become reports that they already had. For all they knew, the local language didn't even have tenses.

But in fact Trimble was just deflecting the question. He was the only person present who knew that there really was another large American party heading into the jungle, because he was the only person present who happened to have passed through Havana, where he'd heard several relevant details of a chartered vessel that had docked there for engine repairs less than a week earlier. The guy who might have been in the best position to clear all this up was Poyais O'Donnell, an Irishman who lived in the town of San Esteban. He was the fixer who had arranged for five hundred Pozkito natives to perform as extras in the movie. But when they arrived in San Esteban, O'Donnell wasn't there. He'd left a message for Jervis Whelt, the young director, saying that he'd been called away on urgent business but everything had already been settled with the Pozkitos. So they couldn't ask him to solve the mystery of "the other Americans."

In addition to ten actors and four actresses, the *Hearts in Darkness* crew was as follows: director, first assistant director, second assistant director, unit production manager, cinematographer, dialogue assistant, script clerk, head cameraman, two assistant cameramen, crane operator, crane steerer, gaffer, assistant gaffer, key grip, two assistant grips, pace man, two electricians, sound engineer, assistant sound engineer, sound-boom man, sound-cable man, hackle man, assistant hackle man, special-effects man, prop man, assistant prop man, set dresser, assistant set dresser, fixture man, carpenter, assistant carpenter, painter, makeup man, assistant makeup man,

wardrobe man, assistant wardrobe man, hairstylist, assistant hairstylist, two stuntmen, animal handler, developer, projectionist, fire-
man, still photographer, accountant, secretary, doctor, dentist, head
chef, executive chef, two kitchen assistants, store man, assistant
store man, interpreter, two accommodations men, laundry man,
and two personal assistants to members of the cast. Though called
"men" by studio convention, fifteen of the crew were women. There
was also Trimble, which made a total of seventy-nine people now
disembarking from a ship here at the dicey headwaters of this tributary of the Río Patuca.

"I'm not going to bother about learning everybody's names," one
of the actresses had declared. "We won't be out here long enough,
and there are too many of us." But Trimble had not only learned all
the names, he'd opened a file under each one. That was just how his
brain worked. By his reckoning, seventy-nine was round about how
many people there were in New York who were famous enough that
on a slow day they could get into the gossip column just for having
a birthday party. None of the *Hearts in Darkness* crew would ever
warrant a place in the stories he'd take home to the *Mirror,* but when
he overheard something juicy about a carpenter or a kitchen assistant, he couldn't just disregard it. Until this trip, Trimble had never
in his life traveled further than Atlantic City. Perhaps he should
have been intoxicated by the "mighty jungle." But in fact he didn't
particularly notice the difference. What interested him was people.
Everything else was just wallpaper.

At least fifty of the natives were supposed to meet them and
unload the ship, but so far there was no sign of anyone at all, although the greenery was so thick that the entire population of
Staten Island might have been hanging back just out of sight and
you wouldn't have had the least idea. About half the expedition was
milling around on the slippery bank and the other half was still on
deck. Most were dressed for a normal summer day on the studio lot,
and an uncaptioned photograph of the scene might have been taken
to show a pleasure cruise that had veered psychotically off course.
As Trimble ambled down the gangway he found Whelt in a huddle

with his prime minister and his pope: Kermit Rusk, the unit production manager, and George Aldobrand, the Englishman who played Coutts's sister's ex-fiancé, the male lead role in *Hearts in Darkness*.

"Either O'Donnell gave the wrong instructions or they didn't understand him properly," Rusk was saying. "But they must be waiting for us at the pyramid." People sometimes still called it that even though everyone knew by now that it was not a pyramid but rather had two stepped sides and two sheer vertical sides; strictly speaking it was a triangular prism. "We'll send a few guys down there to fetch them." He had one of those phlegmy voices that makes it impossible to concentrate on what a guy is saying when you first meet him because you're so busy mentally imploring him to clear his throat.

"Without guides?" said Whelt.

"The map shows that the site is due east from these headwaters. Not too far. In the meantime we put everybody back on the ship to make sure nobody wanders off."

"I'm not getting back on that blasted ship," said Aldobrand.

Some of the cast, knowing that Trimble was the only American reporter for a hundred miles and they would otherwise be entirely lost to the press for the duration of the shoot, had already begun to make subtle bids for his attention. But not Aldobrand so far. Back in Bournemouth, he'd been an aspiring music-hall performer whose manager had dropped him on the basis that he was "too handsome to be funny." From the time he arrived in Hollywood, however, the legend was that he had never been turned down for a single part. He had a scene in *Hearts in Darkness* in which he had to put on a bow tie while he delivered a complicated monologue to the actress playing Coutts's sister Marla, and although for the most part Whelt had conducted his script rehearsals with no props or costumes, the dialogue assistant had insisted that Aldobrand use an actual Gieves & Hawkes to run through that scene, because on *The Big Shakedown* the atmosphere of professionalism and respect that was so important to a functioning movie set had never quite recovered after they all found out far too late that Charles Farrell wasn't capable of emitting anything more than guttural moans while he was in the process of tying his shoelaces. As it turned out, though, Aldobrand had to be coached to tie his bow tie much more slowly, and with both hands instead of just one. Otherwise it was unsettling to watch, everyone said.

"With all due respect, Mr. Aldobrand, do you want to unload the vessel yourself?" said Rusk.

"We've been traveling for eons. These people want nothing more than to see for themselves what we've had our hearts set on all this time." By this stage of the afternoon there was such a limpness to the way people fanned their faces and waved away mosquitoes that the crowd seemed to waggle like a giant sea anemone.

Rusk nodded at the director. "It's your decision, Mr. Whelt."

Whelt did not seem to Trimble like a guy who was good at adapting to unexpected circumstances. "Maybe we should just wait here," Whelt said. "The natives may be on their way."

"Wait?" said Aldobrand. "For how long? No. If that was the prevailing attitude around here, this temple would never have been found in the first place. Anyway, the insects won't be so bad once we get away from the water." He took the megaphone Rusk had been carrying and raised it to his mouth. "Listen, everyone: our concierges may not have arrived yet but we're bally well pressing on! Bring whatever you feel like carrying. Everything else we'll send for later." There was a smattering of applause.

So behind a drill bit of machetes they tramped into the jungle. Trimble found himself near the front next to Myslowitz, the émigré set dresser, who kept grumbling that back in Germany, because of "that *Hochstapler*" Leopold Jessner and his productions of Shakespeare, the fashion had been for every single play to be performed up and down a flight of steps, and he had looked forward to escaping such inanity forever in the United States, only to get hired by this movie of all movies. But the general good humor lasted far longer than Trimble would have predicted, and Aldobrand moved up and down the line giving encouragement: "Remember, we're almost the first white men ever to set eyes on this place. You can tell your grandchildren that." Someone voiced a flight of fancy about a gang of Hottentot adventurers coming across the stump of St. Patrick's Cathedral in a thousand years' time. After about half a mile, when their destination began to rise into view between the towering kapok trunks, there was pointing and hooting. And if it was possible for the seventy-nine to believe that their supposed precursion by the "other Americans" was merely a trick of the light, the intruder that is just your own reflection in the mirror at the end of the gloomy corridor, then it was possible, too, to believe that the ruins had been folded in on themselves by some refractory property of the tropical air. So that was what they told one another until the evidence of their senses became so hard to deny that even Aldobrand fell silent.

There was only half a temple.

And over the sifting and popping and nagging and burping of the forest, they could hear the sound of a jazz band.

In those early days, not a lot of people thought to ask themselves why the Pozkitos decided to interpret Coehorn's vague instructions by completely dismantling one of the temple's two great staircases before moving on to the other, rather than just starting at the capstone and working their way to the bottom. After all, the two approaches would expend about the same amount of labor, and to a "civilized" mind that has been taught to trust the symmetrical and distrust the arbitrary, it would feel much more logical to take it, as musicians say, from the top. But a few days later, a story started going around of a Pozkito boy who had been seen to eat one whole hemisphere of a papaya before starting on the other (instead of working his way around the equator as if it were an apple), and this may have added some weight to the theory that the Pozkito people had some sort of racial disposition toward bisectional progress, even though the truth was probably just that the Pozkito boy was avoiding the mushy half of the papaya. In any case, for most of the arrivals at the Mayan site, the events of those first few days were so unexpected that they didn't pause for much geometrical analysis. The ladies and gentlemen of *Hearts in Darkness,* in particular, had nothing in their minds when they emerged from the trees except "Half of our temple is gone!" They were robbed of the tourist experience that they deserved after their long journey, the gut-punch of awe. Because that temple was quite something when it was still intact: two hundred feet high, two hundred feet wide, four hundred feet long, with sculptures running up the mossy balustrades and a peripteros not unlike a miniature Jefferson Memorial crowning the upper terrace where the two staircases met. And all this, impossibly, in the middle of a ravenous jungle. But the newcomers never really saw what was there. They only saw what was missing. One half was mundanely, predictably solid. The other half was a screaming gap.

Leland Trimble prided himself on never being surprised by anything. And indeed, because he had already known about "the other Americans," he was better prepared than his companions to see forty, maybe fifty whites standing around an encampment at the foot of the temple, as an uncountable number of skinny Pozkito men in loincloths labored around them like ants plundering a wedding cake, some rolling logs and some pulling ropes and some chiseling stones, to the accompaniment of a pianist, bassist, clarinetist, and drummer improvising on a gypsy air. But there was one detail of this tableau that, by contrast, would not have meant much to any of his companions but that absolutely staggered Trimble. And this was that the guy supervising all this work was Frank Parker, the nightclub singer, who must have followed him all the way to Spanish Honduras to get revenge for that item in the gossip column. Trimble's instinct was to turn and run before Parker noticed him. And yet when Whelt rushed up the slope, Trimble couldn't stop himself from following. Because whatever happened here was going to be important later.

Whelt was shouting and waving his arms. "Stop this!" He raised the megaphone. "Stop this right now!" So immediately Trimble knew that Whelt was going to lose. He sounded like a pacifist or a vegetarian. The "other Americans," many of whom had been playing cards or sunbathing, were looking around in bemusement as more and more of the seventy-nine stumbled out of the jungle like a halfhearted ambush. And the Pozkitos weren't paying any attention at all.

Sometimes, back in the city, when two people out walking their dogs were about to pass in the street, you'd see the dogs start yowling the instant they caught sight of each other—no negotiations, just straight to war, running on the spot, claws practically sparking on the sidewalk, as if they didn't know they were on leashes and all they had ever wanted in the world was to drag themselves a quarter of an inch closer to the other dog's jugular vein—sometimes just a preposterous little meringue of a dog, a poodle or a Pekingese or a Pomeranian like Scofield, up against a Doberman, and yet neither bothered to acknowledge the imbalance—this hatred so total that you'd think one dog must have murdered the other dog's father or raped his wife or forced his department store into bankruptcy, when in fact they'd probably never seen each other before in their lives, and the only explanation was that each had scented in the other a terrible incommensurability at the deepest levels of dog music, dog mathematics. That was what happened when Whelt and his counterpart looked each other in the eye for the first time. They didn't quite start to growl. But Trimble could feel their hatred crackling across the air between them, a hatred that neither of them would have been able to explain, a hatred, like a love, that no one outside it would ever really comprehend, but that was instantaneous and undeniable and overwhelming.

"Who are you and who are all these people?" said Whelt.

"My name is Elias Coehorn Jr. and these are my employees. You'd better have a good answer in return."

So it wasn't Frank Parker after all. Trimble now had to concede that I'd had it right in the meeting at the *Mirror:* the guy he'd seen getting dragged away from the octopus-wrestling match was in fact the Coehorn boy. But as nutty as Parker's presence here would have been, Coehorn's didn't make a lot of sense either.

"My name is Jervis Whelt. I am the director of the Kingdom Pictures motion picture *Hearts in Darkness.* This is my cast and crew. We are here to shoot on location at this Mayan temple." Whelt sounded as if he thought he would be fine so long as he could keep on stating factual propositions.

"I'm sorry but as you can see you're a little late. We're taking it home with us. You ought to have got here last week."

"We didn't see any other boats."

"You obviously weren't looking very hard. We moored downriver and took a shortcut overland."

By now Rusk had caught up. Whelt turned to him. "Get our interpreter."

That was when Coehorn saw Trimble. "Don't I know you from somewhere?"

The interpreter wasn't far behind. Rusk brought over the nearest Pozkito laborer, a glum-looking guy with an underbite. "Ask if he knows anything about the five hundred natives that Poyais O'Donnell hired to work for us," said Whelt.

After conferring with the laborer, the interpreter said, "He says he's one of them."

"What do you mean?"

"This is it. They're all here."

"These are the same natives we hired?" said Whelt.

"Yes."

"That can't be right."

"It certainly can't," said Coehorn. "The Irish go-between hired these natives for us. These are our natives, not yours."

Overhead there flew a macaw with prismatic feathers, like an advance scout for a rainbow. "Ask him who he thinks he's working for," said Whelt.

More conferral. "Both."

"Both?"

"He says first they're working for this man"—Coehorn—"then they're going to work for you"—Whelt.

"But we need the temple here so we can shoot our motion picture," said Whelt. "How does he think they're going to work on our motion picture if we can't shoot it because they've already taken the temple away?"

More conferral. This time the translator shrugged. "I guess either he didn't understand the question or I didn't translate it right."

"Did you pay Mr. O'Donnell his commission in advance?" said Rusk.

"I believe so," said Coehorn.

"Did you ever actually meet him in person?"

"He was away—"

"Away on urgent business. Right. That son of a bitch."

"The natives will have to put the temple back together," said Whelt.

"We only have two weeks of shooting scheduled here," added Rusk. "Once we're through, you can do whatever the heck you like with it."

"Do you really expect us to sit around buffing our fingernails for two weeks?" said Coehorn. "I'm not staying here one day longer than I have to."

By now Trimble was feeling almost disappointed that Frank Parker hadn't come all the way to Spanish Honduras to take revenge on him. Not much in life was more important than getting even, and he always respected a guy who didn't so much take a tooth for a tooth as he took a whole smile.

Rusk said to Coehorn, "If you don't want to wait for us to finish you could go away and come back again."

Coehorn smirked, and turned to the interpreter. "Tell our Pozkito friend he can go back to work."

"He's our interpreter!" said Whelt. "You can't use our interpreter! No, tell him they won't get any money from us if they carry on working for these other people."

"Tell him the same thing from me," said Coehorn.

"Tell him we'll double their wage."

"Emphatic ditto."

Whelt pulled Rusk a short distance away, and Trimble followed. For a moment Whelt just stared into space, as if the technicians inside him were performing some sort of emergency recalibration. Then he said quietly, "How much cash do we have?"

"Not much. We weren't expecting to need any. Just a little emergency fund in case anything went badly wrong in Panama or La Ceiba. And a little silver and gold for the same reason."

"Send someone back to the ship to fetch it all. Quickly."

"The natives may not know what to do with a hundred-dollar bill. I think O'Donnell was going to pay them in, you know, fish-hooks and beads."

"Just get it all. Jewelry too. Watches. Strip the cabins."

"Folks are not going to be very happy about that."

"We can buy it all back once we get word to Mr. Spindler to send more money. And bring liquor, salt, mirrors, flashlights . . . anything the natives might value. We won't put it all on the negotiating table right away, but we need it in reserve."

"These other guys may have the same idea."

"Then we'll just have to outmatch them. There's no other way." Whelt looked at Trimble. "Why do you keep following us around?"

But at that moment Aldobrand arrived to reconstitute the troika. "What the deuce is going on? Why are they striking our set?"

While Rusk explained the state of affairs, Trimble saw an anole running across the ground so he stamped on it—a Brooklyn cockroach instinct.

"Well, whether or not we can persuade the Indians to put it back together again," said Aldobrand, "what's important at this juncture is that at the very least they don't take any more of it apart. Wouldn't you agree?"

"Yes," said Whelt. But the Pozkitos still hadn't stopped toiling.

"Then it's time to chain ourselves to the gates."

"Pardon me?" said Rusk.

"Like the suffragettes." Once again, Aldobrand grabbed the megaphone. "Listen, everyone: last one up the steps is a saddle-goose!"

The cast and crew of *Hearts in Darkness* just frowned back at Aldobrand, possibly struggling with his picturesque vocabulary. But then he made his dash, and they understood. There was a stampede. Soon, the entire party was spread up the stone steps of the surviving staircase like the audience at a Greek auditorium, with Aldobrand hiking all the way up to the upper terrace, the edge of which was now a precipice overlooking the absence of the staircase on the other side. Trimble himself, however, took the bottom step, as if he'd merely sat down for a cigarette on the stoop of a brownstone, feeling that it was better not to commit himself. Perched on the next step up was a dowdy girl he didn't recognize.

"Hey, I don't think I've seen you before," he said.

She swallowed. "No, well . . . haven't you? I suppose I'm not . . . that is, I haven't been around much. Um." Like Aldobrand she had a posh British accent, and for some reason her voice quavered as if he'd just accused her of drowning a baby.

Trimble said flirtatiously, "You sound like you're guilty about something." The girl blushed and avoided his gaze. But not in the alluring way girls did that sometimes. He took out a handkerchief to blot his forehead. Aldobrand was assuming that the army of Pozkito men weren't so loyal to Coehorn's enterprise that they'd just drag everybody back down by the hair. From what he'd seen in those wretched little settlements on the banks of the Patuca, the Pozkitos didn't deserve their reputation as the local Peace Society. They were more than capable of violence. He could picture them running Tommy Gagliano off Broadway.

But the next morning they were all gone.

∽

The girl Trimble met at the foot of the temple was Joan Burlingame, virgin, Mayanist, and now defector. Last Easter a librarian friend at Cambridge had taken her to see the archive of Charles Darwin's papers that was in the process of being recataloged at the University Library, and among them Burlingame had found particularly memorable an 1831 letter in which Darwin had transcribed some of his father's objections to the young man accepting a place on the *Beagle* as a supernumerary naturalist: for instance, "that they must have offered to many others before me the place of naturalist; and from its not being accepted there must be some serious objection to the vessel or expedition; and that my accommodations would be most uncomfortable; and that it would be a useless undertaking." She thought of this letter when she was trying to promote the Coehorn expedition to her mother and father, who made the same sort of reply that Robert Darwin once had: that Joan couldn't possibly be anyone's first choice for a scheme like this, and the fact that they'd offered it to her proved there must be something wrong with it, and that in any event she would be certain to hate every minute, since she didn't even like going to the seaside.

Despite agreeing with most of that, Burlingame did after a long battle manage to persuade her parents. The principal of Newnham College and the head of the Department of Archaeology and Anthropology, meanwhile, needed only polite letters from the Eastern Aggregate Company soliciting the temporary release of their student for an endeavor of great scholarly importance and educational value. These were sent by the same efficient secretary who arranged for Burlingame a passage to New York and a trunk full of brand-new field equipment. However, each time she worked up the courage to ask if she could speak to Mr. Coehorn again, she was told he wasn't available, and he didn't come to see her during the two days she spent in a Manhattan hotel, which she was too nervous ever to leave since there was no one to tell her where to go. So it wasn't until her first afternoon on the chartered steamship to La Ceiba that she found out the actual purpose of this expedition: to disassemble a Mayan temple.

Burlingame kept reminding herself that if it were not permissible to bring relics home for safekeeping, the British Museum would be nothing but empty halls. Just like the nymphs of Notcote, the tribesmen here were demeaning their ancestral pile, and whatever Lord Byron might have said about "Thy walls defaced, thy mouldering shrines removed by British hands . . . and snatch'd, thy shrinking Gods to northern climes," etc., he had never met a Pozkito. So far, Burlingame's observations did not at all match what she knew about the tribe from Bridewall. She had seen no evidence of sensuality, jubilation, communism, but rather violence, rigidity, greed. But either way one's conclusions about the responsibilities of the conscientious white man must be the same.

When she was five years old her father had bought her a ticket for a church raffle and during the drawing of the numbers she had won a bottle of champagne. Everyone had looked at her and laughed, which had made her cry, and then the prize with its pretty gold foil had been taken away, which had made her cry even more. But just as it was now obvious to her that a child could not be permitted to keep a bottle of champagne, it should be obvious to the Pozkitos that they could not be permitted to administer the estate of their more advanced ancestors. Or at least that was what she forced herself to believe, until she was actually standing in the clearing, watching the first few blocks being hauled down from the ruin. She realized that this temple was the sublimest thing she had ever seen and she had set eyes on it for the first time at the very last moment of its inviolacy, the very last moment before a pillage in which she was herself complicit, so that the temple in all its mountainous weight now seemed to her paradoxically ephemeral, a dream that shattered in your mind as you tried to recall it, a deep-sea fish that prolapsed to death as soon as it was brought up into the light.

Even then, Burlingame didn't make a fuss. She just scribbled what notes she could and assisted with the project of diagramming the temple so it could be reinstalled on the North Shore of Long Island according to the serial numbers being painted on each stone. If it had to be taken apart, she thought, it might as well be put back together accurately. She still couldn't shake off the feeling that this was not why she had come here; that this was not why she had worked so hard for the chance to study at Cambridge with Bridewall; that this was not, all in all, why she was on this earth. But she was also aware that nothing could be more futile than making a protest with Coehorn, who had come here with no other objective than to take the temple away, and who still, as far as she could tell, had no idea who she was. Even when the rival party from Los Angeles made their baffling arrival at the temple, and it became clear that they wanted it to be put back together, which was what she longed for too, Burlingame didn't feel that was any use to her, since her parents had brought her up to remember her loyalties.

But then came the moment when the actor called for action, and she realized the newcomers were about to put the surviving ruins under guard. She looked up at the newly exposed inner face of the half-temple, which wasn't mossy and flat like the orthogonal sides but rather raw and irregular, umbrous, good for bird nests, resembling something between a basalt cliff and a tenement house whose side wall has been bared by the demolition of its neighbor. Mistaking her for a comrade, someone slapped her on the shoulder and said, "Come on!" Once again she felt the weight of the bottle of champagne in her little arms, and this time she hugged it tightly to herself and ran.

☙

The Pozkitos were nowhere to be found.

Five hundred men missing from the site, and yet from what Trimble overheard that day, not a single American from either faction could actually recall seeing any of them leave. For even the most observant, there had been no more than a half-conscious impression of dwindling, like the constellations fading in the hour before dawn.

And the Pozkitos had taken their loot with them.

For most of the previous evening, the leaders of both expeditions had bargained (through their interpreters) with representatives of the Pozkitos, offering more and more and more in exchange for either the disassembly or the reassembly of the temple. First it was all to be paid on completion, then half on completion and half in advance, then, desperately, all in advance, that same night. When the auction ended after several hours, both bidders were so mentally exhausted that they fell asleep in their mosquito-net bivouacs a little fuzzy on the latest developments but nonetheless almost a hundred percent certain that they'd won. What neither of them could believe was that they'd been reduced to begging illiterate tribesmen for the privilege of enormously overpaying them for manual work. Maybe that was why it didn't occur to them to hold anything back. They'd come from a country where people would hitchhike a thousand miles just to pick beets. Who could imagine these natives having the guile or the initiative to skip out on such a cushy job?

But now, at sunrise, as the temple cast a long shadow over the trees, not a single one of them was left.

"We hande[d] over everythi[ng]," Rusk said indistinctly. "Everythi[ng]!" When he was vexed he had a tendency to stuff more chewing tobacco into his mouth than he could really manage.

"I say we pick half a dozen men from each side and send them into the jungle to find those Indians," said Aldobrand.

"Then what?"

"Bring them back here along with everything they've stolen."

"How are twelve white men going to discipline five hundred natives?"

Aldobrand looked at Rusk as if he didn't understand the question.

"You're just trying to whittle us down," said Coehorn. "I'm not sending anybody away from here."

"We don't need the natives, Mr. Rusk," said Whelt. "There are nearly eighty of us. We can rebuild the temple ourselves. Remember what you said about the Labor Day Hurricane." One night aboard ship, Rusk had told a story about traveling through the Florida Keys to search for his cousin a few days after the big hurricane of 1935. Watching the disorganized efforts of the Coast Guard, he'd become convinced that if you put a movie studio like Kingdom Pictures in charge of rescue and evacuation, they would do a far more efficient job than the government, because studios knew better than anyone how to feed and shelter and transport masses of people on a tight schedule and a tight budget.

"No, I'm afraid nobody will be rebuilding anything," said Coehorn. "You squatters may think you're very clever but two can play that game." He gestured at the exposed half of the temple's acreage. The ancients had laid their foundations on top of a mixture of white clay and broken pottery, recently plowed into broad furrows by the raft-like palettes on which the Pozkitos had been dragging the great stone blocks away from the site. The whole tract was still strewn with debris, not only ropes and tools and timber and empty inga pods but also what looked at a distance like tarnished silver. Now the "other Americans" were hastily shifting their encampment there so that the deconstructionists would sit in the way of the reconstructionists just as the reconstructionists already sat in the way of the deconstructionists. Earlier today Trimble had observed the first tentative and peripheral fraternization between the two expeditions, but he knew that wouldn't last. Absently, he sucked his little finger. He had awoken to find the tip encased in a sort of fibrous thimble, presumably spun by some insect with unfathomable motives. His back still ached from sleeping on stone.

"You're not being rational," said Whelt, glaring at Coehorn.

"Don't talk to me about 'rational,' " said Coehorn, glaring back. "You've traveled two thousand miles from Hollywood to shoot a movie at this pyramid? Haven't you ever heard of plywood? Haven't you ever heard of *sets*?"

"As long as this goes on, everyone's snookered," said Aldobrand. "Someone will have to do the decent thing."

"We're not leaving," said Whelt.

"We're not leaving either," said Coehorn.

And they didn't.

PART TWO

The heat, we might add, is terrific, but make-ups
manage to survive. The jungle is as verdant as ever,
but mosquitoes never bother any one.

(From Bosley Crowther's review of the film
Law of the Tropics *in* The New York Times, *1941)*

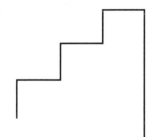

THEY'VE SENT ME AN ASSISTANT.

I went in this morning and there she was. It was as if someone had taken the image of an assistant I had in my head and made her flesh: twenty years old and so molten with youth under that prim gingham dress that she's almost painful to look at, like an ingot just pulled from the furnace, but also earnest and efficient and sincerely happy to have the job. Her name's Frieda and she lives with her parents and her two little brothers not far from my apartment in Springfield. I asked her who'd given her the security clearance to work in the warehouse, and she said it was a man named Mr. McKellar. So even after he claimed he was powerless to help, Winch came through for me. Of course, my new assistant may double the chances that I'll find what I'm looking for among "all the evidence in my case," but that's like buying two lottery tickets instead of one. If it takes five years to defeat the warehouse instead of ten years, my liver will still kill me long before we finish: it's not just the drinking, it's the drinking on top of the organ damage I suffered after I almost bled to death from an abdominal puncture in '57. The girl's help will be as futile as everything else in my life.

All the same, she's nice to have around. It wasn't until I tried to imagine what the evidence warehouse must seem like to her that it occurred to me I should at least get a coffee machine and a radio. I spent the morning teaching her how to work a flatbed editor. At lunchtime, after she ate her ham sandwich, I noticed her painting her right thumb with a clear liquid from a bottle, but it didn't smell like polish. When I asked her about it she blushed and told me that she's never grown out of sucking her thumb, so now she glazes it with colocynth vinegar twice a day, but it doesn't work so well any more because she's started to like the taste. My God, the sweetness of this girl. Just breathing the same air as Frieda might give me another few months on this coil, like old King David rejuvenating himself by lying beside the virgin Abishag; but I decided then that I wouldn't want her to stay too long with me even if she were willing. I'm not going to sit there day after day watching the light gradually fade from her eyes. That will be her husband's job.

She hasn't asked me yet why I only have two-thirds of a left ear, but she did mention that I sound "sort of British sometimes." I explained that I was begotten in a small colony of the British Empire: my late mother. And even after a decade of American schooling, I never entirely shook off her voice. Later, when I joined the Office of Strategic Services, my half-accent turned out to be an asset, because I fit right in among the northeastern aristocrats who talked like Douglas Fairbanks Jr. I once mentioned that to my mother and she happily took full credit, as if she'd had it in mind all along to train me for an organization that didn't yet exist. And I couldn't argue, because she'd tuned me exactly right. My mother grew up on Berkeley Square, like the song, and talked exactly how those Brahmins wished they could talk. An old man in our neighborhood once told me that listening to her haggling over the price of pastrami gave him more pleasure than any music he'd ever heard.

My mother was born into wealth, but by the time she came to New York there was nothing left. In 1912 her father took out enormous short-term loans against his estate to buy a stake in a British-American syndicate planning a historic consolidation of Atlantic shipping lines. The venture should have made him one of the richest men in London, but one of his American partners swindled him with the connivance of a bribable judge. Rather than rely on lawyers, my grandfather crossed the Atlantic to recover his investment, by force if necessary. But before he could locate his former partner, he came down with tuberculosis. My mother followed him to New York to nurse him until he died. By then the house on Berkeley Square was gone and the only inheritance was debts. But in the meantime my mother had fallen in love with a skating-rink porter, and she never went home.

I gave Frieda a two-sentence version of the story. But after that she kept asking for more details. I guess it's romantic.

The only thing I don't like about Frieda's arrival is that I'll never again be in a position where I can do Winch McKellar a favor in return. It was McKellar who recruited me into OSS in the first place. I first got to know him in the thirties when I was still at the *Mirror* and he was wasting his father's money investing in cabarets, becoming in the process one of those guys who are ubiquitous in the city for absolutely no good reason. We loathed each other.

But in the spring of 1943 I was back in New York on leave from the 2nd Photo Tech Squadron. At about four o'clock on Monday morning, the girl I'd spent most of the weekend with kicked me out of her suite at the Waldorf-Astoria, and there was only one place I could think of to get another drink in that part of midtown. When I turned the corner onto 49th Street, I saw there was already somebody standing in front of the entrance to the old Bering Strait Railroad Association of North America headquarters. In the slump of his shoulders I could read the same disappointment I felt myself a moment later when I realized we were looking at a perfume store.

"When did this place shut down?" I said.

"You leave New York for a while—"

"This is what happens. Right."

"Was it because of that poor bastard who died in the tank?"

"Are you kidding me? That was in '38. This place hadn't even peaked out yet."

"That was five years ago? The killer octopus? Jesus Christ, I'd like that time back." Finally he turned to look at me and his eyes widened behind his glasses. "Zonulet?"

I chuckled. "McKellar!" We embraced, and from then on all our previous hostility was no more than a vicious rumor that somebody else had started. I was still in my rumpled first lieutenant's uniform, but McKellar wore civilian clothes. "You in service?" I said.

"Sure."

"Where?"

"Same place you ought to be. Where are we going to get a drink? I'm not walking all the way to Broadway."

"I just came from the Waldorf."

"Is the bar there open?" McKellar said. The gonions of his jaw were so wide-set and pointy you could have opened bottles on them.

"No, that's why I didn't stay. But there *is* booze in that building."

"That much we do know."

On the way there we saw a fish-delivery truck pulling in around the back of the hotel, and we managed to sneak inside through the loading dock, which may not have been the most dignified use of our combat training that either of us had ever made. Soon after that we were opening a stolen bottle of sherry in the Waldorf's umbrella room. "This would be quite the romantic escapade if only you were a lady," observed McKellar. The room was still in the process of being adapted to the recent fashion for young engaged couples to walk around under tandem umbrellas, which was one of those developments that made me feel pretty content to be going back to war.

"Let me guess," I said. "You're with the Oh So Secret?" A nickname for the Office of Strategic Services.

"The Oh Such Snobs. Right. And I think you are exactly the fellow I needed to bump into." He looked down at the mackerel in his hand. "I don't even remember picking this up." He put it down. Then he poured some sherry on his index finger and dabbed it on my forehead.

"What the hell are you doing?"

"I'm anointing you. Holy orders. Now I can tell you the classified stuff and if you breathe a word of it the statue of Surgeon General Benjamin Rush on E Street will strike you down with a bolt of lightning."

"Is that official procedure?"

"Yes, under War Service Regulation My Big Dick. Listen, we're taking Sicily next month." The island had a scattering of partisans, radicals, turncoats, and Allied infiltrators, McKellar explained, but nothing resembling a coherent local support network for Operation Husky. What OSS hoped to give General Patton was a way of cinching everything together after the landings. And that was why they needed the Mafia. "We've been working with the junior wops over here to keep the ports tidy since '41. Sicily's different, though. All the *padroni* there hate the Moose so we thought it would be easy. But we keep hearing that no one will talk to us unless we go through Andreotti. Supposedly he's the only boss in America they all still respect. You know who Andreotti is?"

The smell of rain in here was distilled to an overproof. "Of course I know who Andreotti is. I was a crime reporter for eight years. Andreotti threatened to personally strangle me I can't even count how many times. Once it was because of a misapprehension and he apologized afterward."

"He apologized?"

"He sent two hookers to my apartment as a gift. I was out. They waited outside on the stoop all evening. I almost got evicted."

"OSS is all Yale boys—we don't have the right contacts for this kind of thing. And the FBI haven't helped any. Can you get us a friendly sit-down with Andreotti?"

I looked at my watch. "Not in the next three hours."

"That's when your leave ends?"

"Yeah."

He patted me on the shoulder. "Actually, your leave ends right now. I'm transferring you. The mere fact that you weren't with OSS already shows there's something wrong with the way we recruit." We drank to it, and that was how I began a career in intelligence that one day would smash like a meteorite into the semi-temple in Honduras.

But if, to some of us, the temple offered a long, complex fall, to others it offered a short, simple one. Around three years after my reunion with McKellar, in 1946, when a bloody and exhausted Hauptsturmführer Kurt Meinong staggered out of the trees and set eyes on it for the first time, what held his attention was not so much the monument itself as the human figure who stood at the edge of the terrace on top, two hundred feet up, silhouetted against the setting sun, unmistakably about to jump off.

Nine days before that, Meinong had arrived at what was supposed to be the last sanctuary he would ever require. To receive a rapturous welcome at Erlösungfeld, he would only have had to explain that he was a nepotal descendant of Augustus Meinong, the Saxony horse breeder who had come to Spanish Honduras in 1848 to found this devout farm colony in the forest. But after he revealed that he'd spent the last six years fighting for the glory of the Third Reich, the Erlösungfelders treated him like he was Jesus Christ on a furlough. Over a supper of salted pork in the meeting house that evening, many of the women wept as he recalled the night he first learned of his brother's sacrifice at Dramburg, and when he was obliged to confirm that everything they had heard about the Soviet rape of the Fatherland was true, and much worse besides, one farmer got so angry he literally started tearing out his hair. Several times Meinong was asked to narrate the specifics of his own war service, but although he'd noted with relief that the Erlösungfelders spoke forthrightly about Jews, there were children at these tables.

Because the majority of German immigrants had been expelled from Belize and Guatemala earlier in the war, but no comparable persecution had taken place in Spanish Honduras, it was felt by many in Erlösungfeld that Augustus Meinong's choice of this country all those years ago must have been not just felicitous but divinely inspired, and now that they would have the honor of sheltering this handsome knight of the realm they were all the more sure of it. If any Americans came looking for him, they said, or the local police, they would rather raze the settlement than give him up. Kurt did not expect that such a gracious gesture would be necessary, since he'd been careful on the way here, but he also knew it would be too dangerous to leave for quite a while, so he had better start getting used to émigré life in Erlösungfeld. They were extremely boring people, but he could live with that.

On the third night he lingered at the meeting house for quite a while after the women had cleared the tables. When only half a dozen men were left sitting on the terrace, one of the farmers produced a bottle of sugarcane schnapps. Rather sheepishly, as if he expected Meinong to condemn them as apostates, he explained that although Erlösungfelders did not drink among themselves, they brewed small quantities of spirits for their visitors. Meinong nodded as if he believed this story, wondering whether they'd had any other visitors since the last century.

They talked about Hitler and all that he'd done for Germany. Meinong kept his feelings about the Führer's volatility and egotism to himself. There had at one point been discussion, the farmers admitted, of traveling to Europe to fight for the Reich, and Meinong could tell they still felt guilty they hadn't. Of course, they were all eager to hear about his service in detail. When, just as a digression, he lamented how much of the war he'd had to spend in close contact with Jews, the farmers expressed their sympathy; but Meinong, now on his fourth large glass of schnapps, didn't find their sympathy quite heartfelt enough, and after it occurred to him that none of these men had ever met a Jew in person, he decided to make sure they understood exactly how stomach turning the experience had been, day after day, week after week. Before he knew it, he was telling them about his duties in the pathology section at Location D.

For a long time after he finished talking there was no sound but the scrubbing of crickets. Meinong drained his glass of schnapps and shakily poured himself another. The farmers exchanged glances, and one of them muttered a word that Meinong didn't quite catch. Then, with an almost telepathic synchrony, they got to their feet, picked Meinong up, and carried him to the ferny perimeter of the village.

Meinong was almost able to believe that this was an impromptu victory parade, the way a soccer team would sometimes bear their *Stürmer* around the pitch after a goal, but there was something too rough about their grip on his arms and legs. And when he found himself prone on the ground, with the brawniest of the farmers holding him down, he knew he'd made a bad mistake.

"'You shall not pollute the land in which you live,'" said the farmer with his knee on Meinong's back, "'for blood pollutes the land, and no atonement can be made for the land for the blood that is shed in it, except by the blood of the one who shed it.'" Some of the other farmers had already tied a noose, and now they threw it over the thickest branch of a kapok tree.

"They were just Jews!" wailed Meinong.

"They were women and children. You admitted that."

"It wasn't our land anyway. It was mostly in Poland. 'Beloved, never avenge yourselves, but leave it to the wrath of God.' Remember that? Romans, I think. 'Leave it to the wrath of God, for it is written—'" But then the Bible quoter cuffed him in the mouth.

Ever since he was in the SS, it had been an unwavering part of Meinong's toilet each morning to slide a razor blade inside the left wing of his shirt collar instead of a silver stay, and at Erlösungfeld he hadn't given up the habit any more than he had given up brushing his teeth. Now it saved his life. He waited until the noose had been tested and a stool put beneath it. When the Bible quoter on top of him shifted his weight in order to haul Meinong up, Meinong got one hand free. He slid the blade out of his collar, reached behind his head, and blindly made three quick slashes where he thought the Bible quoter's face and throat might be. The Bible quoter shrieked and fell backward. Then Meinong was off and running through the cane fields.

He had assumed the Erlösungfelders would turn back once he was off their land. But they were like bushmen chasing an antelope. Never could he have imagined he would have to flee for so long. Minutes turned into hours, hours into days. He grew almost wistful for the embrace of the Soviet army. The chase became the house in which he lived: he ate there and rested there and once, at the height of his delirium, masturbated there. Sometimes he was almost sure that the farmers must have given up, but then a ruckus in the distance would tell him they hadn't. They made no attempt at stealth, and sang hymns to keep their spirits up, so he would hear them even when he was so far ahead that he couldn't understand how they could possibly have stayed on his trail.

The end didn't come until the afternoon of the sixth day. By then they were deep in the jungle, deep enough that you could feel the pressure of it rising in your eardrums. He wished that instead of trying to lose the farmers in the wilderness he'd aimed for La Ceiba and taken the risk of trying to escape on a boat. The dirt and sweat and dried blood seemed to hang on him heavy as flannel, the skin beneath a Proterozoic mudscape of cuts and blisters and swellings and bites, an organ on his outside more livid and tender than any on his inside. Apart from the ants he picked off his arms there was nothing to eat around here but a few unripe papayas on the trees; yesterday he hadn't been able to keep any food down, but today he didn't seem to be throwing up any more, which he thought might be a bad sign, like when you're so cold you stop shivering. He knew he couldn't go on much longer. Every single step now was an epic in itself, a coin stolen from God's inside pocket. His pursuers were close enough behind him that there was no question of sitting down against a tree to recover his strength. No question at all. But he did anyway.

When he opened his eyes again, the farmers were no more than twenty yards away, their number somehow reduced from four to three. He wondered about the death they would give him, and was grateful that because of their clumsy hands and limited imaginations it couldn't possibly be as slow and precise and almost fugal as some of the deaths he had helped to give others.

Then *bang, bang, bang, bang,* and all three of them fell down. The reports sounded not unlike a Mauser. From out of the trees rose a feathery shock wave of birds.

Two small men came into view. They were clearly savages, with mahogany skin and black hair and bare chests decorated with necklaces. But they wore khaki field trousers and leather boots and carried bolt-action rifles. In a few seconds they would see Meinong. He had to get up. He had nothing left, absolutely nothing, and yet he refused to die. So he levered himself to his feet, and, with the gait of a puppet being dragged across a stage, he shambled away. He heard more shots as he went, and he half-hoped one would hit him, but he kept running.

And so at last he came to the temple.

There was some sort of shantytown here, or perhaps two shantytowns—one spread up the stepped hypotenuse of the temple and the other across the flat field beside it—and dozens of people, fully clothed Caucasians, moving among the huts and lean-tos like peasants in the ruins of Rome. He could smell wood fires and stewing meat. The existence of the great stone wedge out in this impossible place might have inspired some awe or confusion in Meinong if he hadn't been so distracted by the figure at the very top. Even from down here there was something about the figure's posture that made it obvious he or she hadn't just gone up there for the view.

"Who are you?"

The sandy-haired fellow who stood in front of him had spoken in English. Kurt tried to remember the name on his forged ICRC papers. But he couldn't. He was just too tired. "I am Hauptsturmführer Kurt Meinong," he said in a voice wizened almost to nothing by thirst.

"Where did you come from?"

Kurt gestured behind him.

"You came from the jungle?"

"Yes."

"But you're a white man. I mean, where did you come from before that? Did you come from . . . out in the world?"

"Yes."

"We haven't seen anyone from out in the world since . . . well, since we got here. Eight years. It's so damned strange to see you . . . so if you've been out there, you know what's happened? Since we left?"

"Yes."

The fellow looked panicked for a moment. Called upon to ask a question, any question, his mind had naturally gone blank. "Uh, what about Hitler and Czechoslovakia and all that stuff?" he said at last. "Was there a war? When we left they were saying there might be a war. You sound European. We haven't had any news."

"No news?" said Meinong, beginning to understand that this conversation might have consequences. To match the final physical and spiritual efforts he had just made, he would have to launch a final mental effort. He thought of a history of the Siege of Paris he'd read in which it was recounted that the worst trial wasn't the famine or the shelling but simply the isolation from whatever was going on outside the city's walls. "You've had no news? For eight years?"

"Nothing whatsoever."

"Yes, there was a war," Meinong said carefully. "Russia invaded Poland in 1939. Then Japan made a surprise attack on the United States. Together Stalin and Hirohito hoped to take over the world."

"What happened?"

"We beat them back."

"You fought? You personally?"

He wasn't going to make the same mistake he'd made at Erlösungfeld. "For the German-American Alliance, yes. It was a long, awful war. At least fifty million dead."

"My God."

Before this fellow could ask any more questions, Meinong pointed up at the top of the temple. Now that he'd completed the infernal triathlon, he was going to faint, and he wanted to know if anyone was going to intervene in the suicide. "Are you aware that—"

But then the figure leaped out into empty air.

☙

Around the same time Kurt Meinong arrived at the site, Elias Coehorn Jr. was holding a special evening breakfast in his bungalow. His three dining companions were his friend Irma Kittredge, *New York Evening Mirror* reporter Leland Trimble, and Walter Pennebaker, the former head bookkeeper from the Lollipop on 47th Street and the closest thing Coehorn had to a secretary of the treasury. The intimate gathering was to toast Pennebaker's departure. Tomorrow he was going back to New York. For the very first time in the eight years they'd spent here, Coehorn was sending someone home. It was the cognac that had given him the idea.

If you didn't count the vibration purges he used to undergo every two weeks in New York to guarantee a charmeuse complexion well into middle age, Coehorn had only ever made one long-term investment. One snowy afternoon in 1936, back when among his father's templar order of personal accountants there were still at least a couple who could be tricked into advancing him cash, he'd been on his way to meet a friend whom he'd promised to compensate handsomely for kindling a symbolic funeral pyre in her apartment during her birthday party in order to emphasize some rhetorical point that could not now be recalled. But on Park Avenue he'd bumped into another, older friend, freckled Brimslow Rennie. The Rennie family had lost everything after Black Tuesday, and Coehorn hadn't seen Brim in years.

Brim explained that the following morning he was sailing for France because he'd just purchased a small cognac distillery in Charente-Inférieure from its bankrupt alcoholic owner. "I'm going to turn the place around," he said through his lisp. "I'll be in profit in four or five years for certain. The first thing I'll do is buy back Mother's pearls." What Rennie didn't yet have, however, was money to replace the distillery's rusty stills with modern equipment, and having found no investors in New York he was hoping that somehow he'd be able to raise it from his fellow passengers on the steamship. When Coehorn asked what he could expect in return for six crisp bills he happened to have in an envelope in his pocket, his friend replied that a three-hundred-dollar stake would get him six cases of cognac every New Year's Eve for life, starting in 1946, the first year that the 1936 eau-de-vie would have aged in the barrels long enough to be worth drinking. Judging that if anyone could make a success of this, diligent Brim could, Coehorn handed over everything he had on him, went home pleased with himself, and then forgot about it for several years.

But on December 31st, 1945, during preparations for that night's masked ball, it occurred to him for the first time that he hadn't left any instructions to forward the cognac to Spanish Honduras. In fact, if he was out of touch for long enough, Rennie might conclude that Coehorn's cognac could just as well be sold to someone else. And that was what got Coehorn wondering about what else had been going on his absence. He was almost thirty-four, and by now most of the padlocks would have come off his trust fund. Also, he was pretty sure that every five years or so his father was in the habit of updating his will. Before another New Year's Eve passed Coehorn wanted to reassure everyone in New York that he was still absolutely in the process of exporting the temple to Braeswood and that as soon as he was finished he would return like Odysseus to take his revenge on the cognac's other suitors and enjoy what was his.

Even if all he mailed north was some chunk of corbel that had broken off during the initial deconstruction, a paperweight of Mayan limestone, at least no one could deny that he'd made a start on the job. Like erosion by the elements it might be slow but it was also irreversible. All this time, he'd refused to allow even a single member of the expedition to leave the site, since Whelt already had a dangerous advantage of numbers, and he knew that if one guest slipped away from your dinner dance with the air of having something better to do then all the others would soon follow. But these days his rivals seemed so pallid and threatless, quivering up there on the steps like a cat stuck in a tree. So when it occurred to him that by employing Pennebaker as a courier he could be rid of him for a few months, that decided matters for good.

"The question, obviously, is how he should present the history of the expedition when he gets back to New York," said Coehorn to his guests. "We can't go into so much detail that it gets boring. We can't narrate every minute of the eight years we've been here. Especially that early period—'38, '39—there was so little of interest going on."

෨

December 2nd, 1938

Carrotwood Hospital
5600 Samuell Boulevard
Dallas, TX
United States

My love,

The last time I wrote you, they were still telling us they were going to take a sack of mail back to San Esteban which is the little town we came through on the way here where I met that bleaty witch lady I told about before, & they'd have it sent north. But now with everything that's been going on Mr. Rusk says there won't be any mail going back to San Esteban for the time being. So I guess I'm just going to have to fold this letter up & file it in my jewelry box next to the first one.

In any case, I don't even know if they let you read the letters I send, I'd venture they probably don't, in fact I'd venture they certainly don't, & even if they did I don't know whether you'd be disposed to read them or whether on the contrary you wouldn't even want to burn them in the fireplace in case by accident you took a breath of me in the smoke. So I can imagine you saying, Why for heaven's sake do I even bother to write. Well, my love, my sweet Emmy Emmy Emmy, for the same reason I talk to you in my head most all the time, because I'd rather talk to you, not there to hear it, than talk to anybody else in the world, there to hear it or otherwise.

We've been here more than three weeks, & the shoot was only supposed to take two. So the real [illegible] of it is that if the folks from New York City had only let us put the temple back together temporary like we asked we could've been finished by now & everybody could've gone whistling on their way. But Mr. Coehorn won't budge. That poor perjinkity boy Mr. Whelt looks like he's stretched on a rack & every minute we fall behind schedule is another turn of the roller, & Mr. Rusk ran out of smokeless tobacco a week ago so now he just chews leaves from the forest & they make his tongue swell up. I like Mr. Rusk, he's blunt most of the time but when you ask him about his old mother & her Persian cats waiting for him back home in Los Feliz you can see he's got a soft heart underneath ha ha.

Mr. Rusk says the insurance doesn't cover more than a week of delays, so we're out of the state of grace, & if there are any accidents now with the cast or the crew or the equipment then Kingdom Pictures won't be compensated

& the whole production might be in trouble, or even more trouble than it already is. But he says there's still enough money in the budget to pay all this overtime, though he won't say how much longer that'll last & we all know Mr. Coehorn's daddy has more money than Kingdom Pictures & the Lord God put together so if it comes down to that sort of contest we can't win.

The bigger hitch is the canned food we brought with us ran out pretty quick & we don't have any natives to butler for us. So Mr. Rusk is organizing posses to go out into the forest & get our food that way, which is just what the New Yorkers are doing too, except we go south & they go north. Lucky for us we have Bit Sewald the prop man, who made the bows & arrows on a caveman movie last year, but he doesn't know a thing about hunting, & we also have Amos Fleming the actor, who doesn't know a thing about making bows & arrows, but he's been hunting since he was a baby he says.

I hear the New Yorkers sometimes come home with nothing but baskets of rotten fruit. But yesterday we got a slumgullion the cooks said was venison except then I heard a rumor that really it was some little wild piggies called tapirs rhymes with papers. Folks don't like to be ignorant of what all they're eating, especially for instance Miss Thoisy who plays Marla & wears her mink stole even in this heat. She was pitching a fit to Mr. Rusk saying, Do you really expect us to eat whatever filthy offal you've dragged out of that forest. Thank heavens for Mr. Aldobrand the Brit who plays Miss Thoisy's ex-husband. Everybody likes him & he always smoothes things over. By the time he finished giving his speech everybody had decided it was real fun to eat like we were on a camping trip.

In any case I heard a whisper that back in Kansas our high-tone Miss Thoisy once nearly went to jail for stealing cabbages off a truck so she isn't one to complain about making do, & believe you me the ones who say at seven o'clock they'd rather starve by half past eight they're gobbling anything that's left. It's a little bland though because the natives took our salt & pepper.

Forgot to tell you we got a new recruit. Miss Burlingame who's a Brit like Mr. Aldobrand & an archaeologist or an anthropologist I can't remember which or maybe both. She's a sweetheart but so jumpy that sometimes you can't even talk to her. She told me she came out here with the New Yorkers to study the temple but when she found out they were shipping it home she decided that wasn't right, like those ladies from the Association for the Preservation of Southern Antiquities. She was hoping to study the natives too but there aren't any so she told me she's studying us Americans instead, & I couldn't tell if she was joking about that or not, probably not because she doesn't make many jokes.

She wouldn't be the only one studying. Mr. Trimble's always paying close attention. He's the gossip man who came along to cover our shoot but he's from New York & he doesn't seem disposed to pledge allegiance to either of the flags. The first time you meet him you can't help but take a liking to his applesauce but pretty soon you feel like a sucker that he ever fooled you like that. When there's a mosquito in your bedroom & all night you think it's crawling on your neck even when it isn't there, well that's how it is after you catch Mr. Trimble watching you while you were unawares just once.

Oh Emmy do you remember the last time before they caught us. When the man on the radio was talking about all the ritzies in New York dancing the Half Doodle & we tried to dance it ourselves but we didn't know the steps so we just swung each other around & I ended up on my back &

Better leave off because there's a girl sitting there sewing & she'll see me blush. But I promise I'll write again soon. Even if I can't send it. I love you Emmeline Sapp.

Yours forever,
Gracie

Jervis Whelt sketches a plan for a second, bigger heliodon to calculate the position of the sun with respect to the position of his camera and his actors . . . Elias Coehorn Jr. lies prone in his hammock letting an ice cube melt on the back of his neck . . . Sound engineer Wayne Dutch tries to sculpt, from memory, the head of his ex-fiancée out of wet clay . . . Leland Trimble strolls through the New York camp beside clarinetist Sandy Mitchell, reminiscing about New Orleans, a city he has never visited . . . Crane operator Fales Apinews argues with crane steerer Emil Berg about whether it was William Powell or James Cagney who starred in The Public Enemy *. . . Kermit Rusk braids liana bark into rope . . . Joan Burlingame feels guilty for biting her fingernails . . . Assistant wardrobe "man" Gracie Calix folds up the letter to her niece and puts it in her jewelry box . . .*

May 15th, 1939

Carrotwood Hospital
5600 Samuell Boulevard
Dallas, TX
United States

My love,

The most awful awful awful thing happened. Mr. Rusk is dead. He was showing a few of us his new perpetual motion machine when all of a sudden he curses & grabs the back of his neck, first time I ever heard him curse. He shows us all a scorpion that must've been hiding in his collar, just a baby one. He chuckles & tosses it off the edge. Then about a minute later he gets a sort of dreamy look on his face & says he has to lie down for a minute or two.

I help him back to his cabin & almost as soon as he gets into bed with his clothes on he's asleep but still mumbling & already hotter than hate. I stayed with him all night but he just got worse & worse, jolting like he was bouncing off an electric fence sometimes, once without even opening his

eyes he reaches out & grabs my wrist so hard I think I got
a sprain, & then by dawn it was over. That man worked
so hard for us all & now he's gone. I'm desolated Emmy I
truly am.

I'm worried too. I know it isn't right when he's barely in
the ground to think of anything but the man's own life cut
short & his old mother back in Los Feliz not even knowing
but I think the rest of us are in bad trouble now. There were
two men in charge of this shoot, Mr. Whelt & Mr. Rusk, &
Mr. Whelt does just as much as Mr. Rusk did if not more,
I'm not sure he ever sleeps, but the difference is Mr. Whelt
doesn't care about anything that doesn't show up on camera.
An empty stomach doesn't show up on camera so he doesn't
care about an empty stomach, even his own. That lens is
his only eye. It was always Mr. Rusk who organized the
trapping & the foraging out in the forest & let me tell you we
have all the preview we need of what happens when there's
no Mr. Rusk because there's no Mr. Rusk for the New York
folks, never has been, & that's why their trapping & foraging
just sputtered out a while back when they got tired of going
out into the forest all the time. Now they buy most of their
food from us. What do they buy it with, they buy it with
ice. Yes Emmy you read that right: even though the New
Yorkers only thought they'd be in the jungle for two weeks
they brought an ice-making machine all the way here, hand
pumped & runs on ammonia, because Mr. Coehorn doesn't
like to go without a couple of Horse's Necks every evening
except of course it's no use for that any more because the
natives got all his brandy.

We gladly send over a few hampers for each sack full
of ice, but the ice-making machine can only make so much
ice every day & it's not enough to buy all the food the New
Yorkers want at the price we give them so they have to
barter with what all else they got. We thought they'd handed
everything over to the natives just like us but it turns out
they still have all kinds of department-store this-and-thats

the natives didn't want because they didn't understand
what they were for. Orange bitters, Alka-Seltzer, ear plugs,
perfume, Dubble Bubble, pumice stones, chess sets, hair
pomade, dried lavender, Benzedrine, [illegible], Chinese
fans, oh & rubbers, I'm sure some of the crew over here
brought rubbers themselves, a man must dream after all ha
ha, but only a few, whereas Mr. Coehorn packed a whole
box, & maybe rubbers aren't as important as food but Miss
Droulhiole the assistant make-up lady is already so big that
we all agree she must've got storked on the ship over here
& not by that handsome gentleman from the United Fruit
Company who bought us all drinks in San Esteban, & also
I heard there's a girl over yonder in the same predicament,
so you can draw your own conclusions.

Mr. Whelt didn't bring any sundries like that because
he didn't figure they'd be important & maybe they aren't
but folks are hankering for them, oh my goodness how
we're hankering for them now we've been out in the jungle
for months. The New Yorkers have this special money like
play money they call scrip that's printed on artificial silk, &
some people here were saying we should have special money
too, but Mr. Rusk & Mr. Whelt wouldn't have it, so we hand
everything out just about equal, & it may sound a little New
Deal but I'm glad we do because folks are still cordial to
each other over on this side.

But one day everything's going to run out. I don't just
mean the D. Bubble & such. We're almost out of film. You're
wondering, how'd we gobble so much film when we haven't
even started making the movie, but it's all test shots, Mr.
Whelt keeps making test shots with stand-ins cause he says
if he makes enough test shots then when the New Yorkers
finally give us the temple back we'll be so prepared we can
make the whole movie without one minute or one frame
wasted. The lights sure do bring out the moths.

Mr. Whelt didn't mean to come anywhere near using up
all the stock but there's less than we thought cause a few

cans got exposed by accident & Mr. Rusk God rest his soul
only figured it out a few weeks ago doing an inventory.
Just today I heard Mr. Whelt asking Mr. Yang the developer
how you make celluloid film from scratch, out here in the
jungle he meant, what a lot of horsefeathers, but he was
dead serious, so Mr. Yang had to tell him that to make
nitrate film you need silver chloride & nitro-somesuch &
you can't exactly cook those up in a skillet. He & Mr. Yang
were having this discussion only a few hours after Mr. Rusk
passed which I didn't think was too respectful but when
something like that happens it's like Mr. Whelt doesn't even
notice or he pretends he doesn't, I remember him looking
more upset about the film finishing sooner than he thought
than he did this week about Mr. Rusk finishing sooner than
he thought.

Paper too. Maybe bringing a printing press all the
way to Honduras seems about as silly as bringing an ice-
making machine, but you need it for call sheets & script
revisions & memos & so on when it would take too long to
have somebody type it up five sheets at a time on carbon, so
we brought a printing press & about twenty reams of paper.
But there was a week in February when there was a bad
wind blowing through & folks were just feeling ornery as all
get out, I think Mr. Whelt & Mr. Rusk were scared for their
authority no matter how many fine words Mr. Aldobrand
said, so they had to hush people down & in the end they
say OK from now on everybody can use the paper for what
all bodily contingencies they must, no more dead leaves.
They were only meaning to give out one sheet per body per
day, but there's a stampede up the steps & before long it's
all gone & all I managed to get my hands on was a few torn
pieces left over. I know I said folks are still cordial to each
other over on this side but not that day they weren't.

I did bring some nice writing paper of my own to write
you on but I didn't bring enough cause I never expected
to be here so long & that's almost gone now. Then the

other morning I was talking to Miss Droulhiole about the
paper running out & she asks me what I need paper for &
shamefaced I have to explain that I still write letters even
though they won't be sent & she tells me she does just the
same. I didn't think anything of it but that night Trimble
comes along & says a little jungle bird told him I'm short of
writing paper for writing to my dear ones & he'd like to make
me a gift of a few sheets.

They're scented & I can't understand for the life of me
how they held up so long under these toad-stranglers we've
been having. I ask him what he wanted for them & he looks
offended & says, Nothing, nothing at all. Now Emmy I knew
I oughtn't to put myself in any sort of hock to that man but
I was thinking how if I ran out of paper I wouldn't be able
to write to you any more & my dear heart it makes me so
glad to write to you, so I took it. He wouldn't tell me where
he got it, & the next day I asked Miss Droulhiole if she said
anything to Trimble about the paper & she swore she never
did.

I better explain what I meant up there by perpetual
motion machine. Mr. Rusk named it that but he told us it's
not really a perpetual motion machine because a perpetual
motion machine is powered by nothing but its own self &
his machine is powered by rain. Let's see if I can explain
how it works. It's a block & tackle for pulling heavy loads
up from the bottom of the steps to the top. There's a barrel
at the top of the temple that fills up when it's raining, &
the barrel is roped through a pulley to a sled, so when the
barrel's full you take the catch off the block & pay out the
rope so the barrel drops down the flat side & pulls the sled
up the steps, & when the barrel's nearly at the bottom it runs
out of rope underneath & tips over so all the rainwater spills
out, & when it's empty it's light enough so the weight of the
sled with nothing on it sliding back down the steps pulls the
barrel back up the flat side to the top of the temple. Did you
get all that. I'd draw you a little diagram but you know I'm

not much for drawing. Guess it doesn't matter if you can't picture it, I ought to remember just because I want to picture everything that's going on where you are it doesn't mean you want to picture everything that's going on where I am.

The other morning a few of us were sitting around gabbing about what it must've been like for the Mayans who built this place all those years ago & how long they lived & whether a Mayan mother would lose more babies in the cradle than an Okie mother & so on. You can imagine Emmy there were a lot of opportunities for indecorous talk in a discussion like that & I don't claim much education myself but sometimes the ignorance around here can make your eyes spin in your head. Can't even remember how we got ourselves on to the subject, but Mr. Dutch the sound engineer, he announces that a lady can have a baby a year for ten years, but she can't have one baby & then wait ten years & then have another baby, because a lady's ovaries, he said, are like canned ham, it lasts a long time before you open it but once you open it you just have to keep eating it, at least a little off the top every so often, or it starts to go bad. We say to him, No, Mr. Dutch, that isn't even how canned ham works, let alone a lady's ovaries, but he's just stuck on it.

So I tell him my parents had my brother when my mother was nineteen & I don't know why but after that they didn't have another til my mother was forty-one & they had me, & my brother has a daughter of his own, which means I have a niece only a year younger than me, & because of some bad feeling in the family I didn't even meet her til around the time we were both finishing high school, so it wasn't like meeting a niece or even a sister, just a charming new friend with a bit of a resemblance.

& oh my goodness Emmy by then the things I was saying were of no pertinence at all to Mr. Dutch & his theory of the ovaries but sometimes when I get an excuse to talk about you I just can't stop til I'm stopped. If Mr. Dutch didn't interrupt

with in fact the female tubes are more like a sleepy bear then
I might could've just kept on, I would've told them about
how you looked that first time I saw you, with the lily pollen
stains all over your dress, about how I saw you looking
back at me & I didn't dare hope your heart was stamping &
whinnying like mine was. When I think on that my darling
that's when I'm saddest that it all turned out like it did. I'd
better finish now. I love you Emmeline Sapp. I know you
don't believe in God but saying a prayer that won't be heard
isn't any sillier than writing a letter that won't be sent. So
remember Mr. Rusk in your prayers.

Yours forever,
Gracie

*Elias Coehorn Jr. plays a round of the card game Canfield
with caterer Art Canfield, which continues to amuse him
every time . . . Masseuse Patricia Boniakowski wonders if,
seven months ago, back in her apartment in Astoria, she
might have left her curling irons on . . . First assistant director
Rick Halloran celebrates after successfully snatching a live
fish out of the river with his bare hands for the first time
after so many weeks of failure . . . Jervis Whelt asks Freddie
Yang to explain to him in greater detail the principle of
electropositivity in metals . . . Leland Trimble haggles over a
pair of opera glasses with Coehorn's friend Irma Kittredge . . .
Joan Burlingame realizes she has forgotten the collective
noun for frogs and would have no way of checking if for some
reason it became important to know . . . Virginia Droulhiole's
baby kicks . . . Gracie Calix folds up the letter to her niece
and puts it in her jewelry box . . .*

～

"Actually, I remember quite a lot going on in '38 and '39," said Irma.

"Regardless, you must get through it as briskly as possible," Coehorn told Pennebaker. "Chop chop, just the facts."

"What about something a bit more impressionistic?" said Irma. "You know, what life was like for a range of different people. A sort of cross-section."

"I can't think of anything more tiresome," said Coehorn. "Much better to—"

But he was interrupted by his head chef wheeling a serving cart into the dining room, or not so much wheeling it as grinding it, since by now it had only one wheel that still turned.

On the serving cart were four plates under blackened pewter cloches and a jug of cloudy red liquid with a lot of ice cubes, condensation cascading down the outside.

"Now, how long have you been working on this?" said Coehorn.

"About eight months," said the head chef.

"Justify your labors."

"To eat, we have dry-cured peccary ham and poached wild duck eggs on an unleavened manioc-flour muffin with a Hollandaise sauce made from wild duck egg yolk, breadnut butter, and juice of the unripe marlberry. To drink, we have manioc spirit and pickled casana juice seasoned with palm-frond charcoal, chili pepper, more unripe marlberry juice, and a Worcestershire sauce made from manioc vinegar, inga sugar, striped anchovy, pokeweed garlic, bamboo charcoal, and various other jungle spices."

Coehorn looked around delightedly. "Has everyone got it?"

"No," said Irma, who was wearing a gown she'd sewn from the lining of one of Coehorn's old ruined suits.

"Eggs Benedict and a Bloody Mary!" said Coehorn. "Just like they serve at the Waldorf. Notwithstanding a chemical outrage I once suffered in a limousine, it's the best hangover cure in the world. In fact it may even beat the outrage."

"I don't think I ever drank a Bloody Mary before," said Trimble.

"Well, even in New York you can't get one just anywhere. There's only a small fraternity of qualified bartenders."

This evening breakfast to toast Pennebaker's departure was a sufficiently special occasion that Coehorn hadn't felt any hesitation in further glamorizing it with the premiere of the Eggs Pozkito and the Pozkito Mary. No one but he and the head chef knew quite how disproportionate a share of the settlement's productive capacity had been diverted toward this enterprise over the last eight months (although Pennebaker must have suspected). But it was worth it, because this breakfast was Coehorn's temple to the gods. Just as the Mayans' own temple—in common with the Hanging Gardens of Babylon, or Braeswood and the neighboring estates along the Gold Coast—could have been built only by a civilization with the surplus resources to indulge even its most grandiose fancies, so this breakfast had been made possible only by the current prosperity of the camp. Back when they were all still grateful for every fried wasp this would never have happened. In other words, the meal over which they would be discussing how to convey Coehorn's visionary leadership to those back in New York was itself that leadership's best symbol and substantiation. Unfortunately one couldn't carry a poached wild duck egg two thousand miles. So here they were composing an official history instead.

"Pennebaker, when you're sitting there with my father, or with one of Trimble's colleagues from the *Mirror*, or with whomever else wants to know—when you're sitting there and your diction is temporarily intelligible between mouthfuls of funnel cake—I think you'll have to start by explaining what good capitalists we are," said Coehorn as his head chef poured four glasses of Pozkito Mary, careful not to spill a drop.

At all the mines, quarries, plantations, and logging camps operated by subsidiaries of the Eastern Aggregate Company, and at some of the remoter factories and canneries, scrip was in circulation. Even in the states where it was illegal to pay workers in scrip vouchers that could only be spent at company stores, you could still offer advances on wages in that form, and workers always took advances when they could get them. To discourage counterfeiting, most denominations were printed not on paper but on rayon, an innovation unique to Eastern Aggregate. Elias Coehorn Sr. didn't give a lot of homilies, but one day when his son was about fourteen he had produced a ten-dollar voucher blotched brown with blood. "Last month a lumberjack in Alaska was stabbed to death by two other men who wanted to take this from him. His widow mailed it to me for reasons of which she could not give a comprehensible account in her letter. But do you know why I'm showing it to you, boy?" Young Coehorn had shaken his head. "This is worthless to you and me. There is no store in the state of New York that will accept it. Somewhere I have a hundred uncut specimen sheets of identical bills. But in Alaska it was worth killing for. This scrap of artificial silk was worth killing for for no other reason than because I said so. I could do the same for any object in the world that's big enough to stamp my name on it in six-point type. I could do the same for any dead leaf clogging our gutters. Do you understand? That is the power you may inherit one day. You must be mindful of that."

In the unmindful years that followed, the lesson might not have had its intended effect on Elias Coehorn Jr.: rather than helping him to see dead leaves as potential banknotes, it helped him to see banknotes as no more than mulch putting on airs, especially when, to take one instance of many, he encountered a friend in the street who wanted to refurbish a cognac distillery. During a meeting about the Honduras expedition so tedious that Coehorn thought he could feel his cerebrospinal fluid beginning to coagulate, the Eastern Aggregate logistician opposite him had said, "Usually when we send people out a long way from any banks, we issue scrip, but you won't be down there long enough to need it. Now, these import liability warrants we talked about on the telephone—" Coehorn stopped him. "I want scrip." He realized that he did, after all, want to experience for himself this particular privilege of his father's: if he was to have a kingdom, even for a few days, then it should have a royal mint.

But just as the manager had said, within the initial timetable of the expedition, there wasn't any use for scrip. On the ship and at the site there were no company stores. Everyone just took whatever supplies they needed. Only after the native grifters made off with their loot did Coehorn decide to issue currency. The maxim of the settlement was not going to be a communistic "From each according to his ability, to each according to his need," and some medium of exchange was required to allocate what resources they had left (or even just to get a poker tournament going to pass the time). And in retrospect this decision was a stroke of genius, because it produced a toytown version of a free market.

Not entirely free, of course. The Eastern Aggregate camp could also be regarded as a planned economy, with Pennebaker as its chief planner. Coehorn regarded accountancy as a superstition and forward planning of almost any kind as an embrace of death. Pennebaker, on the other hand, had dreamed since he was a child of becoming a bookkeeper so he could frolic in credits and debits for the rest of his life. At the camp, it was always Pennebaker who reminded Coehorn that they needed to sell more ice to the Angelenos, or that they couldn't be so generous with the reserves of bubble gum, or that they were devoting too much foraging time to obscure seasonings like pokeweed. And he was as pesteringly attentive to the welfare of the citizenry as he was to the welfare of the state, even though people hadn't come all the way to the jungle just to be told to brush their teeth or get some rest or save some of that for later when they might be hungry again. It was intolerable. That he was always right simply made it worse. Even Irma agreed he had to go.

"Well, Mr. Coehorn," Pennebaker said, "I guess I'll begin by getting everybody up to speed on the difference between fiat money and specie money in this particular context. We had the company scrip, but out here it didn't really seem to have any value, because—"

"Oh my God, Pennebaker, I'm already falling into a coma," exclaimed Coehorn, his head in his hands. "This is worse than a logistics meeting. I said one or two paragraphs! What was that? Six paragraphs already?"

"No, Mr. Coehorn, that was only . . . seventeen words so far."

"Eighteen words too many. Let's just scratch the economics."

"If you'll allow me, Mr. Coehorn, I think my experience from the *Mirror* might come in handy here," said Trimble. "As a newsman, you learn pretty soon that if you want to tell a really contortuplicated story, you have to tell it through human beings, not facts and figures."

Another reason Coehorn had no misgivings about sending Pennebaker away was that he got such good counsel from Trimble. It had emerged that the ratty little fellow could be quite astute, and although Trimble moved amphibiously between the two camps, Coehorn knew that deep down he was a New York man and he had New York interests at heart. Coehorn could only pity the *Hearts in Darkness* crew in that respect, because if there was anyone who had their interests at heart it certainly wasn't their boy king Jervis Whelt. "Trimble's right," he said. "Start with something interesting. I know the imminence of your reunion with your beloved funnel cakes may be clouding your judgment but do try to apply yourself to the problem."

"Just to be clear, Mr. Coehorn, you want me to pass over '38 and '39 as fast as I can," said Pennebaker.

"Yes."

"Then I slow down as we enter the early part of this decade."

"No, not necessarily. I don't remember those years being very eventful either."

࿇

[illegible] 26th [illegible]

Carrotwood [illegible]
[illegible] Samuell [illegible]
[illegible] TX
United [illegible]

My love,
    Ever since [illegible] ran out [illegible] trying to invent [illegible] even when [illegible] experience making paper [illegible] type of trees [illegible] catty whompus [illegible] it hardly [illegible] & the pen goes right through [illegible]
    o to hell with it

Virginia Droulhiole plays peek-a-boo with her son Colby . . .
Elias Coehorn Jr. receives fellatio from croupier Carl Ivo . . .
Irma Kittredge warms up her bathwater in a boiler made
from one of the generators that used to power the floodlights

before the fuel ran out . . . Jervis Whelt, kneeling on the upper terrace, where there was once a handsome peripteros until one half was disassembled and the remaining half collapsed during a storm, draws a map of the other encampment . . . Walter Pennebaker estimates the metabolic fuel value of jungle honey in calories per ounce . . . Leland Trimble comforts sobbing carpenter Dick Schwalbe . . . George Aldobrand plays cricket with a tapir-hide ball of his own construction . . . Gracie Calix wads up the letter to her niece and throws it away . . .

September 3rd, 1942

Carrotwood Hospital
5600 Samuell Boulevard
Dallas, TX
United States

My love,

So much to tell. I haven't been able to write for a while because it took so long for the papermaking unit to learn how to mix the slurry so the paper doesn't fall apart when you write on it & then for the first few months they were only making a few sheets a day so there was none for poor old Gracie. I didn't like to write on the mushy paper because you couldn't make out the words, which shouldn't matter because Emmy my darling you're never going to read these letters anyhow, so I could write on the rain with my finger for all the difference it makes, but I can't help wanting to write real letters, so I guess in my heart of heart of heart of hearts I still think one day I'll get these letters to you & maybe I'll even be sitting there watching you read them. Somebody needs to knock some sense into me wouldn't you say Emmy.

I ought to start from the beginning but I don't even know where that is. Well here goes. The folks at Kingdom Pictures were expecting us back by Christmas '38 with a few cans of

film so they could start shooting the scenes at the beginning
of the movie set in New York. Emmy did you know they
always shoot movies out of order, I sure didn't before I
got into this business, & now for all you know I wrote the
end of this letter before I wrote the salutation ha ha. But
Christmas '39 & Christmas '40 had come & gone & Mr. Whelt
said he's sure Mr. Spindler will be understanding of the
difficulties we've faced out here in Honduras but all the same
it won't be to the movie's advantage to have fallen so far
behind schedule. So what he wants to do is go back with the
whole movie shot, so that all Mr. Spindler has to do is put his
seal on a final cut before they send it out to theaters.

We still can't shoot the temple scenes because we still
don't have the whole temple. But Mr. Whelt said there's
no reason why we can't shoot the New York scenes with
the Coutts family since they were only going to be shot on
a sound stage anyway, we just have to build a few sets &
props & such. The problem is there wasn't much film
left after all Mr. Whelt's test shots, not nearly enough to
shoot even just these New York scenes. So what Mr. Whelt
invented is a little like those *"tableaux vivants"* we used to
see at county fairs you know the ones, except I remember
the ladies weren't [illegible] to move a muscle for reasons
of decorum but Mr. Whelt makes sure there's half a dozen
actors all moving around & talking like cattle auctioneers to
get across as much in five or six seconds as they normally
would in a half a reel.

Film isn't the only thing we're short of . . .

[section abridged]

About a month after that, when it seemed like things
couldn't get much worse, Mr. Aldobrand had his face
ripped off by a monkey. Yes you read that right. He was out
foraging, his third trip out that day they said & no surprise
knowing how hard he works for the rest of us, when this
critter just jumps on him out of the trees for no reason
at all & before they can get it off him it's already taken

his nose & his upper lip & most of his cheeks. He was so cheerful about it when Dr. Zasa was working on him back at the camp, even though he must've known the doctor couldn't do much more than put a bandage on it, Not to worry, my face is insured at Lloyd's he says & I think he was joking though I guess it could be true because I heard Mary Pickford insured her hair. Mr. Apinews who was with him when it happened wouldn't quit talking about how sore he was the monkey got away before they could revenge themselves on the little so-and-so.

A few days ago Dr. Zasa decided he should take the bandages off, not that I really believe he had any idea of the [illegible] time to take the bandages off an injury like that, he's only a studio doctor not a surgeon. Oh Emmy it's beyond my powers of description to tell you what Mr. Aldobrand looks like now & I'm glad it is because just to write it down would be a kind of cruelty I think. We ought to be treating Mr. Aldobrand the same way we treated him before but the truth is if I just look straight at him for a second I have to run off on my own somewhere & sit down & shake for a few minutes.

If our high-tone Miss Thoisy had the same happen to her she'd wish the monkey had killed her instead because nothing means more to her than her looks, but Mr. Aldobrand is so much the opposite that he goes around as if he couldn't care less, which sounds sort of salutary for the rest of us but really we wish he'd show a little more of a reaction, cause it doesn't feel right.

When folks first saw his new face they were saying it's finally time to send somebody back to America, we ought to send Mr. Aldobrand to see the doctors who put Mr. Spindler's face back together after the airship accident. Mr. Aldobrand wouldn't hear of it of course. He wants to make the movie. But what nobody's disposed to mention is how can we make our movie when our leading man looks like that. Mr. Halloran wants to cast somebody else in the part

but Mr. Whelt says you can't make a big change like that
without Mr. Spindler's permission because they'll already
have mentioned Mr. Aldobrand in the advance publicity
materials. Instead he wants to put a new scene in the script
where Mr. Aldobrand's character has his face ripped off by
a monkey on the way to the temple, but I'm not sure that
would pass the Hays Code & besides I think he's forgetting
that Mr. Aldobrand's character has to marry Miss Thoisy's
character at the end of the movie not float off dead down the
Río Patuca like Lon Chaney in *The Phantom of the Opera* oh
why did I ever write that down I feel guilty already.

You can't tell but I had to quit writing for a minute just
now because Trimble came in. This is my confession, I told
you a lie at the start of this letter, or no I didn't tell you a lie
but I left something out. The papermaking unit are making
more paper than they used to but still hardly enough to go
around. So I'm writing to you right now on paper Trimble
brought me.

After the first time he did that I swore I'd never take
anything from him ever again but I guess I couldn't keep to
it. Yes Emmy I made a deal with the devil so to speak, but it
isn't too serious. Sometimes Trimble asks me what I heard
about something from somebody, or sometimes he gets me
to tell somebody something about something else but pretend
it wasn't him I heard it from. That's all. I still hate him like
poison but I don't fret about it much because it's no injury
to anybody it's only gossip.

I do call it uncanny how Trimble always knows so much
he's got no business knowing, not just about us but about
the New York folks too because he spends just as much time
down there as he does up here, but he's a born newspaper
man I guess.

God almighty what I'd do for a cigarette.

Last night a few of us girls were sitting around the fire
making arrows, I was sharpening a fishbone to make the
type of arrowhead you need for bowfishing, when out of

nowhere Miss Raye who plays one of the temple nightclub floozies just starts bawling fit to pop an eyeball. We ask her why & she won't say right away but then a little later she says, When are they going to come for us, we've been out here so long it feels like we're stuck here in purgatory, it doesn't make sense, isn't anybody wondering where we are, I've got friends back in Hollywood who must have gone to the authorities we've been missing for so long, why aren't we in the newspapers, why aren't they sending search parties, how could Kingdom Pictures abandon us out here, etc.

So we tell her, We'll be home as soon as we finish the movie, they're just waiting for us to get the movie in the can, which is what folks tend to say around here when anybody starts talking like Miss Raye was talking. But then a couple other girls admitted they've been nursing the same sentiments. And soon we're all saying, Yes, yes, if only we could go home. But I only said it to fit in. Because the truth is I don't want to go home. Miss Burlingame too, I didn't hear much conviction in her voice. Maybe a lot of the girls there were only saying they wanted to go home because everyone else was saying it. You end up in Hollywood because you wanted to get away from something but you don't have to be there long before there's something there you want to get away from too. That's how life is. I haven't personally got anything against Hollywood yet but I really don't care where I am if I can't be with you the only star in my sky.

Yours forever,
Gracie

Joan Burlingame tries to coax Jervis Whelt into taking a nap . . . Rigger Mick Ofshe ejaculates into a spider's web to see what will happen . . . Colby Droulhiole sings a song his mother taught him . . . Elias Coehorn Jr., having vomited inside his cabin, endures the smell until somebody arrives to bury it for him, rather than demean his station by burying it himself . . . Actor Amos Fleming, a compulsive reader who thought this trip would be a wonderful opportunity to spend a few weeks immersed in the Complete Works of Shakespeare and therefore brought no other book with him, starts it over for the fifth time, feeling a loathing for its author like none he has ever felt for a living human being . . . Carl Ivo guts a catfish . . . George Aldobrand uses a mirror to brush insects off the numb part of his face . . . Gracie Calix folds up the letter to her niece and puts it in her jewelry box . . .

☙

There's an apocryphal story about a certain CIA analyst who supposedly still works down in Foggy Bottom. (Of course, every story I'm going to set down here about the agency is apocryphal in the sense that it's unverifiable, but this one in particular does not have the stench of truth to me. Then again, not much does any more; I think my nostrils are burned out.)

The story goes that about ten years ago two police detectives in New York or Chicago or some other City of the Plain were investigating a string of very clinical sex murders when a tip or a hunch or a lucky break led them to an apartment where they found a garrote or a hunting knife or a can of harrowing photographic negatives or some other indication of the occupant's guilt. But they also found thousands of pages of typewritten notes about various scenarios for the escalation of the nuclear arms race. Even at a glance the detectives could perceive such professionalism and detail in these notes that they began to wonder if they might have stumbled across a senior KGB agent who'd been assassinating local blondes according to some esoteric Russian agenda. They handed the suspect over to the FBI and the FBI handed him over to CIA, but when CIA interviewed the suspect about his notes they discovered he didn't know any state secrets, or at least none that he hadn't deduced on his own. He was merely an enthusiast, a kind of gentleman scholar possessed of a tenacious and dissective intelligence. Analysts at the agency who received photostats of his notes tended to agree that never in their whole careers had they seen work of such high quality, and in the end it was decided that for the sake of the long-term security of the United States, the suspect should not be tried for his crimes but instead should discreetly be given a job. He now has his own basement office where he writes long reports to be summarized for the attention of the president, and the "mainframe computer" that's being built at Langley for processing data in bulk has been designed to simulate his mode of reasoning as closely as possible. Sometimes the story ends here, but sometimes it's claimed that twice a year, on Christmas Eve and Independence Day, the analyst is escorted to a randomly selected town in the Midwest where he's permitted to indulge his other hobby for an evening so he doesn't get too pent up. Also, he's right behind you. Boo!

I'll believe it when I meet the guy. Still, that story always makes me think about the personalities that accomplish a lot in this business. Trimble, whether I want to admit it or not, would have been an asset to the agency. But if Frieda, my assistant at the warehouse, ever asks me about a permanent job, I won't encourage it. Her heart's too big. This morning, when I tried to call Winch McKellar to thank him for sending her, his girl wouldn't even put me through. I understand he can't admit he helped me out. I'm typhoid now. But it shows how the agency has changed in the last few years as a result of Branch 9's ascendancy. An officer of McKellar's seniority shouldn't have to worry about who he talks to on the telephone. Regardless, I told Frieda I'd spoken to Mr. McKellar, the man who organized her security clearance, to assure him she was working hard for me— and, good grief, whenever she shows me that smile of hers, I can feel my sins sluicing off me like birdshit under a jet wash. The archangel Gabriel wouldn't dare ask this girl out on a date because he'd feel like too much of a bum. In any case, she stays home almost every night to help her three little brothers with their schoolwork. So she'd be busy.

Trimble, in the years Gracie Calix describes in those letters, was like an avatar of the Central Intelligence Agency, not the actual government bureaucracy but the paranoiac's vision of it as an immanence or supernatural law. Almost anything that happened at the temple, no matter how trivial: if Trimble wasn't responsible for it, then at the very least he knew about it. Eastern Aggregate scrip was not yet in use among the Californians, so in theory there was no cross-border currency, but Trimble had established himself as the Federal Reserve in an economy of rumor. And although Coehorn and Whelt were both statesmen of sorts, there was no one else at the temple with Trimble's totalizing ambitions, so he was almost unopposed in his project.

My task here is a reckoning of that project's magnitude, but given all of the above, the immediate question is not how Trimble did so much, it's how he did so little. From his arrival in 1938, it took him until 1944 to acquire both the *Hearts in Darkness* crew's Incipit portable printing press and a steady supply of paper, the two modest prizes toward which he'd been working almost that entire time. If Elias Coehorn Sr. had made such draggy progress, no one would ever have heard of Eastern Aggregate. But the population of 131 at the site wasn't New York or even Hershey. They lived frugal lives, centrally administered, without much vice. Trimble could only be as dynamic as the system itself. It was as if he'd sat down at one of those old treadle-powered sewing machines to find that the crankshaft barely touched the flywheel and there was barely room to move his foot, so he just had to flex and wiggle for six years until by agonizing degrees he'd transferred enough energy into the machine to get it running.

Trimble was a hoarder by nature. But hoarding wasn't easy, because it wasn't as if he had a lease on a warehouse out there. Any stockpile in a tent or cabin would have been noticed right away, and out in the forest there were no hiding places from human and animal foragers. If Trimble hoped to corner a commodity, he had to cache it with other parties, a hoard in only a virtual sense.

So Trimble mostly hoarded what he could hoard in his head, and his head made this new "mainframe computer" at Foggy Bottom look like a knot tied in a handkerchief to remember an errand. No Russian novelist ever understood his characters like Trimble understood these people. He knew the real father of your baby. He knew you couldn't tell left from right without glancing at the notch on your hand. He knew that even though you said you were happily married back in New York, you'd actually been exiled to a rooming house after inadvertently passing on to your wife the gonorrhea you'd picked up from another man. He knew that when you told the story about being one of the only bystanders to survive the massacre at Owl's Head Pier, you always left out the detail about using a fat lady as a shield. He knew you couldn't go a day without chewing that sour purple leaf, even if you had to go so far into the jungle to find the bushes that you sometimes got almost irretrievably lost. He knew you'd asked another man if he wanted to be an accomplice in a rape, and then afterward pretended you were joking. He knew you gambled with loaded dice. He knew you liked to bait your outstretched tongue with chewed papaya and then wait for an insect to land there before gulping it down like a lizard. He knew you'd been given your very technical job only because of a clerical error and so every day you gave thanks that filming hadn't started yet. He knew you stole leftovers. He knew you would have got the monkey off Aldobrand a lot sooner if you hadn't been so rapt with fascination. He knew you were afraid of the dark. And, above all, he knew that if he threatened to gossip about it, you'd do almost anything he wanted, which included telling him someone else's secret that you'd sworn on your life never to reveal. Furthermore, for every fact he knew that was true, he had another fact that he'd invented but that he would have no trouble making other people swallow. My old *Mirror* colleague had been conniving enough back in New York, sure, but still clumsy sometimes. The isolation here had sharpened his game, like a summer tennis camp that went on forever. He didn't make mistakes any more.

The reason it was necessary for me to abridge two paragraphs from Calix's letter of September 1942 was that she attempted there to recount the events that led to Trimble finally taking control of the printing press. Calix was a lucid analyst who gave it her best try. And for all her naïveté, she was faster than many at the camp to understand his nature. But that section of her letter is nevertheless almost unintelligible. Who can blame her? Trimble's project, from the perspective of any individual at the temple, must have been like one of those puzzles in a magazine where they print a magnified detail of some household object and invite you to guess at the whole, except in this case the object was not a toothbrush or a nylon stocking but a monstrosity budding in the darkness.

When Trimble first asked Whelt if he could borrow the portable printing press for the good of the camp's morale, the director replied that the reporter's presence on the shoot was tolerated only for its advance-publicity value and that Kingdom Pictures equipment could not be subject to frivolous wear and tear. And Whelt was one of a handful of people at the site over whom Trimble couldn't get any leverage. Coehorn, on the other hand, was unpredictable but on the whole easy enough to puppet. Trimble had learned how to pander to his vanity, the focus of which had shifted in this period from his dress and grooming to his qualities as a benevolent leader.

Around that time, Whelt was plotting to send two men downstairs on a moonless night to steal a gallon of ammonia from Coehorn's hand-pumped ice-making machine. Trimble, of course, heard about it. So he arranged for the men to be caught in the act. This was the first such transgression by one camp against another since the two expeditions had arrived, and it came as a shock to almost everybody.

Coehorn, furious, demanded a ransom for the return of the burglars he'd arrested, to be paid in food deliveries over the course of a year. It was an exorbitant penalty. "When we heard what he was asking," Calix writes, "I'm ashamed to say there were some of us who were ready to leave those men to their fates down there. But not me & not Mr. Whelt." Trimble suggested to Coehorn that, since the two men were to be returned right away, he should demand collateral for the future schedule of payments. Something Whelt couldn't replace. Not camera or sound equipment, because Whelt would never give those up. But perhaps his printing press . . .

And so the Incipit was duly handed over as a surety. Meanwhile, the ransom payments were crushing enough to invert the economic standings of the two camps, boosting the New Yorkers above the Angelenos. "We were already doing all the trapping & foraging & fishing we could," Calix writes, "& we still barely had enough left over to buy ice from the New York folks. Now we have to put their supper on the table day after day as well as our own. It's a ruination to us. People say it's like Black Tuesday all over again. & it stings double because for so long it was the New York folks who were the Okies of the jungle because they were so lazy but now it's been turned upside down & all for nothing." All for nothing? Not to Trimble. Because the printing press was his now.

Unfortunately, if any copies of the *Pozkito Enquirer* have survived to this day, they haven't found their way to the warehouse or to my private archives. By the time Trimble published the first weekly issue, I think almost everyone at the temple must have been aware on some level that they were living under a tenebrous new dictatorship. But this awareness hadn't quite condensed into speech or even conscious thought. These people knew, each one, that Trimble was blackmailing them. They knew that the blackmail was making them miserable. They knew that their neighbors also seemed miserable. But they couldn't complete the syllogism and see that Trimble was blackmailing their neighbors too, because he'd helped each of them to feel either that their secret was uniquely shameful—that no one would ever forgive them for it because no one else could possibly be hiding anything so bad—or that their debt to him was uniquely grave.

When they first set eyes on that newspaper, with its blurry and uneven but still horribly legible type, that was when they must finally have realized that Trimble had the whole outpost afraid of him. But the moment the possibility of collective resistance was born was also the moment its little heart stopped, because it was one thing to have your secret whispered from tent to tent and cabin to cabin, mixed in with all the other peelings and ashes of village social life, but quite another to have it set down there in irrefutable print where every other human being in the universe would see it by lunchtime. Forget the basic absurdity of the *Enquirer*'s existence, and the disgust with which its editor was regarded. The first time a man sees his name disgraced in a newspaper, it doesn't matter if he knows no one will believe it—it doesn't even matter if he's looking at the only copy ever printed—he will still feel shaken beyond reason. This is because the setting of text in columns under a headline is essentially a magical act. I was a reporter once too and I know. Perhaps Aldobrand and Thoisy and a few other Hollywood veterans could resist the effect, in the same way that a Jivaro warrior who is hexed often enough by his enemies is believed to grow a sort of protective callus around his kidneys. But not the rest of them. If you'd displeased Trimble in the last few months, maybe you'd been waiting to see what would happen, or maybe you hadn't even realized your mistake. Either way, here was his retribution, as public as an old-fashioned hanging.

In both camps, people tried to denounce the newspaper to a higher authority. It didn't yet seem plausible that Trimble could openly defy Whelt or Coehorn, and although the copy was in the same jaunty style as the gossip column back at the *New York Evening Mirror,* no one in their right mind could fail to see that this was a malign document. But when the first issue of the *Enquirer* was shown to Whelt, he just scanned it without much interest and handed it back, failing to understand how it was relevant to his film. And when it was shown to Coehorn, he chuckled his way to the bottom of the page and said that Trimble should be congratulated on the idea and he hoped they'd all be good sports about it.

☙

September 19th, 1944

Carrotwood Hospital
5600 Samuell Boulevard
Dallas, TX
United States

My love,
    Lyndon was so afraid it would get in the newspaper. If everybody knew, he used to say, this was before I ran off to Hollywood. If everybody knew that his wife and his wife's niece had But he never could finish the sentence. I know you've already put the whole episode out of your mind as best you can, he said to me, but a man's reputation, that's

forever. Put it out of my mind! Sure, I put it out of my mind.
Put it out of my mind so well I still haven't forgotten an
inch of your body eight years later, I mean it Emmy, not an
inch, yes we all know there are parts of you that if a half-
blind boy saw just once through a black veil in not much
moonlight he'd still be thinking on it when he died an old
man in front of a firing squad but I can still turn myself over
just picturing the bottoms of your heels or the backs of your
earlobes or the bald place like the curve of a river where
your hair parts on the side of your head.

What I mean to say is I didn't understand then why
Lyndon was so afraid of the newspaper. I understand now.

We all try not to read it. I promise we do. We know that
if we all just quit reading at once Trimble would most likely
shrivel up & wash away in the rain. But every week when the
new number comes out I don't know what to tell you Emmy
but it feels like it would be easier to quit breathing than to
look away. At the bottom of the steps here we've got a turkey
coop full of jungle turkeys, they have technicolor wings & a
gobble that gets faster at the end like a coin when it falls on
the table just right, & one night Mr. Hickock the grip was on
watch when a jaguar got past him & he tried to fight it off
but it took most of the turkeys. Or so he said. Well the top
story in the *Pozkito Enquirer* this week was that Mr. Hickock
fell asleep boiled on yam gin & forgot to close the door so the
turkeys just wandered off on him, & when he woke up he
realized his mistake, so he gave himself a few cuts with a
knife & then took one of the turkeys that was too [illegible]
to skedaddle & tore it up with his bare hands in the coop so
it'd look like a jaguar got in.

I know to you it can't sound like the blackest sin in the
world after all we've been through & besides who did he buy
the moonshine from none other than Trimble most likely.
Mr. Hickock is just a human being like us all. But what you
have to reckon with is we are hungry, so powerful hungry
all the time, & without those birds we'd spent months &

months rearing we'll be even hungrier for a long stretch to come, not to mention we use the feathers for fletching. Mr. Hickock always used to pride himself more than anything on his trustworthiness & clean living & this is what he did. So that night, after the newspaper came out, Mr. Hickock just ups & walks out into the jungle.

He didn't have any destination & he didn't mean to come back. Dr. Zasa saw him go but he didn't think anything of it til somebody found a note in his cabin. So the doctor & some other men went looking for him in the jungle. I can tell you there were a few around here happy to see him gone like that after what they read in the newspaper but Mr. Hickock is our friend & in any case we can't afford to lose another strong pair of hands. When the men went out to rescue Mr. Hickock I think they figured they were going in defiance of Trimble, because Trimble tried to ruin him with that newspaper. But when they brought him back the next morning all scratched up & staggering, it was a miracle they found him at all, Trimble seemed happier than anybody. He gives Mr. Hickock a big hug & tells him he'll make sure he gets second helpings at dinner. Afterward I understood it, Mr. Hickock dead is out of Trimble's power, & Trimble doesn't want anybody out of his power.

You want to know if I'm worried I'll ever see my own name in those unholy pages. Well Emmy I think for once in my life I've been smart. For a long time I didn't tell the folks here anything about where I came from. Why for goodness' sake would I. But after a while I could tell Trimble was sniffing around. He wanted something on me just like he's got something on everybody else. So one night not too long ago I told Miss Raye I ran away from my husband to go to Hollywood because I wanted to be an actress, & I'm sobbing like a naughty Catholic at confession, & I keep saying how guilty I felt about it. Now I know Miss Raye's done a hell of a lot worse than that in her time & so have almost all the folks here so when she's comforting me she must be thinking,

This girl's a real bluenose if she thinks that's so bad. But that's just what I want, because now Trimble must think if he wants to scare me he just has to make a threat about how he'll put it in the newspaper. As if I could care less ha ha.

So you see I'm clear of Trimble pretty much. I still do a chore for him once in a while but not because I have to. Oh Emmy my conscience you want to know how I can still do anything for that man now we've all seen him for what he is. But you should've seen me last week when I put on the lipstick he gave me, not the Okie lipstick we make out of achiote seeds but I mean real Max Factor, I don't know how there's still real Max Factor in this jungle after 6 years, & of course I couldn't put it on in the camp because everyone would know who I got it from, I had to take a wander into the trees when I wasn't needed. I brought a little piece of mirror I saved from one that broke, so I made sure to get it just perfect, & I couldn't see my whole face all at once but when I was done I swear I looked prettier than Miss Thoisy, maybe that isn't saying much any more because believe it or not Miss Thoisy still insists on going around with that mink stole even though by now it would be a great compliment to say it looks like something you'd fish out of a sewer drain, but I swear I did, & it felt so sweet my darling, all I could think was how much you'd want me to kiss you if you saw me like that, about my lipstick putting a blush on your neck. I don't want to say what I do for Trimble but if he ever asks me to do anything that'll be any injury to anybody I say no so I'm not as bad as some.

The thunder outside. You know Mr. Upritchard has kidney stones & Dr. Zasa says they'll pass in a few weeks but when I see him lying there with the torments of hell in his face it makes me think he'll just up & die like Mr. Rusk.

I dreamed about you last night Emmy. We were in a dance class & the monkey that took Mr. Aldobrand's face was teaching everybody the Half Doodle & it squawked at us every time we stopped dancing, but at least you were with

me. You know I was going to come for you. I was going to get
things ready for us to go away & then come for you. That's
why I came out & said what I said to Lyndon & the others. I
thought if I told the truth they'd be watching us both but if
I lied then one of us could help the other. I wasn't trying to
save myself I was trying to save us both. You know that or
leastways I tell myself you do.

Yours forever,
Gracie

Jervis Whelt hoists a copper rod up toward the lightning . . .
Fales Apinews loses the bet he made with himself about how
long he could go without thinking about his toothache . . .
Leland Trimble gropes for a dropped apostrophe . . .
Rick Halloran decides to abandon his attempt to make
a mousetrap from the sprung jaw of a piranha . . . Joan
Burlingame deseeds a chili pepper . . . Keith Upritchard longs
for death . . . Carl Ivo walks down to the river intending to go
fishing, but finds, instead, an empty basin, a stranded ship,
and a great concrete dam . . . Gracie Calix folds up the letter
to her niece and puts it in her jewelry box . . .

He read the letters

Emmy he read the letters

OH GOD EMMY he read the letters

He's been reading them ever since I've been writing them.
I was SO STUPID Emmy. My jewelry box. Why did I think

I wasn't sending them anyway & I wasn't ever going to so
why didn't I just burn them or

[illegible]

Last night he came to me when I was on my own & he says he has a little favor to ask. I thought it was just going to be some tattle about somebody like usual. I guess it was but not like usual. He wants me to say Mr. Aldobrand misused me. Came up behind me out in the trees & put a stake to my throat & misused me. He tells me all the different ways I'm supposed to say Mr. Aldobrand did it & it's like nothing I've ever heard in my life.

I know why. We all like Mr. A. so much & Mr. Aldobrand never does anything wrong so he's near enough the only man here who could still stand up to Trimble if he ever was disposed to.

I say, No Mr. Trimble I'm not going to do it, Mr. Aldobrand never did anything to me, I don't care how much ice & lipsticks you've got this time. And he smiles & says, But Miss Calix we all know nobody will touch Mr. Aldobrand because of his face & by now he's as rucked & twisted on the inside as he's rucked & twisted on the outside, you haven't paid attention to how he looks at you dames lately but if you do this thing for me you'll be saving some sister of yours from the inevitable when Mr. Aldobrand just can't hold it any more. And I shake my head & tell him to get out of my cabin, I can hardly speak I'm still so sick to my stomach from all his filthy talk. But then he says, You know you'd be in quite a jam if word was to get out about you & your niece. I wouldn't want to see you in a jam Miss Calix. We've always got along so well.

He knows Emmy. He knows all of it near enough.

One curiosity I used to have about Trimble was whether the other girls were giving him their ministrations so to speak. He gets what all he wants here & men want what men want & Trimble's only half a man but I know he wants it too because you can see it in his ugly face any time a girl bends over or her strap comes untied. So he must be happy as a flea on a farm dog, I thought. But what I couldn't figure was

why he never asked me to do anything like that for him, &
I know that sounds awful vain because I'm not the prettiest
girl out here, but I've owed him before & back in Hollywood
when you owe a man for something it's the first thing he
thinks of, happened to me more times than I can count on
the Kingdom Pictures lot.

Now I know why he never asked. He doesn't want to
ask. He wants you to ask. He wants you to beg. I did beg &
I could tell that was what he liked the most. Last night I tell
him he can do those things to me, those things he wants
me to pretend Mr. Aldobrand did to me, he can do all of
them, so long as it stays a secret & you stay a secret too. But
he says he wouldn't think of treating a lady like that. So I
really started to plead, I took off my blouse & I told him I
wanted him to do it to me, I told him I was hurting for it.
It's the most shameful [illegible] I've ever done, worse than
anything I ever had to do in Hollywood because it was for
Trimble. He still said no. He said, I'm flattered, Miss Calix,
but that's not the sort of favor I asked you for. You know
what I want you to do.

I can't do it Emmy. I bore false witness against you & look
what happened. You're stuck in that place & all because of
me. I meant well but it's the worst thing I ever did.

But I can't see my name in big letters on the front of the
newspaper next week. I can't have everybody knowing. I
can't. I can't. I can't. That's why I don't care that we still
haven't gone home, because out here in the jungle nobody
knows. It's a slap in the face of Jesus for kin to lie down
with kin Emmy not to mention woman with woman or that's
what they'll say because that's what they always say to us.
They can't understand we didn't have any choice. They can't
understand our love was truer than anything they've ever
felt in their wretched lives.

There isn't any way out now. Not for me.

Oh sweetheart why did I have to end up in Hollywood
free as the wind & you behind those walls in Dallas. It's

not right. Why wasn't it the other way around. You never would've have got yourself into a mess like this. I know you must hate me for it. You must have nothing else to do there but hate me. You must deal your hate out over & over like a game of patience. I try to tell myself different but I know.

After I finish writing I'm going to tear this up so nobody ever finds it.

I'm sorry Emmy. I'm so sorry. I still love you.

Elias Coehorn Jr., Leland Trimble, Irma Kittredge, and Walter Pennebaker sit down to a dinner of Eggs Pozkito with Pozkito Marys . . . Joan Burlingame settles an argument about the foraging schedule between Joe Hickock and Lionel Zasa . . . Head chef Sal Delabole whisks the "Hollandaise" . . . Colby Droulhiole stands motionless so as not to startle the diaphanous butterflies that have settled on him to drink his sweat . . . Kurt Meinong limps for his life . . . George Aldobrand punches a cougar in the nose . . . Freddie Yang closes his eyes to practice navigating the new darkroom by touch one last time . . . Gracie Calix folds up the letter to her niece, the easier to rip it into confetti, then leaves her cabin barefoot and climbs the steps of the temple, keeping her eyes down not only because she'd rather go unnoticed but also because she doesn't want to see anything that might give her second thoughts now that she's made her decision, except that it's a pointless measure because if there's anything that's going to bring her to a halt it's not these hungry men and women in their crooked shacks, it's the view from the terrace right at the top, out over the other settlement and the forest canopy and the hills in the distance, never a better impersonation of paradise than in this gentle early-evening light from a sky that's beginning to turn orange, but she's crying so hard that just wiping enough tears from her eyes to see properly feels like bailing out a boat, and when she looks down she isn't scared at all by the drop but she knows that if she stands here too long somebody is going to wonder what

*on earth she's doing (she can't bear the thought of getting
"rescued" like Mr. Hickock), so with nothing more profound in
her head at that last moment than "Get on and do it, Gracie,"
she takes a deep breath, steps forward, and jumps . . .*

☙

"Anyway, breakfast has been waiting politely for far too long," said
Coehorn, breaking off from the debate about how best to narrate the
story of the expedition up to this point. "Eight months in the making
and we shouldn't delay even a moment longer." He raised his glass
of Pozkito Mary. "Here's to a good story, well told!"

"To a good story, well told!"

Each of the four took a long, luxurious drink. Then Trimble went
white, Coehorn slammed his fist on the table in horror, Irma had a
coughing fit, and Pennebaker retched all over his Eggs Pozkito.

After they had recovered, Pennebaker was ordered to taste some
of the eggs from Coehorn's plate, and he reported in a strangled
voice that if anything they were even less of a success. When the
head chef came back into the dining room, the other three guests
watched Coehorn, waiting to see whether he would erupt in anger.
They didn't even realize that this was a double blow to him because
clearly he would now have to delay the twelve-month project of
research into Lobster Thermidor that he'd intended as a sequel. Still,
he'd always felt that one should show more good humor about the
failure of something expensive than about the failure of something
cheap. "Send the leftovers up to Master Whelt with my compli-
ments," he joked. "And bring us something simple to eat and to
drink as quick as you can." This wouldn't necessarily prevent him
from informing the head chef later that his scrip wages would be
docked. In any case, whatever his nagging bookkeeper might say
about the misallocation of resources, the sizable write-off didn't
trouble Coehorn, because his kingdom was in such good health at
the moment. "Now, where were we?" he said.

"The silver lining around all these clouds we've had tinkling on
us," said Trimble. "If we'd just come here, took the temple, got home

in time to listen to the *United Fruit Company Radio Hour,* that's no story. But what you had to contend with, Mr. Coehorn, it's front-page stuff."

"Exactly right," said Coehorn. "We begin with those good-for-nothings tailing us here. Then something on how I had the idea of occupying this ground like an army so they couldn't put the temple back together. Then how I've been propping them up for the last eight years because they simply don't know what they're doing out in the jungle, and they're no more grateful than Lenin was after Hoover sent him all that famine relief. Really, Pennebaker, what I want you to emphasize is that, yes, it's the ladies and gentlemen of Eastern Aggregate who are my guests—they mean more to me than anything and I've barely slept a minute since we got here because I'm so determined that everyone should have a good time—but all the same, Whelt's gang are human beings too, and however lousy their behavior, I've still taken it upon myself to make sure that each and every American in this jungle—"

They were interrupted by the head chef running back into the bungalow. "A lady's taken a dive off the temple! Right off the top!"

"Where did she land?" said Irma.

"I didn't see. Must have been somewhere in camp."

Irma's feet had been bare on the jaguar-skin rug but now she was slipping her sandals back on.

"Where are you going?" said Coehorn.

"Where do you think?"

"We still haven't had anything to eat."

"For heaven's sake, Elias, somebody may have died!"

"But it's only one of the Banisters," which was Coehorn's nickname for the Angelenos on the stairs. He knew how vital it was to take the initiative at the very beginning of a crisis in terms of reassuring people that they didn't have to pay any attention. But Irma just glared at him. "Oh, all right."

The sky in the west was mixing an Old-Fashioned and below that the tree-covered ridges receded into the mist. Already you could feel the thrum of a crowd that longed to center itself on something but had been suspended in the moment before it figured out exactly what. "What's everybody waiting for?" said Coehorn. "The body will be right at the bottom of the wall. It's not as if there's room up there for a running start."

"Actually, Mr. Coehorn, I think this lady could have landed as far as thirty or forty feet away from the base of the temple," said Pennebaker.

"Don't be preposterous—no one can leap thirty feet out into empty space. Not even you, Pennebaker, if you saw someone throw a funnel cake off a roof."

"But, Mr. Coehorn, horizontal velocity is independent of gravitational acceleration, so a falling body will maintain—"

"Nobody gives a damn about your folklore! How many times do I have to tell you that?"

Coehorn and Irma paced the width of the temple and back, however, without finding a body among the limestone scree at its base. So a dozen men attempted a sort of dragnet, and even that seemed like an absurd recourse, since the camp wasn't so broad that it would be at all difficult to spot an object the size of an adult female among the huts and shelters and looms and kilns. Still, Coehorn allowed them to pick their way back as far as Pennebaker's fantastical forty-yard line before he said to the head chef, "Clearly you saw an eagle or something like that flying overhead and you mistook it for Dorothy Poynton."

"No, Mr. Coehorn, I wasn't the only guy who saw her. I've talked to two others now. It was a woman. We're sure it was a woman."

Coehorn raised an eyebrow. "So you're telling me a woman jumped off this temple and just . . ."

The head chef nodded. "Yes, sir. Just vanished."

❧

Here are some instructions on how to make film stock in the jungle.

1. Abandon your attempts to fix nitrogen from the air using lightning. Even after several months of work on the copper nitrogen-fixing rig you built from spare lighting equipment, you haven't

found a way to capture enough of the ammonia for it to be practical. Yang will feel divided, because on one hand he won't particularly like the idea that he survived a lightning strike for nothing, but on the other hand he'll be pleased that he won't have to risk getting struck a second time. The first time, the pink tattoo of broken capillaries didn't fade from his shoulder from nearly a month; they were in a forked pattern just like a bolt of lightning in the night sky, as if Yang's skin were itself a kind of film stock for photographing the storm. You share your craving for nitrogen with all the plants of the rain forest, where there is never enough in the soil. Yang will mention that if you had enough power you could use the Birkeland-Eyde process, fixing the nitrogen with a 6,000°F electric arc, and briefly you will wonder if it might be possible to convert the Indians' dam into a hydroelectric power station, but you have neither the necessary equipment nor the necessary friendly relations with the Pozkitos.

2. Do not abandon your attempts to extract ammonia from urine. Yes, at first it was as unproductive as the nitrogen-fixing rig, even after you went out into the forest and constructed a ten-gallon urine tank from kapok wood sealed with pine resin. But after Upritchard is toppled by his kidney stones, you will hear Zasa mention that the ammoniac odor from Upritchard's urethra suggests that his kidney stones might be struvite stones, which is bad luck because struvite stones are particularly difficult to pass. Under intense questioning, Zasa will tell you that from what he can recall, struvite stones are thought to be caused by microbes in the urinary tract, although he can't be quite sure of that without his reference books and there's some chance he might be mixing up struvite with cystine. Take a urine sample from Upritchard in the hope that the microbes infesting the man's renal system are of an especially hardy and rapacious breed. Add the sample to the urine tank, along with a gallon of tapir blood which may help to nourish the colony. After about a week, you'll find that the urine tank will produce plenty of ammonia as long as it's regularly topped up with tapir blood. This last task is an inconvenient

one because the reek from the tank will depopulate the forest for about a hundred feet in every direction. One day, suggest to Yang that it might be wise to post a guard there in case someone tries to steal the precious urine from the urine tank. He will look back at you in silence for a while.

3. Discover that, when the cast and crew were instructed to hand over all their money, jewelry, and watches to bid for the services of the Pozkitos, Adela Thoisy held at least one item back. This won't be the first time you've made a discovery of this kind, but it will be the first time it matters. The item is a LaCloche Frères platinum and diamond necklace given to Thoisy by one of her lovers back in Hollywood. Reassure Thoisy that subsequent events justified her decision, even though an irrational part of you will wonder if somehow it could have been exactly this shortfall that made all the difference. Take the necklace from Thoisy for safekeeping, promising to return it to her untouched, then pry out the diamonds and painstakingly hammer the platinum thinner and thinner until you've made a sort of flexible trellis. Heat the catalytic platinum as hot as you can over a charcoal fire, pump the ammonia from the urine tank across the folded trellis, and bubble the resulting nitrogen dioxide through water to produce nitric acid. It will take several months of trial and error to make this work, and you and Yang will have to get used to weepy blisters all over your forearms and persistent shortness of breath. When Burlingame urges you to quit before you permanently invalid yourself, reply that you can't make a movie if you don't have any film. Realize that it may have been for the best that you didn't get the ammonia that you plotted to rob from Coehorn's ice-making machine, because that source was necessarily limited, whereas this one is renewable.

4. With several other men, take hammers, picks, and spades down to the drained riverbed to begin mining for rock salt. The moss and vines will not yet have had time to sprawl across the dry ground

here so it will be the barest terrain you've set eyes on since the New Yorkers first denuded half the temple's foundations. Why the Pozkitos decided to alter the course of this tributary with a dam, nobody knows, but the source of their seed capital for the cement and construction equipment is bitterly clear. Burlingame warned you that it's even harder to eke out enough food now that there's no water nearby for fishing, but catering on location is the responsibility of a production manager, not a director, so as usual you put it out of your mind. Anyway, you need sodium chloride more than you need fish. As you excavate, mostly by moonlight because of the summer heat in the daytime, you will suspect that the Pozkitos sometimes watch you from the parapet of the dam, which rises blankly over the basin like a movie theater's projection screen. Sometimes you will hear the echo of what sounds like gunfire. The ship on which you arrived, already picked clean of every last ounce of metal, fabric, and glass, will list further over to port with every day that goes by; Yang will remark that it would be exciting to film the moment it finally capsizes, so remind him sternly that there is no dry shipwreck in the script of *Hearts in Darkness*. When you wipe the dirt off the foggy pink crystals of halite, they will look to you like scale models of Upritchard's struvite stones. Ask yourself whether more of the shoot's chores couldn't be delegated to microbes of different kinds, given that Upritchard's former tenants are contributing more to its progress than Upritchard himself ever did before his death. Recalling that cheese is produced by fermentation, you will wonder whether there might not be a microbe somewhere in the human body that would transmute rotting vegetable matter into a nutritious jelly. You will still be thinking about how greatly preferable it would be to eat a nutritious jelly twice a day instead of unpredictable meals when you arrive back at the camp and Burlingame asks you how much food you think can be saved if part of the new mine's output is traded to the other camp for use as table salt, curing salt, bleaching salt, and so on. Ignore the question, which has nothing to do with the movie.

5. Collaborate with the members of the papermaking unit on the production of cellulose from pinewood pulp. The cellulose they were using for paper stock is too coarse for your purposes, so it will take several weeks of experiments to improve it. Burlingame will warn you that they are exhausted, and when you reply that they are only giving you twelve hours a day, she will point out that they also have to carry on making standard paper stock, so they don't have any time to sleep. Since you rarely if ever find sleep necessary, this complaint won't interest you. Also, you don't quite understand why you seem to have so many conversations like this with the Englishwoman these days, since she didn't come with you from Hollywood and she has no official role on the shoot. (Occasionally you've wondered if it might be because she wants to go to bed with you; she doesn't seem like she wants to go to bed with you, but then again that blond reporter you met at the Spindler mansion in '38 didn't seem like she wanted to go to bed with you either, right up until the moment when it became obvious that she wanted to go to bed with you immediately, so it may be that there's just no way to tell.) Ask one of the members of the papermaking unit why he is still making standard paper stock, which has no conceivable application in the current circumstances, instead of devoting all his physico-mental resources to the cellulose experiments. He will seem reluctant to answer, but after a while he will mumble something about Trimble, who is the reporter from New York.

6. Render gelatin from tapir hide and bones. This process is so elementary that there is no need to explain it here.

7. Ensure that, during the negotiations over the hostages from the botched ammonia robbery, one of your go-betweens surreptitiously took some shavings of silver from one of the suits of Mayan ceremonial armor lying around the other camp. Pour hot nitric acid over the silver to make silver nitrate crystals. Dissolve these in warm water, and also dissolve some powdered salt in warm tapir gelatin. (Instead of laboratory equipment you will be

using Yang's developing kit. Many of these steps must take place in complete darkness.) Using a buffer of lemon juice and soda ash, mix the two solutions together to form a precipitate of silver chloride. Separately, pour hot nitric acid over the pressed cellulose to make nitrocellulose. Carefully trim the sheets of nitrocellulose to a 35-millimeter gauge with nail scissors before rubbing them with cabbage-palm oil as a plasticizer. The first time you try this, before you realize how important it is to keep the nitrocellulose damp, you will be fortunate enough to lose no more than the top joint of the third finger of your left hand in the explosion. That day, Burlingame will beg you to stop, and you will for a while, because it's difficult to work with any precision while your hands are bandaged. Allow yourself this interval to contemplate your situation. The moderately complex requirements of the film stock's manufacture up to this point have helped you to understand that a frame of exposed film is like a set of encyclopedias in the sense that a frame of exposed film contains almost everything that has ever happened. Of all the possible universes God could have made, there are so many in which that frame never comes to exist, and so few in which it does, and in this context the only meaningful qualities of our own universe are those that determine its status with respect to that binary. The megaphone yell of "Quiet on set!" is vacuous because it assumes a simple distinction between set and not-set. In fact, the set includes any entity that stands in any causal relation to any frame of film. Which means that to make exactly the film you want to make, to attain total control as a director, either you have to shear off every one of those causal relations or you have to extend your authority over every one of those entities. Sometimes the useful self-containment of the *Hearts in Darkness* shoot reminds you of the orphanage in which you grew up. When Jerome carried on hunting robins even after the matrons had fitted a bell to his collar, it felt like a triumph in which all the boys could share, but now that you're the one in charge, you'd rather strangle a cat than let it walk through a shot. In movies, everything is there for a reason; in life, almost nothing. You got your name the same way all the other foundlings at your orphanage got theirs: a matron ran her finger down a list of Civil War brevet generals in a book and happened to stop at Jervis Whelt. You would never direct a script in which any of the characters were named so arbitrarily.

8. Coat the nitrocellulose base with the silver chloride emulsion and perforate the margins. Congratulations! You have made film stock, and you are ready to start filming again. Just remember the Whelt Rule, and everything will be fine.

೧೨

"Joan, get in here."

"May I open the door?" Burlingame knew how angry they'd be if she let in daylight from the anteroom when she wasn't supposed to. (This was the same day in 1946 that Kurt Meinong arrived at the temple in time to see Gracie Calix throw herself off the top.)

"I told you to get in here, didn't I?"

She opened the door. The roof hatch of the darkroom was propped open and the two men stood there under a shaft of dawn. There had to be enough space in here for two men to grope around at once, so this cabin was one of the longest in the camp: it extended out over multiple steps with a scaffold underneath to hold it up.

"Sorry to yell at you, Joan, but you've got to see this," said Yang. She came forward, and Whelt passed her a ribbon of photographic negative. "It's okay to touch it," said Yang. "Just hold it by the edges. Yeah, up to the light."

The stock was as exact in its dimensions and finish as you'd expect given the personality of its manufacturer, and yet it nevertheless had the primordial quality of a rind of snakeskin you might find out in the forest. The sixty or seventy frames here showed Yang walking toward the camera while waving his arms and sticking out his tongue. They'd run the camera with a hand crank, since of course the generators hadn't been in use for years. Even at less than an inch high, in inverted grays already beginning to fog, the images had a startling, almost three-dimensional clarity, like the bas-reliefs on the Frieze of Parnassus.

"What do you think?" said Yang.

"I don't know the first thing about film, but I think it looks marvelous."

"Just 'marvelous'? Do you know how long we've been working on this?"

"'Marvelous' is really rather emphatic where I come from."

"Joan, where you come from, nothing this exciting has happened in eight hundred years and that's why you don't have a word to describe it. We've made film in the jungle. We've made film in the jungle and it looks better than any Eastman Super X I ever laid eyes on. Whelt, tell her your theory."

"In 1925, a researcher at Kodak found that you get the best film speeds if you use gelatin from cows that fed on wild mustard seed," said Whelt. "The sulfur from the mustard makes the silver halides more sensitive to light."

"There's no mustard out here, but whatever the tapirs eat, it must be twice as good."

"Does this mean you can start filming?" said Burlingame. Outside this cabin, with famine never far away, the question would have been laughable, not to say offensive. But she knew Whelt thought of nothing but *Hearts in Darkness*. In 1938, when she first met him, he had understood that people could not be fed and sheltered in retrospect by a film that might one day come to exist. Now that awareness was lost. The closer his ship came to collapsing into the barren earth, the tighter he gripped the wheel. What Burlingame couldn't understand was that although Whelt had probably eaten less and slept less over the last eight years than anyone else at the site, he seemed to have aged less too, as if it were only by the accumulation of labeled film canisters that his body was willing to acknowledge the passage of time. What she also couldn't understand was why she had come to spend so much of her time mothering the director. Yes, if something needed to be done and no one else was doing it, she felt like a skiver unless she did it herself. But to scour a few crusty dinner bowls was one thing; to assume the guardianship of an adult male was quite another.

"We have almost everything we need," said Yang. "We can even record sound negatives if we want. Even if we dilute the fixer we have left we'll be out of developing chemicals soon, and assuming there's no bush out there with hydroquinone in its berries we can't make any more, but just because we can't watch the rushes until we get home, that doesn't mean we can't shoot the movie."

"We just need more silver," said Whelt.

"It wastes a lot of silver, making the silver chloride like this. An ounce of silver ought to go a long way but we only got a few feet of film this time. If only we had one whole suit of armor we could make enough to finish the movie as soon as we put the temple back together. That's assuming we don't need too many takes. But after all the test shots we've done . . ."

In other words, they weren't actually any closer to returning to work. Burlingame remembered a joke her father used to make: "If we had bacon we could have bacon and eggs if we had eggs." From one point of view, this project had never been more urgent. Yang had discovered that some of the Kodak film they'd exposed in their first year at the site had already begun to decompose in the muggy air, speckling brown and giving off a smell like dirty socks. Whelt would have to reshoot all those scenes, which would at least solve the continuity problem of Aldobrand's disfigurement, if that role wasn't to be recast. But from another point of view, the stakes of this project were, as usual, nil. If the sheer heat of their hatred for Coehorn hadn't vaporized him by now then it probably wasn't going to vaporize him any time soon, so how were these two going to get their hands on a full suit of silver ceremonial armor, let alone the temple itself?

But of course Yang was as excited as a schoolboy, and even Whelt looked satisfied for once. He could never outwardly relax, she knew, but the calm in the deep of his jitters was the Rule in the deep of his metaphysics. All smash hits, the director had told her, followed the Whelt Rule, and any folktale that had endured long enough in a culture to be transcribed by an anthropologist must be regarded as a smash hit. So if somebody went to the trouble of converting the plots of all the folktales of the world into Whelt's special notation, they would necessarily recognize the Rule in every single one of them. For her part, Burlingame was skeptical that all folktales really could be made to line up with perfect posture like that. She'd read too many that were fascinatingly lopsided and scoliotic. That aside, it seemed to her that the real question was exactly what type of rule the Rule was supposed to be. Did Whelt truly believe that all human beings in all times and places must prefer plots that followed his Rule? Did the Rule, in other words, reflect some immutable feature of the human mind? Once, after a rather challenging piece of "new music" at a piano recital, her uncle had declared that even a Martian would prefer conventional harmony because conventional harmony was based on simple mathematical ratios. So would even a Martian prefer conforming plots? Often, Whelt seemed to be too practically minded to interest himself in these speculations. He could still recite the ten highest-grossing films for every year going back to *Birth of a Nation* in 1915, and that metric, he sometimes implied, was the Rule's only importance. But at other times he talked about the Rule as if it were a radiant categorical imperative.

Surprisingly, her discussions with Whelt had given her a new framework for understanding the Pozkito cosmogony. According to the accounts she had read, the Pozkitos didn't believe that the gods had created material stuff, only that they had designed the Platonic forms. Except it was more like calibrating the laws of physics, or inventing the rules of a game, or . . . It wasn't easy to pin down. But now Burlingame understood that, in essence, the Pozkito gods had stipulated the range of available narrative units, just like Whelt's notation, or Antti Aarne's *Verzeichnis der Märchentypen*. They had set the patterns of behavior into which things would inevitably fall for the rest of time. Despite this accomplishment, the gods' powers were not to be exaggerated. They were closest, perhaps, to the *asuras* of the Hindus or the *lares* of the ancient Romans. The Pozkito attitude to them was not worship or fear so much as pragmatic alliance.

Of course, Burlingame had hoped to find out a great deal more. But there were no Pozkitos around to study. So instead she studied the Americans.

She stole her observations furtively. There were two reasons for that. The secondary reason was that, with paper at such a premium, she hadn't wanted anyone to learn that she still had a supply of 280-page Alwych all-weather notebooks, the very last of which she was now horrifyingly close to filling. But the primary reason was that if they found out they would probably be indignant and it would isolate her. At Cambridge it had been a commonplace to joke about studying the fellows at High Table as if they were headhunters, but the joke was funny only because everyone knew that anthropology was by definition the study of primitive peoples. All good fieldwork began with a brave man making a long journey into a dusky place. And she knew the Americans wouldn't want to think of themselves as a tribe of that kind. Only once, so far, had she let slip what she was doing, and she still regretted it. She didn't know what it was about Miss Calix that sometimes made her gabble herself into indiscretion.

That she was preoccupied with the assistant wardrobe "man" this morning, however, was perfectly natural, because Calix had been absent from her cabin the previous night and seemingly hadn't been seen by anyone at all since around sunset. Knowing there was no point raising the subject with Whelt and Yang, she congratulated them once more on their achievement and then excused herself.

Outside, clouds as slight as dandelion seeds speckled the whole sky. The first person she saw was Joe Hickock on his way downstairs. She knew he'd still be feeling sour about the disagreement last night. There were times when Burlingame wished she could just go quietly out into the forest and take care of the week's foraging, gardening, hunting, and trapping for everyone at the camp, which would be so much less unpleasant than settling all these arguments about who wasn't doing their share. Because that wasn't quite feasible, however, she often had to play the umpire between two angry men who before long would hate her even more than they hated each other. Her first instinct this morning was to turn away fast enough that she could plausibly pretend not to have noticed Hickock. But conscientiousness forbade it.

"A very good morning to you, Mr. Hickock," she said. But he just nodded at her and carried on his way. Praying he wouldn't make this too hard, she called after him, "Mr. Hickock, I wonder if I could—"

"What?" He was a tall man whose eyes looked as if they were perpetually exhausted by the crushing weight of his brow.

"I'm so frightfully sorry to hold you up but—"

"You're going to tell me I should be out looking for bird nests right now."

"No, Mr. Hickock, not at all."

"So what is it this time? A ticket for littering? You've always got something to say, haven't you, Burlingame? Always something. Can't ever let anybody walk on by."

Burlingame swallowed. "It's only that Miss Calix hasn't been seen since sunset yesterday and even if it's not time for a search party, I think we must all at least—"

"You're worried she might have had enough of all this. Done something about it."

For a moment Burlingame didn't understand what Hickock meant, and then with a chill she realized he was talking about suicide. She could no more imagine a girl as vivid and pretty as Calix choosing to annihilate herself than she could a butterfly flying deliberately into an oil lamp. Even if the possibility had ever occurred to her, she wouldn't have been so crass as to raise the subject with Hickock, who had walked out into the jungle that night in 1944 and still carried himself like a man who never expected that failed attempt to be forgotten, almost in defiance of a community that might otherwise have been willing enough to forget it. "No," she said, "I meant . . ." She meant that Calix could have been mauled by a jaguar or bitten by a snake or tied to a tree by one of the New Yorkers. But she was now too mortified to finish her sentence.

"You ever think that sometimes a person makes a decision? They make it, not you, and if you don't like it, well, *I'm so frightfully sorry, Miss Burlingame*," Hickock said, imitating her accent, "but you can go fuck yourself. It's their life. You've got no right. You think you're everybody's mother around here, but you ain't. You stick your nose into every little thing that goes on, and nobody knows why, because you didn't even come here with us, you're just some old maid who we caught like a bad cold because the pricks over there wouldn't have you. If the girl's gone, let her go. You think I'm joining your fucking search party? Why can't you just let somebody get what they want once in a while?"

Burlingame turned and fled up the steps.

She'd understood that her busybodying wasn't always welcome. But she'd hoped that in the long run people saw that it was for the good of their little clan. To hear that she was resented so fiercely was to feel as if the temple had just been picked up and dropped on her. Even the words "old maid" stung, which was silly. Yes, she was twenty-nine and it had been twelve years since her first and only kiss, but almost everybody here had put their private lives away in the icebox, because that was the nature of the expedition. (Moreover, she was alone more or less by choice: she knew she was plain, but there were so few ladies here that even she had endured plenty of passes over the years.) Behind those personal insults was the dreadfulness of what he'd implied about his desperate act a year and a half ago. Could it be true that he wished he hadn't been fetched home by his friends? She'd always assumed that people who were saved from suicide were grateful for the rest of their lives. And then there was his beastly tone and language, as if she weren't worth anyone's politeness, which made her so indignant she wanted to alert a policeman or at the very least a friend, but of course there was no one here who would care if she told them about it. She felt dizzy with the crashing plural hurt of it all. When she arrived panting at the upper terrace, she was relieved to find that there was no one else around, because she planned to sit there and weep until there was nothing left of Joan Burlingame but one of those little museum placards that read "EXHIBIT TEMPORARILY REMOVED."

One thing was for sure. She was never, ever going to intervene in anybody else's affairs again. Not without a written invitation. The last time Rusk's rain-powered pulley system had been used, she noticed, the ropes had been left snagged up, but she certainly wasn't going to do anything about it. She wiped her nose with the back of her hand, wishing she was within fifty miles of a clean handkerchief. And then, faintly, from no direction she could identify, she heard a voice wailing for help.

☙

"I can't think of anything else, so I suppose that's the end of the tour," said Coehorn later that day.

"Thank you again," said Meinong. "This is a remarkable place." They were standing on a viny ridge that had a good view across the two-acre camp to the temple. At their backs the jungle grizzled and whined. This morning, after sleeping for something like fifteen hours, Meinong had awoken in the infirmary cabin afraid that somehow he was back at Erlösungfeld, and he was ashamed to recall that when the door creaked open he had cowered in his bed, expecting the next face he saw to belong to one of the farmers. But it was just Coehorn, the leader of this camp, coming in to check if he was awake. After that, sipping from a bowl of broth, Meinong asked several questions about where he was, but none of the answers made sense, so even though he felt as if he'd been shot, stuffed, mounted, and then shot again for good measure, he still insisted on getting up for a walk around the site with a borrowed cane at his side.

"You know, that might be another way for Pennebaker to do it," said Irma.

"Do what?" said Pennebaker.

"Sometimes if you want to figure out how to explain something you just need to wait until somebody new arrives and you're showing them around. When Pennebaker's in New York he could pretend he's giving a tour just like you just gave Kurt. 'Over here . . . On your left . . .' And they'd get a picture in their imaginations."

"But nobody made a note of what I was saying just now, and I don't think I could do it so well a second time," said Coehorn.

"Oh."

"Excuse me, but did I just hear you say that Mr. Pennebaker is going to New York?" said Meinong.

"That's right," said Coehorn. "They must be wondering what's become of us so we're going to soothe their curiosity."

"Will he be coming back?" He kept his tone even.

"No," said Coehorn.

"Yes," said Pennebaker. The man reminded Meinong of a buck-toothed and clerkish old colleague of his at Location D: when he made some trivial correction, he did his best to be casual about it, not because he understood that you didn't remotely care, but, on the contrary, because he assumed you'd be humiliated by your error and thought he was helping you save face. "I'll have to make sure the supplies are delivered here safely," Pennebaker continued. "Kerosene, rifles, disinfectant . . ."

"Gramophone records, cognac, pajamas . . . ," said Coehorn.

"Carpentry nails, bandages, prescription eyeglasses . . . ," said Pennebaker.

"Lipstick, Benzedrine, *The New Yorker* . . . ," said Irma.

"And of course enough funnel cakes to fill Carnegie Hall!" said Coehorn.

"Kurt probably doesn't know what a funnel cake is," said Irma.

"It's a type of cake," explained Coehorn. "Pennebaker loves them, don't you, Pennebaker? He cries himself to sleep every night because it's been so long since he last ate a funnel cake."

Pennebaker did not smile so much as winch his lips into a mirthless cringe. Waving away a botfly about the size of a canelé, Meinong noted that many of the stouter blocks of limestone from the Mayan ruin above had been put to use here as side walls or mezzanines, so that the random positions in which they'd been abandoned by the savages eight years ago had been allowed to determine the whole plan of this holiday camp. He did not think it likely that the Russians in Berlin would be quite so lackadaisical about the rubble of Speer's marvelous *Reichskanzlei*. Back when he was traveling through Puerto Cortés with forged Swiss papers, he had been trapped into sharing the only available taxi outside his hotel with an American businessman. Unprompted, the businessman started talking about the steamship voyage he was about to take to Europe. He made his living as an exporter of agricultural tools, but his largest buyer, the United Fruit Company, had just switched over to another company who claimed their "hygienic" equipment would retard the spread of a leaf blight called white sigatoka. So he was going to try his luck in Berlin, where he thought there would be a robust market once all the factories were pulled down and the workers returned to the countryside. After this second offense, he said, the world would surely never again allow the German people to do anything but till their land like medieval peasants.

"Hey, look," said Irma. "The temple—something's going on up at the top."

"Is it another magical fairy flying off into the empyrean?" said Coehorn. "Don't waste my time. I've still got a crick in my neck from yesterday evening."

"No, it looks like they're coming down this way."

The other three followed her gaze. Irma was right. Two men were being lowered like window washers down the face of the temple, although at this point their platform was still only a few feet from the top. "If it were after dark I'd say it was another incursion by stealth," said Coehorn. "But they're in plain view."

"Come on, Elias," said Irma. She and Coehorn hurried off for a closer look, perhaps forgetting that Meinong couldn't keep up on his shaky legs.

When the other two were out of earshot, Pennebaker said, "You know, I've never eaten a funnel cake. Never in my whole life."

"Oh?"

"I've never even seen a funnel cake. I've tried pretty hard to remember what I might have said to make Mr. Coehorn think I loved funnel cakes so much but I still don't know."

"Have you ever tried to correct his misapprehension?"

"I did once but he thought I was just embarrassed about the teasing."

"Will you sample one of these funnel cakes when you are in New York?"

"I never thought of that. Do you think I should?"

Meinong shrugged. "How soon do you expect to get back here?"

"It shouldn't take me more than a couple of months, depending.

I'm especially looking forward to finding out what happened in the war. Everybody wants me to bring back some news. I mean, we all appreciate hearing about it firsthand from you, we really do, but my brother's in the army and I want to know where he got sent off to fight. By now he probably speaks a little German! I don't mean any offense, but I never would have thought there'd be a German-American Alliance, not after the last war. But I guess that was just a disagreement among cousins—whereas you take the Russians, or the Japanese . . ."

Pennebaker burbled on. Meinong's estimate was that each of these witless Yanks had once possessed at least a respectable intelligence but then voluntarily renounced it: Coehorn because it had complicated his egotism, Irma because in the long run the least exasperating way to maintain their friendship had been to abase herself to Coehorn's level, and Pennebaker out of servility to the other two. He wondered who was really running the place. Tomorrow he would find someone to give him a proper tour of the camp on the staircase. Aside from a few of the bamboo scaffolds propping up the huts at the very bottom, which were dug into the earth just below, that camp had never been allowed to overspill the temple itself. To stand at the bottom and look up at the steps was like the approach by boat to one of those coastal villages in the Cinque Terre with the terraces stacked picturesquely on a rugged slope. Whether he decided to settle up there or down here, he believed this could be a better sanctuary than Erlösungfeld. At least if there were no disruptions. He regarded Pennebaker for a moment and then hobbled on.

ᔕᔕ

When she'd opened her eyes in the night to see a skull grinning back at her, Calix had understood right away that she'd entered the country of the dead. But then dawn had come, and she'd reached out to snap an incisor from the skull's crumbling jaw just to prove to herself that in fact she'd been turned back from that country at the border.

It's not the fall that kills you, it's the landing. That was what people always said. And she'd had no fall to speak of, but a hell of a lot of landing to make up for it.

This was what must have happened: hours earlier, as she'd shuffled to the edge of the temple, a lasso of rope from Rusk's rigging had crept up around her ankle, and she'd been in such a mess she hadn't even noticed. The upper tackle, which hadn't been stowed properly the last time it was used, had about fifteen feet of loose rope left in it before the truckle hit the brake. So when she leaped off, the thrilling interval of weightlessness or flight had only lasted an onionskin of an instant before the line went taut and she felt a jerk on her left leg, and then she was swinging back down toward the temple in a vertical arc like a wrecking ball on a chain. By the time she smashed into the limestone, her kneecaps, which hit first, were above her face, which hit second. How many times she might have bounced, she couldn't know, because she was knocked out by the impact. She was left dangling against the temple like a cliff climber whose abseil had gone unspeakably awry.

Later, in the moonlight, she moved in and out of a half doze with no sense of time passing. All her blood had thickened in her head like the last of the catsup, except for some she could feel crusting over in her eyes. Her entire body was in such a tremendous amount of pain that for a long while her state of suspension upside down by one ankle nearly two hundred feet off the ground seemed, in comparison, barely worth mentioning. In particular, her left leg felt like more break than bone, and her right leg had nothing to support it, so she tried to prop it up against the cool stone at her side, but every time it slipped off, its useless weight ripped at her thigh muscles until she thought she was going to retch over her own face again.

When she was more awake, she mewled with all her strength, but she was no louder than a bird call in a night full of bird calls. Even before the sun set she would have been hard to make out against the notchy surface of the temple's front elevation, and now she was as good as invisible. The next time she lost consciousness might not be the last, but one of these times probably would be. The longer her bowels pressed down on her lungs, the harder it was to breathe; that was what killed you, she knew, if the Romans crucified you upside down like Saint Peter.

She needed to get back up onto the temple. And of course one thing she did have, the only thing she did have, was a rope. But she hadn't climbed a rope since she was a kid, and kids can climb anything. Also, that was with her little feet scrabbling under her. She'd never tried to climb a rope with just her hands. Even to do that, she would have to jackknife in half at the abdomen to get her hands up as high as her left ankle, where the rope started. She knew before she tried it that she wouldn't have the strength, but she tried anyway. The exertion made her snarl like a woman in labor and she still couldn't hoist her torso up even the tiniest distance or get her hands anywhere near the rope.

"Emmy," she said, and hung there gasping for a while.

It made her think of the Chaplin movie where he got hoisted upside down from the bunting at the opening ceremony for the department store, except it wasn't as funny. She realized that if she could walk her hands up the side of the temple, she would be levering herself inch by inch with mostly her arm muscles instead of clenching herself up all at once with mostly her stomach muscles. There were plenty of handholds in the broken masonry. However, she saw the problem with that as soon as she made a preliminary attempt. Usually when you were climbing a wall you kept most of your weight on your feet while you were making progress with your hands, but, short of hanging by her toes like a monkey, she couldn't use her feet upside down. So she would have to brace her forehead against the temple to take some of the weight off her arms. Even if she found a few hospitable ledges, this was going to get harder and harder as she went on, because as her torso ratcheted from vertical to horizontal, she wasn't going to be resting her head on the wall so much as just jamming it against the wall crown first, relying mostly on friction between limestone and matted hair. And when her head inevitably slipped, her arms alone wouldn't be strong enough to hold her up, so she would just flop right back down, and her entire body weight would yank against her left leg again. Just the thought was enough to make her whimper aloud in horror.

She should just dangle there until either the rope broke or she passed out for good.

No, she shouldn't, because she didn't know how long that was going to take, and in the meantime this pain wasn't going to go away. The climbing wasn't impossible, after all. It could certainly be done. By a circus acrobat. After some practice.

She started again, hand over quivering hand, in earnest this time but more aware with every passing second that this was not going to work.

Then she found the gap.

At first it felt like just an especially large cranny. But as she groped further into it, she realized it had to be part of the architecture of the temple. It was deep enough that she couldn't reach the back with the tips of her fingers, tall enough that she hadn't found its ceiling yet, and maybe about eight or nine inches wide.

This loophole was wide enough for her head but not her shoulders, so she would only fit if she came at it as if she were lying on her side. If she wedged herself in there, and if there was enough slack in the rope, she might be able to turn a slow cartwheel until she was the right way up, gaining a little elevation in the process. She still wouldn't necessarily have the strength to climb back up to the terrace, but at least she wouldn't be hanging by her ankle any more, and she might get within reach of the rope without having to fold herself in half. Every so often there came that distant popping, like firecrackers, that you heard more and more often these days when you were high enough on the temple for the sound to reach you. The small fraternity in the *Hearts in Darkness* crew who had seen active military service were insistent that it was gunfire coming from somewhere in the jungle, but there was still debate because gunfire seemed so hard to account for.

She put the palm of her left hand flat on the floor of the gap, and then straightened her arm to jack up her torso, because the higher she entered, the more rope she'd have to spare. By the time she locked her elbow straight, enough of her weight was on that arm to make it tremble under her. With her right hand, she felt inside the gap for a handhold on the wall, and when she'd found one that seemed good enough, she started to drag herself head first into the darkness. A mosquito settled on the caruncle of her eye, which was suddenly so sensitive that she was sure she could feel the mosquito shifting its weight from foot to foot like a golfer as it got ready to bite. This was another irritant to be ignored, just like the survival instinct warning her not to get into a space so small that she might not be able to get out again, which in any case had fallen silent as soon as all her other survival instincts rounded on it with fury in their eyes. She stuffed herself inside until she was up to her waist, and soon began using her elbows to work her torso higher, keeping her shoulders at a diagonal against the vice of the walls so that she couldn't slip. Her intention had been to rotate until she was head over heels, but long before that there came a point when she was close enough to prone that almost none of her weight was on the rope around her ankle any more. For the first time, as the blood flowed back in, her left leg could relax into its desolation, and a sensation went through it that was a type of pain the same way the temple was a type of bird nest. She passed out again, and it wasn't until a few hours later, when the setting moon shone directly into the gap, that she woke up and got acquainted with the skull in its shiny helmet.

"You got any brothers or sisters, Miss Burlingame? Younger ones?"

"No. Nor elders. Why do you ask?"

"Because if you did, I expect you'd know you can't give someone a bath without looking at them." Burlingame blushed, and Calix felt a little wicked for making fun of her, but the situation was undeniably ridiculous: while she lay there naked under a sisal blanket, Burlingame was sponging the sweat off her bruises with her eyes averted. "You ever tried to wash a dish without looking at the dish?"

"In any given week I wash quite a number of dishes in almost complete darkness."

"Besides, you oughtn't to be going to the trouble. I'd say you did your good deed for the day when you heard me chirping in my nest and got me rescued." It was midmorning, and about twenty-four hours had passed since Calix had been brought here half conscious. Outside the hut she could hear voices, and she wondered if she was a subject of gossip.

"Well, I can scarcely ask one of the men to do it. Anyway, they say the German fellow who came into the other camp was given the best of care. It wouldn't do to let them show us up. How do you feel now?"

"Like I got one of those Swedish massages from every man, woman, and child in Sweden. But better than before." Her nurse was so proper that Calix couldn't resist prickling her some more. "You still aren't looking. You keep missing spots."

Burlingame swallowed and ran her tongue from left to right between her lower lip and her teeth, then very deliberately, as if recalibrating an observatory telescope, turned her gaze down toward Calix's torso. This venture was so visibly costly to Burlingame that straight away Calix felt remorseful for making her do it, and even, for no good reason, a little ashamed of her nakedness.

She'd brought a miserable silence upon the both of them. And the motion of the sponge had changed, as if Burlingame were now trying to pretend it wasn't warm flesh she was varnishing but only some sort of furniture. Calix put most of it down to Burlingame's native prudish qualities, but all the same it wasn't the most reassuring feeling in the world to have someone react with such squeamishness to your injured body. To fill the silence as the sponge bath entered its abdominal chapter, she said, "What were you doing up there, anyway? Up at the top of the temple. You never said."

"Just collecting my thoughts."

"Quiet up there, isn't it? And the view's peachy."

"Sure is."

"They should install a set of those nickel binoculars."

They were both aware that quite soon the sheet was going to have to fall below Calix's hips. Calix wasn't sure why this awareness should weigh so heavily, but it did. "What about you?" Burlingame asked, dipping the sponge in the bucket again. "Before you fell?"

Calix smiled. "That's nice of you, Miss Burlingame."

"What do you mean?"

"Nice of you to pretend. But there really isn't any obligation." She was getting goosebumps on her stomach, and although she didn't think there was anything inherently licentious about goosebumps, she still wished to God they would retract.

"You're talking quite over my head, I'm afraid," said Burlingame.

"I'm sure everyone knows why I went up there and everyone knows I didn't just fall."

The sponge was now almost at Calix's pubic bone.

"If you were incautious of the height and you leaned out too far that's no reason to—"

"I jumped," said Calix.

The sponge halted.

From the anguish on her face it was clear that Burlingame wished her fiction could have been maintained for just a little longer. "You had a . . . moment of madness."

"It wasn't just a moment."

"But of course now you're glad you were saved," Burlingame said, her voice on a tightrope.

"You mean, would I try it again?"

"Would you?"

"If you tried to do what I tried to do, and something happened to you like what happened to me, would you take it as a sign that you ought to dust yourself off and give it another go-around?"

"No, I certainly wouldn't."

"Well."

Burlingame put the sponge back in the bucket and left it there. "You always seemed like a cheerful sort. But . . . of course they say, don't they, that . . . um."

"I got in a bad fix with Mr. Trimble."

"Trimble?"

"Yes."

"I don't see what sort of fix could possibly be so bad that you'd—"

"Mr. Trimble has a great talent for fixes. He is a top man in the fix business." Calix did not detect complete comprehension. "You understand, don't you, Miss Burlingame? You know about Trimble. You must know."

"Know what?"

"Oh, now, come on, Miss Burlingame! Folks might not talk about it much but everybody knows and there's no use pretending otherwise. Mr. Trimble is the master of this plantation. We're all his slaves. We all belong to him. Up here and down there the same."

"You're being rather hyperbolic."

"No, I am not. You can't really be telling me you don't know. You've seen his newspaper. Mr. Trimble's an evil man and he gets most everything he wants and there's nothing anybody can do it about it any more."

Burlingame looked at the ground for a while. "Perhaps I did know. I have known, dimly. But I've been making heroic efforts not to think about it. I suppose I mustn't be a very good observer, as ethnologists go. But I never thought I was, really." She drew in a long breath. "And you mean to say that you . . . tried to do what you tried to do because of Trimble?"

"I didn't see any other way out of where he'd put me."

"If you had lost your life it would have been because of that man?"

"I carry my own load."

"Just for the sake of his . . . his bloody . . ." Burlingame looked up. She was now meeting Calix's eye for the first time since the sponge bath began. And Calix was astonished, even alarmed, by the suddenness of the change in Burlingame's expression. She'd only had her head bowed for a short time, but somehow she already had the flushed and teary face of someone who'd been conducting a screaming argument in a high wind, and there was a rage in her green eyes that Calix could not reconcile with what she knew of this timid Englishwoman.

"You all right, Miss Burlingame?"

"I'm going to find Trimble. I'm afraid your bath will have to wait."

"Oh, no, Miss Burlingame, you mustn't!"

"You needn't worry. He can't blackmail me. I'm quite safe. I've never done anything interesting in my life, you see." And with that she was gone.

☙

The clouds were brandishing rain when Burlingame found Trimble further down the steps, chatting with Berg the crane steerer.

"I really must talk to you, Mr. Trimble."

"Of course, Miss Burlingame." Trimble slapped Berg on the shoulder. "See you in church, pal."

Now they were alone, or at least at a distance from all the usual bustle of an afternoon on the temple. "It has come to my attention . . ." Burlingame was confused to find herself using vocabulary she associated with school assemblies, but nothing else seemed to be available. "It has come to my attention that by your actions, deliberate or otherwise, a young member of the crew has come to great harm."

Trimble shook his head and gave a little whistle. "Honestly, Miss Burlingame, I feel like I just took a medicine ball right in the gut. That's the last thing a guy wants to hear on a beautiful morning like this. But if you could tell me just what happened and maybe tip me off about how to put things right then you'd be doing me a very signal service."

"Miss Calix. The wardrobe girl. As you may already know she is convalescing in bed."

"Sure. They say she's lucky to be alive."

"That's right."

"She took a real tumble."

"Yes."

"But now she's going to make it through okay," said Trimble. "Sounds like just the sort of heart-cozy I like to put on the front page of the *Enquirer.* I'm looking forward to writing it up. Apart from that I don't see what it's got to do with me personally."

"You will not put it in your newspaper. You will leave Miss Calix alone."

"Leave her alone? If it's okay with you, I'd rather not. She's a pal of mine."

"No. You will stop all this. You will shut up your workshop of calumny." Where she might have fished that phrase from she had no idea. She was still quite surprised at herself for using the word "bloody" a few minutes ago.

"You've knocked me for a loop here, Miss Burlingame. I just can't make out what you're getting at. Well, you know the old saying— 'divided by a common language!' "

"You put people in fixes. You're an evil man. Everybody knows."

Trimble gazed at her. She could see she was close to exhausting his patience. "Everybody knows, huh?"

"Yes."

"Everybody knows and everybody feels the same way as you do?"

"I believe so."

"Hey, Ricky-Boy." Burlingame looked behind her. Halloran, the first assistant director, was on his way up with a megaphone in one hand and a ball of twine in the other. The *Hearts in Darkness* crew had lived for so long on this stepwise estate that their gaits had changed. When they went out into the forest they had stair legs instead of sea legs. The topology would be encoded in the film itself, if it was ever finished: all the dolly shots in Whelt's recent storyboards were lateral, as if the camera were sidestepping along a tread, and all the pans were either horizontal or vertical, to match the rectilinear grid of limestone blocks underfoot. Even after all this time, however, it felt to Burlingame as if interactions in the camp retained a faintly provisional quality, because it was a rule of human life that a meeting on the stairs never signified much. They all longed for *esprit de l'escalier,* a reward deferred forever because they never truly reached the bottom step.

"Good timing, Rick," said Trimble. "Spot me that bullhorn for a minute, will you?" Halloran hopped up rather slavishly to pass the megaphone to Trimble, and Trimble held it out to Burlingame. "If everybody feels the same way as you do, you should get them all involved. Start a political party. How about it, Burlingame? Don't be shy. Tell them about me. Tell them what you say they know. See how far you get."

"No!" Burlingame turned. The cry had come from Calix, who was descending toward them with a plank of pinewood under one armpit instead of a crutch. The rise of each step was so high that she wasn't so much hobbling as vaulting. She was wearing the clean clothes that Burlingame had brought to the infirmary cabin for her to put on later, although her skirt was on backward. "Please, Miss Burlingame. Just leave off. Mr. Trimble and I can settle it between ourselves." Halloran must have made a creditable guess at what was happening, because he gave Burlingame a solemn nod, meaning that she must take Calix's advice.

Without having decided what she was going to do, Burlingame took the megaphone from Trimble. For all its tinplate heft it did not feel quite real. The truth was that nothing had felt quite real since Calix folded the hem of the sheet down to her waist. Burlingame had once read about an Albanian king who'd escaped so many assassination attempts by his own generals that he'd installed a hydraulic mechanism beneath his throne that made steel grills spring up around him on all four sides if he pressed a switch in the armrest. Burlingame felt that was just how she had always reacted to shocks, emotional or otherwise. She would not have survived the emergency of Calix's bosom if in that instant she had not separated herself from reality inside an impregnable cage, so that she could touch Calix's nakedness where absolutely necessary but it could not touch her. And now, although Calix had put on a blouse, Burlingame's cage had not withdrawn. There it was still, between her and the weight of the megaphone, between her and the facticity of her actions, between her and the inconceivability of calling a man evil to his face. The trouble was that it hadn't worked quite as designed. The cage might have protected her from immediate destruction, but not, in the end, from the image of the soapsuds running down the sides of Gracie's breasts, and not from this fury, this deep rib-cracking fury at the thought of the girl being driven to such despair for another's silly profit. For a long time she had felt keen to become friends with Calix, but that could not account for what was happening to her. So unprecedented was the intensity of these feelings that Burlingame almost wondered if something from the jungle might have worked its way into her brain. And all the while, everything else felt weightless, fictional, neutralized beyond the cage, just because it wasn't Gracie's body or Gracie's life. Trimble still wore a smirk of absolute assurance that she would not call his bluff when, as if full of helium, the megaphone simply lifted itself to her mouth. "Er, good morning, everyone," she said. "Can I have your attention, please?"

For the first time she realized the practical advantages of possessing the sort of English accent that Americans found impressive. The megaphone had turned a good number of heads. She walked along the step until she was right at the edge of the temple, a pulpit from which the echo of her voice might reach some of the New Yorkers too. "Could I please have your attention?" she called again. "Your immediate attention."

Gracie, who had finally reached her, put a hand on her arm. "No, Miss Burlingame! I won't let you get yourself into this kind of trouble. Not on my account. You don't know what he'll do to you."

"It's all right, Gracie." The warmth of the hand on her arm only urged her on. Through the megaphone again: "Mr. Trimble has given me permission to speak to you all about the state of affairs here in both our two camps." She glanced over at him. The smirk still on his face seemed to flicker in place like a buzz saw in motion. "I really must have everyone's attention for what I'm about to say. Gather round, if you please." She knew she wasn't qualified for this. When she tried to think of speeches, all she could remember was school assemblies again, prize givings, graduations. That, after all, had been her life before the temple. But didn't that mean she was intelligent, at least? Intelligence wasn't nothing. She waited until quite a crowd of people had stopped their work or come out of their huts, including at least a dozen down in the other camp.

"We are all very grateful for Mr. Trimble's hard work over the past few years," she began. "He has made a diligent chronicle of the goings-on in our little community. After a hard day's work, who of us has not looked forward to settling down with a copy of the *Pozkito Enquirer*? Mr. Trimble deserves our sincerest thanks." She started to clap, which wasn't easy because she held the megaphone in her left hand so she had to slap the back of her wrist with her right. Here and there, others joined in the applause, but she soon let it finish. "However, I'm sure Mr. Trimble will not object if I should go so far as to suggest that perhaps the time has come for . . . Well." A raindrop goosed the back of her neck. She faltered. If a real downpour started she would be outvoiced, she would have to stop, she would be allowed to stop and it wouldn't be her fault. She no longer felt that drunk's invincibility, and there was a part of her, not such a small part, that would welcome a summary dismissal by the sky.

Trimble took the opportunity to step forward. "Thank you so much, Miss Burlingame," he said. "I'm touched, really I am." He reached to pull the megaphone out of her hand.

But Halloran, six foot four and sturdy, blocked his way.

Trimble looked at Halloran as if this had to be a joke. And Halloran was squinting and chewing his lips like he had a bee trapped inside his face. But he didn't budge. As she'd already admitted to Gracie, Burlingame had remained willfully oblivious to Trimble's program. But one proposition of which she felt almost certain was that in all this time he had never resorted to violence. And so it was strange to see on Halloran's face—and this was a man who had served in the infantry—the sort of grimace that you might otherwise associate with the animal terror of impending dismemberment. Trimble was feared, she realized, feared like death, this rodential gazetteer who had so little power to do anything that really mattered.

Burlingame looked at Gracie, who had tears in her eyes, and then looked back out across her audience. In the last minute or so it seemed almost to have doubled in size. She tried not to pick out individual faces because she knew that would deter her. Into the megaphone she said, "You all know Miss Calix. You all know that Miss Calix nearly lost her life last night. We each carry our own load, of course. But nonetheless I have been led to understand that Mr. Trimble, for all his good intentions, must take some share of the blame." The right angles of the temple steps meddled with the acoustics so that sometimes her words would come booming grandly back at her but if she let the angle of the megaphone dip a few degrees she felt as if she were talking into a pillow. "Miss Calix was in a state of despair. She is a young woman of strong character and gay disposition. Why should she have been in such a state? Why should this have been done to her? What drove her up there last night? What I mean to say is . . ." By now Burlingame was having trouble keeping her voice from cracking. "Because this young woman, this dear friend of ours, once made an error. Some trivial error, no doubt. And much as he did to Mr. Hickock a few years ago, Mr. Trimble forced her into a position of—"

"Miss Burlingame—" said Gracie.

She felt rain again, and spoke faster. "I don't know what it was she did. I don't have any right to know. None of us do. But I'm quite sure it was nothing. She didn't deserve this. What happened to her must never be allowed to happen again."

"Miss Burlingame, my niece is confined to a mental asylum because I had sexual relations with her for months and months and then when we were caught I told everyone she forced herself on me," Gracie said.

Burlingame stood there open-mouthed for a moment. Thankfully her audience could not have heard what Gracie said. But Halloran had heard, and he was now staring at Gracie as if she'd just licked her lips with an eight-inch forked tongue.

"Gracie . . ."

"I couldn't have you do this for me not knowing. He's going to tell everybody anyway."

"How do you like that, Miss Burlingame?" said Trimble. "Is this little tramp still your 'dear friend'? This cradle-robbing muff-diving falsidical Dixie tramp?" With a snarl he pushed past Halloran, so that his face was only a few inches from Burlingame's, and she felt very aware of her position right on the edge of the temple, a hundred feet off the ground. "You still want to stand up for her? Knowing what she did? Your 'dear friend' tore the frock off her little niece and laid her down and ate her cunt up. A hundred times in a row, probably. I did her a favor. I found that out and I didn't tell nobody. And if she'd taken a running jump off the top and it was because of me then maybe I would've been doing her a favor that way too. You think about that, Miss Burlingame, before you say anything else." He smiled. "Or maybe that don't put you off. Maybe that's part of the appeal. Just speculating." He seemed almost to be sniffing for a scent. "Yeah. Yeah, I think so. You know, I think that's it. I should have guessed. When she needed a nursemaid, you weren't too slow to step up, were you? When her drawers were falling off her and she needed a nice long sponge bath between her legs."

Without meaning to, Burlingame glanced at Gracie, and then turned away, mortified. She could forgive the girl anything, but she could not herself expect to be forgiven. There was no hydraulic cage any more, and no king inside, just a few bent medals glinting from a small pile of ash. Nobody at the temple was immune to a coup d'état except this warlock who knew your secrets before you knew them yourself. This time, Halloran didn't stop Trimble from grabbing the megaphone out of her slack hand. He raised it.

"Sorry for the interruption in the show just now, ladies and gentlemen. We had a little conferrumination to finish in the wings. But that's over now. What I want to do is give you all an exclusive preview of the front page of tomorrow's *Enquirer*. Miss Calix and Miss Burlingame here, they ain't just fast friends, you know. They ain't just a couple of gals looking out for each other in hard times."

But even with the megaphone his voice could hardly be heard, because by now at least a hundred men and women, above and below, Angelenos and New Yorkers, reconstructionists and deconstructionists, were chanting, "Out! Out! Out!"

☙

Pennebaker had been scheduled to leave camp at daybreak. So the previous day he had declared his intention to go to bed early, meaning about eight in the evening, in order to be well rested for his long journey, and Coehorn had declared his intention to go to bed late, meaning about seven in the morning, in order to be present for the send-off. However, just before Pennebaker retired, Coehorn had asked him to rehearse his opening remarks to the New York press one last time. Pennebaker's recall was perfect, but hearing him yet again made Coehorn realize there were still one or two *mots* not quite *juste*. He told Pennebaker that he wouldn't dream of keeping him from his bed, but in the time it would take him to brush his teeth and change into his pajamas, they could collaborate on what their rivals might call a last-minute script polish.

Seventeen hours later, there was no longer a script. Not even the barest statements of fact had survived. Coehorn had chewed so much of the sour purple leaf—at first to feel more creative, and later to stay awake—that by now he could not stop grinding his stained teeth. He'd begun to understand that he had no hope of rewriting Pennebaker's remarks until he'd completed the project of mapping and repairing certain previously unsuspected fissures in the structure of English itself. But he still felt fully confident that they would see Pennebaker off before noon.

When Lon Maisoneuve came into the bungalow to report the hubbub outside, Coehorn instructed everybody to ignore it. This felt too familiar. "First there was that circus trick with the Incredible Vanishing Leaper," he complained, counting on his fingers. "Then the platform being lowered down. And now some other crisis. They're obviously just craving attention."

"Really, Mr. Coehorn, I haven't seen a crowd like this in one place since the day we got here," said Maisoneuve. "A lot of the Banisters have come down off the steps."

"You mean the temple's unguarded?"

"Closest it's ever been, I'd say."

Coehorn got to his feet. Here was an excitement he hadn't felt since those first clashes in 1938. Not long ago it had struck him that, like his father, he had founded a corporation. The industry in which the corporation did most of its business was the satisfaction of his whims and languors, and in that respect it might resemble a sort of burlesque of Eastern Aggregate, but it was no less functional or self-sustaining. He would never underrate his achievement. And yet he still wanted the temple as badly as ever. Shielding his eyes against the daylight he hurried out of the bungalow. He was ready to seize the moment, even if the last seventeen hours hadn't set much of a precedent in that regard.

But as he rounded the southwest corner of the temple with Irma and Pennebaker at his side, the first person he met was a tall man whom he recognized as one of Whelt's stooges.

"Mr. Coehorn, I've been sent to tell you that, with all due respect, you'd better not get any ideas," the man said. "We're watching, and if we think you're looking to try anything funny, we'll be back up there holding you off before you can say 'Jack Robinson.' What's happening now is for our people and your people alike so you can just forget all that for the time being. No touchdowns in halftime."

"What do you mean, 'what's happening now'?" said Coehorn.

"We're getting rid of Trimble." The man tried to sound stern as he said this but his glee was so uncontainable that his voice warbled in the middle. He gestured behind him. Coehorn could see that Leland Trimble was being manhandled toward the perimeter of the clearing, with another big Angeleno clutching his left arm and Mac Parke, Coehorn's own athletic trainer, clutching his right. Pressing at their rear like a wedding party were scores of others, close to the entire population of both camps, craning their necks or jostling forward or spreading out at the sides to get a better look. There was a lot of noise, but he couldn't make out any individual cries, only a sort of swarmy, hysterical jubilation.

"What is this?" said Coehorn. "Is this some Indian ritual we've suddenly adopted? Are we driving a scapegoat out of the village in the hopes of a good harvest?" Striding forward, he raised his voice. "Stop this at once!"

Trimble looked up. His hair was disheveled and he'd lost a sandal but he seemed to be unharmed. "Mr. Coehorn!"

The sky was the color of the temple and Coehorn's face was damp, but by the standards of the jungle this wasn't rain yet, just something the sky had to push out before it really started, like the water left behind in the showerhead from the last time you used it. By now he was close enough to speak directly to Parke. "Let him go! Do you really think anyone who dines at my table is going to be humiliated like this? What the hell is wrong with you?"

"That's it, Mr. Coehorn," said Trimble. "Talk some sense into them."

The procession had stopped. "We've all decided, sir," said Parke, who most of the time was nothing but plasticine features and dumb obedience, like a cut-rate golem. "He's got to go."

"You've 'decided'? Have you forgotten who you work for? If for some reason Trimble isn't welcome up in the cheap seats any more, that's fine. We've got plenty of room for him down here. In fact if you're not careful he will have your cabin, Parke."

"He's done things."

"Done what? Published a newspaper? Brokered any number of complicated deals between the two camps? He's indispensable."

"You don't know, sir. You wouldn't understand."

"I understand perfectly well. I know what I'm looking at. This is mob justice, and it's disgusting. For eight years we stay basically civilized and now this. What are you proposing to do? Feed him to the jaguars?"

"No, sir. It's exile. He only has to leave the site. He can go wherever he likes. But he can't come back."

"How will he survive in the jungle? Look here, just because one isn't infatuated with another person's company that doesn't mean one has the right to send them off into . . ." Coehorn remembered Walter Pennebaker was standing beside him. "The point is, I won't allow it."

Irma took his arm. "Elias," she hissed.

"What is it, Irma?"

"Elias, look at me." He did, and was alarmed by her eyes. "Let this happen."

"What?"

"Let them send him away."

He could feel her fingernails digging into his bicep, and he wanted to look away from her but somehow he couldn't. "Irma, what in the world has come over you? I've never seen you like this."

"I'm not going to tell you again, Elias. Let. This. *Happen*." She was hissing now, and that last word was the tip of a switchblade held right up to his cornea.

The crowd had fallen almost silent. They were watching to see what he would do. He reached out to give the reporter's hand a good shake. "Best of luck, Trimble. Look me up when we all get back to New York."

Coehorn didn't stay to see what would happen. Instead, attempting to recover a modicum of authority, he insisted that Irma and Pennebaker return to the bungalow with him. At their backs, Trimble could be heard yelling, something about somebody's lovechild, something about somebody's probation terms, but Coehorn didn't listen. They trotted along most of the way because the real rain had started now, the hyperemesis, the tommy-gun barrage, the collapsing aqueduct, the doubled gravity. Everywhere, cabins would be springing new leaks, always directly over your bed, your table, your trunk. The sight of the water rivering down over the antique limestone made Coehorn nostalgic for New York sidewalks in the spring. "Your bags are packed, Pennebaker?" he said when they got inside. "You have the stone? You're ready to go?"

"I sort of thought we were putting it off until tomorrow," said Pennebaker.

"It's not even noon. There are hours of daylight left."

"But Mr. Coehorn, I haven't slept."

"You can sleep tonight. Better not to waste any more time."

"And we haven't finished working on the stuff I have to say."

"Oh, I can't spend one minute more on all that," said Coehorn, waving his hand. "Just think back over our discussions and select the best and most truthful material and put it in an intelligent order and I'm sure we can trust you not to disappoint us."

෧෨

Although he knew it was futile, Yang spent a long time trying to talk Whelt out of going down inside the temple. His first argument was that they didn't need any more silver. After the suit of armor that Gracie Calix had discovered had been winched up and filleted of its bones, what remained was about forty pounds of metal, which would make more than enough silver nitrate film to shoot the rest of *Hearts in Darkness* (just as soon as all the other obstacles withdrew). But Whelt, who so seldom showed any hungers at all, talked

_____ silver like a greedy prospector. Even if they didn't find another
_____ least be a few trinkets. If
eft, they had to have it.
as too dangerous. Perhaps
more than that, or perhaps
) well was in fact as hollow
: did indeed have an inter-
mble the hotellish corridors
Whelt might easily get stuck
nb back up. (Halloran joked
semble the other half of the
:d an icy stare from Whelt.)
night find himself lost down
e camp had no rope available
. But Whelt said there was no
s "perpetual motion machine"
:ould also be helpful for com-
cay," two tugs for "Please send
ugs for "I am beyond rescue so
ier leave me to die." This caused
had to send someone inside, it
ire, because they couldn't afford
dn't trust anyone else to do it in
ired by irrational fear.
rations following Trimble's ban-
carnival, with singing, dancing,
bers of the crew were somewhat
iat they might be expected to do
ame, Whelt was soon up on top of
e around his midriff. Because the
nitration of the Mayan suit or armor was not yet under way, he wore
its engraved headpiece as a protective helmet. Yang had nagged him
into agreeing that if he did find catacombs to explore, he would
nevertheless return from this preliminary descent within an hour.
He climbed down to the suspended platform they'd constructed the
previous day to rescue Calix, and the last remark he made before he

disappeared into the silver mine was, puzzlingly, "This reminds me of the time I was invited to Mr. Spindler's house."

After an hour of waiting, Yang reeled up the line about eighty feet, until it was almost taut, and then gave it a tug. Whelt tugged back once, so Yang payed the rope back out. After two hours, Yang went through the same procedure, and again Whelt tugged back once—rather irritably, if that was possible. After three hours, ditto.

After four hours, Yang tried to reel up the rope yet again, but this time it just kept reeling and reeling until he held the frayed end in his hands.

෨

"You know how to get to the river, don't you?" someone had said, and he'd nodded. None of them were intending to escort him all the way, but Trimble nevertheless walked quite a distance on that bearing just in case he was followed. They really believed he was going to leave the site for good. They were wrong and they could stay wrong.

If he felt like it, he could go anywhere. He'd never bothered to pick up more than a few words of Pozkito, but he knew he could walk into that Indian guerrilla camp beyond the dam, a white man in tatters without so much as a wormy cherimoya to trade, and within a year he'd be their commandant. Or he could raft down toward San Esteban until he found some real business under way—timber, cattle, sugarcane, loans—it didn't matter what, just as long as people did well enough out of it that they had something to lose. If that got boring he could take a steamship back to New York, become editor of the *Mirror,* or president of the stock exchange, or mayor of the city, or whatever he wanted. He'd already proven his capabilities beyond doubt.

But if a collection agency put a padlock on your store, you didn't just shrug your shoulders and call your cousin in Poughkeepsie to ask about a job. You stayed on the block; you watched; you waited; you pissed on your shoes sooner than take your eyes off that store. Because it was still yours, and so was everything in it, and before long you were going to find a way to take it back. To geek out on the temple now would have been a waste of eight years' work. His whole operation had worked on the principle of ownership without possession, and he was entirely comfortable letting other people look after his holdings for him. If those holdings weren't all piled up in his cabin at once, that didn't mean they weren't his, and if he couldn't go near the temple for a while, the same applied.

They probably thought it was a withering indignity to be dragged away shouting like that. But sometimes back in New York he might get bounced from three nightclubs in one night, and he always outlived his lifetime bans. He told himself not to resent how they'd treated him. They couldn't possibly understand how much he'd given them, and in their position he might have done just the same. But of course he would have done it sooner and he would have done it better. Where they merely pricked he would have impaled. His old friends didn't seem to understand that he would have no choice but to get even with them, and so they hadn't gone nearly far enough to make sure he wouldn't dare come back. They weren't just ungrateful like children, they were soft like children, too. He'd seen it in the earnestness with which they'd asked that silly question—"You know how to get to the river, don't you?"—so that they could congratulate themselves afterward for their generous behavior. They'd never admit how sheepish they had felt in those last moments when they were alone with him in the trees, like a few God-fearing junior salesmen showing a hooker the door after the fun got a little out of hand. But he knew them. By the very feebleness of their attempt to pull him down, they'd proven how easy it would be to climb back up.

At regular intervals over the last eight years he'd spent entire days or nights crouched in the boughs of a tree at the edge of the clearing, watching the site from a distance through the opera glasses he'd bought from Irma, trying to understand its clockwork better. Everyone except him thought of the two camps as separate, independent, because they hadn't seen how even tiny events in one were connected to tiny events in the other. If he noticed anybody going anywhere or doing anything that he couldn't immediately explain, he made sure to find out more the next day. He wanted omniscience, and most of the time he had it. Now that he couldn't interview anyone directly any more, he'd have to do a lot more peeping at the ant farm. But he knew there wouldn't be much going on this afternoon because of the weather, so at this stage it was probably better to turn his attention to food and shelter and weapons. He was about to set off north when he became aware of movement on the hunting path nearby.

If it had been any further away, he couldn't have heard it over this drenching rain, which turned every bower in the jungle into a private booth. He got down and crawled a few yards through the undergrowth in that direction until he could see who was coming without being seen himself.

No one would be out today without a good reason—you could practically drown out here just by yawning too wide—and he might have guessed it would be Pennebaker. The bookkeeper looked miserable but determined as he trudged along with a rucksack on his back and a pith helmet on his head, a quarter of a mile down, only two or three thousand to go. Cradled like an infant in his arms was the chunk of Mayan limestone that Coehorn had chosen to send back to his father. Trimble took some satisfaction in knowing that the balance of power at the site was about tilt wildly, not only because that treacherous lush had lost his two best advisers in one morning, but also because the *Hearts in Darkness* crew might at last start paying attention to Burlingame. The meek really shall inherit the earth, apparently.

Then, between the trees, Trimble caught sight of somebody else further up the trail. Meinong, the German army officer, was hurrying to catch up with Pennebaker.

Trimble had kept a close eye on him in the days since his sensational arrival. He was smart, observant, patient, slippery. Was he, like Trimble, ambitious? Would he, like Trimble, make the most of his gifts? He hadn't yet given any sign, but it wasn't hard to imagine him as a rival.

Not until Meinong was just behind him did Pennebaker hear the footfalls and turn. "Oh, Mr. Meinong! Did Mr. Coehorn send you after me? Did something happen?" Trimble could only barely make out the words.

"Yes, Mr. Pennebaker," said Meinong. "There is some concern that Miss Lopez's performing mouse may have stowed away in your rucksack."

Pennebaker's reply was inaudible.

Meinong said, "Perhaps you could check the rucksack just once more all the same."

"Okay." Pennebaker looked down at the stone. "I'm not supposed to let anybody else touch this until I get to New York, but maybe you could hold it for a minute?"

"I should be happy to, Mr. Pennebaker," said Meinong.

Pennebaker passed the stone to him before shrugging the rucksack off his shoulders and swinging it around to his front. He was fiddling with the buckles when Meinong brought the stone down on his head with both hands, cracking his right socket and bursting the eyeball.

The accountant dropped the rucksack and toppled over. As he lay there, slack, the rain swilled from his ruined orbit a mixture of dark blood and vitreous yolk. He was probably kaput already, but Meinong nevertheless knelt down, raised the stone over his head, and slammed it down once more.

With that accomplished, he grabbed Pennebaker's body by the ankles and began to drag it away from the hunting path. As quietly as he could, Trimble slid backward, just in case Meinong came in this direction. The rain forest was like the Bowery: if you left anything unattended in the street for an afternoon it would get stripped down to a grease stain. Still, if Meinong was as clever as Trimble estimated, he'd at least deal with the brass fittings in Pennebaker's rucksack and the fillings in his teeth, either of which would be enough to prove the skeleton wasn't Pozkito when it was found one day with weeds growing through the eye sockets. Honduras might well have scavengers that ate metal but Trimble hadn't heard about them yet.

"Hey! Who's that?"

Trimble looked up, startled, and so did Meinong.

Joe Hickock, the grip who had reacted so melodramatically to that row over the fugitive turkeys in '44, was approaching with an ax in his hand. For all four men to coincide on the hunting trail like this was quite a mischance, but then again this was the quickest and most familiar route to the river, and no one risked an avant-garde shortcut in a rainstorm. Meinong let Pennebaker's feet drop and moved forward to intercept Hickock. "*Ja, hallo,* I am Herr Meinong. I don't believe we have met."

"You're the new guy they were talking about? The German?" From where Hickock was standing, he wouldn't see Pennebaker's body unless he looked over to his left.

The next exchange was inaudible.

Then Meinong smiled. "The food they serve in our camp, it is not so easy on the stomach."

"You walked all this way just to take a crap?"

"I thought it best, yes."

"That bad, huh?"

"What about yourself?"

"I came looking for Trimble. He came this way earlier on. Have you seen him?"

"No, I haven't. Why are you trying to find him?"

Hickock narrowed his mouth. "I meant to have a talk with him before he left. That's all. No sign of him?" He looked around. That was when he caught sight of Pennebaker's feet. "Hey, what the heck . . . ?"

Meinong bowed his head and charged at Hickock, tackling him in the chest.

Trimble thought back to that night at the Bering Strait Railroad Association when he'd won a stack betting long on the diver against the mollusk. This fight was going to be enjoyable enough to watch, but it was a shame he couldn't put any money down. If Trimble himself had been caught in the same predicament as Meinong, he could have talked his way out of it, but he had to admit it would have been harder for this stranger with a foreign accent, who was now kneeling on Hickock's torso.

With his left hand Meinong had Hickock's right wrist pinned to the earth and with his right hand he was prying his fingers away from the handle of the ax. But that meant Hickock's left hand was free, and he could reach up just far enough to knock Meinong in the jaw. The third time he did that, Meinong looked unsteady for a moment, and Hickock jacked his knees to tip Meinong off him.

Each scrambled to get on top of the other; each maintained his own grip on the ax handle; each clawed at the other's eyes, nose, throat with his free hand. They were so slathered in mulch that their two bodies together might have been some octopod newly burped from a mudpot. And Hickock, who'd already torn open Meinong's left nostril, must have been stronger, because he forced Meinong down and knocked his front teeth down his throat with one punch. As Meinong wriggled, he fit the heel of his hand under Hickock's chin and tried to push him off, but he couldn't do much. They were both roaring as they strained against each other like some misaligned machine. Then all of a sudden Meinong let himself go limp. Hickock jerked forward a few inches. And his shoulder came down hard on the head of the ax, which was upturned in the soil.

Hickock fell sideways, his eyes screwed shut with the pain. Meinong wrenched the ax out of Hickock's shoulder. Now the weapon was uncontestedly in his grasp. But by some furious effort of will, Hickock managed to haul himself most of the way upright before Meinong did, clamping down on the gash in his shoulder with one bloody hand. So Meinong, who was on his back, was flailing up at Hickock, who was still down on one knee but nearly on his feet. This was awkward, and if Hickock had been quick enough, he could have snatched the ax out of the German's hands. But instead Meinong rammed him in the groin with the blunt end of the handle.

Hickock collapsed again, and now it was Meinong who got back up on his knees, panting. He had his back to Trimble, who realized that there might still be time to intervene. Trimble didn't know exactly why Meinong had intercepted Pennebaker. Perhaps this supposed war hero didn't want the outside world to know about the two camps, or perhaps he didn't want the two camps to know about the outside world, or perhaps both. Regardless, he was playing some kind of long game. Hickock had some unfriendly intentions toward Trimble, sure, but he didn't have the right instincts to be a real threat. Meinong, on the other hand, could very well take advantage of Trimble's absence, undo some of his hard work, complicate his eventual return. If Hickock was the one who got home alive instead of Meinong, there might come a time when Trimble would be thankful for that. All he had to do was snake forward and yank one of Meinong's legs out from under him. That little prank would probably be enough to give the American the upper hand. A nice patriotic idea.

But he stopped himself. Hickock couldn't know he was here. He thought of the youthful Coehorn, whom he'd mistaken that night for Frank Parker, failing to break up the wrestling match.

And then it was too late to get involved, because Meinong swung the ax down on Hickock's skull like the mallet of a fairground high striker, hard enough that the blade broke off the rotten handle.

Trimble wondered how the German expected to handle this. If Hickock's absence was noticed today, then a lot of people might surmise, accurately, that he'd gone out to take his own revenge on Trimble and something had gone wrong. They'd be regretful, until they realized one of the axes was missing too, at which point they'd be livid. That was if Meinong could return to the camp without anyone noticing he'd been gone. But in fact Meinong would get back there with mud in his hair and a face like the cherry pie the dog found on the sideboard, so everyone would see he'd been in a fight, and he would need to come up with a story. If Trimble had to bet on it, he'd say that Meinong would succeed in persuading the others that his injuries had nothing to do with Hickock's disappearance, but there would certainly be some suspicion.

Once again, Trimble started backing up through the bushes to make room for Meinong to schlep the bodies away from the path. Then Meinong looked toward Trimble.

He must have heard movement. The rain was still chattering on the canopy, and Trimble thought he'd been quiet—but obviously not quiet enough. He stayed absolutely still.

Meinong started walking toward him. In a matter of seconds he would flush Trimble out like a bevy of quail. The ax might be broken but Trimble wasn't likely to win a fight; you might say that in murder terms Meinong was on a little bit of a roll.

He jumped up and ran for his life.

Running through the jungle was always a waking nightmare. The empty air turned solid as an enormous wasp nest loomed out of the mist, or the solid ground turned hollow as your foot crashed through a squirrel's burrow. Vines snared your ankles and branches slashed your eyes and you sprained joints you didn't even know you had. He was making so much noise in the hell gym he couldn't even hear if Meinong was behind him, but still he lurched onward.

Then he was falling.

He had come to a long, steep incline of the kind you did not often find in this terrain, and his momentum had pitched him right over it. His thigh smacked into the earth and then his shoulder and then his forehead and then his ass as he rolled and bounced and tom-tommed down this hillside that seemed to carry on halfway to the Mariana Trench. He realized he was screaming.

Finally he came to a stop.

He felt like the proverbial penny dropped from the top of the Empire State Building. His body was a trade fair for the pain business, exhibiting every different type of sting and twinge known to modern man, and he already knew that when he woke tomorrow morning it would seem easier to hold his breath until his heart stopped than to crank himself upright. On the bright side, it probably hadn't been as bad as slamming face-first into the temple and then hanging upside down by one ankle all night, like a dope. Also, he had quite a head start on Meinong now, assuming the German didn't choose to come down in the same elevator. He listened hard but he didn't hear any movement further up the slope. For the moment, he was safe.

ও

By daybreak the rain had stopped but the mist was thicker than ever. A clammy and enfeebled thing, the sun, dragged itself up out of the night. A clammy and enfeebled thing, Jervis Whelt, dragged himself up out of the temple.

The previous evening, Yang had gone straight to Burlingame to give her the news about the rope, and she'd persuaded him they should keep it to themselves for twelve hours instead of snuffing out the festivities. "We won't send anyone in there to look for him until first light, so we're stuck for the moment," she'd said. "And until then it's pointless to cause a panic. They don't all have to know yet. It might sound heartless, with Whelt down there alone, but really I think the heartless thing would be to make everyone cancel their fun for a vigil. It's been so long since people have looked happy. And the two camps are mixing for once." So Yang had spent the night fretting in a wigwam on the upper terrace, and when Whelt did at last flop from the temple's cleft, the developer was there to give him water and shout for help. Weighing ninety-nine pounds and nine ounces, the newborn was lifted from the platform on the same stretcher that Calix had once occupied, and he was put to bed in the same infirmary cabin.

Today, however, Burlingame did not intend to give any consequential sponge baths. She urged Whelt to sleep but he refused to close his eyes, and when she touched his forehead it was so hot she flinched. Burlingame did not, of course, believe in the Mummy's Curse of *Daily Mail* legend. And yet, as envious as she felt that Whelt had been the first to properly explore the temple, she wasn't sure if she would have had the courage to go in there all by herself. She was unsuperstitious but she was not above the creeps. Now, in some sense, such fears had been substantiated. This wasn't just thirst and fatigue. Whelt looked as if he had knots tied in his arteries. He must have roused some old venomer or pathogen from its bed in the dust. If he hadn't come back, she wondered whether they really would have risked sending another soul into the darkness to see what had become of him. A brave man makes a long journey into a dusky place . . .

"Bats," he croaked, as if she'd just asked him a question.

"Pardon?"

"Think about the bats, Burlingame."

"That's what happened? A bat bit you?" She knew that if he had rabies he would certainly die here.

"No. There were no bats in there. That's exactly what I mean. Think about it. Why not? It's cavernous—in the sense of literally cave-like, I mean, not in the sense of spacious—and it's dark and there are no disturbances. Every bat's dream house. Why have we never seen them flying out of the temple at sunset?"

"I don't know."

"They're afraid."

"Of what? What did you find in there?"

"Apart from silver, you mean?"

"There was more silver?"

There was a degree of satisfaction in Whelt's voice as he delivered this news, but Burlingame could tell that something else was limiting his exuberance. "Yes," he said. "There were more suits of armor. Dozens of them. A whole infantry company's worth. Silver by the ton. We can make millions of feet of film. Tens of millions of feet. Tens of thousands of reels. But that's not all. You know about the Pozkito gods, don't you?"

"I know a bit."

"I met them down there, Burlingame. While I was in the temple I met the gods."

☙

Of all the proxy wars in which the United States has involved itself during my lifetime, the smallest to date is the Bangassou Civil War of 1951. It began after a French mineral-exploration firm announced that this piddling independent sultanate had between twenty and thirty thousand tons of uranium beneath its hills. The sultan at the time was friendly to the local French colonial powers, and thereby diplomatically and commercially accessible to the United States, so right away the USSR started trucking hampers of arms and cash to his enemies. He was soon deposed, and escaped to Paris, where I spent a few hours with him one afternoon. By then the agency was backing his nephew. Not a lot of reliable reports were getting out of the region, but the sultan knew that back home his former subjects were slaughtering one another with foreign weapons. Proxy wars are nasty, shabby affairs. If the belligerents down there had described themselves as pawns of the superpowers, even that would have been a little self-aggrandizing: at best, they were the buttons and nickels you play with when you've mislaid some of the original pieces. "It would have been better if we'd never found the uranium," the sultan said to me in his soft voice. "Not just better for me. Better for everyone. There are some curses I wouldn't wish on my worst enemy. My wife assumed it would corrupt me. She was looking forward to that." The following year the CEO of the French firm was charged with investment fraud after it turned out that in fact Bangassou had uranium reserves of no more than one thousand tons. By that time the sultan had been shot dead on a massage table and nearly half the surviving population of Bangassou had fled across the border into the Belgian Congo. The debacle forced the resignations of three of my colleagues who probably should have run a few more checks before they got so carried away pushing back against the Kremlin. As far as I know not a single word about the Bangassou Civil War ever appeared in the American press. The annals of CIA are gilded with such triumphs.

It would have been better if Whelt had never found the silver. Not just better for everyone. Better for me.

Uranium, gold, diamonds, rubber, oil: if you're a young nation all of these will glimmer like white lead in your mother's breast milk. And that lode of Mayan silver certainly had its deforming effect on *Hearts in Darkness.* But I'm the only person left who still chokes down the silver every day of his life.

Since they first let me into the warehouse a few months ago, I've worked my way through something like a thousand hours of footage, which is about a fiftieth of the three hundred million feet of 35mm that Whelt shot at the temple between 1938 and 1957. As I've said, the tribunal can't proceed until I've had a chance to consider all the available evidence. So that's how I'm condemned to live out these last few seasons until my liver takes its revenge on me: watching the unedited rushes of *Hearts in Darkness,* searching for the photographic evidence that would vindicate the testimony I submitted to the tribunal. My forensic audit requires a systematic chronology of the footage, but if God had knocked the world off His workbench and it had shattered on the ground He could not have had a bigger job piecing history back together. As a boy, I loved going to the movies, but I hated jigsaws.

Admittedly, my days have been a lot more pleasant since Frieda arrived. But on Tuesday she never came into work, and now it's Thursday night and I still haven't seen her. Three days. The warehouse feels empty without her, but I'm not concerned just because I miss my assistant. I'm concerned because I know how conscientious she is. If she were sick in bed I'm almost sure she would have got word to me. I'm too tired and queasy to feel predatory toward Frieda, but she's so enchanting I have to feel something, so instead I feel fatherly—that's my dime-store psychoanalysis. And perhaps I'm just an overprotective parent. All the same, she's exactly the type of girl that the universe likes to desecrate just to prove a point, and I can't help worrying about what might have happened to her. I know my orchid lives with her family in Springfield, but I never took down her telephone number or her address. So earlier this evening, as a last resort, I called Winch McKellar to ask him.

"I didn't send you any assistant," he said.

That didn't surprise me. "I understand you can't admit it because you have to keep up appearances. All that horseshit. But we both know there's nobody else who could've done me that kind of good turn. I wouldn't call for any other reason, I promise you I wouldn't, but she hasn't come to the warehouse the last three days. She's pretty young. I know Springfield isn't the Bronx but I just want to make sure she's all right."

"I didn't send you any assistant. Even if I wanted to, it would be impossible. That material is classified. Do you think they'd bend the rules for you of all people? There's no way they'd let some college girl in there."

"Well, the fact is, they did. She's been doing terrific work."

McKellar's voice softened. "If that's true . . . All I can say, Zonulet, is be careful. College girls aren't as innocent as they used to be.

Take it from me. I know how faithfully you've guarded your virtue all these years and I wouldn't want you to be led astray."

I chuckled, knowing this might be the closest McKellar would ever come to acknowledging the favor he'd done for me. Of course, if he'd really intended to gift me an easy lay as well as a helping hand, he'd recruited the wrong girl.

Straight after that he was back to business. "Listen, I can't help you with this or anything else. Please don't call me again until your tribunal is over."

"My tribunal will never be over," I said, but he'd already hung up. Notwithstanding that joke about college girls, nobody would have guessed that until a few years ago we'd been best friends. Short of driving around Springfield shouting out of my car window, I'm not sure what else I can do about Frieda. I'll just have to hope she comes in tomorrow, or on Monday, and all this fuss was for nothing.

As McKellar kindly reminded me, the evidence in my case is classified. Which means that I may or may not be guilty of "unauthorized removal and retention of classified documents or material," a federal offense. This evening, I smuggled a few frames of film out of the warehouse. I took two silly precautions. The first was to hide them in my underpants, even though the guard never pays me any attention. The second was to choose only frames so over- or under-exposed that they show nothing but white or black and therefore cannot sensibly be regarded as classified material, even though I know that wouldn't be enough to exculpate me if somehow they were discovered in my apartment. I risked it because I needed to take a closer look at them in private. When I put a strip of 35mm on the flatbed editor today, I thought I saw something on the viewing screen that I recognized from Honduras. Not something the camera put in the negative. Something living on its surface.

I'm almost certain, for two reasons, that I must be wrong about what I thought I saw. The first reason is that the film was brewed in the jungle out of antique panoply and tapir gristle and nephrolithic urine. Over the years the recipe was continually adjusted to taste.

This is a pre-industrial, home-cooked product, like something you'd buy from a stand by the side of the road, and so of course there are irregularities in texture and appearance. The reel in question may simply have come from a loused-up batch.

The second reason is Halorite 1219. Nitrocellulose is passionately flammable. It can combust for no good reason, and once it starts burning you can't stop it because it makes its own oxygen. However, before the *Hearts in Darkness* film was shipped from Spanish Honduras back to the United States at the end of 1957, every inch of it was sprayed with a proprietary halocarbon fire retardant called Halorite 1219, which is manufactured by Apex Chemical in Michigan but has never been cleared for civilian use. I had no personal involvement in that phase of the operation, but I couldn't object to the choice, because I'd been a loyal Apex Chemical customer going back to my days at the *New York Evening Mirror*. It was from their catalog that I ordered the benzoic oxymorphone I used regularly in both eras of my career, and I believe they also developed the active ingredient in an emergency hangover cure I took once or twice. The Halorite coating significantly degrades the image quality, and I'm sure the fumes do much the same to my renal tissue, but it's a necessary evil: without it, that warehouse would be a bomb on a short fuse. The salient point here, however, is that no living organism could survive on a surface sprayed with Halorite. And yet I've brought those scrags of film home with me because I have to be sure.

Not only am I an alcoholic who's too sick to drink, I'm also a career spy with no security clearance, which is just as liable to give a guy the shakes. I'm judiciously paranoid even at the best of times, and right now my assistant is missing and I have contraband in my apartment. I hope I can be indulged, therefore, if I admit to a preoccupation with the cream-colored convertible Chevrolet Bel Air that's been parked in different places on my quiet street the last three nights. I know a stakeout car when I see one, even if I can't necessarily explain why.

∽

Once again my thoughts have turned to the whelp from the agency who'll be responsible for searching through my papers after my death. He may be skimming this journal like a ninth grader with a book report due in the morning. But I hope that, on the contrary, he's too afraid he might miss something important if he doesn't cross-reference every detail, and this assignment annexes his weekends, curdles his dreams, makes him wish to God he'd chosen a different career.

In that case, he certainly won't have forgotten about Meredith Vansaska, my former colleague in the newsroom of the *New York Evening Mirror*, who is not irrelevant to this history just because Trimble nabbed her berth on the SS *Alterity* in 1938. The full chronology of her life is a context in which some skimming may, in fact, be acceptable, because for nine years after that she got no closer to the temple. But then one morning in 1947—quite out of the blue, in the most inauspicious circumstances, like a block of Mayan limestone dropping from the cloudless Santa Monica sky—the temple got closer to her. Two minutes before it happened, she was still smoking a cigarette in the living room of an apartment at the Miramar Hotel while she and the piano player waited for Wilf Laroux to finish masturbating.

They were now working on the chapter of Laroux's autobiography that would cover the season in 1918 when he played his first big part on Broadway. Because his diaries showed that he ate almost every night at the Chalfonte on 45th Street, he had called down to the kitchen of the Miramar for a breakfast of Tyrolean beef hash with sauce gribiche and white asparagus. Because his diaries showed that the song he most liked to dance to at Pluto's was "Your Lips Are No Man's Land but Mine," the pianist was playing it for the twenty-eighth time in a row. And because his diaries showed that the person with whom he most frequently had sexual intercourse during that year's production of *The Rainbow Girl* was Verree Dietz, he was now in the bedroom pleasuring himself to a contemporaneous photograph of the actress.

Vansaska very much wanted to dismiss this method as ridiculous. The trouble was that it worked so well. Every day, the forty-nine-year-old actor would come rushing out of the bedroom of the apartment, an old publicity shot and a warm hand towel lying jilted on the carpet behind him, and he would explode into reminiscence. Before he went through the ritual, any questions about his past would elicit only the muzziest generalities, and half the time even those contradicted one another. (The diaries were not much help because he'd never bothered to put anything down except unannotated ledgers of auditions, paychecks, songs, dinners, and sexual partners.) After he went through the ritual, he didn't turn into Proust all of a sudden, but he could at least achieve an elementary nostalgia, and for the episodes that really meant something to him he might produce a rather marvelous bouquet of sensual detail. The price of this, however, was that Vansaska had a hard job assembling the sort of background facts upon which her journalistic training insisted, because Laroux was so besotted with his own sensorium that he had no patience left over for any events or relationships that he had not directly experienced. Husserl, the great sleuth of the phenomenal consciousness, described his preparatory investigations as an *Egologie,* or "egology," and the term had not caught on, but Vansaska, who had read a little Husserl at Radcliffe, felt that Laroux was one of the world's foremost egologists.

She hadn't planned on becoming a ghostwriter of autobiographies. But at present she had no other means of supporting herself and nobody else to support her. At the beginning of 1939, four months after her reckless afternoon in the motel with that long-lashed young film director she met outside Arnold Spindler's mansion, she still hadn't worked up the conviction to break off her engagement with Bryce. So she had asked her loving virgin fiancé to arrange an abortion for her. This was the cruelest thing she had ever done to another human being, but it was for the best, because he told her that if he did as she asked he could no longer become her husband. There were two terminations that winter, but at least Bryce, after the amnion of his devotion was finally lanced, could get up and wipe himself off. And indeed by the time America entered the war they were both happily married to other people.

The actual procedure made for a bleak season, and she felt the loss for much longer than she'd insisted to herself she would. But in the ranking of horrors it was nothing compared to crouching in the back of that cab as it pulled up to the gate of Creedmor State Hospital four months prior. When Trimble had tricked the driver into taking her there as if she were a patient to be committed, he couldn't have known that all her life she had been scared she would end up in exactly such a place. But perhaps he'd made a lucky guess. After the misunderstanding was sorted out, she told the driver that at best he could expect to get his license revoked and at worst face charges for kidnapping. But in fact when she got home and realized she wasn't going to the jungle after all she did no more than call in sick to the *Mirror* so she could pull the curtains in her apartment and spend four days sleeping and crying. She felt she had been toyed with in order to remind her of a rule of life: you can light out for a hiding place but what you always find instead is just what you are trying to hide from.

Bryce had known his new wife since freshman year at Harvard. Vansaska had known her new husband for two weeks before their wedding. He was a cowboy, an actual cowboy, with big rough hands like in a dime novel about a cowboy with big rough hands, whom she met in a bar near Grand Central. The eighteen months they spent together were the most blissful of her entire life. She would give him one of her favorite poets to read, or show him how to eat an artichoke, or leave him alone with three of her most acid girlfriends at a party, and watch him square up to the task with the sort of good humor—earnest and self-mocking and clumsy and capable all at the same time—that she hoped she would have shown picking her way across a gully in an evening gown. Those were the times she felt the most deeply for him.

But then, all at once, like the lights coming up at the end of a movie, their love just came to a stop. They both realized it almost simultaneously and they parted without rancor. At the time, neither of them felt diligent enough to organize a divorce (although she expected to get a letter about it from him one day when he met someone else) so instead he just went straight back to New Mexico and later joined the army. She felt it had been a good marriage, much better than any of her friends'. By then she was estranged from her parents and she wanted a new start, so she moved to Los Angeles to take up a job at the *Herald Examiner.* The black basalt prison felt distant there, and she decided to stay. She grew to love the stretch and diffusion of it, the long walks she took in the dusk from her place in Silver Lake, meeting almost nobody but the dogs who seemed to her so much more real than the owners they towed along behind them like mannequins on wheels. Around the end of the war she moved across to the *Times,* where, having nothing better to do with her lunch hours, she began an affair with her editor. She'd assumed that they both understood it was strictly utilitarian, but when she broke it off he got so angry he found a pretext to fire her. With less than sixty dollars in her bank account, she started calling around for favors. At last a friend at Dial Press back in New York recommended her for the ghostwriting job, and she was summoned for an interview to the bungalow apartment at the Miramar where Wilf Laroux was staying until the renovation of his mansion was complete.

The memorious egologist burst from his chamber, his hands still fumbling with the cord of his dressing gown. "The New Amsterdam Theatre!" he exclaimed. "Opening night!"

Vansaska stubbed out her cigarette and picked up a 2B pencil to start taking shorthand. The pianist played on.

". . . and that was how Verree got her start, of course," said Laroux a little while later, "because she was understudying for Ada Coehorn and the day before we opened the woman just vanished. To tell you the truth I was happy about it. She was so thick with Verree I could never get Verree alone. They were always curled up together in her dressing room talking about, you know, whatever it is that women talk about. One night I had such trouble peeling them apart that I just gave up and went to a cathouse."

"Ada Coehorn?" said Vansaska. "Did she have anything to do with the Eastern Aggregate Coehorns? Didn't Elias Coehorn once have a wife who was an actress?"

"I never met any of her clansmen," shrugged the exact opposite of an omniscient narrator. "But she wore a lot of diamonds. Rockslides of diamonds. She was a lovely thing, even better looking than Verree, really got your marrow melting. I tried to make her at a party once and she said, 'I'm sorry, Wilf, but I belong to someone else.' I'd already noticed she wore a ring. 'Didn't you hear?' I said. 'The statute of marriage expired at midnight. They forgot to renew it. Everybody in the state of New York is unmarried until they sign a new bill in Albany tomorrow morning.' That was a line I used a lot back then, and it did make her laugh, but then she said, 'Oh, I don't mean my husband.'"

"So she had a lover?"

"Maybe. Once during the rehearsals I walked in on her screwing Arnie What's-His-Name."

"Who was that?"

"An impresario type. He produced a lot of the shows at the Knickerbocker. That was the last time I ever saw him in New York, as a matter of fact, up to his balls in Ada Coehorn. Then some time in the twenties, right after I moved to Hollywood, I ran into him again. He was a big shot at some studio by then . . . Oh, it's tap-dancing on the tip of my tongue. Sweetheart, hand me my diary for '29."

"I don't know if this is necessary, Mr. Laroux. We're making terrific progress on 1918."

"But you're always saying you want all the boring details." He flipped through the diary. "Johnny, give me 'You're Getting to Be a Habit.' You know that one, don't you?" The pianist played the opening chords. "Mary Rialto," said Laroux. "Chicken-and-ham galantine."

"Pardon me?"

"Mary Rialto. Chicken-and-ham galantine. Mary Rialto. Chicken-and-ham galantine. Mary Mary." He closed his eyes, and his hand began to slide toward his crotch. "Mary Rialto."

"Let's get back to *The Rainbow Girl,* please," said Vansaska sharply.

"Mary Rialto. Yes, that's it. That's the stuff. Mary Rialto."

"Do you want us to, uh, step outside for minute, Mr. Laroux?" said the pianist.

"No, keep playing. Mary Rialto; Mary Rialto. Mary Rialto.

Chicken-and-ham galantine. Mary Rialto." Then Laroux's eyes snapped open. "Arnold Spindler! The head of Kingdom Pictures! It was an overcast morning with the smell of gardenias in the air and I was up for the part of a navy captain in a movie that at that time they were calling *Officer on Deck—*"

But Vansaska had put down her pencil. "Arnold Spindler was having an affair with Ada Coehorn?"

"Yes. I've forgotten why that seemed interesting a moment ago. Where were we? Johnny, play 'Your Lips Are No Man's Land but Mine' again. Thank you. Now, Jim Huneker was in the audience that night and he had published the most unforgivably snotty review of our *Julius Caesar* so in the interval I sent a boy to him with a note that said . . . hold on, let me remember the phrasing exactly . . ."

Vansaska could laugh all she liked at Laroux, but it wasn't as if her own memory was a device of industrial precision. The long-lashed boy, the promise of the jungle, the ride to the asylum, the abortion, the broken engagement: even after all this time she still had a feeling in her skull like coat hangers rattling on a closet rail whenever anything reminded her of those months (whereas she would struggle to come up with a single impression from the pastel expanse of 1944). The period was so intense it seemed to deserve a name, like *la Terreur*, and she sometimes thought of it as "the Pinch," borrowing a term a friend of hers had coined. Arnold Spindler's disputed sanity was far from the only story she'd pursued at the *Mirror* that had come to nothing. But it had stayed with her longer than any other—not only because, in general, artifacts dating from the Pinch were exceptionally well preserved, but also because, in particular, she associated Spindler's *Hearts in Darkness* with the escape to the Torrid Zone that would somehow have fixed everything in her life (or so she had felt at the time and perhaps felt still).

She was an adult and she could give a sensible account of the events of the Pinch. And yet she also felt that she understood nothing of those events, that she was as bewildered as an animal. A connection or a logic seemed absent, grievously absent, absent like something stolen. Spindler's fate was the sort of mystery you could summarize in a two-sentence lede, but everything adjacent to it was the sort of mystery where you couldn't even articulate just what was so mysterious. She had no good reasons for thinking that somehow if she solved the former it might help her to solve the latter. So this was foolishness upon foolishness. No, her world would not be mended by the jungle. No, it would not be deciphered by a studio boss. She knew she should grow out of her fixations. But that wasn't easy.

She'd waited a long time for *Hearts in Darkness* to come out, anticipating that she would go alone to torture herself at least two or three times—but it never did. So at last, one slow afternoon at the *Los Angeles Times,* she went down to spend a few hours with the news librarian in the clippings morgue. She couldn't find a single reference to the movie after that initial announcement. Kingdom Pictures had never released a full cast list, but she knew that George Aldobrand and Adela Thoisy had been cast in the lead roles, and it turned out that after 1938 neither of them had ever appeared in another movie. Aldobrand was featured in "Say, Whatever Happened To . . . ?" in *Photoplay* in '44, but the column contained no new information and implied that his career had simply "hit the skids."

What surprised her the most, however, was a story in the *Times* itself about the board of Kingdom Pictures electing a new chairman, because she couldn't believe she hadn't heard about it at the time. Arnold Spindler was mentioned only in passing as the founder and former chairman. Had he died or just stepped down? Either way, what was the cause? Had he shown himself in public at any point? The story didn't bother to answer any of these questions, nor did it acknowledge the theories about Spindler that at one time were so commonplace in Hollywood. The writer had left the *Times* and Vansaska couldn't get a telephone number for him, but she asked the current head reporter on that beat if he knew anything more about Arnold Spindler or *Hearts in Darkness* or George Aldobrand or Adela Thoisy. Patronizing as ever, he informed her that the war had put America through a centrifuge and sometimes the leads you might have been able to find before Pearl Harbor just weren't there any more and never would be again. This seemed pretty defeatist to

Vansaska—Los Angeles wasn't exactly occupied Tokyo and VJ Day wasn't exactly Year Zero—but she knew from her own reporting that in certain cases it was close to the truth. They called it a clippings morgue but it was more like a cemetery, marking time with its expansion. The librarian had a year-round cold and if you spent too long in there with him you'd catch it too.

Since then she'd largely succeeded in pushing Arnold Spindler to the back of her mind. But Laroux had undone that in a few words. "I'm sorry to interrupt you again, Mr. Laroux," she said, "but I have a few more questions about Ada Coehorn."

"I thought you wanted to get back to *The Rainbow Girl*. Ada Coehorn never went onstage in *The Rainbow Girl*."

"She vanished before opening night. Right." Vansaska knew that when Laroux said "vanished," he didn't necessarily mean that Ada Coehorn disappeared without a trace, only that he never saw her again with his own eyes and therefore as far as he was concerned she passed out of existence. "Did anyone ever explain where she went?"

"I can't see what this has to do with the story of my life," said Laroux. "I don't remember anything else about Ada Coehorn or where she went or who she was fucking."

"But I guess Verree Dietz would probably know. What happened to her?"

"She stayed on Broadway. For the best, I think. She was a little older than me and I'm not sure she would have taken to Hollywood."

"Could I telephone her? Strictly for background, you understand. I'm a newspaper reporter and I guess the old habits die hard," she added, smiling humbly, trying not to sound too eager. "I just wouldn't want to get any of the facts wrong."

"Please stop wasting time. First of all, we're writing a book about Wilf Laroux, not Ada Coehorn. Second, Verree wouldn't talk to you. She always hated tripe-hounds. And third, even if she did, she wouldn't have a single kind word to say about me. So you can forget about your 'background.' Understand?"

"Yes, Mr. Laroux," said Vansaska. "I'm sorry, Mr. Laroux."

. . .

Of people entering late middle age it was sometimes said that their face told the whole story of their life; for a twice-married former Broadway actress and "clip-joint queen" like Verree Dietz to have maintained such wholesome and unfussy good looks at the age of fifty-five made Vansaska feel optimistic that sometimes, like an autobiography, that story might be rather selective in its content. "What do you want?" Dietz said, standing at the door of her apartment.

"Good afternoon, Mrs. Dietz. My name is Meredith Vansaska. I'm a writer—"

"I'm sorry but I don't talk to writers any more."

Vansaska didn't literally put her foot in the door, but she made a sort of feint in that spirit, which was just enough to stop Dietz from shutting it in her face. "Wilf Laroux sent me."

That was clearly a name Dietz hadn't heard for a while. "Wilf? Really?"

"Yes. I'm ghosting his autobiography, and he asked me to talk to you."

Dietz smiled and shook her head. "You must be a very patient and creative young woman. I once asked Wilf about his childhood. He could muster precisely one story about his mother, except he turned out to have mixed her up with his nanny, and precisely one story about his father, except he turned out to have mixed him up with Mark Twain. But he's not going to recruit me as one of his research assistants. I hope you didn't come all the way across the country for this."

"I did, yes." She thought of herself as wearing a diving suit with a breathing tube that stretched thousands of miles back to Silver Lake. On this visit she would not see any friends or family, nor entertain any recollections of her past, nor breathe so much as a molecule of frozen New York air, because she was not really here. She had taken a week's unpaid vacation and bought a round-trip sleeper ticket she could scarcely afford for the sole purpose of following a "lead" with which she had no real reason to concern herself, and this folly would be kept pure and confined. Walking through Manhattan, she made sure to zigzag through the grid—down one block, across one block, down one block, across one block—because superstitiously she felt it reduced her chances of bumping into anyone she knew. "And I have a letter from Mr. Laroux here," she said. "I can't tell you how keen he is for me to talk to you."

Reluctantly, Dietz took the letter and looked it over. Vansaska had been professionally contracted to imitate Laroux's voice, so those three typewritten paragraphs should have been as easy to fake as the signature underneath. However, when Laroux wanted anything at all, even a meaningless favor from a total stranger, he spent his charm so profligately that Vansaska wasn't sure what register he would have left to fall back on in a situation like this when he needed to persuade a perceptive old friend of his sincerity. All the same, she felt she'd done a creditable job.

Dietz looked up. "And why didn't you telephone before you arrived?" she said. "I suppose because you wanted to put this forcibly into my hands as if you were serving a subpoena?"

"That was Mr. Laroux's suggestion, yes."

"All I can say about this document is that Wilf must have changed. Whether for the better or worse I wouldn't venture to say. You can have one hour."

"Thank you so much, Mrs. Dietz." When she stepped into the apartment, Vansaska said, without thinking, "Oh, are you in the middle of . . ." Moving, she might have said, or spring cleaning or refurbishing, but she tailed off because none of those quite made sense. Couch, chair, writing desk, bookshelf: the living room had exactly four objects of furniture, two small paintings on the walls, and not a single ornament or knickknack. But this wasn't an attempt at the sort of European rigor that was fashionable along certain highbrow foothills of Hollywood. The place just felt evacuated.

"In the middle of what?" said Dietz. "Take that off," she added, meaning Vansaska's winter coat, and gestured to the chair. "I do have an idea of what people expect from an obsolete actress who lives alone. Framed playbills and newspaper clippings and signed photographs of myself. Old props and presents from my dead admirers and perhaps a corgi mummifying under the chaise longue. That's about what you had in mind?"

"Not at all . . . ," said Vansaska, without enough conviction.

Dietz sat down opposite her on the couch. "Have you ever been to a movie at the Loew's Park Theater over on Eighth Avenue?"

"I don't think so."

"No, of course not, you're much too young. For some reason that theater is almost exclusively patronized by people older than the Brooklyn Bridge. And if you go there and watch how they behave, you realize that almost everyone who lives in New York City long enough eventually goes crazy. Money doesn't help you. Not by itself. There are only two things that do. One of them is children, and I don't have any of those."

"What's the other one?"

"A place upstate, and I don't have that either. So I just do what I can. I live in an apartment that looks like this because I believe that in an apartment that looks like this I am less likely to go crazy. I may have taken it a little too far. I don't think it would really do any harm to hang more than two pictures, for instance. But those are the best two pictures I own and I haven't finished looking at them yet. Perhaps when I finish looking at them I'll put up some others. I just don't want to live inside one of those Egyptian pyramids where all your valuables are buried with you and every last detail of your life is carved on the walls. I've been to apartments like that and those are the apartments where people go crazy as they get old. Then they go to Loew's Park Theater and spit at the popcorn girl. Now, produce your notebook or your tape recorder. What do you want to know about Wilf and me?"

Vansaska had decided that she would ask a direct question about Arnold Spindler only if the subject hadn't come up naturally within fifty minutes of her allotted sixty. As it turned out, however, she didn't have to wait that long. After less than half an hour, Dietz said, ". . . and he used to get so worked up because he couldn't always have me exactly when he wanted me. But even if I had been as obsessed with Wilf's penis as Wilf was himself, I had a duty to Ada. In those years she had very few friends and certainly no other real confidante. Granted, she had a tendency to talk in circles, for hours and hours sometimes, but she was in an impossible situation."

"What sort of situation?"

"Well, it's of no relevance to the Ballad of Wilf Laroux."

"But Ada Coehorn left the production quite abruptly, didn't she? That's how you ended up playing the role opposite Mr. Laroux."

"Yes," said Dietz, "and let me assure you, this is the one occasion in the entire history of the theater that the understudy wasn't pleased to see the principal depart." Ada Coehorn and Arnold Spindler, she explained, had at that time been lovers for eleven years, ever since they met at an audition in 1907. Their affair had continued undiscouraged after they both got married to other people and Ada bore a sickly son for her husband, Elias Coehorn. The latter had first identified her as a potential acquisition when he was obliged for business reasons to sit through a performance of *When Knights Were Bold* in a private box at the Garrick, and thereafter he pursued his takeover bid mostly through her parents. That Arnie and Ada's affair was common knowledge on Broadway didn't seem like an immediate liability because, although Coehorn had permitted his wife to maintain her acting career, he declined to have any contact whatsoever with her colleagues. And when she and Arnie wanted to dine together in public, they often took a trolley up to Little Mongolia (which at that time, before its dwindling, still had plenty of cozy restaurants) and afterward strolled hand in hand over the footbridge to watch the circus riders practicing, so there wasn't much chance of anybody recognizing either of them. From time to time Ada's husband did send men from Eastern Aggregate's Good Conduct Division to shadow her, but in general they were easy enough to avoid, distract, or pay off. Then, at last, came the apocalyptic afternoon when a soft-footed and indivertible young Good Conduct agent named Phibbs caught them together in a dressing room after a rehearsal for *The Rainbow Girl*.

Careful to make clear that he was aiming his pistol only at Arnold's head, never at Ada's, Phibbs wouldn't let them leave the chaise longue until his employer could arrive in person. For nearly two hours they lay there naked and scared like foxes run to ground, until Elias Coehorn Sr. came through the door.

Exactly one month later Ada broke her neck after falling from a turret window. Her husband had ordered that for the indefinite future she was to be confined to Braeswood and all her correspondence was to be read, so the intervening sequence of events was known only because before her death she managed to smuggle out a letter to Dietz in her son's Latin tutor's briefcase. And the most surprising part of this story was that she had succeeded in convincing Coehorn that this was the first time she had ever sinned, that there had been no ongoing affair. This man who overlooked nothing and presupposed nothing, who saw new opportunities and cheaper alternatives where others saw only a cataract haze of sentiment and precedent and social norms and received wisdom, who would have made Jesus Christ Himself submit to a standard aptitude test if he'd asked for a job in the mailroom—this man who'd built an empire on undistorted judgment—even this man was apparently not immune to wishful thinking when it came to his empress.

As a result, Coehorn did not have Spindler destroyed. Instead, that balmy evening after the rehearsal, he merely took the adulterers downtown to the Spindler residence and forced them to watch while he raped Spindler's wife on the dining room table.

Vansaska gasped, and Dietz gave a small nod. "With regard to what happened afterward," she went on, "there are two possibilities. One is that, a few weeks later, Coehorn's agents turned up some firm evidence that Ada and Arnold had been going together for years, and when the boss found out he had them both killed. Or perhaps he even took care of it personally. You know, people in show business will joke about anything. Anything! But when Coehorn's wife was in our midst I didn't hear anybody joke much about that man. He was frightening even from a distance. I never did see Arnie again after that winter."

"That was because he went to Hollywood," said Vansaska. "Mr. Laroux met him there once. He became quite a potentate."

"Really? Well, I think that just about rules it out. A man truly afraid for his life would have run a lot further than Hollywood. If

Coehorn had wanted to find him there, he would have found him. QED, if Spindler survived it was because Coehorn didn't particularly want him dead."

"And the other possibility?

"What Coehorn did to Spindler's wife . . . The way Ada wrote about it in that last letter . . . She was laid absolutely to waste. She blamed herself for it. Furthermore, she was never going to see the love of her life again. She was never going to act on the stage again. And perhaps for the first time she fully understood what sort of man her son had for a father. But it is all a darkness, of course. We can't know. What does seem to me unlikely is that the whole matter concluded with Ada's funeral. Arnie Spindler may have made something of himself in Hollywood, as you say. But imagine the hatred between those two men. Darling Ada gone and each blaming the other for it. That sort of hatred can have a very long run." Dietz looked at her. "My my, young lady, how your ears have pricked up. It's only now I see how interested you are right this minute that I realize how bored you must have been before. All those dutiful questions about Wilf. What are you really here to find out?"

"This is all for Mr. Laroux's book." And I wasn't bored, Vansaska wanted to say. I wish you had an hour on the radio every week where you told stories and explained how not to go crazy.

"Wilf's name hasn't been mentioned for quite a while. You've made no attempt to bring me back to the point. Quite the opposite."

"It's background."

"No. No, I don't believe it is. You're not the first writer I've dealt with, you know." Dietz stood up. "False pretenses aren't clever. They are merely rude. I think you'd better go."

The following Monday morning, back in Silver Lake, Vansaska got up a little early to attend to the condition of her house before she left for the Miramar. Over the weekend, for the first time in her life, she'd bought herself a plant, and she was at the sink filling a saucepan with water when she heard the telephone ring.

"I got a call from Verree Dietz over the weekend," said Laroux down the line. "She said she was paid a visit by a writer who had supposedly been sent to interview her on my behalf. This writer had a letter from me—on my headed stationery, no less—explaining how much I wanted Verree to offer some reminiscences for my book."

"I'm sorry, Mr. Laroux," said Vansaska. She wouldn't beg, she decided.

"You've betrayed my trust. I believe you may even have committed a crime. I'm astonished that my editor should ever have recommended you. My next telephone call will be to Dial Press, and I hope they spread the word about you. Good day, Miss Vansaska."

There followed two types of morning silence. The first was the silence of a telephone handset replaced without jingling on its cradle, because Vansaska was reminding herself to take a positive outlook, and a positive outlook was so fragile that it would shatter the moment you lost concentration, so the tension of it in her muscles made her very careful about small actions. Never again, at least, would her stomach turn at the mingled odors of semen and interwar restaurant cooking. But in the second type of silence, the fathomless silence that always follows a bad phone call, she could hear the black basalt prison assembling itself block by block outside her window. To drown it out she lunged to turn on her radio, and heard the familiar theme music of the *Apex Chemical Breakfast Bulletin*, a slow ascending scale followed by a glissando back down. She wished she could call Dietz and ask her whether devoting yourself to an old mystery was the sort of thing that drove you crazy or, on the contrary, the sort of thing that kept you sane.

⌒⌒

Something terrible has happened.

My hand is shaking as I write this. If I had any sense I would burn this memoir, but I have to find a way to understand what I saw this morning and I can't talk to anybody about it. I'll try to be as straightforward as I can.

I arrived at the warehouse around eight o'clock, nodding hello to the guard as I went inside. I hung up my coat and I took a sip of coffee from my Thermos flask. When I glanced at the flatbed editor I saw that it still had a strip of film loaded into the plate. This was out of the ordinary, because when I go home for the night I always make sure to unload the Steenbeck and put the film I've been working on back in its canister. So my first thought was that the previous night I must have been too distracted, and I reproached myself for my carelessness. I turned on my machine, the one with sprocket wheels specially modified for fragile negatives, and the frame behind the prism was projected onto the viewing screen. Four realizations came to me in succession, and although they cannot have taken more than a few moments in total, they felt like they were spaced widely apart.

First, this footage was in color, so it could not be from *Hearts in Darkness.*

Second, it showed a naked girl. Her mouth was gagged and her hands and feet were bound. Her eyes were wide with fear and bloodshot from crying. She was slumped across the lap of a larger figure, whose head was cut off by the top of the frame. They were on a bed.

Third, the girl was Frieda, my assistant.

Fourth, the bed looked like the bed in my apartment. The larger figure had my build and his hands had my complexion and he was wearing one of my suits.

I turned the speed switch on the editor to begin playback.

The larger figure took one of Frieda's breasts in his hand and squeezed it, making her wince. For another minute or so he continued to fondle her. Then with the other hand he reached behind him and picked up a kitchen knife. I recognized the knife because I have sliced lemons with that knife. Frieda tried to squirm away but he grabbed her under the armpit and yanked her up toward him. He pulled the knife across her throat. Blood spurted from the gash and the light began to fade from her eyes. The footage ended.

There was a ringing in my ears. I thought I was going to faint. But I managed to unload the film from the plate and stuff it into my pocket. As I passed the guard again on the way out of the warehouse I said, "Taken ill," in a hoarse voice. I didn't realize until I got to my car that I'd forgotten to put on my coat and my keys were still in the pocket, so I had to march past the guard two more times.

The suit from the film is still hanging in my wardrobe and there are bloodstains on the lining of the jacket. The kitchen knife is back in the drawer but as far as I can tell it's clean. The sheets on my bed are also clean but I found more dried blood on the underside of the headboard. Frieda's body is nowhere in the apartment. If something happened here, someone has done a good job, but not a perfect job, of tidying up afterward.

Someone.

I have no recollection of kidnapping and murdering a twenty-year-old girl. I have no recollection of cleaning up the scene or disposing of the corpse. I have no recollection of setting up a movie camera in my bedroom. I have no recollection of fostering any desire or intention to do any of those things.

Frieda was my assistant. That is what I do remember. But yesterday McKellar told me again that he didn't send me an assistant. He told me it was unrealistic to imagine that anyone like Frieda could have been allowed into the warehouse with me.

If you believe the agency's psychologists, I have been mentally unsound at least as far back as my first visit to the temple; even when I'm attempting to give the honest testimony of my own senses, I still cannot be trusted as a witness; I am erratic and delusional. That's what they intimated, a little euphemistically but nevertheless assuredly, in their testimony to the tribunal. They were just saying what Branch 9 told them to say. Nevertheless, I have to concede that in at least one respect they were right. Ever since I "met the gods," my brain hasn't worked quite like a normal person's does.

In all my reflections on the qualities the agency looks for in an employee, there is one opinion of mine that has not wavered: the best of us must have a part of our personality that looks at the human beings around us as no more than objects colliding in space, that operates without morality or emotion, only purpose and will, like an educated tarantula. I'm trying to remember where I first heard that story about the psychopath the agency hired as an analyst.

The cream-colored Chevy is still parked down the street.

∽

When the rumors went around Cambridge that the vice chancellor had suffered a nervous breakdown, Burlingame's friend Claire had said to her, "It shows, doesn't it, how near we all are to losing our senses if the wrong thing happens?" Speak for yourself, Burlingame had wanted to reply. She had always felt almost oppressively sane, like the only sober person at a party. Yesterday, with Gracie, she'd behaved just as her mother would have, trying to cleave the girl's attempted suicide from the rest of her life as a "moment of madness." But assuming that certain acts were insane by definition was as circular as assuming that your calculating machine must be faulty just because it gave you a figure that didn't suit you. And now here she was with Whelt, wondering how much of this epiphany she could blame on his fever. A Pozkito tribesman reports a conversation with the gods and he is sane. A clerk from Tooting reports a conversation with the gods and he is mad. A pope reports a conversation with the gods and he is sane. A film director reports a conversation with the gods and he is . . . what?

It wasn't as if there was such a profound contrast between this new focus and the obsessions of the past. Today, the patient sounded so rational you could have mistaken him for the doctor. In fact, Burlingame didn't even feel as if she were privy to the full stretch of Whelt's rationality, because she could tell that most of it was still busy reanalyzing precedents and permuting outcomes. She knew he should be resting for the sake of his health, but she also knew that he was set on talking whether she responded or not, so she did her best to question him as seriously and attentively as she would have questioned any other anthropological interviewee. "Let's go from the beginning," she said. "While you were in the temple you met the Pozkito gods."

"Yes."

"You only heard their voices? Or you saw them as well?" The humidity had brought her out in her usual sizzling rash, and outside the thunder rolled on, nearing and receding and nearing and receding like a sentry on patrol.

"I was with them," Whelt said. "As close as I am to you now. There were at least two of them, maybe more. They had accents, but I could understand them pretty well—except that they told me their names several times and I just couldn't seem to fix them in my mind. No one else can be allowed to go down there, Burlingame. That's imperative. Tell Yang and Halloran. You know I've spent all my life purging unreason from my thinking. I'm the only man here who can say that and I'm the only man who can risk spending time alone with the gods. Anybody who left them any openings would have lost his mind in there."

"But that's just what surprises me. I always thought of you as a freethinker."

"I am familiar with all the arguments for and against the existence of a Judeo-Christian creator. Those arguments have no bearing on the gods of this region."

"What did you talk to them about?"

"Burlingame, did you ever wonder why we arrived one day after the New Yorkers? Instead of a week after, or two weeks before? Hasn't that always seemed a bit too exact to be just bad luck?"

"Well, yes, now that you mention it, I have wondered. Quite often." It was the second great puzzle, to be turned to as a sort of refresher when you were bored with the first great puzzle—the question of why, in eight years, nobody from back home had ever come out to the temple to find out what had become of them all. Eight years stalling and staling, she thought, which aggregated to about one average human life frittered away per nine residents, or nearly fifteen in total (in addition to the smaller number of lives lost in the conventional sense). Such an unthinkable gush of dead time, like walking through one of those foot tunnels under the Thames where you couldn't acknowledge the weight of it pressing down over your head or you'd scream. And yet she'd discovered in herself another viewpoint, a sort of belvedere fixed up out of soft-boiled parrot eggs and the smell of Gracie's hair, from which she could look down and feel prouder of their home with every day that passed. They had come here with high ambitions but they had not achieved them, and in that respect the worst you could say about the temple was that it was part of the general run of things. If time was wasted here, perhaps time was wasted almost everywhere.

"Did you have any theories about the coincidence?" Whelt said.

Burlingame hesitated. "We can't possibly know. It was all arranged so long ago and so far away. But I suppose it's crossed my mind that . . . well, that Coehorn's father might have heard about your expedition, or Arnold Spindler might have heard about Coehorn's expedition, and for some reason one of them had a desire to confound the other. They were both rich men with all sorts of international business interests. They might have had some professional enmity. Some grudge."

"No. That's not it. The gods have 'international business interests' of their own. They explained everything to me, Burlingame. It seems so obvious now. I don't know why we couldn't see the trap for ourselves. The Whelt Rule was the biggest mistake I've ever made. We'll have to start the picture again from the beginning. Do it completely differently this time." There was not a speck of fever in his gaze, which was hard, bare, too bare, like exposed wiring. "The gods did this to us. They brought us all here for a reason."

PART THREE

Do not stray from the subject; omit the extraneous.

(From the Central Intelligence Agency's
Style Manual & Writers Guide for
Intelligence Publications, *8th ed., 2011)*

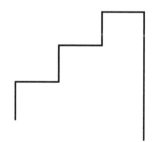

WILSON STOOD ON THE BALCONY OF THE AMERICAN CONSULATE WITH his bald pink knees thrust through the ironwork. He had become trapped there while leaning over the railing to talk to me. Two prostitutes were already greasing the sides of his kneecaps with cabbage-palm oil in preparation for tugging him free. "Please don't worry about me," he called down. "This happens quite often. Like a bally snare trap, this ironwork. I keep meaning to get it replaced." Both prostitutes now bent to encircle his waist with their arms. "Ready, ladies: one, two—three!" Craning my neck to watch, I felt a warm drop of lubricant splatter on my forehead like an unction as Wilson's knees slipped clear. For an instant it looked as if all three of them were going to topple over backward on the balcony, but Wilson executed a *pas de bourrée* of undeniable elegance and kept the others steady with his hands on their shoulders. With all the resonance of a mallet on sheet metal, the church bell began to clang for morning mass. Today was Sunday, February 5, 1956, my fortieth birthday.

A short time earlier, getting down from the dented old McCormick truck that had brought me to the main square of San Esteban, I had said to an old man, *"Donde queda el consulado americano?"* My driver had been to the town before but he didn't know.

"I can get you a girl much cheaper," the old man replied, also in Spanish.

To describe the truck as temperamental would have been condescending; rather, I had the impression that it had been earnestly wrestling with a deep crisis of personal faith about the very principle of internal combustion as a motive power. As a result, the eighty-mile overnight journey south from Trujillo had left me in no mood to waste any more time. "I'm not looking for a girl. I'm looking for the American consulate. Understand?"

"The girls I know are also much prettier," said the old man. I dismissed him and moved on. An Indian boy wearing nothing but a muddy vest and a straw hat, previously absorbed in tying together some cockroaches by the legs with a piece of thread, abandoned his work and ran after me begging for coins. When I said no, three more boys made the same request, as if encouraged. A barber—who must have been able to see that I had a fresh crew cut and an even fresher shave, because I'd seen to myself with a razor out of sheer boredom during one of the McCormick's intermittent crises—offered me the full works, and then, persistently, a generous discount on the full works. From my travels in Cuba I was already familiar with the vacuous bustle of this kind of tropic square, the ritual and the reflex action, a null economy in which every figure in every negotiation tended toward zero, like a parched man swigging from an empty canteen in the hope of masticating a dry cracker. And yet it was also true that every settlement on the edge of the jungle shone with a sort of unearned glamor, not only because of its intimacy, like a tyrant's doorman, with the adjoining horrors, but also because of the memory—faded, garbled, borrowed—of the explorers who once made it their final nominate waypoint before they disappeared in search of El Dorado, the White City, the Kingdom of Prester John, the Fountain of Youth, the Hesperides, and/or the Garden of Eden.

At last I found a waiter smoking outside a cantina who could tell me how to get to the American consulate, although he, too, mentioned something about whores. When I followed his directions to the building with the pediment over the front door, and my knock was answered by a woman in a moth-eaten negligee eating a cherimoya, I was ready to acknowledge that the problem must lie with either my pronunciation of *consulado* or with its local idiomatic meaning, but then Wilson called down from the balcony.

Over glasses of chilled horchata in the drawing room, having changed from shorts into slacks, he explained how an Englishman came to be running a brothel out of the American consulate in San

Esteban. "Ever since I was at prep school I'd always wanted to be a writer," he told me. "A serious one, like Dostoevsky or Kafka." He had a boyish face and ears like ruddy oyster mushrooms. "But all I seemed to be able to come up with were humorous stories about school sports' days and so forth. They were quite well received in some quarters but they weren't what I dreamed of doing. So I thought I'd better go out and see something of the world. I got a job with my uncle's match company because they do some business in Tegucigalpa. Quite soon I decided it didn't suit me but by then I was making a few shekels on the side as a string man for a couple of American papers. Always looking for the sick-makingest side of everything in case there was something I could glean from it. At any rate, one day I got wind that there was a doctor in a town called San Esteban who'd invented a cure for leprosy. Off I went. Well, do you know how many San Estebans there are in Spanish Honduras?"

"No."

"Quite a few! I didn't realize before I left but there are quite a few. For all I know this doctor really is doing marvelous work in one of the others, still unburdened by publicity. Anyway, by the time I got here and twigged this was the wrong one, I'd run out of traveling money, but old Tussmann, the American consul here, needed a man who spoke good English. At that time Tussmann was allowing his young wife—I'm not sure which of them initiated the arrangement; mustn't pry, that's my rule—but he was allowing his wife to receive gentleman callers on a freelance basis in one of the guest rooms. Then after Tussmann died, she more than ever needed to support herself, and to be quite honest so did I. One thing led to another. Naturally I've written to your Department of State to see if they feel like replacing Mr. Tussmann, but I still haven't had a reply, and in the meantime I feel we're very much living up to the spirit of his mission here if not the letter. The female sexual organ is, after all, the universal consulate. Don't you think?"

"What if a lady knocks on your door?" I said. "Or a pious family man?"

"We also maintain an extensive lending library."

"How long are you planning to stay in San Esteban?"

"As long as I bally well can. I'm very happy here. The only deficiency, really the only one, is that I never get any decent material for my fiction—which was supposed to be my reason for leaving England in the first place."

"Really? In a place like this?"

"I've turned out quite a number of little comic sketches but there's not much to distinguish them from what I used to write about Walton-on-Thames. You know, eccentric sorts next to a river."

"But the isolation . . . ," I said.

"Yes?"

"The vice, the torpor, the decay. The white men feeling greater and greater contempt for their own values. The sense of the numinous as horribly distant, or at times, on the contrary, horribly close. You don't see it as a kind of . . . allegorical hell?"

"Now that you mention it . . ." He mulled that over for a little while. "No. Anyway, if I'm ever in a dirty mood, I just remind myself how fortunate I am to have found my vocation. I can't recommend this line of work highly enough."

"Snatch on tap?"

"Pardon? Oh, I see!" He laughed as if genuinely delighted by the expression. "No, no, no. I don't indulge. It would show favoritism. But the company of the ladies never fails to enchant. Now, I've blathered on long enough. You must have business in San Esteban, and something tells me you're not a fruit man." By this I took Wilson to mean an employee of the United Fruit Company, rather than a homosexual. "What can I do for you?"

"I'm looking for an Irishman named Poyais O'Donnell. Know him?"

"Of course! Everyone in San Esteban knows Mr. O'Donnell. He's one of the pillars of our little community. And the only other chap within an egret's flight who appreciates a cup of tea. Not that we ever get any real tea down here. Are you a friend of his?"

"I'm a notary agent for the firm of Letterblair, Handsom and Lowe. There's a probate dispute involving another branch of the O'Donnell clan who emigrated to the United States during the famines and got rich. No one seems to be able to agree on the exact furcation of the family tree. I've been sent to interview Mr. O'Donnell, see what he remembers, get a sworn statement, find out if he's kept hold of any photographs or papers. There may be some money in it for him."

"Sounds rather Jarndyce and Jarndyce," said Wilson.

"I wouldn't know."

"Well, I'm afraid it's rotten timing, because Mr. O'Donnell left just this morning to see to something somewhere or other. But he's sure to be back before too long. He always is. Are you in a tremendous hurry? Would you like to leave a note for him?"

The large mirror over the mantelpiece was spotty with oxidation. In my experience, the belief that rust was somehow contagious like mildew was remarkably common, even among well-educated grown-ups. Perhaps because there was a deeper truth to it. Rust could indeed be contagious, especially in places like San Esteban. You could catch rust if you hung around here too long.

On the other hand, my horchata was delicious. "No," I said. "I'll wait."

A week before I arrived in San Esteban, I had watched a young man creep into a police morgue in Havana with the intention of doing outrageous things to a corpse. He was visibly nervous, as any young man will be the first time he embarks on such a venture. Havana nights were never peaceful, but this morgue was in the basement, so nothing could be heard but the young man's footsteps and the electric hum of the refrigerator cabinet. Religious iconography was not permitted in government morgues, but without it Cubans tended to be a little skittish when they found themselves alone with the dead, and when the beam of the young man's flashlight moved across the wall it revealed the standard unofficial compromise, a fire hose that had been threaded around some nails hammered above its reel so that it made the shape of a chubby-fingered Mano Poderosa. He put down his briefcase, swung open the doors of the cabinet, and one by one checked the faces of the eight cadavers shelved on trays inside until he recognized the object of his quest: a well-muscled specimen with a swarthy complexion and a few days of stubble on his scowling face. Holding the flashlight in his mouth, the young man pulled the tray halfway out of its housing, knelt down to open his briefcase, and produced from it an eyeliner brush and a bottle of indelible ink.

"I'm afraid I cannot in good conscience let you go any further," I said.

As the young man whirled around, the flashlight slipped out of his mouth and I heard the lens crack on the concrete floor. "Who," he huffed in panic, "who—who's there?"

"Just an onlooker with a natural concern for the sanctity of the dead."

The young man turned to scurry away. But before he could get out through the doorway, Winch McKellar stepped into his path. "Not so fast, buddy."

The two of us had been lying in wait for about half an hour. "Turn the lights on, would you, Winch?" I said.

He did so. Now we could all get a better look at each other. The interrupted desecrator was so scrawny you could have fit a sheaf of him on one of those cadaver trays. I already knew his name—Hank Tapscott—and his occupation—officer of CIA, just like Winch and myself. With respect to the corpse, whose arms were marked with tattoos and whose chest was marked with bullet wounds, the corresponding details were a matter of public record. About forty-eight hours earlier, he'd been gunned down in flight from a double-murder scene, and afterward he had been officially identified by the police as a local vagrant known to them from earlier petty offenses.

But why a local vagrant would have got it into his head one night to equip himself with a semiautomatic, break into the Zamoranos mansion on Calle 17, and assassinate the industrialist Vicente Zamoranos and his wife Floramaria while they lay in their hundred-gallon bathtub together, nobody had yet explained.

And why a local vagrant would have tattoos in Arabic script on his biceps—prison or merchant navy tattoos, by the looks of them—nobody had explained that either.

"Step aside!" Tapscott said to McKellar. "You have no right to be here!"

"Granted, but neither do you."

"I said step aside!" Tapscott tried to push past McKellar, so McKellar gave him a hard shove. As he stumbled backward, I wheeled him around to the nearest of the morgue's two autopsy tables and forced him down so he was bent over it with his chin resting on ventilated steel rim. He tried to rise, but McKellar lined up for a right hook between his eyes, and he faltered.

"I am here on State Department business—"

"So are we, buddy," I said. "I'm a case officer here in Cuba. You're on my patch. So why don't you tell us exactly what business you're referring to?"

Tapscott didn't speak.

"I know you can't see his face from there," McKellar said to me, "but he's giving us what I'd characterize as a thin, contemptuous smile."

"We know you work for Branch 9," I said. "We know they sent you over here to clean up after this mess with the Zamoranos. We know you bribed the police to misidentify this guy who—I now can't help but notice—doesn't even look especially Cuban. Egyptian, maybe, or Libyan, if I had to guess."

On the night the assassinations had taken place, I'd been down in Pinar del Río, a hundred miles to the southeast. I had first visited the town two years earlier to investigate rumors of Soviet-sponsored agitation in the tobacco plantations, but I kept finding excuses to return because I so enjoyed climbing the ridges nearby. McKellar managed to raise me on the telephone from CIA headquarters in Foggy Bottom and explained that from what he was hearing—and Winch had a gimlet ear—certain documents found on the body of the assassin had proved worrisome to the Branch 9 boys, so with the connivance of the deputy chief of mission at the American embassy in Havana they were launching an urgent Spicko (meaning a cleanup operation, after the Apex Chemical detergent powder). He arranged to rendezvous with me in the capital the following afternoon. The first thing he told me after he got into my car outside the airport was that Tapscott, a Branch 9 cub, had been sitting a few rows behind him on the flight from Washington National. We were too late for those identifying documents, which the police must have destroyed before they could be entered into evidence. So instead we started following Tapscott around.

By this point it was common knowledge in the agency that Branch 9 was running some sort of training camp out in the jungles of Central America. But specific details were like hens' wisdom teeth. Lately, however, various wayward graduates of the camp had been turning up dead or jailed in the strangest places, Tunis and Juba and Luang Prabang. And when one of these strays got mixed up in something that threatened to spark a lot of publicity—say, the assassination of two members of Batista's inner circle—Branch 9 would dispatch one of their own to tamp down any potential revelations about the freelancer and his curriculum vitae. In the past, they'd done a pretty spotless job. But this was the first time it had happened on my turf.

Branch 9 had begun in 1951 as a task force within the Western Hemisphere Division of CIA. Not one of the officers assigned to it had been a particularly noteworthy character. But in those offices, between those men, something dark and furious must have been birthed, because over the next few years the task force had extended its mission, hoarded its power, shaken off any oversight, until it was ascending through the body of the agency like some hungry teratoma or parasite homunculus. I'd never seen anything like it in all my years in intelligence. By now Branch 9 wasn't a task force, it was a nascent branch of government, an *imperium in imperio* with an outsized influence over the foreign policy of the United States.

McKellar and I were both ambitious. " 'It is essential to the future of every free society,' " my old friend liked to say, quoting one of the founding principles of CIA, " 'that the agency should help to maintain their institutions and their national integrity against aggressive movements seeking to impose totalitarian regimes upon them.' And it is essential to the future of the agency," he liked to add, "that you and I become director and deputy director some day."

But although in all our years at CIA we hadn't wavered from

that aim, neither of us had yet been appointed chief of station any-where, or even deputy chief of station, let alone any position of real clout back in Foggy Bottom. Within the agency, McKellar and I had accumulated a great deal of power, but it was a power of a chthonic kind, seldom observed, seldom acknowledged. And, unfortunately, chthonic power didn't get you promotions. In the Barrio Chino in Havana I had seen them burning hell money, the banknotes that could only be spent in the underworld, and in hell money I regarded myself as a billionaire. Fifty was the sort of age at which a job like director of Central Intelligence began to suit you, so in the next decade I would have to find a way of converting all my hell money into something the federal government would accept as legal tender. With Branch 9 running the banks, that would not be possible. In fact, we could see a future in which all the promotions and bud-gets and clearances would go straight to the Branch 9 cronies and the rest of us would be left to fight over the scraps, a future in which anyone who dared defy them would be forced briskly out of the organization. The agency was only ten years old, but there was already a graveyard, figuratively speaking, of guys who'd fallen victim to its internecine politics; I'd made McKellar promise to slit my throat and dump me in the Chopawamsic Creek before I ended up like one of those sad sacks, drinking myself to death in some basement office with drippy pipes, mumbling to myself about all the betrayals I'd suffered.

Sometimes I joked that if I put as much effort into my responsi-bilities in Havana as I put into spying on my own colleagues back home, every seditionist on the archipelago would probably just give up in despair. But my priorities were well founded. In the long term, the enemy was world communism, but in the short term, the enemy was Branch 9. And McKellar and I believed that the training camp in the jungle was turning into Branch 9's biggest liability. In other circumstances, I might have been very curious to know exactly who the dead gunman was, and exactly where he hailed from, and exactly who hired him to rub out the Zamoranos. But right now, all of that was secondary.

"You've been working hard on your Spicko," I said. "Branch 9 sent you here because they don't want anybody finding out that this fucker was one of the family."

"If you're suggesting we had anything to do with killing the Zamoranos—"

"No, I'm not. I'm only suggesting you'd rather this guy didn't exist, because your training camp was where he learned to shoot. And if somehow that came out in the investigation, it would cause you a lot of embarrassment. So you had the cops write him up as some bum off the avenue. Except there's still the small matter of the tattoos. A lot of people are going to see them before he's in the ground, and maybe not all of those people take bribes."

"What were you going to do about them?" said McKellar. "All that Arabic. It's so squiggly."

"Yeah, I'd really love to know," I said.

"Come on, Hank. Tell us."

"As a matter of genuine professional curiosity."

"Please, Hank."

"We're begging you, Hank, just give us this one—"

Tapscott muttered something.

"Huh?"

"Waves," Tapscott said irritably. "I was going to make the Arabic stuff into waves, all right? Like on the ocean."

"Not a bad idea," I said. "If it was me, I would've just burned everything off with salicylic acid and called it a day, but I applaud your attention to detail. Now that we've broken the ice, Winch and I just have a couple of other questions we'd like you to answer. This Branch 9 camp in the jungle. Where is it, and who set it up? Was it Atwater?"

I had known Colonel George "Jawbone" Atwater in OSS. Beneath a banal and droning manner he concealed a preternatural thirst for blood; he was one of those guys for whom peacetime was a drag and wartime was better but the Book of Revelation would have been just perfect. Some years later, during the final weeks of the Bangassou Civil War—when the place had been blown to shivers, but nobody knew yet that the uranium under the hills was a chimera—Jawbone got so impatient for results that he drove across the border on a motorcycle and personally took command of a loyalist paramilitary outfit called La Garde de Nuit, by all accounts an ineffectual bunch up until that point. The agency wasn't usually too finicky about incidental casualties when the freedom of an entire people was in the balance. However, some photos got back to Washington of the aftermath of a Garde de Nuit raid on a convent that was thought to have arms hidden in the cellars, and these photos must have been truly spectacular—enough to turn some almost unturnable stomachs— because when Jawbone refused on principle to disclaim his part in the raid, it was decided that he could never again run operations in the field. Except that decree hadn't lasted very long, because I knew he'd helped to train the rebels who ousted Guatemala's President Jacobo Árbenz in 1954, and his name kept coming up in connection with Branch 9's guerrilla camp.

"I'm not telling you a goddamn thing. And when I get back to Washington . . ."

But then McKellar undid his tie pin and held up the sharp end so it glinted in the light.

"Oh, are you going to torture me with that?" Tapscott said with a smirk in his voice.

"No, we're not going to torture you," McKellar said. "We don't operate like that."

"What are we going to do?" I said. I could feel Tapscott tensing as if he had it in mind to break away from me, so I locked his arms up even harder behind his back.

"We're going to tattoo him," said McKellar. " 'CIA Branch 9' on his forehead. It might not be good for his cover, but it'll be a fine testament to his loyalty."

"Don't you need special equipment for that?" I said.

"No, you just kind of poke it in. I bet that's how this guy"—the cadaver—"got his."

"But, Winch," I said, "one of the first rules of interrogations is that you leave no marks. Tattooing a guy's face could hardly stand in more severe contradiction to that rule."

"That's true," McKellar said, dipping the tip of the pin into the bottle of ink. "But if he doesn't like the design, he can just make it into waves or something like that. Keep still, please, Hank. Don't worry—it won't hurt nearly as much as you'd think, and this pin is solid silver, which has an antiseptic property."

Tapscott held firm until McKellar made the second dot on his forehead. Then he shouted, "Hey! Hey!" He breathed heavily for a few seconds. "All right. All right, you traitorous sacks of shit. Just don't tell anybody you heard it from me."

"I give you my word that we won't."

"You two are fucked in the long run anyway, you know that?"

"Be that as it may. This camp . . ."

"It's in northeastern Honduras. Out in the ass-end of nowhere."

"Who set it up?" I said. "Was it Atwater?"

"No. The camp existed long before Branch 9."

"So who runs it?"

"Indians."

"Don't give me that."

"It's the truth," Tapscott said. "They're called the Pozkitos. The camp's been there since at least the middle of the forties. They were training anybody who'd pay. Branch 9 didn't come aboard until later."

"After Guatemala?"

"Before."

"Indians?" McKellar said. "Come on. You can't just set up a guer-rilla training camp overnight like it was a shoeshine stand. Where would they get the guns from? Where would they get anything at all?"

"Maybe they had an investor. I don't know. Anyway, now Branch 9 is their only client. Branch 9 are training up a standing army for United Fruit."

McKellar and I exchanged a glance. Key to the ascendancy of Branch 9 within CIA was their close relationship with the United Fruit Company. Although its aftermath had been a little prickly, the United Fruit–backed Guatemalan coup of 1954 was regarded in Foggy Bottom as a model for future operations: American intelli-gence and American business working as equal partners to advance their joint interests around the world. "Just look at Guatemala . . ." was a phrase you heard in those corridors with pestiferous regularity. And if it was their work on the coup that helped put Branch 9 on top, it was United Fruit's influence at the State Department that helped keep them there. Eisenhower recognized CIA's value, but on the whole he preferred to advance his foreign policy through State, with the result that there were certain steps we couldn't take without State's participation. These days, a triangle operated in which Branch 9 would tell United Fruit what they felt was necessary; United Fruit would go to State to ask for it; and State would call on Branch 9 to do it. This worked a lot better for Branch 9 than going to State directly, which is what the rest of us still had to do.

"What the hell does United Fruit need with an army?" I said. "With Árbenz gone, there isn't a single government in Latin America that won't suck their banana." In a country like Honduras, where United Fruit was one-sixth of the economy, where they'd built all the railroads themselves, they could do whatever they wanted. Among leftists the company was nicknamed *El Pulpo,* the Octopus.

"Things can change pretty fast. They've seen that before. But, hey, I'm not disagreeing with you. This army always sounded like a boondoggle to me. Their biggest enemy is white sigatoka, and you can't shoot that with a rifle."

"How did Branch 9 get friendly with these Indians?" McKellar said.

"REMOTER."

"That a code name?"

Tapscott nodded.

"For what?"

"I don't know. Only the top guys know about REMOTER."

"Is it an operation or a person or what?"

"I don't know."

"Would you prefer serif or sans serif?" McKellar said, stirring his pin around in the ink bottle. "I think serif would look better on you."

"I'm telling you I don't know! It's just a word I've heard people say sometimes. All I ever picked up is that REMOTER's what got us involved with the camp in the first place."

"All right," I said. "This camp. Do you know exactly where it is? Did you ever see it on a map? Latitude and longitude, maybe?"

"No. But there's some godforsaken little town on the banks of Patuca. San Esteban, I think. The camp must be over that way because the fixer we used was a guy who lived there. He knew the jungle and he knew the Indians so he'd set himself up as a liaison and we carried on using him even after Atwater arrived. Poyais O'Donnell. Irishman with no loyalties. I heard that back before the war he was mixed up in some—"

"*¿Quién es usted?*"

I looked up. A night watchman stood in the doorway of the morgue, goggling at our *ménage à trois*—or *à quatre*, if you counted the corpse.

We talked our way out without too much difficulty. Tapscott took the opportunity to slither out of our grip, although at least McKellar managed to dump a few ounces of ink down the back of his white seersucker suit as he left. In any case, he'd already given us so much that we didn't care.

Sometimes, you just have to sever one tendon and all the rest will soon snap—and McKellar and I were convinced that, for Branch 9, the guerrilla-training camp was that tendon. Once we found it, we could begin sawing away at it. I hadn't yet met the expatriate Tapscott had named but I'd met many like him and the very definition of a fixer was a man who could be bought. Even the hours until morning now felt like an almost unendurable wait, because the sooner I could get on a flight to Honduras, the sooner our rally would be at hand.

Three weeks after I arrived in San Esteban, however, half a night's delay no longer seemed quite as significant.

Wilson kept assuring me that in all the time he'd been a resident of San Esteban, this was the longest Poyais O'Donnell had ever been away on business. Every morning he prognosticated that the Irishman would return either that day or the next, unless perhaps he'd been detained by some misfortune or emergency, in which case at the very least news of him could be expected. In my years at the agency I'd learned that the ingenuous bonhomie of the upper-class Brit was a more resilient technology for concealing an agenda than perhaps any other ethnic mien in the world, but there was no question in my mind that Wilson's earnestness was authentic. Because he was currently the only other white man in San Esteban, we ate and drank and played rummy together quite often, despite two social obstacles.

The first was that he was a lifelong teetotaler who'd never even tasted the local cane liquor. The second was that my fairly generic cover identity as a notary agent hadn't been built to stand up to more than a few conversations—moreover, because my trip to San Esteban had no official sanction, it wasn't backstopped at the agency—so when I was called upon to tell stories from my invented past, I was adding terraces and conservatories to a pup tent. I had no trouble improvising, but I also knew that when you cobbled a stop-gap into a permanent architecture, when you allowed a short delay to molder exponentially, you were generating, under that surface drowse, all manner of tensions and contradictions.

I still hadn't detected even the faintest subsonic vibration of a guerrilla training camp somewhere to the northeast, and I didn't want to wait for O'Donnell forever, out here at the foxed edges of the atlas, where the eastern seaboard could fall to the Soviet tank corps and I'd probably hear the news several days later from some crone at the market, where the humidity not only made the afternoons feel endless but went so far as to warp the clockwork of my wristwatch as if in general contest with anthropic time, where the drawing-room mirror continued to tarnish at its imperceptible pace, where I had nothing to do but take strolls around town like a widower in retirement and back in my rented room I got so bored that in my lowest moments I genuinely contemplated starting a novel to see if I could get further than Wilson. But I also didn't want to go back to McKellar with nothing after wasting three weeks on this escapade. So I was still there on March 26th when the American boy flopped into San Esteban like a hairball coughed up by the forest.

I believe I was the first person in town to set eyes on him. Almost everybody else was in the plaza watching a cockfight that, as far as I could tell, was the local equivalent of Sugar Ray Robinson against Jake LaMotta. O'Donnell lived in a two-story house not far from the consulate, but I'd learned that he also maintained a storehouse on the riverbank. Having already broken into the former one night without finding any useful clues, I saw this as a good opportunity to make a discreet search of the latter. So close to the jungle there was a perceptible change in the insect demographics, and I was plucking some sort of marauding flechette out of my ear when I heard movement from the tree line.

The boy must have been around fourteen or fifteen years old. His skin was as tanned as if he'd never spent a day indoors—not to mention filthy, and crosshatched with weals and bites—but underneath all that he was a Caucasian with a neat haircut. The cut of his ragged vest and pants reminded me of the styles of my own youth, but they were made of some coarse woven fiber that wasn't cotton or linen. With wide eyes he staggered forward, as if his sheer curiosity at the sight of me was enough to overcome his obvious exhaustion.

"Is this New York?" he said in English.

"This is San Esteban, kid. Who are you? Where the hell did you come from?"

"My name is Colby Droulhiole. I came from the camp." And then I had to lunge forward to catch him in my arms before he toppled face-first into the mud.

Those were the last words I got out of the boy for a long time. Wilson and I installed him in one of the "guest rooms" at the consulate. The jungle can turn any Anglo-Saxon into a swoony Victorian lady, constantly in need of bedrest, but this case was more severe than most: somehow young Droulhiole had held off his fever long enough to make it to town, but by the time we took off his clothes he was already broiling so badly you might have thought his insides were undergoing some unspeakable pupation. Even though, in the days that followed, his sheets were changed with great efficiency (no bordello under Wilson's punctilious management could be unaccustomed to a brisk turnover of linens), it sometimes felt as if what we really needed was an entire civil-engineering infrastructure—dams and aqueducts and storm drains—to contain the volume of fluid that was pouring out of his body: the typhoons of sweat and the unceasing trickle from the anus and the blisters so dropsical that you had to pop them into a towel or the pus might splatter your hand up to the wrist. A recent fatal bar brawl had left San Esteban without a trustworthy MD, but it turned out that Wilson's geishas, and indeed Wilson himself, swore by a soup made from the flower of the kapok tree. Apart from that, there wasn't much to do but pour water down the boy's throat and dab ointment on his sores. Sometimes I overheard the women whispering to each other, and none of them believed he would recover. He was just too weak.

Of course, I was rooting pretty hard for the boy, because there were a lot of questions I wanted to ask him. When I searched his pockets and his rucksack, I found a reel of catgut, bandages, spare socks and underpants, soap, candles, rock salt, some wooden darts and stakes, a kind of obsidian shiv, a navigational star chart, a detailed but imprecise hand-drawn map of the American tropics, the dried-up carcass of a scarab with a deformed horn (perhaps a strange good-luck charm, like a rabbit's foot?), and a few other odds and ends. All of these things were handmade. If he'd packed any food, there was none left.

He'd told me that he'd come from the camp. But he wasn't some Libyan filibuster. He was a rangy teenager who spoke in an American accent. So I couldn't understand what business he had training to be a guerrilla, and I couldn't understand why he or anyone else would think he could possibly survive a jungle trek, this tenderfoot scout out here on his own with no compass and no printed map and no weapons or tools you couldn't find in a Bronze Age display at a museum. If the Pozkito/Branch 9/United Fruit training camp was as deep in the wilds as I had estimated, he had done extraordinarily well even to make it to San Esteban. And yet, for all my curiosity, his own story didn't matter very much, provided he could give me a firsthand account of the camp.

Every day I sat with Droulhiole. I wanted to make sure that, if he ever woke up, mine would be the first face he saw, and he would imprint on me like a hatchling goose. When he murmured in his sleep I could never make out the words but nevertheless I would press my ear to his mouth as if to a seashell and hear the jungle in his guts. Then, around the time the girls went downstairs to the drawing room to await the river traders, I would walk home to my rented room to have a few glasses of guaro before going to bed. I'd told Wilson that, because I was the one who found the boy, I felt a personal responsibility for his well-being, which of course Wilson found quite proper. Nobody except me knew what the boy had said before he collapsed.

On the afternoon of the sixth day of the vigil, Wilson's housekeeper Reyna saw me coming out of the washroom of the consulate and told me that Wilson was looking for me because he had some news. I thanked her and encouraged her to look in on the boy. Downstairs, I found Wilson in his study.

"How's the patient?" he said.

"Stinks worse than ever."

"Today I was reminiscing about how Mother always used to give me a little present after we came home from the dentist. Made the horror of the drill feel quite inconsequential in retrospect. If he does pull through, we must make sure he has his pick of the ladies for a few nights. As a reward for his fortitude. He'd enjoy that, I suppose? My own school years feel terribly distant now, and every generation is so different from the last, but boys of his age do still go in for that sort of thing, don't they? It hasn't been displaced by . . . I wouldn't know—crystal-radio sets and so forth?"

"I think fifteen-year-old boys still go in for exotic pussy, yes."

"Splendid—it's settled."

"Reyna tells me you have some news?" I said.

"Oh, yes! I think you'll be happy about this—"

But then Reyna herself appeared in the door, looking distraught. "El chico," she said. "Creo que está muriendo."

Wilson and I followed her upstairs as fast as we could. In the last few minutes the boy's condition had indeed come to a crisis. I could see his muscles cramping and quivering like a seizure at half speed, and his face had turned the color of dishwater, and Reyna had turned him on his side so he wouldn't choke as he vomited a clear bile, the viscous dregs of a dozen cups of kapok-flower soup. I put a hand to his forehead and found his temperature had fallen so precipitously that his skull should have cracked like quenched steel.

"I don't think there's much we can do," I said.

Wilson told Reyna, who was already praying under her breath, to get the priest. After that he and I stood there in silence, hands in our pockets, fixing the boy with the strenuous attention of the utterly impotent, as if watching a house burn down.

But by the time the priest arrived, the boy looked healthier than any of us.

He was still unconscious, but now it was a tranquil sleep; for the first time, I could hear him quietly snoring. The color had returned to his face and his temperature was more sensible. Evidently all that strife earlier had been a final push, a Liberation of Paris. The priest was sent home again, grumbling about the wasted house call. Wilson told Reyna that she and the others weren't to celebrate until the boy had incontestably recovered. "But it does look bally promising, doesn't it?"

After Reyna was gone, I said, "You had some good news for me. I guess I don't dare hope that the name O'Donnell is about to come out of your mouth."

"I'm afraid he's not back, no. But our little town has gained another rummy player, at least for a few days. There's a chap passing through—an American, like you. I met him at the market today. He's a salesman. Seemed personable, if rather guarded. Always nice to have a splash of new blood—socially, I mean."

"Who does he work for?"

"He didn't say. But when he lent me his magnifying glass I couldn't help but notice it said 'Property of Eastern Aggregate.' That's a New York firm, isn't it?"

"Yes, it is." I kept my voice steady but all of a sudden my nerve endings were trembling as if I'd caught a fever of my own. My whole time in Honduras I'd carried a Browning semiautomatic at my hip, but not until now had I ever really been aware of its weight.

That night, I didn't leave the sickroom to go back to my own bed. So I was waiting there around three in the morning when they came for the boy.

"We can see that the perceptions of our senses, even when they are clear, must necessarily contain certain confused elements," Leibniz writes, "for as all the bodies in the universe are in sympathy, ours receives the impressions of all the others, and while our senses respond to everything, our soul cannot pay attention to every particular. That is why our confused sensations are the result of a variety of perceptions. This variety is infinite. It is almost like the confused murmuring which is heard by those who approach the shore of a sea. It comes from the continual beatings of innumerable waves."

Quite so. I had once met an ambassador who had declared with great authority that true intuition, of the sort a spy must exercise, was "primal, ancient, almost mystical." Which proved to me that this ambassador had never in his life experienced anything like intuition firsthand. Actually, intuition was a rigorous computational process involving enormous quantities of data. It simply wasn't always recognizable as such because it didn't waste its time writing reports to its superiors to justify its findings; that was what intuition had in common with yours truly. (And nobody had ever described my methods as "primal, ancient, almost mystical," except, of course, in a sexual context.) For that reason, I couldn't have explained why the words Eastern Aggregate rang the bell for last call in San Esteban.

Nevertheless, intuition was how I came to be sitting there on the floor next to the door of the boy's room, up against the wall on the hinge side so I wouldn't be in sight if it opened. I hadn't moved in several hours except to borrow his bedpan. The last of the river traders had left the consulate around two, and since then I had heard no voices from below, only the crickets and a rooster on night watch. There was no light but moonlight in the room and most likely no light but moonlight in the whole house. I wasn't on edge any more. In fact, I had always found there was something about these intervals that really cleared your head, evened you out, let you feel the grain of the minutes passing, like sitting in a girl's apartment waiting for her to come back with bagels and lox.

I didn't hear the stairs creak until the feet responsible were almost at the landing outside. Slowly, I slid up the wall to a standing position. The handle turned and the door swung open and a man stepped into the room. He was of a much heavier build than Wilson and he held a pistol. When the zbyszko took one more step forward, so that he was clear of the door, I spritzed him in the face with benzoic oxymorphone. Despite his bulk he folded up neatly.

My plan was to question the Eastern Aggregate man after he woke up. Was he here to kill Droulhiole or just kidnap him? Was Eastern Aggregate working with Branch 9 and United Fruit? How had they learned of the boy's presence here so soon? I had already pried his pistol out of his hand and I was about to pat down his pockets when I heard movement over my head.

The consulate had only two floors. Someone was on the roof.

Now I wasn't so relaxed. I glanced at the window, which was hinged and had no lock. I considered firing blindly through the ceiling with my Browning, and I considered waiting next to the window for the second man to climb down through it. But if there was a second man, I couldn't be sure there wasn't a third. Then I heard the first man groan. I cursed the benzoic oxymorphone, which must have denatured in the heat. It occurred to me to simplify the exercise by shooting the first man in the kneecap or even the head. But as soon as I used my own gun, any other asshole who had one would probably use his too, and until I had no other choice I wouldn't run the risk of losing my ward to a stray .38 in a dark room.

Instead, I just kicked the first man in the head hard enough to replenish his blackout. Then I went over to pull the sheet off the boy, before splashing most of a jug of water in his face. "Get up. You're late for school." He just blinked at me. "I said get up."

"Who are you?" he said. This was the first time he'd been fully conscious in six days. I had to yank him out of bed by the armpit. He tumbled to the floor, nude. I bent down, reached under the foot of the bed, and hoisted it up onto its headboard, with the mattress and frame leaning against the window.

"Come with me," I said. "I mean right fucking now, friend." I grabbed his arm and pulled him toward the door. When he stumbled over the man on the ground he almost fell headlong again—but that hurdle was nothing compared to the stairs. One might almost have said he took the stairs like someone who'd never encountered a staircase before, except that didn't quite cover it, because somehow he managed to take the stairs worse than someone who'd never seen a staircase before. Even allowing for the darkness and for the boy's wasted muscles, I was astonished by the consistency with which he lost his footing on every eight-inch tread. But at last we got down to the foyer of the consulate. I threw open the front door and came out moving in a crouch, sweeping my Browning left and right and up to the rooftops. As far as I could tell, the street was deserted, so I beckoned to the boy to follow. For a moment—naked in the moonlight, trotting along in waggly imitation of my own combat prowl, bewildered by his surroundings—he resembled a sylvan mammal that for the first time in its life had braved a human settlement in search of food. Before we left, I picked up a piece of broken masonry and hurled it through one of the ground-floor windows. Whoever was on the roof might have a harder time getting away once the household was roused.

After that it was only a matter of stealing a horse.

I was not so naive as to assume that just because I'd nursed Droulhiole back from the brink of death, protected his identity as best I could, and rescued him from two or more intruders with guns, I could expect any gratitude. The boy was in his teens, after all. That he would be so uncooperative that I would actually have to resort to an interrogation room, however, I did not anticipate. While we were on our way to Tegucigalpa in another rackety old McCormick that I'd hired (along with its black driver) in Catacamas, I asked him again and again about the guerrilla training camp in the jungle, and he kept insisting that although he knew of some Indians running around with rifles, he had never had anything to do with them.

"Kid, you might not remember, but you already told me you came from the camp, back when you were in a more forthcoming state of mind. There's no use changing your story now."

"But I meant a different camp," he said.

"Oh, and what camp is that? Summer camp? Camp Waskatoon-Hey-Ho for Boys?"

"The movie. We were making the movie. You must know the movie."

I didn't let that divert me. "What about before that? Where did you come from?"

"I came from the camp."

"I meant before the camp," I said. "Where were you before the camp?"

"Nowhere. I was never anywhere before the camp."

"God almighty. All right, let's come back to that later. You said you were on your way to New York."

"I was on my way to Hollywood."

Over the past several hours, Droulhiole had shown all the symptoms of a mental condition that one might describe as the exact opposite of intuition: when a person gives up hope that any aspect of their waking life will ever be intelligible to them again. And most of these questions—these pretty simple questions—made him quail as if I were giving him a surprise exam on Leibniz's metaphysics. Only when we were on the topic of his destination did he give unmistakable signs of telling a lie. He had that adolescent boy's condition of looking entirely chinless when he wasn't sure of himself, as if his lower jaw could retract all the way into his body.

One possibility was that he'd been trained at the camp to play a character under interrogation. Back in San Esteban, however, he'd been terrified of our stolen horse (a terror that would have been justified if he had known how raw it was going to rub his undercarriage over the next few hours, but at that point he did not) and he'd asked me if it was a "giant tapir." He still refused to admit that he had ever seen one before, even in pictures. If that was part of his cover identity, it was a rather avant-garde cover identity. What had they told him at the camp? "Whatever you do, soldier, even if the bastards hang you upside down and put matches under your fingernails, for God's sake don't let on that you've ever seen a horse!" The truck was apparently a revelation to him too, and electric light bulbs, and my Zippo.

A second possibility was that he'd been brainwashed. A third was that he was, in the words of the agency's counterintelligence interrogation manual, "a schizoid or strange character [who] lives in a world of fantasy much of the time. Sometimes he seems unable to distinguish reality from the world of his own creating. The real world seems to him empty and meaningless, in contrast with the mysteriously significant world he has made." And a fourth possibility was that he was mentally subnormal. By now I'd supplied him with both clothes and salve. Our driver, who spoke no English, was attempting to overtake a caravan of mule carts laden with bananas. We were passing them so closely that I was able to lean out through the truck's window and grab a fruit, though it wasn't ripe enough to eat yet. In Honduras it was customary to bury a traveler where he fell, so there were graves by the side of the road, wooden crosses shored up by piles of stones. Beyond, green piney hills rolled into the distance, the sane and reasonable luxuriance of a forest that's open to the sky, not clenched overhead like the jungle's tesselar canopy. "Hollywood," I said. "Once again, kid, I must remind you that you are trying to sell me the cat meat after you already sold me the beef. By your own admission you were going to New York."

"That's not right. I must have been a little moggadored. I was sick."

This was something else I couldn't account for: my passenger kept using slang—like "moggadored" to mean confused—that I hadn't heard since before the war. Back in America that usually meant a person had grown up rich. "Okay, let's just say you were 'moggadored' and you meant to say you were going to Hollywood. Why Hollywood?"

"To tell everybody about the camp," he said.

"To tell everybody about the camp that you refuse to tell me anything about."

"To tell everybody about the movie. The progress on the movie. You must know the movie!"

After we'd been around that mulberry bush half a dozen times, I ran out of patience. Previously, I'd intended to check into a hotel suite in Tegucigalpa to let the boy complete his convalescence. Instead, I directed our driver to the agency's headquarters downtown (acquired in '52 from a gold-prospecting company), where they were certain to have at least rudimentary detention facilities. If anyone should ask, the boy would be a reform-school inmate from Sacramento who'd run away to join the Guatemalan communists and seen a few things he wasn't supposed to see.

I left Droulhiole alone for an hour or so before I came in with a lunch pail of egg baleadas and two bottles of beer. He was staring at the mirror window that took up most of one wall of the interrogation room, stretching from the ceiling about halfway down to the floor. Having no free hands, I kicked the door closed behind me. "You're thinking we wouldn't have a mirror that big just for guys like you to check their zits," I said. "We call that the Fourth Wall. If you've never been in a room like this before, you've probably never seen one. From this side it's a mirror, but from the other side it's a window. There's a little observatory next door. If my colleagues want a peep show, they only need to pull up a seat in there, and you won't ever know they're watching us."

"You must have used a lot of silver to make a mirror that big," Droulhiole said. He didn't seem to have understood me. Somehow even sitting in a straight-backed chair he managed to look as awkward as a raccoon stuck in a cat flap.

"I think they make them with aluminum now, not silver," I said. "But only a little of that. It's mostly glass." This only made the boy stare more intently at the mirror window. I followed his gaze long enough to catch a glimpse of myself. Lately I was losing my hair from my temples even faster than I was losing it from my crown. "If you're wondering if you can break it: trust me, you can't. Pound on it, throw the chair at it, whatever you like. Doesn't matter. It might crack, but it won't break. Anyway, how are you feeling, Mowgli? I know you haven't eaten for a while. Are you hungry?"

"Yes."

I sat down myself. "Well, it's not quite lunchtime yet. Let's commence with where you were going, because on that subject you're a man divided against himself, and that isn't good for the constitution. You start telling me the truth, you can eat, all right? You keep telling me the truth, we can finish our business here, and maybe we can even put you back on the road to New York or Hollywood or wherever it was you were headed. But until then, here we are, and here we'll stay. As long as it takes."

"You're not on the foraging rota today?" he said.

"I'm not."

"Tomorrow?"

"No."

"The day after, then."

"No."

"Oh, are you injured?"

"No . . . no, kid, this is my job. So you're stuck with me. And try to bear in mind that if it weren't for the guy you're looking at, you would've died on the riverbank back in San Esteban."

For a while Droulhiole looked down at the table. "You won't tell anybody?"

"You have my word."

"New York first, then Hollywood. That's where I was going."

"Terrific. Now we're getting somewhere. So why didn't you want me to know you were going to New York first?"

"I was supposed to travel directly to Hollywood to tell everybody about the progress on the movie. That's what I promised Mr. Whelt I was going to do. But before I left, Mr. Coehorn had a talk with me. He told me eight years ago they sent Mr. Pennebaker to New York but he never came back like he was supposed to. Mr. Coehorn said Mr. Pennebaker must have gone native. He must have forgotten himself among those people. Mr. Coehorn told me I had a special duty I couldn't tell anybody about. I was to travel up the river and appear in New York as if by accident and reestablish my acquaintance with Mr. Pennebaker and find out what had happened and then . . ." He tailed off. "Also, Mr. Coehorn told me Mr. Pennebaker would be fat

and half naked and smeared all over with, uh, with funnel cakes—
that's a type of cake—just fit to make you puke. Is that true? Is that
what Mr. Pennebaker is like now?"

There we sat, on opposite sides of the table, thoroughly baffled
in our different ways. "I'm afraid I don't know any Mr. Pennebaker,"
I said.

"I met Mr. Pennebaker when I was younger but I can't really remember his face or his voice or anything like that. He's just a name
to me, I guess. Anyhow, I asked Mr. Coehorn how I could be sure
that I wouldn't forget myself too when I got to New York, and he told
me not to worry, because I haven't grown up with all the luxuries
you have here, the funnel cakes and the cocaines and all that stuff,
so they won't be such a temptation. You know, he's right, I couldn't
even tell you what a cocaine looks like."

"I see."

"Say, how much longer do you think it would have taken me to
get to New York if I hadn't been taken ill? Mr. Coehorn said it would
take a long time, but I tend to be faster than the older folks. I figured
if I could find somebody in, uh, Cancún with a boat who'd row me
across to Florida, I could cut the trip right down. How close are we
to New York now? I saw a lot of tall buildings."

For a moment I imagined myself as my old mentor Professor
Mathers interviewing a Tucano tribesman, listening to his version
of recent history, taking notes, sifting through the allegory and the
exaggeration, flaring his nostrils at "the stench of truth." Anthro-
pologists weren't supposed to draw conclusions from lone subjects,
ever since the Provençal scam artist George Psalmanazar not only
convinced everyone in Queen Anne's London that he was a Formo-
san expat but made a best seller of his *Historical and Geographical
Description of Formosa*. Knowledge began with consensus, the over-
lap of two or more minds, otherwise it was no better than the solip-
sistic universe of the "schizoid or strange character." And yet when
the agency debriefed a Soviet defector, he would often describe some
department of the Kremlin that was as obscure to us as Formosa
was to the Stuarts, and we would have to decide whether to take
him at his word. Like the Directorate of Support inspecting a confer-

ence room for bugs, we would narrow our paranoia to a tight beam, double-check every inch of the transcript for gadgetry. Of course, we also had guys of our own, many of them frustrated novelists, whose job it was to punch up cover stories, to bottle the stench of truth like a musk and spray it where necessary, to supply all the arbitrary and redundant details that give the feel of reality. So we knew, roughly, what was feasible in that respect (though if the Russians should suddenly advance the technology of fiction it wouldn't be the first time). But what about *The New Adventures of Tarzan* over here? I had been so convinced that he came from the training camp. But the longer he talked, the harder I found it to believe that his account of himself could possibly be pure invention, either his own or anyone else's. To me, it positively reeked of truth.

I pushed the lunch pail across the table to Droulhiole. "Try one of these baleadas, kid, and by all means wash it down with a beer. I don't want to butt in with any more questions. I just want you to explain to me who you are and where you came from. And I want you to start from the very beginning."

Three hours later I was on a secure line to McKellar back in Foggy Bottom, having summarized, as best I could, what Droulhiole had told me. With the telephone cradle under my arm and the cord stretched taut I was pacing back and forth across the empty office like a dog on a chain, and talking so fast I hadn't let him break in once. "I know it sounds crazy. I know you're going to tell me that nobody in their right mind would believe it. But I do. Damn it, Winch, I do. And do you know what this means, if it's all true? Branch 9 has neighbors. About 150 white American neighbors. Like a convent school next door to the whorehouse. Do you know how many different ways that gives us to make Branch 9 rue the day they partnered with those Indians to run the training camp? We have pieces on the chessboard now. We have pieces on the fucking chessboard! The Dullards will forgive Branch 9 a lot"—meaning Secretary of State John Foster Dulles and Director of Central Intelligence Allen Dulles—"but if we play this right we can start the kind of jumblefuck down there they will not have the option to forgive."

"I hope so, pal," McKellar said, "but you're going to have to do it on your own. I'm shipping out to Jakarta next month. I would have told you sooner but I didn't know where to get hold of you."

"You're kidding me," I said.

"No."

"How did this happen?"

"How do you think? Branch 9 fixed it."

"Those fucking maggots!" I shouted, thumping the desk with my fist. "Winch, I feel like I just got word that you died. Indonesia. You don't know shit about Indonesia."

"I certainly don't. But at least Laura's excited."

"You're telling me I have to take on Branch 9 by myself? I'm good at this job, but have a sense of proportion, Christ. I can only be in one place at a time." All my excitement about Droulhiole had flushed away. I sat down heavily in the chair behind the desk. So rarely did I permit myself anything less than total self-confidence that even a temporary diminution staggered me like a migraine. McKellar and I had been separated before, but never by half a world. For the first time since my birthday eight weeks ago I became aware of myself as forty years old. No seniority in Foggy Bottom. No home. No family. Not many friends. I saw myself from the outside, a lone subject, hoarsely insisting upon the reality of "the mysteriously significant world he has made," nobody to reassure him but his own face staring back from the mirror wall . . .

"This is just a pothole," McKellar said. "We're still on the road. You and me. Deputy director and director by 1964. New York for Christmas and sherry in the umbrella room at the Waldorf-Astoria."

That was all it took. My crisis was already over. I lit a cigarette and leaned back in the chair. "Promise me you'll write every day, sweetheart."

"Of course."

"Put lipstick on before you kiss the envelopes."

The baleada vendor across the street started up his chant again, so loud, penetrating, and relentless that I wasn't sure how anybody in these offices managed to sustain an unbroken train of thought. There was something badly wrong with an organization that could silence a leftist radio station for the sake of American foreign policy interests but could not silence *"Baleadas con huevos!"* "You said these camps are out in the northeast," McKellar said.

"The kid drew me a map. He doesn't understand scale, but aside from that he's a born cartographer. All we need to do—all I need to do—is establish some kind of influence over them. Without making such a commotion that Branch 9 and the Indians get wind of it."

"This is the middle of the jungle you're talking about, with no communications," McKellar said. "You'll be cut off from everything that's going on in DC. Not to mention you might get bitten by a jumping viper. This isn't going to be an easy op to run. And you can't bring anyone else on. How are you going to keep both ends up?"

"Didn't Sturgis have almost exactly this problem with those Kuomintang who were hiding out in northern Burma in '46?"

"Yes, and from what I remember he got them all killed."

"Huh."

"And what are you going to do about the boy?"

With all the melodrama I'd almost forgotten that my new asset was still sitting downstairs. "As far as we know, pretty much nobody west of my left shoe knows about these two American camps, and that's how we want to keep it. I'm going to take the kid to Isla de Pinos. Find him a nice cabin on the beach somewhere nobody speaks English." Neither Branch 9 nor Eastern Aggregate would have any chance of finding him there.

"You really think nobody in the States knows about the camps?" said McKellar.

"If they do, they've been keeping quiet about it for eighteen years."

"What about this individual your boy was trying to find?"

"Mr. Pennebaker? If he'd ever turned up in New York with a story like that, we would have heard about it. And I don't have time to look for him. But I'm going to put a PI on it just in case."

"Wasn't there a Pennebaker who was head bookkeeper at the Lollipop before the war? It's not a very common name."

"Who knows?" I said. "Maybe they're related." My flask was empty so I opened the bottom drawer on the off chance of a bottle of rum but found only a pair of metalworker's earmuffs.

"Listen," McKellar said, "you remember that weasel Tapscott mentioned something called REMOTER?"

"Yeah."

"I've found out a little more. REMOTER is the codename for an individual. I don't know which individual, but apparently there were meetings in New York in '53. Branch 9, United Fruit, and REMOTER sat down together. They made an agreement for Branch 9 and United Fruit to take a joint 50 percent stake in the training camp."

"So REMOTER was one of the Indians?"

"Maybe, if you can believe some Indian from the back of beyond ended up cutting deals in a hotel suite in Manhattan. Sounds cockamamie to me. But that's the last help I'm going to be able to give you for a while, buddy. You're on your own now."

We stood in the shade of the warehouse to watch the men force-feeding the airship, gorging it as it lay on its side in the dust, plucking every so often at its underbelly to even out the swell. At first it didn't look like much more than a discarded stocking, but then, in a manner that seemed biological, almost indecently so, it began to writhe, bloat, iron out its creases, double in size and double again, stiffen the cartilage of its tail fins, rear up until it was bigger than you ever would have believed it could get, a blind white grub a hundred feet long, reborn from the darkness of its packing crate and now glowing under the Southern California sun. The guys in overalls turned on the propane burner between the blower and the airship's mouth, and from where I stood I couldn't see the flame but I could see the muddled air and within minutes I saw the effect on the airship as it rolled a little, bounced a few times on the tarmac like something just come to rest, and finally began to haul itself upright, testing first the weight of its own hide and then that of the gondola with which it was saddled. No one was actually flying today, however, so before long the men turned off the burner and started circling the pressurized airship, sometimes upright, sometimes on their hands and knees, pressing their ears to its flanks.

"What are they doing?" I said.

"Listening for leaks."

"Does that really work?"

Albee chuckled. "Sometimes." He was a tall, chunky guy who tended to stand with his feet wide apart, unshakeable, as if in an emergency you could slip the airship's bowline under his chin and use him as a mooring tower. Earlier this afternoon he had, as ever, refused to confirm to me whether or not his company was working on a flying car. "How about it?" he said. "Think she looks fit for purpose?"

"She's quiet?"

"Big slow-revving ducted fans. Heck of a lot quieter than any airplane engine. And of course when you're just hovering she doesn't make any noise at all. The problem is she's slow. You'll be lucky to get fifteen miles an hour."

"I can live with that. She steer all right?"

"Not in a high wind. But the rudder's a good size. What kind of weight are you carrying?"

"Just me, my gut, and about another sixty, seventy pounds of equipment."

"She won't even notice."

Albee knew better than to ask for specifics. His company had a long-standing relationship with the agency, and he had the authority to sign over the airship as a donation in kind. That worked out well for me, because I didn't have a budget for my operation in Honduras, and it worked out well for Albee's company, because the airship hadn't been taken out of storage in over a decade but they would still get a tax write-off according to some fairy tale estimate of its peak value. I walked over to stroke the airship's warm envelope, a heavyweight cotton varnished with iron oxide, butyrate, and fire-retardant halocarbons. "You can paint her black for me before I ship her down to Honduras?"

"Nine thousand square feet of canvas, almost," Albee said. "But if that's what you need. Put enough boys on it, shouldn't take us more than a few days."

This warehouse represented the very back of the attic here, and was situated accordingly, so we rode some kind of two-man battery-powered tricycle back to Albee's office. The seagulls of Redondo Beach made regular patrols of the complex to shit on any novel threats to their sovereign airspace that had emerged from the hangars that day. I wondered whether the company's planners had deliberately set out to erect such a faithful imitation of the studio lots to the north or whether in fact the tribute had been unconscious. Once we were seated upstairs, in a sunny office with balsa-wood scale models arrayed along the shelves like specimens in a natural-history museum, I took out my cigar cutter to cut a Petit Upmann for each of us. "They've been sitting in the archive all those years?" I said. "Perfectly good airships? Can't anybody find any use for them?"

"There was an evaluation during the war. But it didn't come to anything, and these days nonrigid thermals are about as fashionable as the Half Doodle. Nothing wrong with the concept. I'm sure one day they'll come back around. It's funny, though—nothing for years, and now two of you in a month."

I had been about to pass him his cigar, but that stilled me. "Two of us?"

"Oh, it's nothing. There was a lady, that's all. She had a few questions. You know how we developed those airships originally? When I was just out of school, I got a job at Gardena Aviation. Tiny outfit but in '28 we won a contract from Kingdom Pictures to develop a camera blimp. They wanted something nonrigid so you could fold it up and drive it out into the desert on a trailer; thermal because around then you fellows"—meaning the federal government—"were talking about buying up all the helium; and quiet so you could just hang it a hundred feet up and it wouldn't interfere with the sound recording. Well, that airship you just saw is more or less the airship we designed."

"That was the one that crashed? With Arnold Spindler inside?"

"Yes. After that there was a lawsuit, of course. That was the end of Gardena. Our patents got sold off. They were passed around for a while, but by the time I ended up here they were here too. Reunited!"

"So you're giving me an airship that's primarily famous for crashing," I said.

"No, no, you don't have to worry. That crash was the product of special circumstances. Never should have happened. That's what this lady wanted to know about. The crash. She was writing a book, she said. But I could tell she was a crackpot. She had that googly look in her eyes. And she smelled like laundry you forgot to air out after a wash."

To seek an audience with Arnold Spindler—that name from another era—had been Droulhiole's stated mission in Hollywood. Nothing for years, and now two in a month. "What was her name?" I said.

Albee, who by now had taken his cigar, blew a smoke ring that testified to a long career in aerodynamic engineering. "Oh, I didn't take the trouble to remember. Say, you can settle this for me—is it true most of the flavor is in the wrapper?"

"Can you find out for me?"

"About the wrapper?"

"About this writer's name."

Albee shrugged, not knowing why I was pursuing the subject. "I guess I could ask my girl to look in the datebook." He pressed a button on his intercom. "Felicity, sweetheart, could you remind me of the name of the lady writer who came to talk to me a couple of weeks ago?"

"Certainly, Mr. Albee." A pause, in which I had the feeling that something was passing over my head, vast and soundless and camouflaged against the sky. The intercom spoke again. "Her name was Meredith Vansaska, Mr. Albee. Is there anything else I can do for you?"

There are some houses that give you such a forceful vision of your corpse lying undiscovered for several weeks after your death that you can't possibly walk past them without resolving to talk to your neighbors more often or at the very least to sign up with a cleaning service. Here, the front door was ajar, but the chain was on, perhaps because the wood of the door was so warped that it would have been hard to shut properly. I knocked, but there was no answer. If you looked through the big windows on either side, or peered through the gap between the door and the frame, you could see only leaves, as if the whole place had been barricaded with philodendrons. But the lawn behind me was a parched brown, in contrast to its immaculate neighbors. After several weeks in the tropics, the silence of Silver Lake, the absence of stray dogs and street hawkers, felt like the result of some purge or rapture. "Hello?" I called. "Vansaska? Are you there?" There was still no answer.

I took out a rubber band, reached around to the other side of the door, and fumbled out of sight until I had one end looped around the slider at the end of the chain and the other end around the door handle. Then I turned the handle from the outside so that the slider was pulled along to the end of the receiver and the chain came loose.

I stepped into an atmosphere so thick I felt chloroformed—or rather chlorophylled.

It was as if the director of a failing botanical garden had decided to bring the entire collection home to live with him. Ferns, orchids, figs, bromeliads, ficus trees, violets, palms, succulents, cacti, some potted on the floor and others hanging from hooks, some dead and others flourishing, some nearly my height and others small enough for my buttonhole, scores upon scores of plants, a hyperbaric greenhouse, a slum crammed with every race and nationality. The bungalow itself seemed to be disintegrating into compost, with condensation running down the walls and mold dappling the cornices and plaster bellying from the ceiling. Sacks of nitrogen fertilizer were piled by the doorway and there was a film of mud underfoot. I used the toe of my shoe to tear up a spider web connecting the stalk of an aroid palm to the spout of an overturned watering can. Because I couldn't even see as far as the other end of the living room, it was by the rustling of the foliage that I first perceived her approach.

"Zonulet?" she said, shambling toward me in a stained blue kimono. Her hair was lank and she did indeed have what Albee had so compassionately described as a "googly look in her eyes," a look that reminded me of certain women I'd met as a crime reporter, not the violent ones but the ones who were strangled by some vine of grief. "You're so much older."

"It's been almost fifteen years," I said.

"Yes, I suppose that is the relevant statistic."

I wasn't sure it was, actually. Something else at least as pitiless as time had blasted my former *New York Evening Mirror* colleague into this condition. When I looked at her I felt fear. Not just worry, like when I was on the phone with McKellar in Tegucigalpa, but fear. Not just fear for her, but fear for myself. I wanted a swig from my flask but I knew it wasn't very good manners to let an old friend see that you couldn't even stand to look at them without groping for some Dutch courage. "This is where you live?"

" 'Framed playbills and newspaper clippings and signed photographs of myself. Old props and presents from my dead admirers and perhaps a corgi mummifying under the chaise longue.' "

". . . What is that, a poem?"

"Why are you here?"

"Pleased to see you too," I said. "Come on, we'll go to a hotel and then later on we can see about cleaning this place up. Can you pack a bag? I'll pack a bag for you. Where's the bedroom?"

"I'm not a child."

"You can't stay here. It's not . . ." It's not sane. "It's not healthy for a person." I took her arm.

"Don't touch me," she said, pulling away without vigor. "Why are you here? I assume you came with some other purpose than to serve me an eviction order."

"I came to catch up with an old friend. But that doesn't really matter just now. What matters is taking you somewhere you're less likely to die from either a swamp disease or a collapsing roof."

"This is my home. These are my plants. If I weren't comfortable here I would already have left. I'm perfectly aware of how it must look to you." Her voice was as toneless as if she were reciting from a script.

I realized I might have to come at this less directly. "Can we just talk, then? Can we sit down somewhere?"

"If you like."

She led me to the bedroom, which was just as thickly vegetated, although at least the bed made a clearing in the center. Littering the floor was a corona of hamburger wrappers, soup cans, cigarette butts, pencil erasers, tissues, underwear. What troubled me even more than the squalor itself was her total renunciation of embarrassment or self-consciousness about a visitor setting eyes on it. We sat down side by side on the bed's edge, which didn't feel any less provisional than standing in the living room. "Did you lose someone?" I said.

"What do you mean?"

"I mean did somebody die? Or run off? A kid of yours, or a husband . . ."

"No."

"Parents?"

"My parents are dead, yes." She yawned, beginning to wilt sideways. I saw that I shouldn't have let her return to her nest.

"How long ago?"

"My father in '48, my mother in '49."

She couldn't still be in mourning. And yet I knew that the woman I remembered from our *Mirror* days—a keen reporter, a good sport, a pretty face who'd never had much trouble filling her dance card— wouldn't have just cracked up for no good reason. "What is it, then? What happened?"

"Nothing. Nothing much has ever happened, really."

"The plants, then. Why the plants?"

"I never went to the jungle, so . . . The old woman who lived below my piano teacher—after she died, her grandnephew . . . I've always remembered it. I've always wanted to go to the real jungle."

"That's what this is supposed to be? The jungle?" For someone who'd never seen it firsthand, she'd done a fine job dressing the set. If you had asked me, before I saw this bungalow, whether a human author could ever produce a fully convincing imitation of nature's chaos, I would have said no, but now I wondered if it just took the right state of mind. "Vansaska, for Christ's sake, if you want to go to the jungle so much, why not just go now? Go today! We can go together! I can get us on a plane to Cancún and we can drive down through the Yucatán. Won't cost you a dime. Shit, we're only a couple days' drive from the redwood forests up the coast. You ever seen those? I swear it's just like being in the tropics except you don't sweat so much."

She shook her head. "No. No."

"No what? You could be in the real jungle tomorrow! Why not? Give me one good excuse."

"No. No." She seemed to be refusing not only the offer but even to let the topic enter her head, hunching over self-protectively as if the conversation itself were a threat to some internal poise.

"Vansaska, beautiful, just listen to me. I can see you're at a low ebb here—"

All at once her posture changed, and for the first time she really looked at me, not sideways from a half-bowed head but straight at me with a fury that in an instant had burned off the haze from her eyes. "You think this is low? You asshole. Do you have any idea what a Battle of Normandy Ascent of Everest Theory of fucking Relativity accomplishment it is every minute of every day that I don't eat that whole bottle of Nembutal in the dresser? This is low? I am alive. I am alive and I have not yet taken any decisive steps to amend that state of affairs. I am not even in an institution. This is as good as it gets. This is summa cum fucking laude. And you come in here uninvited to complain about my fucking houseplants?"

I exhaled heavily. "Jesus Christ." I took out my flask. "Sorry." And yet I was glad I'd said what I'd said, because she was so much more lucid now that she was roused. "Not to dispute your assessment," I said, "but I happen to know you went to see a man about an airship a few weeks ago. What I mean is, you were not only alive, you also made it as far as South Bay."

"That feels like a very long time ago. I have good weeks and bad weeks. This is not a good week." She rummaged in the sheets behind her to find a headband before scraping her hair back into it so impatiently she pulled out a few blond strands in the process. "How do you know about that?"

"I was with Albee a few hours ago. He mentioned you. He said you wanted him to tell you about Arnold Spindler's airship crash. He said you were writing a book."

"I tell people that because I don't have press credentials. There's no book."

"So it's . . . what? Just an interest of yours?"

"You could say that. Some days I feel like it's the only thing in the world keeping me from taking the decisive steps I mentioned. But if you want to call it an interest, call it an interest. I've spent the last ten years looking into Arnold Spindler and Elias Coehorn. It's been slow, because most of the time I'm not up to it. But I have a hot cockle here, Zonulet."

We both smiled at that nostalgic expression. "What's your hot cockle?" I said.

"The man they pulled out of the wreckage of that airship was not Arnold Spindler. Or, to be precise, they pulled two men out, and one was Spindler and the other wasn't. The one who got photographed on the stretcher, and recuperated in the hospital, and went back to the mansion in Bel Air: that wasn't him. What happened to the real Spindler after the crash, I don't know. Whether he was alive or dead, I don't know. But no one ever saw the real Spindler again. The crash was a setup."

"So who was the other guy?"

There was ten times more life in her voice now: "An impersonator. Spindler never looked quite the same after the accident. His skull was a different shape. His right eye was smaller and lower down."

"Because he smashed himself up in the crash."

"It was a way to cover the switch. No surgeon could have made the impersonator look exactly like the real Spindler. But Spindler with a scrambled face was an easier commission. Hence the airship crash. Also, it was a lot tidier to make the switch out in the Alabama Hills than it would have been if his limousine got T-boned on Sunset Boulevard."

"Albee told you all this?" I said.

"No, but everything he told me fits with what I've already found out. He has a lot of doubts himself about what happened that day."

"This was '29. Correct me if I'm wrong, but New York money didn't start coming into Hollywood until the early thirties. That's how Kingdom Pictures got so big. Before that, who would've had enough at stake for these shenanigans?"

"It wasn't about money." There was something almost involuntary about the way she'd taken up the old rhythm of the newsroom, like a drummer tapping his fingers on a countertop.

"What was it about?"

"Revenge. Paternity. Have you ever heard of a movie called *Hearts in Darkness*?"

Droulhiole had spent three hours telling me about it in the interrogation room. But Droulhiole was a secret. Droulhiole didn't exist. "No."

"In 1938 Kingdom Pictures started production on a movie called *Hearts in Darkness*. They assembled a cast and crew. When I was in Hollywood that year I . . . met the director. He was going to shoot it on location at a Mayan temple in Honduras. Bev wanted me to report on the shoot but I didn't go, remember? Anyway, the movie was never finished. And none of those people ever came back from the rain forest. Around the same time, an expedition left from New York with exactly the same destination. They never came back either. Elias Coehorn Jr. was leading that expedition. The only legal heir of one of the richest men in America disappeared into the wilderness, along with at least a hundred others, and as far as I can tell no one has ever published a word about it in an American newspaper. In 1940 the family of the actress Adela Thoisy hired a search party to go into the rain forest. There's some evidence that the search party was massacred by one of the native tribes out there before they even got as far as the temple."

Nice to have corroboration that Droulhiole wasn't a Psalmanazar. Also, it probably meant that Pennebaker had never surfaced in New York, although I would keep my freelancer on it just in case. "I don't understand what this has to do with the airship," I said.

"The Spindler expedition and the Coehorn expedition set out for this temple at the same time. But that wasn't the first opportunity anybody ever had to use those two names in the same sentence. Back in the teens, Spindler had a long affair with Coehorn Sr.'s wife. Later Coehorn found out about it, and he raped Spindler's wife to punish him, and Coehorn's wife threw herself out of a window. That was 1918. Spindler fled to Hollywood and started Kingdom Pictures. Eleven years later someone arranged for Spindler's airship to go down so that from then on they could puppeteer his corpse, figuratively speaking. People say Spindler used to pride himself more than anything on his dignity and straightforwardness and good sense in the middle of all those hysterics on Broadway. Imagine the sort of revenge where you don't just kill someone and have done with it, you carry on afterward. You turn his name into a punch line. You make sure that anything he ever accomplished will be subordinate to the stories about his craziness. You own him dead for longer than he owned himself alive."

"And when people met Spindler after 1929—"

"Hardly anybody did."

"But when they did. You think he was played by that impersonator?"

"Yes."

"And you think Coehorn did all that?" I said. "Granted, the rich do find odd ways to keep themselves occupied—but what's your reasoning? Spindler must've had other enemies in Hollywood. And if Coehorn had already got back at him once, why would he have waited eleven years to do it again?"

"There are photographs of Spindler from when he's a boy. He starts puberty late. Before puberty he has the most nondescript face you've ever seen. After puberty something distinctive comes through in the features."

"What are you saying?"

"If puberty brought so much out of him then it's reasonable to suppose that in a son of his it would also—" But then she stopped herself and gave me another hard look. "What did you say you were doing here? In California, I mean."

"I told you. I came to see Albee."

"About what?"

"I work at the State Department now. His company does some business with us. Lately there's been some interest in one of the old Gardena Aviation thermal airship designs—from us and, as it turned out, from you. 'Nothing for years,' he said to me, 'and now two of you in a month.' Quite a coincidence. So I thought I'd pay you a call."

"You're lying. Or at least you're streamlining considerably. I've known you longer than almost anybody, Zonulet, remember? Why are you really here?"

I had to give her something. "When I say State Department . . ." I cocked my head.

"I see. That doesn't surprise me. You'd be good at that."

"Ever since the war."

"Where do you live now? Washington?"

"I'm a sort of circuit rider."

"You could help, you know. Some car salesman gets his passport stolen in a cathouse in Mexico and the federal government springs into action, but a hundred Americans die in Honduras and somehow it's like nothing ever happened. As I said: this story is all I have now. Don't you look in the mirror sometimes and think, 'Thirty more years? They expect me to go through thirty more years of this? Thirty at least?' "

"No," I said. "I never think that."

"Sometimes I have a sort of vision, of a stack of diaries, thirty of them, those big desk diaries like my mother used to have, all blank, all empty, and I'm an ant who has to crawl across every single one of those empty pages before I'm allowed to get to the end. Unless . . . unless I decide I don't have to." She paused. "Put it this way. I don't often find reasons to leave this house. I've given over the best part of my inheritance to errand boys sent by grocery clerks to deliver bags and collect bills. When I do leave, it's because I'm trying to find out what happened in '38. But I don't have any leads left. Your pal Albee was the last one. Someone has rather methodically snipped off most of the loose threads. I've run short of places to go. But it seems to me that if anyone should know what happened to those Americans in Honduras, it's you people."

My old friend had given me almost everything she had and I'd given her nothing whatsoever in return, just as if I'd been pumping some whiffled attaché in a hotel bar. I could have told her that those Americans were mostly still alive. I could have told her that there was a boy living in a cabin by the beach on the Isla de Pinos who'd grown up on the set of *Hearts in Darkness.* I could have told her, at the very least, that she wasn't wasting her time, that she should keep looking, that if she could substantiate her hunches she would have a story that would make the bones of Beverly Pomutz rise up out of the earth to buy one last exclusive for the *New York Evening Mirror.* The greatest kindness in the world at that moment would have been just a few words out of my mouth, a breath of life in this miasmal air.

But I knew Branch 9 was waiting for me to get careless.

I didn't even want to risk asking any more questions, in case she detected a second time that I knew more than I was admitting. And as our conversation about Arnold Spindler began to sputter out, so did Vansaska herself. I tried to keep my hostess engaged with chitchat about the years since we'd seen each other, our old colleagues, the state of the newspaper business, life in Los Angeles. But the longer she went without talking about Arnold Spindler and *Hearts in Darkness,* the further she sank back into her previous condition. Melancholy came on like hypothermia, her spirit withdrawing inside her inch by inch until once again her voice was flat and her eyes were dull and her muscles were slack. Before I left, I repeated my offer to take her to the real tropics, even though I knew her response would be the same. Soon there was nothing else to do but tuck her back into bed. Once again, I found myself standing over a chronic drowser in dirty sheets whose jungle malady was beyond my expertise. "Keep at it, sweetheart," I murmured. "Keep at it if you can." Then I gathered up the trash around her bed and carried it out to the garbage cans beside the house.

·   ·   ·

At long last, the temple came into sight.

Three hours earlier, just before midnight, I'd taken off from a barge anchored in the Ebano Lagoon, about eighty miles east of Trujillo Bay along the north coast of Honduras. This was my fourth sally, and my last chance for almost a month, because by the following night the moon would start waxing too bright. I had some faith in Droulhiole's amateur cartography, but he'd been working from memory and without instruments. If his map had been precisely accurate, the temple ought to have been forty-six miles from the lagoon at a 197-degree heading. In practice, I was a rookie pilot navigating a thermal airship with only a directional gyroscope and a pitot-tube speedometer on cloudy nights that were calm but never entirely windless, which meant that the indeterminacy of my course was probably about commensurate with the indeterminacy of his map, and the most I could do with those numbers was set the mood for the evening. On each slow flight I described a long teardrop shape, skimming about four hundred feet above the canopy, and so far I hadn't even managed to locate the tributary of the Patuca that was supposed to guide me toward the temple. I had agency-issue eye drops to improve my night vision (which gave me glittering paisley floaters when I closed my eyes, perhaps because I took three times the recommended dose); all the same, with clouds masking the starlight, the darkness was vertiginous, a nearly fathomless blackout on every side of the airship's cramped gondola, the dim red glow of my instrument lights like the last ember of an extinguished universe. During the war, I'd spent a year in the 2nd Photo Tech Squadron of the Air Force before McKellar recruited me for OSS, but I'd never actually been up in one of the P-40s from which most of the reconnaissance pictures were taken. Now, at last, I'd come to understand how truly severed from the earth you felt when you were lofting over obscure terrain with nothing to guide you home but a quivering needle. Fortunately, I had twice the fuel I needed, and all the yammer of the forest to keep me company, reaching up like sirens and car horns to a window on the fiftieth floor.

I'd just taken a gulp from my flask when I saw it. The senses are always so eager to please, and dozens of times each night my eyes had traced right angles in the stipple of their own straining. But this was different. I could make out an adumbration of the landscape that was neither treetop nor empty air. I turned the rudder to swing the airship to the west.

Before long I was close enough that a flickering spark came into view below. After turning the rudder again, to make sure my black whale wouldn't swim directly over the site I raised the field binoculars that hung around my neck, and made out a white man tending a fire on a stone step.

I had found the temple.

According to Droulhiole's map, I was on the opposite side of the ruin from what he'd described to me as "the camp with all the Indians wearing green," which had to be the Pozkito/Branch 9/United Fruit training camp. Bent over because the gondola's ceiling was too low to stand up straight, I went around behind the pilot's seat to shove my cargo out of the open rear hatch. As it fell from the gondola, the static line deployed the crate's black parachute. The loss of sixty pounds of ballast sent the airship lurching skyward. Steadying myself on a handrail, I reeled the static line back inside the hatch. About ten seconds later I heard the crack of branches as the crate hit the canopy. By then I was back in the pilot's seat, holding down the rudder to make the interminable starboard turn—the Roman Catholic Church could reverse itself faster than this airship—that eventually would point it back in the direction of the coast.

The craft was designed to suppress not only the thrum of the engine, as Albee had promised, but also the flash of the burner. I couldn't be quite certain that some first-rate pair of eyes down there might not still catch sight of the vessel—as faintly out of place against the sky as the temple was faintly out of place against the forest—but a hundred-foot shadow lumbering over the horizon would be a singularity so immune to explanation that any rational person would discount it as a phantasm.

Inside the crate was an RS-1 field radio, the same model we used behind the Iron Curtain, comprising a receiver, a transmitter, and a hand-cranked power supply (all waterproof) with a range of seventy-five miles, along with four gooseneck flares, two Zippo lighters, and a pound of Hershey's chocolate. Stapled to all six sides of the crate were copies of the following notice: "This is a radio. HIDE EVERYTHING YOU HAVE FOUND HERE SO NOBODY CAN FIND IT, AND TELL *NOBODY* ABOUT IT. After you have studied the operating manual in private, use the radio to contact me. I can supply food, medicine, weapons, tobacco, alcohol, news, and correspondence from the United States, or anything else you require. If you follow these instructions *CAREFULLY,* you will become the most powerful individual at the temple."

The radio was a dart thrown blindfolded. But it was the best option I had. I couldn't approach either of the two settlements openly, in case Branch 9 was watching. And even if I'd had a direct telephone line to Coehorn or Whelt or Burlingame (names I knew from Droulhiole) I wouldn't have used it. Too often when you made an overture to some footling provincial boss you promoted him in his own mind, alerted him that he had something America wanted, so that all of sudden he thought he was Napoleon Bonaparte and became correspondingly tiresome to bargain with. Instead, I intended to worm my way in from the periphery. Of course, there was a chance that whoever found the radio would be such a poster boy for good citizenship that he'd take it straight back to camp. But if I knew anything at all about human nature, that notice on the crate was enough to win over nine people out of ten. I just had to hope my new asset didn't turn out to be either too stupid or, worse yet, too smart.

In Trujillo, I'd hired a skinny half-Jamaican guy called Pavo for four dollars a day, because he struck me as sharp and dependable when I talked to him in a cantina. Any kid off the street could be my airship groom, but I needed somebody I could also trust as my radio operator. For hours at a time, whenever I was off shift, he would have to sit there listening for a transmission from the RS-1 that might never arrive.

As it turned out, however, I was the one wearing the headphones when it came in, the first word that followed Droulhiole out of the jungle and into my embrace: "Testing."

This was the third night after I'd dropped off the field radio. I was in my cabin aboard the lumber barge I'd leased, and my feet were up on my TBX receiver while I read the new Scribner's translation of Leibniz by the light of a gas lantern, so when I heard it come to life I had to twist around so fast I practically unsocketed myself at the waist. The receiver ran off a battery but I was cranking up the transmitter by hand as I shouted, "Yes, I read you, come in, come in!"

"Who's on the other end of this?" A man's voice, with an unmistakable Brooklyn accent, and also a crust on the glottis as if maybe it hadn't got a lot of use lately.

"Your new best pal."

"Is that right?"

"Pleased to meet you," I said. "Pleased as hell."

"And where are you, new best pal?"

"Somewhere between you and the good old United States. Not too far. Are you alone?"

"I sure am."

"Nobody's going to catch you with the radio?"

"No."

"You've hidden the crate and the parachute?"

"Yes."

Pavo appeared at the door of my cabin, and I gave him a thumbs-up. "Must have been quite a surprise to find them, I guess?" I said.

"A lot of funny things happen in the jungle."

The voice was starting to remind me of someone in particular, but I couldn't think who. "So I'm told. Well, let me give you the essentials of the situation. I'm an interested party with resources at my disposal. I want to make sure the outcome for all of you at the temple is the best it can be. And to do that I need a man on the ground I can trust. Are you that man?"

"At your service."

Of course I would have preferred to interview for the post like I had with Pavo, but in this case I would just have to play whatever cards I was dealt, even if they were nothing but a deuce and two old bus tickets. "Terrific," I said. "I hope your cranking arm isn't tired yet, because I need to ask you some questions about the lay of the land down there. And then we're going to come up with a plan together. By the way, did you enjoy the chocolate?"

"I ain't eaten it yet."

"Really? No need to ration it out. There's going to be a lot more where that came from. Or anything else you want. Anything at all. Remember that. Now, tell me a little more about yourself. Which of the two expeditions do you belong to?"

"I came here in '38 with the Kingdom Pictures crew. That don't mean I belong to them, though. I pack my own lunch."

"And what exactly . . ." But then the words faltered in my throat and my hand faltered on the crank handle. Because I'd picked up another staticky signal, this one transmitting across a distance of eighteen years, and it was a recollection of a specific voice: a more youthful one, more insinuating, more inflated in its confidence, but nevertheless very similar indeed. Eighteen years was a long time, but back at the *New York Evening Mirror* I'd got so used to the sound of this voice, in your ear day after day like a gabardine-sleeved tentacle still mucky from its spawning bed at the bottom of the Gowanus Canal. I tried to put the thought out of my mind, because there was no sane and well-ordered universe in which it could possibly be the same one.

And yet I had to ask because I had to be sure.

"Trimble?" I said. "Is that you?"

When I heard footsteps behind me I assumed the librarian had come back so I didn't even look up from the viewfinder. My camera was mounted on a copy stand between two lamps, all pointing down at the album open on the table. The copy stand was crafted like a Chippendale, and the furnishings of the corporate library in Eastern Aggregate's Manhattan headquarters were in general exorbitantly grand and Oxbridgean, perhaps in order to foster the feeling that the collected ledgers and records of the company should be regarded, in some sense, as classics. Nearly all queries were answered by telephone, and as far as I knew I had the place to myself aside from the superabundant library staff. But then somebody made a polite cough, and I turned.

"I'm very sorry to interrupt your work, Mr. Zonulet. But I was hoping you might permit me to introduce myself." Despite the luxe carpentry of the copy stand, one of the two lamps kept losing its angle because of a broken spring, and the guy in front of me produced a similar impression, with a light-bulb head that seemed to overburden his scrawny neck. He was in his mid-fifties and wore a suit of a fussy, old-fashioned, expensive cut that fit in well with the decor. "John Phibbs," he said. "I'm one of the vice presidents of Eastern Aggregate."

We shook hands. "Pleased to meet you, Mr. Phibbs. To what do I owe the honor?"

"The head librarian tells me you are taking some photographs of our wage vouchers from the interwar period."

"That's right."

"I'm extremely curious as to the purpose."

"I hate to be awkward, Mr. Phibbs, but the librarian probably also told you that I'm here on State Department business. So I can't go into detail. But let me assure you that your company's cooperation is very much appreciated by the United States government."

"What puzzles me," Phibbs said, "is that the vouchers you're photographing have been out of circulation since the early forties. The company no longer issues private currency of any kind. One would expect that today those items would be of interest only to the numismatical miscellanist."

"Oh, you'd laugh if I explained the reason. It's pretty silly. But as I said, I just can't."

"Of course. I quite understand."

"You said you were a vice president here?" I said.

"That's right. I've been at the company for a long time. I started in 1917 as an operative for the Good Conduct Division. Then for many years I was the personal assistant to Mr. Elias Coehorn, our founder."

"Surely you don't come down to say hello to every visitor to your library? Seems a little below your pay grade."

Phibbs gestured at the copy stand. "And surely this work could be done by any clerk, Mr. Zonulet? It seems a little below yours." He held my gaze for a moment. Then he smiled, and retrieved a business card from his jacket. "But in fact you're quite right. Because of my other responsibilities, I'm obliged to limit the time I spend in this fine library, as agreeable as I may find it. Now, I urge you to telephone my secretary at this number if you need prompt assistance with any matter whatsoever. Good day, Mr. Zonulet, and best of luck with your enquiries."

I watched him walk away, his head bobbing on his shoulders as he moved, and then I turned back to the viewfinder of my camera. "Redeemable on pay day for ONE DOLLAR ($1.00) in lawful money of the United States," declared each scrip note, "without discount or interest, subject to terms of contract, from THE EASTERN AGGREGATE COMPANY," with a five-digit serial number, a date, and the printed signature of "Emerson Opdycke, TREASURER," all superimposed on a red sunburst pattern that radiated from an engraving of the same Lower Manhattan headquarters in which I now stood. Plus, in this case, one further line in italic type. There must have been children born into the villages around Eastern Aggregate coal mines in southwestern Pennsylvania who until they grew up and left home would never even have set eyes on a federal greenback, only this rayon scrip. That much they had in common with Colby Droulhiole. Ostensibly, as Phibbs had said, it was out of circulation now, but I felt that if you asked around after midnight you could find brokers who could tell you the rate of exchange against the hell money they burned in the Barrio Chino.

Phibbs was still on my mind as I adjusted the focus. The Eastern Aggregate Good Conduct Division had been notorious as the most brutal corporate enforcers of the Depression. I had once heard Jawbone Atwater compare them, admiringly, to Ivan the Terrible's Oprichniki. Usually a guy of Phibbs's seniority would prefer to suppress that part of his résumé. But perhaps he felt it compensated a little for his bullyable physique if he hinted that he might once have cracked a few skulls, or at least provided logistical assistance to said cracking.

That is not to suggest that Phibbs had mentioned that detail in order to intimidate me. Intimidation had not been the aim of his visit. Yes, he had wanted me to know I was being watched. But that was, in its odd fashion, an act of hospitality, of respect, like the owner of the restaurant coming over to your table. The point was not just that I was being watched, but that I was being watched from the highest levels, as my status merited.

And that, in turn, is not to suggest that I was happy about it. I now wished that instead of applying for access to these currency albums with my own State Department credentials, I had enlisted some numismatical miscellanist, as Phibbs had put it, to apply on my behalf. The reason I hadn't taken the trouble was that such an obscure request hadn't seemed liable to attract any attention. But I should have given more thought to the implications, especially bearing in mind my run-in with the Eastern Aggregate agent in San Esteban. Vansaska had told me that someone had methodically snipped off most of the loose threads relating to the Americans at the temple. Perhaps that was true. But these leather-bound albums contained samples of every wage voucher Eastern Aggregate had ever printed, including special issues. Phibbs must have thought those special issues were my objective here. In fact, I had been expecting to photograph only generic scrip. Until I reached that page of the album, it hadn't even occurred to me that I would find a 1938 special issue with an extra italic line on every denomination that read, "Issued for Mr. Elias Coehorn Jr.'s expedition to SPANISH HONDURAS"—the first documentary evidence I had ever set eyes on of those New Yorkers who never came back from the jungle.

The agency may to some degree have resembled a dime-novel publisher, with its writers on contract producing fiction by the yard, but to an even greater degree it resembled a movie studio. And if my operation at the temple had been officially sanctioned, I would have had any number of expert prop-makers at my disposal. But because, to use Trimble's dated expression, I was now packing my own lunch, I had to take care of the scrip forgery myself. The deputy chief of station in Tegucigalpa had told me he'd found no reliable printer in the whole of Honduras. I did know a real craftsman in Havana, who would take my negatives and make lithograph plates so immaculate they could hang in a museum. But down there you couldn't get quality rayon of the kind Eastern Aggregate had used, so I had to buy a fifty-yard bolt from a wholesaler in New York's Garment District and export it personally on my next Pan Am flight.

All that was straightforward enough. The problem was simulating how the notes would look after eighteen years of daily fingering in a tropical climate. Of course, the denizens of the temple wouldn't be on the lookout for sourdough any more than they were on the lookout for airships, but if they'd been using the same money for eighteen years—or almost half that, anyway, in the case of the *Hearts in Darkness* crew, who reportedly hadn't adopted it as legal tender until later—they would be sure to notice the slightest difference in feel. Apex Chemical produced a solution specifically for aging paper, but it only worked on non-synthetics. So in New York, I spent an afternoon touring secondhand clothing stores, nuzzling the oldest rayon frocks I could find, trying to attune myself to the decay of regenerated cellulose. And in Havana, after the rayon scrip notes had been printed and cut, I made a series of experiments in artificial weathering, using acids and yeasts and rotating drums.

The result was a dozen different samples with a dozen different textures, like fabric swatches from some futurist tailor. Back at the barge on the Ebano Lagoon, I packed these into another parcel for Trimble, and then dropped them off from the airship, with the light of a gooseneck flare as my target. Later, over the radio, he told me which of the samples was most convincing. I had hoped this part of the plan would take at most two iterations, but I had to go back with a third set of samples before the former blab man was satisfied that I'd found the right weathering procedure to fool his cohabitants.

Regarding Trimble: this did not, for me, constitute an enchanting twist of fate. I'd had no warning of it, because Droulhiole hadn't brought up Trimble's name in the interrogation room, and neither had Vansaska when she reminded me that she was the one who had originally got the assignment to follow the *Hearts in Darkness* shoot back in '38. Dredging my memory, I did retrieve some details of that week. Vansaska and Trimble were both away from the newsroom for a few days, but only Vansaska came back. Then Pomutz, so angry you thought his fillings were going to melt out of his jaw, announced that Trimble had sent him a telegram from Havana. But that was around the same time Frank Parker put the word out that he wanted Trimble in a body cast, and when I thought about Trimble I just couldn't imagine him against any background other than the five boroughs, so it was simplest to assume that this Havana bullshit was only a ploy to throw Parker off. Besides, after Trimble didn't come back to the *Mirror,* it wasn't as if we were sending out search parties. We all hated him. Some people liked him the first time they met him because he was so confiding, so ingratiating, so informal, and realized their mistake only later on—though my own instincts had been swift and accurate. In the thirteen years I'd been in the intelligence services, I had met torturers and child killers and at least one amateur cannibal, but none of them ever got on my nerves quite like Trimble.

Sometimes I marveled at that figure. Only thirteen years since McKellar press-ganged me in the umbrella room of the Waldorf, and it felt more like a thousand. Only ten years since Harry Truman chartered a peacetime intelligence service, and the agency felt as historied as the Knights Templar. So much had happened. And that dilation of time was reflected back at me in the mirror every night. I remembered sitting beside Vansaska and comparing the different ways life had weathered us, its experiments with acids and yeasts and rotating drums. Admittedly, any doctor would tell me I was accelerating my own decline. I drank a lot. And when I drank I almost always drank Scotch and cognac and *añejo* rum, barrel-aged spirits, the older the better, as if I wanted to fill up my body with time itself, equalize the pressure between inside and out. Of course, if I'd invented a technique to age grain alcohol eighteen years in a week, instead of printed rayon, I could have made a fortune.

Although I hadn't yet seen Trimble in the flesh, somehow I felt sure he wouldn't have changed. He really was an imperishable asshole. But no matter how much I disliked him, that wasn't important now. I had worked with him before, and I could work with him again. Furthermore, the plan seemed to me sound. Trimble would use the forged scrip to buy Elias Coehorn Jr., just like a mob boss might buy a local politician. So through Trimble I would control Coehorn, and through Coehorn I would, in the long run, control both camps. My eventual goal was to force the temple and the Pozkito/Branch 9/United Fruit training camp into a much more severe juxtaposition, if possible the sort of blazing jumblefuck that the State Department, even the White House, simply could not ignore, so that they would have no choice but to step in and shut Branch 9 down. And my involvement at the temple might be suspected but it would be impossible to verify.

Perhaps when I took an oath to serve my country as an officer of CIA, I didn't envisage I would ever find myself devoting months of my time to some microfracture on the world map that could not possibly have been more cut off from the foreign policy interests of the United States. But in my view that was the consummate mode of espionage: to exploit the connections between all things, produce the largest effects through the smallest and most indirect causes, like the *gui dao* siege demolitionists of the Three Kingdoms period in China, who according to legend had only to dig up some tree roots close to a fort, dam a stream uphill, mutilate the wings of pigeons that roosted in the battlements, before the walls of that fort would come tumbling down at the tap of a mallet.

And Trimble's next request showed me that he understood this principle just as well as I did.

This was almost four months after we'd started our project. By making small, regular deliveries of the counterfeit scrip, I was ensuring not only that Trimble would remain dependent on me, but also that he couldn't inject it too fast. Anybody who'd passed through a POW camp during the war could tell you that the quantity theory of inflation still held in economies of just a few dozen buyers and sellers. Beyond that, however, I had no control. The operation was a black box. Even if I'd had an infrared camera to take a few reconnaissance shots from the airship, my Photo Tech Squadron analytical training would have run up short against this strange battleground.

I wasn't, thank Christ, stuck on the lumber barge the whole time. In between my contacts with Trimble, Pavo and I would motor a little fishing trawler back along the coast to Trujillo, bouncing into the harbor across the wakes of banana freighters, and twice I flew up to Havana to make sure El Movimiento hadn't been causing too much consternation in my absence, returning each time with an extra trunk full of supplies. Trujillo wasn't much of a town, but by comparison with San Esteban, the site of my previous detention, it was both temperate and metropolitan, with a merciful sea breeze and a small population of Americans, many of whom styled themselves as exporters or brokers but were actually embezzlers or Ponzis on the run.

Pavo kept a jar of leeches who started jitterbugging every time a storm was near, and one day I personally supplied some spare parts for this meteorological instrument when, a little preoccupied with a hangover, I slipped on the deck of the barge and fell into the lagoon. I bounced out faster than a cat but I was already serifed with leeches, which I had to dig out one by one with a thumbnail, saving a few for the jar. That night, after climbing into my hammock, I also felt a maddening tickle on the ball of my left foot. Peeling off my sock, I discovered a less familiar parasite, which I'd missed on my first inspection: a tiny cerulean grub that had bored into me. I shouted for Pavo to come into my cabin and look at it. He recognized the species, whose local name translated as "spite worm." After we burned it off with my Zippo, he explained, the ulcer it left behind would be volubly purulent for at least a few weeks.

I taught Pavo gin rummy. He got good enough to beat me every time. I taught him heads-up poker. He got good enough to beat me every time. I taught him Pennsylvania needledick. He got good enough to beat me every time. There wasn't much else to do. Over a bottle of guaro, I learned that Pavo's father had shot himself two years earlier after the failure of his banana plantation left him in debt to hoodlums. For economic reasons alone, it was hard for a smallholder to hold out alongside the United Fruit Company, but white sigatoka made it even worse. Once, the necrotic leaf disease had terrorized farmer and corporation alike, and if anything the farmers had a better time of it because they knew their plants so intimately. Since around '54 or '55, however, the vast United Fruit plantations had been almost immune. Evidently the company had invented a cure for the sigatoka contagion, but not a single one of their local workers knew the secret. Meanwhile, family farms were as ravaged as ever, often losing entire harvests. After her widowing, Pavo's mother had gone back to Jamaica, where she was born. Pavo didn't feel much hometown fondness for Trujillo.

However, what made it more endurable to me than San Esteban, apart from a better climate and better food, was that I wasn't just sitting on my ass, I was building something, block by block, as fast as it could be built. Maybe I had something in common with the artist who, two-thirds of the way through some monstrous and solitary undertaking, with nobody else to reassure him that "the mysteriously significant world he has made" has any value whatsoever, must grimly reassure himself. Still, given how much faster everything moved in the underlife of the agency, I was conscious that I was missing, in effect, generations of activity. And sometimes, despite my best attempts at patience, I found myself vibrating with boredom. The daughters of Trujillo's wealthier households would spend hours in the morning brushing their fine black hair, and often they sat close enough to their open bedroom shutters that I could watch them as I drank coffee on the balcony of my hotel room. I thought of changing my foot dressing in the open air, as a sort of reply, but I was concerned the girls wouldn't find it comparably romantic.

Short of major developments at Foggy Bottom, I hadn't expected to have any reason to go back to the United States. But then Trimble, in the *gui dao* spirit, sent me to Dallas.

In his latest update over the radio, he'd assured me that the sham scrip was working as intended. Coehorn was impressing everyone with how much money he had in his treasury. "The fine folk over here, they've regained their respect for Mr. Coehorn," Trimble said. "They see he's plutocratical again and they figure he must be doing something right. For a while there they wouldn't do a thing for him. Now he's back to giving orders."

"And he's still in your pocket."

"He's cozy with the lint, absolutely. The problem is the cooze upstairs."

I grabbed for a firefly that had found its way into the cabin of the barge. For a moment it flickered against my cupped hand like a match flame in the wind, and then went out. "Who do you mean?" The firefly, escaping, lit again.

"You want Coehorn running the whole show. Ain't about to happen while Burlingame's on top. Whelt's nothing, but she's the queen bee. Keeps the other camp in line, nice and tight. Doesn't matter how rich Coehorn gets if the Hollywoods are still loyal."

"So we need to reduce her influence."

"Listen. There's a nuthouse in Dallas called the Carrotwood Hospital. And in this nuthouse there's a lady from Corpus Christi named Emmeline Sapp, around forty years old. Or maybe she isn't there any longer, but she was. Locked up back in '36 for being a dike. Wherever she is, you got to get me a photograph. And you got to get me a letter from somebody with a fancy title saying that what happens to her is up to him."

"But I can't possibly go to Dallas. Don't you know Texas seceded from the Union again in '46? They'll never give me a visa to cross the border. I mean, I suppose I could try to sneak in from Mexico . . ."

"Really?" said Trimble, surprised. "Texas ain't part of the country any more?"

"That's correct, Trimble. Much like my balls, which also seceded in '46. For too long they had been denied the right of self-determination."

"Oh. I get it. Another one of those. What a riot."

Although I'd pranked Trimble several times with these sidewise histories, my favorite of the whole bunch had come from Trimble himself: a few times already he'd mentioned the "German-American Alliance" that had supposedly won the war, and even though I was curious to find out where he'd got that idea, for my own amusement I preferred not to set him straight.

Tonight the morbid smell that sometimes blew through the mangroves was especially strong. These swamps weren't as thick as the jungle they margined, but they were even more obnoxious; take something that's already overripe and then leave it in a puddle. Admittedly, the abscess on my foot wasn't much of an air freshener. "Anyway, what the hell does this woman in Dallas have to do with the temple?"

"Trust me on this, Zonulet. This baritone babe is the easiest way to get to where we're going."

I didn't trust Trimble on anything whatsoever. In fact, I was almost certain that he was lying to me—I just wasn't sure about exactly what. But at some point he would need to prove his success in advancing my interests, otherwise the manna from heaven, the cigarettes and chocolate and matches and underwear and cold hard rayon, would cease to arrive. He was smart enough to understand that if he tried to screw me he'd only be screwing himself in the long run. Our interests were aligned. That was much better than trust.

So I went to Dallas.

The Lovelinch Institute had been built according to the *Aufrichtig-kloster* doctrine of postwar therapeutic architecture, which held that corners and turns were redolent of labyrinths; hence this second-floor corridor, which was the longest I had ever seen outside a military installation. From the threshold of Kubie's office, I estimated the distance to the other end to be somewhere between two hundred yards and infinity, and without the windows that ran down one side looking out onto the lawn it would certainly have matched any labyrinth in oppressiveness. This monument to progressive European ideas felt a little out of place in the middle of Texas, and so did its director, whose starchy bearing and rapid, pedantic, slightly anglicized speech made him seem like a Texan parody of a northeasterner (I later found out he was actually from Chicago).

Fine distinctions aside, however, the real incongruity in this particular scene was the water that streamed half an inch deep down the endless hallway.

"I'm afraid you've chosen the worst possible day to visit us," said Kubie. We were splashing along with rubber galoshes over our shoes. "No one has yet been able to explain to me how this was the result of routine maintenance on the hot-water pipes."

"I've come a very long way to meet your patient. A little indoor weather isn't of any account."

"In circumstances like this we give the patients a choice of whether or not to evacuate. For some it's horribly distressing, a kind of apocalypse. But for most it's merely a break in the monotony of life here. Miss Sapp chose to stay in her room. These days she has quite a robust disposition. But please be mindful, all the same, that she is unaccustomed to visitors."

Here I was again, taking pictures of the most obscure holdings in the archive. "What is Miss Sapp's condition, exactly?"

Kubie made a regretful hum. "Her case history is a rather lurid patchwork. With her consent I may one day publish on the subject. In 1935 she was committed to Carrotwood Hospital by her family, suffering from what was described at the time as 'sexual derangement.' Meaning she'd supposedly forced herself on her aunt, who was only a few years older than her. I don't know what happened during her years at Carrotwood—records were only selectively kept. Whether her 'sexual derangement' was 'cured,' I wouldn't venture to say, but by the time Carrotwood was closed by the state, and Miss Sapp came here to Lovelinch, she was in a state of chronic delirium. Phantasmagoric hallucinations day and night. She couldn't function. That was what made her a candidate for the unilateral grada torectomy."

"Unilateral say-it-again?"

"Gradatorectomy. It's a new procedure but I dare say we may one day look back on it as the Lovelinch Institute's chief contribution to the history of psychiatric medicine. In the past, most surgeries of its kind have been bilateral, meaning resections have been made on both sides. But so much is now known about the hemispheric arrangement of the brain that it's possible to be much more precise. In this case, only the left temporal gradatorium has been resected, and the right temporal gradatorium has been left intact. The gradatorium, a structure so named because of its resemblance to—"

"Is this the business with the ice pick?" I interjected.

"I find it deeply regrettable that Dr. Freeman and his transorbital entry are now so closely identified with the lobotomy in the popular imagination," said Kubie with some irritation. "In fact the gradatorectomy is a very complex, very delicate operation, involving a small hole drilled just behind the ear of a patient under general anesthetic. It should be understood that this a modern field with tremendous untapped potential. Not some reckless shortcut of the kind one might have found at Carrotwood."

"So she's fixed?" I said.

"She is far more lucid now than when she came to us. But there are lasting consequences to a gradatorectomy, as there are to any trespass inside the body. Her reasoning has been affected. Let me give you an example. Last week I told her that a ship is presently laying a transatlantic telephone cable along the bottom of the ocean from Scotland to Newfoundland. She did not believe me. No matter how many times I swore to it, she refused to believe that a manmade line could be expected to reliably carry electrical signals for two thousand miles down there among the tube worms and viperfish. Nothing in her experience heretofore has ever suggested that any such thing might be possible."

"I can see her point. It is a pretty strange thought."

"Let me give you another example. Our weekly motion picture screening is popular among most of the patients, but Miss Sapp has no interest in it. She cannot take the pictures seriously. We watched a musical with Ethel Merman playing an ambassadress, I can't remember the title. Miss Sapp made a series of objections. 'Why are they singing and where is the music coming from and how do they know all the words to the songs already? Why do the clouds you see outside the window never change? Why do they not clear up the entire misunderstanding with a simple telephone call? Why, when Ethel Merman introduces herself by some made-up name, does someone not say to her, "No, I recognize you, you are the well-known singer Ethel Merman"?' "

"Again, I can see her point. Those movies hardly make any sense sometimes."

"Perhaps I'm not making myself clear. Miss Sapp will not believe anything at all unless she can verify its workings with her own eyes and hands. Her evidentiary threshold is now insurmountably high. She will not imagine, she will not suspend her disbelief, she will make no temporary concessions for the sake of argument. No anomaly or novelty or fancy can find any purchase in her at all. She is sane now, yes, but perhaps too sane. The world outside this institute is a wondrous and irrational one, and I am not sure whether anyone quite so sane could manage there. Still—there is no doubt that in the final analysis the unilateral gradatorectomy was to her benefit."

There was so little sense of progress as we walked that, even as Kubie gave his explanation, it felt as if the two of us were stationary and the observation windows of the dormitory rooms were spooling past like frames across the gate of a projector. But then something struck the back of my head, and as I turned around, something else struck my hip. I saw two pencils floating away on the current. A door that had been closed when we passed it was now ajar, and a woman peered out at us with loris eyes. Clutched in her right hand was another HB javelin.

Kubie said to her, "I know you don't wish to have your pencils taken away again, Miss Monbut. Please go back in your room. Do some of the exercises we practiced. I'm busy with a visitor but somebody will be along in a moment to help you." The woman darted back out of sight. Kubie bolted the door, pressed an electric switch to summon an orderly to the room, and took out a fountain pen to write a note on the observation pad hanging from a hook. "My apologies," he said to me.

"Not at all. You should try walking past the typing pool at the State Department."

A community like this, I thought, must have its own scrip, albeit perhaps a scrip so esoteric that no two of its tokens looked alike. While we'd been distracted, some other traffic had begun to approach down the hallway: an orderly pushing a patient in the wheelchair. Even from this distance you could see the wheels flicking up a spray of water like a paddle steamer, and the shaved patch, almost luminously naked, on the left side of the patient's bowed head. I couldn't seem to look away from him, because even though he was unconscious I had an unaccountably strong impression that he was about to raise his eyes and stare straight back at me. "Now, here before us is another good example," said Kubie. "This is a man of forty-one, successful in his field, but now reduced almost to catatonia by persistent hallucinations. He sees spirits and demigods. Grand conspiracies. Temporal distortions. Other universes, interpenetrating with our own. He is believed to have accidentally inhaled certain chemicals in the course of performing his job. Just now he was sedated in preparation for his unilateral gradatorectomy. I'm optimistic that after the operation we will see the same level of—"

That was as much as I heard before I blacked out.

Some time later I found myself back in Kubie's office, stretched out on his stiff chaise longue. My suit was damp down one side. In through the open window drifted what sounded at first like some solemn cantillation but resolved itself before long into calisthenics instructions, and along with it the scent of laurels, although I was horrified to see that somebody had taken my shoes off, meaning that the stink of my spite-worm ulcer would soon overwhelm any natural perfume for about a hundred miles. Kubie was tonging ice into a glass of water from a brass bucket in the shape of a pineapple. "What happened just now?" I said.

He handed me the glass. "You fainted, Mr. Zonulet. I have your camera on my desk. I'm afraid the viewfinder is cracked. Do you feel all right? Perhaps you aren't used to the summer climate here? I know it took me a long time to adjust after I transferred."

I smiled. "I spend most of my time in the tropics, doctor. I ought to be able to deal with Texas." I was a pretty self-assured character, but if there was a degree of self-assurance so complete that you didn't feel even a little uneasy about betraying signs of nervous debility in front of an admitting physician at a mental hospital, I had not yet attained it. "Maybe those pencils hit me harder than I thought."

Pavo's leeches were in dispute with the barometer. They were all crowded up at the top of the jar, practically banging their little heads against the lid in their desperation to evacuate. But my barometer showed only a small drop in pressure, not enough to augur a storm. And I couldn't smell ozone on the dusk. Besides, I was impatient. The yield of my trip to Texas wasn't doing any good sitting there beside me in a waterproof envelope.

Emmeline Sapp had not spoken a single word in my presence, consenting with only a nod when I asked if I could take her picture. As she regarded me with her large, dark, almost unblinking eyes, I was curious about what enduring link she might have to the temple, but I knew in the end it was of no importance. The following morning, I drove out west to the Goree State Farm for Women. "Keep on that road until you notice the cabbage fields are full of nurses," the warden's secretary had told me on the phone, referring to the inmates' white dresses. An actual nurse, from the infirmary, helped me choose a few women with burns, welts, or bruises that marred skin of Sapp's approximate complexion, so that the photographs I took could attest to the electroshock treatments, tight leather restraints, and punishment beatings she had supposedly endured. Later, I also forged a sheet of Carrotwood Hospital headed paper to type out a letter from its director stating that a request from the State Department would be sufficient for him to approve Miss Sapp's immediate discharge. Clearly, Trimble intended to blackmail someone at the temple who knew Sapp. I hadn't asked for details but I liked the shape of it. Again, the maxim at work: sometimes you just have to sever one tendon and all the rest will soon snap.

"*No deberías subir esta noche,*" Pavo said to me a second time as I slid the envelope into the supply crate. But nonetheless he helped me nail the crate shut before we carried it out to the deck of the barge to saddle it with its parachute. (Trimble kept nagging me to bring him a linen suit, but although I was willing to provide small luxuries, I stopped short of anything that would advertise too glaringly that he had a supply line to the outside world.) The air felt calm to me—not calm as in "calm before the storm" or "eerily calm" or "too damned calm"—just plain calm.

And that was how it stayed for the first couple hours of flight. By this stage of the Ebano Airlift, I'd had enough practice that I could grope through the moonless jungle as if it were an apartment with the lights off, and I never misidentified the temple in the liminal grain of the night. When the wind began to rise, I wasn't concerned. "Remember, she's a hundred-foot sail you can't douse," Albee had said, but the ducted fans were powerful enough that I could maintain my bearing as long as I kept an eye on the instruments.

Except the wind kept on rising. Even from this altitude, over the drumming of the rain on the airship's taut skin, I could hear the tidal roar of the highest trees straining the wind through their leaves. I turned up the burner in the hope of climbing out of the shear. But higher up it was just as bad. There was no thunder or lightning on the horizon; this wasn't a public spectacle, just the exportation of a tremendous volume of air, after hours and off the books, lubricated by a little water.

I wasn't far from the temple, and I wondered if I could at least keep control of the airship long enough to sight Trimble's flare. Grip the wheel gently with your hands, grip the car sternly with your mind: that was my method on dicey roads, and it never failed. But after a few more minutes the storm was blowing so hard that the rudder was rendered ornamental, and so was the burner, and so was the pilot, really. I couldn't see anything, and I couldn't do anything, except cling to my black planet scudding through the void. By now I was willing to acknowledge that I should have trusted Pavo's annelids.

Still, if I resigned any hope of getting the photographs to Trimble tonight, that didn't leave me with much else to worry about, save the possibility that I wouldn't make it back to the barge before daybreak. Even then, a few cattle farmers sighting an unidentified flying object wasn't enough to compromise an operation like this. (Albee had a few stories to that effect.) Until the weather died down, I just had to concentrate on maintaining a running estimate of my coordinates. My left foot was feeling unpleasantly squelchy, so I unlaced my boot in order to change the dressing on my ulcer.

Then the shooting started.

When I heard the first rifle reports, I wasn't sure if I was the target. But that question was answered in pretty short order by the spotlight. The beam wasn't powerful, but it shone directly at my gondola, and against the surrounding darkness it was like an archangel's lance. I couldn't understand it, because if I knew anything about reckoning, there was no way I could have drifted within rifle range of the guerrilla training camp.

The next sound I heard was a heavy machine gun.

So I didn't know anything about reckoning. Or at least not in a tempest. When I next ran into Albee I would have to ask him about replacing the directional gyroscope with a jar of leeches, fed on my own astute blood. The machine gun fired another burst. I couldn't regard the controls as ornamental any longer, not if they could shift the airship even an inch. I emptied the ballast tanks, to gain altitude, and I hauled the rudder over as far as I could, to offer the vessel's long side to the wind. That way, if the machine gunner had an advanced case of rheumatoid arthritis, I had a fair chance of evading his aim.

If he did not, however, the steel floor of the gondola was no protection against those .50 caliber rounds. No protection for me and no protection for the cotton envelope over my head. I glanced behind me. The spotlight was shining through a neat row of holes in the gondola's floor. Those bullets would have gone through the envelope and out the other side. The airship would react to the leaks as ponderously as it did to the burner. But from now on it had only one vector.

Knowing I wouldn't hear the shot that killed me, I pulled my boot back on, went around behind the pilot's seat, and started unbuckling the supply crate. If nothing else, the exercise reassured me that, should it ever for any reason prove necessary, I would be capable of undoing eight brassieres in less than five seconds under heavy fire. I kicked the crate out of the back hatch, and felt the airship rise, although not as much as I wanted. Nobody shot at the crate as it fell. That was good. But behind me I heard the airship's instrument panel shatter. As best I could, I strapped myself into a parachute harness that was designed for a cube. I cut the static line with my pocket knife, and jumped.

I counted one and two and halfway to three before I released my parachute, because I needed to drop out of the beam of the spotlight.

That left me about four hundred feet from the ground, or about three hundred feet from the treetops, which was barely enough time for the parachute to deploy, let alone slow me down.

Those straps couldn't have been quite even, because one of them yanked me under the armpit almost hard enough to dislocate my shoulder. Moments later, a gust of wind hit with such force that I felt like I was dangling from the string of a kite. The parachute was still opening and I was still descending, but simultaneously the whole tangle was being dragged over the roof of the forest.

For a short interval, the world was nothing but a maelstrom of speed, rain, darkness, gunfire, leaves, and I had absolutely no idea what was happening. Branches caned my feet and then my groin and then my face. Others just snapped under me. Now the canopy of my parachute was out of the wind and into the tree crowns, and this wasn't a continuous fall any more so much as a rapid chain of physics interactions, like the collapse of a trestle bridge.

I was still alive, which meant I hadn't smashed into any of those tree trunks hard enough to break my neck. Of course, if the lines broke or the silk tore I was still a hundred feet off the ground. Or ninety feet now, eighty feet, seventy feet, because by slides and jerks and plunges I was moving down through the trees, though with less momentum each time, until at last the parachute found a set of branches that could be persuaded to share my entire weight.

There I hung, dizzy and limp, no better than a pouch full of bruises, an oversized fruit rotting on the vine. Rain tickled my face, and so did the last few leaves and flowers twirling down from where I'd ripped through the upper foliage. It made me think of the Chaplin movie where he got hoisted upside down from the bunting at the opening ceremony for the department store, except it wasn't as funny.

I was still getting my breath back when I heard in the distance a minor arboreal cataclysm. The airship meeting the forest canopy. I didn't know whether they'd seen me parachute from it, so I didn't know whether anybody was going to come looking for me in this direction. If I needed to defend myself, against soldiers or jaguars, I had my semiautomatic and my pocket knife.

However, I didn't have my flashlight, which I'd left behind in the gondola. I did have my Zippo, but unlike a flashlight it wouldn't be much use held between my teeth, so I was going to have to climb down this tree in total darkness. Before I unbuckled myself from the harness, I searched with my foot for a supportive crotch between bough and trunk, and it wasn't until then that I realized my left boot was gone. I hadn't had time to lace it up before bailing out of the airship and it must have slipped off in the helter-skelter.

I started down the tree. A fall was more or less inevitable, but I managed to put it off for a while. Then a branch snapped off in my hand and I toppled backward out of the tree. But it was no more than fifteen feet down to the damp forest floor, the necessary epilogue of the four hundred.

Grunting with pain, I got to my feet. If I could reach the closest tributary of the Río Patuca, past the Pozkito dam, I could probably catch a boat to San Esteban. That would require me to make a wide loop around the guerrilla training camp to minimize the risk of running into one of their patrols. Trimble, who knew the terrain, could have guided me to safety, but I had no means of finding him.

I hobbled a short distance into the darkness, so that I wouldn't be directly underneath the black parachute draped across the trees. Then I sat down and rested until the sun began to rise on a purged and polished sky. I'd been to the Guaniguanico hills and the Petén lowlands and the Del Norte coast and of course Vansaska's bungalow, but I'd never before been pulled so deep into what the pulp magazines used to call the green inferno. This certainly wasn't my favored zone of operation, but the better I understood it the better I could traverse it, so despite all my aches and itches I tried to turn my concentration outward, to become a TBX receiver, to tune in to all the sounds and the smells, the covert radio broadcasts and propaganda campaigns and diplomatic cables that saturated every frequency of the rain forest. I also listened pretty hard for men with guns who might be coming to kill me.

After four or five hours, when it was light enough that I thought I might be able to distinguish leather from wood, I got up to empty my own ballast tank against the tree. Immediately my holster fell off. Checking the strap, I saw that one of the buckles had snapped, so I threw away the holster and stuffed my gun Mexican-style into the front of my waistband. Then I went off in search of my left boot.

I scanned down on the ground and up in the branches, starting along the path of my windfall, as best I could reconstruct it, and working outward from there. But I couldn't find the fucking thing. My time was limited, because it was idiotic to stay so close to the parachute that marked my location like a pennant. And I was using stamina that I would need later. The storm had wickered the forest floor with dead branches, so that while I was searching my sock was reduced to tatters, and so was the dressing under that, and so was the scab under that. Also, I had to pull out a thorn that impaled my heel like a caltrop. My colleague Don Sturgis claimed to have trekked barefoot through the Burmese jungle for eight days in 1946. Adjusting for his usual hyperbole, he was probably talking about a long afternoon. Regardless, whether or not it was feasible in principle, what seemed to me much more likely in this case was that without a shoe I'd just get slower and slower until I couldn't take another step. But I had no choice but to try. I took off my shirt, ripped off the right sleeve, knotted the sleeve around my sobbing ulcer, and put the shirt back on. That spite worm had really made its point.

Then I heard whistling.

Although I didn't recognize the tune, it sounded to me like an air on a jazz scale. I dropped to a crawl and moved toward it as quietly as I could.

Between the tree trunks there came into view a boy, Caucasian, digging up what might have been a cassava. I knew that both American camps sent out dozens of gardeners, foragers, hunters, and trappers every day. This one was around fourteen or fifteen and dressed in a style that was familiar from my first sight of Droulhiole.

Most importantly, he was wearing handmade leather sandals, and he had big feet for his age. When opportunity knocked, you had to be ready to rob it at gunpoint.

But as I reached for my semiautomatic, I recalled Droulhiole's wonderment at my Zippo. If this boy had also been born here at the temple, the crack of rifle fire echoing across the hills would be familiar to him, but he never would have seen so much as a picture of a pistol. Unless I were able to screen for his benefit a short educational film on the principles of gunpowder propulsion, he would have no reason to be afraid of my shiny tube. And I didn't have even a pinch of benzoic oxymorphone.

Instead, I tossed a handful of sticks so they clattered against a tree over the boy's head. As he looked up, I picked up a heavy broken bough in both hands like a baseball bat, and sprang forward out of cover. I was just about to swing when somebody shouted "Hey!" and grabbed me from behind.

Whoever he was, this guy was big, so big that it was embarrassing not to have noticed he was in the vicinity. The zbyszko wrenched the bough out of my hands and at the same time clamped me across the shoulders. Restrained like that, I couldn't turn around or raise a pistol, so instead I reached for my pocketknife, flicked it open one-handed, and thrust it backward into his thigh. He yowled, and I broke out of his hold—right into the boy's fist under my nose. The punch, which threw me off balance, wasn't bad for a beginner, but then his friend, as if to say "Here, kid, watch how it's really done," pulled me around to deliver an uppercut so hard it could have given my lumber barge a concussion.

What woke me was emerging from the forest into the unobstructed sunlight of the temple clearing. I still didn't know the coordinates of my parachute landing, but they must have been carrying me for quite a while to get here. The boy had my feet and the zbyszko had me under the armpits, so I was facing forward. Never before had I seen the temple in the daytime. And right away I became concerned that for the last several months I had been devoting myself to securing control of an insane asylum.

The atmosphere of the site reminded me of the Lovelinch Institute crossed with the Goree State Farm. We were approaching from the north, so the temple faced us with its flat looming middle. Though I was still woozy, I could see at once that the whole Eastern Aggregate camp was arranged in reference to the temple. By that I don't just mean that, self-evidently, if the temple hadn't been there, the camp wouldn't have been there either. By that I mean that the infrastructure of the camp—not only its cabins and sheds but also its stools and firepits and water butts—expressed an attitude of obsessive, almost worshipful concentration on this wall that kept nothing in and nothing out, this cliff that gave shadow but no shelter, this huge, inert, purposeless blockage, as if, for the residents, it was more fundamental to their balance than the sky or the horizon. Through the camp moved men, women, and quite a few children, in their blurred simulacra of American clothing and haircuts. Like Kubie's patients they seemed to have disappeared beyond rescue into the mysteriously significant world they had made.

Yet, as I observed them heating water or butchering meat or clearing storm debris or performing various small tedious actions that might have involved braiding or peeling or grinding or whittling, I could detect even from this distance an earnestness, an absorption, a gravity, and I realized that if all this was a derangement, it was a derangement I respected. They had held on for eighteen years, not only these New Yorkers but also the Angelenos living up there on the most geometrically inconvenient surface imaginable (assuming there wasn't some lost Mayan torus or hyperboloid even deeper in the jungle). I would have been proud to count myself capable of the same. After all, what was it about the pyramids and wats of dead civilizations that inspired such admiration in the tourist, if not the sense of an entire population neglecting its own immediate needs to labor in service of an idea?

I could feel my gun still in my waistband, the butt under my shirt. My porters hadn't searched me, or at least not very well.

An epidemic of double takes spread through the camp as they carried me down a central thoroughfare. Everyone who saw me broke off from their work to stare. On my left I observed a cabin with a row of clothed dummies on its veranda like a tailor's shop, and on my right about half a dozen banquet tables on wooden decking with a stage at the far end like a nightclub. "He's awake," said the zbyszko. "Drop him." The boy did so, after which I was manipulated until I was down on my knees. "Get the boss." The boy ran off. As a reporter for the *New York Evening Mirror,* I'd never actually met Elias Coehorn Jr., but I'd seen him around, so I knew to expect a less Jewish version of the radio crooner Frank Parker.

Except that the guy who arrived next, at the head of an entourage of four (including the boy), was not Coehorn. He was around forty, and he had what I recognized as a certain kind of authoritative ex-military bearing, that of the discharged officer who has no intention of walking around like a clockwork drummer boy for the rest of his life but is nonetheless capable of growing about a foot in height and clipping a march into his step whenever he feels like some of the old postural equipment might be put to good use. "Who are you?" he asked. "Where did you come from?" He had a German accent. Only his gappy teeth detracted from his impressiveness.

"I prefer to shake hands when I introduce myself," I said, "but this lug isn't giving me the chance. You run this place?"

"Of course he does," said the zbyszko. "Answer Herr Meinong's questions." He gave my arms a yank.

Meinong held up a gentling palm. "I merely assist Mr. Coehorn where I can," he said, in a tone connoting a polite fiction. "You're American?"

"Correct." I was irritated, if not particularly surprised, to find out that Trimble had been lying to me. In his accounts of the power structure of the two camps, no Herr Mcinong had ever been mentioned.

"You were on the aircraft that crashed in the jungle last night, I think?" Meinong said. "The soldiers shot you down." He didn't have the accent of the immigrant German who learned English in America, but of the educated German who learned it in *Gymnasium.* By now we were ringed by gawkers, standing well back.

I nodded. "That's why I hope you can forgive the misunderstanding I had with your friends here. Fraught circumstances, rash actions. You know how it is. But it wasn't at all the first impression I wanted to make. Because, from what I know of your situation out here, I believe I can be of some help."

Meinong licked his lips, making a calculation. "Gag him," he said. The order was so abrupt that no one seemed to understand it right away. "One of you. Get a rag—anything. Gag him. Right away, please."

There was a fuss of activity in the entourage. I wondered why Meinong wanted this interrogation to end before it even began.

Then I remembered Trimble's references to the "German-American Alliance." And I formed a pretty compelling theory. "But I've got so much to tell you all," I said. "I have word from back home."

At that, the fuss halted, and even the guy I'd recently stabbed let his grip on my arms relax. Before me I saw ravenous expressions. Only three of them looked so desperate for news from outside, though. Not the boy, who was merely curious. And not Meinong, who was merely agitated.

"I know you haven't had any other visitors for a while," I added. "Not since Herr Meinong, late of the 'German-American Alliance,' turned up here in the tropics. In around '45 or '46. Have I got that right?"

Meinong asked, "Did you search him?"

I jerked both my hands free, drew my Browning, and shot him point-blank in the face.

I knew the instant the gun went off that I'd been irresponsible. Not because I felt any uncertainty whatsoever about Meinong: I had seen in his reaction that he knew that I knew what he was. Only because it would have been more productive to hold him at gunpoint instead.

But it was an instinct over which I could exert no discipline. Many of my colleagues, after the war, had been perfectly happy to recruit any surviving Nazi who had military or scientific intelligence to offer, as long he was willing to promise that he did not intend to establish a Fourth Reich within the current fiscal year. Not me, though. Not ever. In Europe with OSS, I'd seen a few things.

My hope was that anybody who'd watched it happen would be too surprised to react immediately. And indeed, as I took off running toward a gap in the ring of spectators, nobody moved fast enough to stop me. I was heading for the tree line, and I thought I would make it easily.

Then I passed a cabin and found myself face-to-face with four guys. Two carried spears and two carried bows and arrows. A hunting party.

"Stop him!" came the yell.

I had no choice but to veer left, even though that was toward the temple. An arrow swished past my head. I was running so fast I smashed straight into a bamboo rack on which an animal skin was being dried or stretched, but it slowed me down only for a moment.

Nobody was paralyzed by shock any longer. In fact, glancing back over my shoulder, I saw villagers were converging on me from every direction. Even if I tried to round the temple right at the corner, I would be blocked. I hadn't expected them to be so efficiently synchronized, but then again, these were people who had hunted peccary through the rain forest with Bronze Age weapons for the last eighteen years. I was going to be trapped against the temple's blank wall, and I only had twelve rounds left in my magazine.

Some sort of heavy rigging ran up the full height of the temple. At the bottom was a wooden pallet, with two barrels on it, under ropes stretched taut from each of the four corners to a knot in the middle. At the top, another pallet, also loaded. That gave me an idea. But not a good one.

I spun around. About forty defensive ends were about to pile on the quarterback. There was only one direction I could go. So I made for those barrels.

I had never really understood how pulleys and blocks and tackles worked. But an elevator attendant at the Waldorf-Astoria had once explained to me the principle of counterweights, in the most general terms, years before, when I was whiffled. And that's what I was relying on when I stepped onto the pallet and pushed both barrels over.

Water flooded out of the barrels as they rolled onto the ground. And the pallet, relieved of its weight, creaked into the air.

Hoping to the bottom of my heart that I had given that elevator attendant a good tip, I dropped to a prone position on the pallet. If I got to the top, maybe I could ask for asylum with the other camp.

I'd assumed the counterweight would plunge at more or less the rate of free fall, and my pallet would rise up the temple at the same pace, but in fact the ascent was far too leisurely for comfort. Maybe there was some sort of brake on the rope to prevent either pallet from gaining too much speed before it hit the ground. Still, mine was going in the right direction.

At first the archers below sent arrow after arrow rapping at the bottom of the pallet. But then they started aiming for the rope over my head. A few arrows bounced down around me, and these I snapped in half and threw over the side. The quantity seemed to be easing off, though, perhaps because it was too dangerous to collect them for reshoots while they were still falling from the sky like bullets at a Serbian wedding.

Then, when I was about halfway up the side of the temple, an arrow sliced through one of the ropes connecting the corners of the pallet to the hook. I had to throw all my weight to the opposite corner so that the pallet didn't tip me off the side.

Now I was eighty feet from the top of the temple and they still hadn't made another lucky shot. Seventy feet. Sixty feet. This whole mission had been a treatise on altitude and podiatry.

An arrow notched the rope just above the knot. It held, but the last fibers were screaming in agony. I couldn't keep my weight on this pallet any longer.

I stepped sideways off the pallet and onto the temple itself. Disencumbered, the pallet bumped against the limestone as it lifted past me. I started to climb.

The muscles I'd developed climbing rock faces in the Valle de Viñales had not completely atrophied. And, like anything torn in half, this side of the temple was so ragged that the limestone was generous with handholds and footholds. But it had a damp coat of moss. Except for my right boot, my hands and feet were bare and sweaty. And I was in too much haste to test each hold. I couldn't have given odds on whether I would slip before I was hit by an arrow, but either way I knew I had no realistic chance of covering the whole forty vertical feet. It would be extremely frustrating, I thought, if I didn't live to tell McKellar this story, which was already one of my better ones.

An arrow took off the top of my left ear. I kept climbing.

And then I found the gap.

It wasn't just an especially luxurious handhold—it was so tall and wide and deep that I could fit my shoulders in there. If it wasn't an escape, it might at least be a foxhole. I hauled myself inside.

I smelled a musty odor like soil and truck exhaust, without the tang of guano you would have expected. I squirmed forward until both of my feet were inside with me. Blood was streaming from my ear so I tried to pinch the skin closed. For a little while I lay there getting my breath back. Next time I was in Foggy Bottom I would have to apply to the Technical Services Division for a new body. This one would cost more to repair than it would to replace.

In the dungeon light from the entrance I could see that this wasn't just an alcove. In fact, it looked like it widened as it sloped down into the innards of the temple.

I couldn't go back. So I went forward. "Suppose that there were a machine whose structure produced thought, sensation, and perception," Leibniz writes in the *Monadology,* "we could conceive of it as increased in size with the same proportions until a man was able to enter into its interior, as he would into a mill . . ."

೧

Do you know where you are?
No.

Do you know what year it is?
It's either 1956 or 1959. It could be that it's 1956 and I'm having a vision of something that will happen in 1959. Or it could be that it's 1959 and I'm having a flashback to something that happened in 1956. I can't tell.

What's the very last thing you remember happening to you?
There are two very last things. The last thing I remember in
1959 is licking the film. For almost twenty-four hours before
that I'd been writing my memoir. I didn't sleep, I didn't eat, I
just sat in my apartment and typed. I was so frightened that I
might have murdered Frieda that I put myself into a fugue of
nostalgia so I wouldn't have to think about it. I shut off the
present and went back to writing about the past. My own past
this time, nobody else's. The years I chose, they were the years
when I was still free, still dauntless, still a hero to myself. But
they were also the years when I made the decisions that led
to this terminus.

I started with my first meeting with Wilson, but then I realized I'd better explain what we learned when we interrogated
Tapscott. From there I kept writing in more or less chronologi-
cal order until, in my narrative, I was inside the temple, about
to inhale the fungus for the first time.

I wanted to remind myself exactly what that felt like. And
I had a few crumbs of fungus there in front of me, on the
frames of film that I smuggled back from the warehouse. The
Halorite 1219 fire retardant is toxic. Meaning the fungus from
Honduras shouldn't have been able to survive, let alone grow,
while the film was sitting in that warehouse. But it did.

So right now I'm sitting at my desk. It's a few minutes since
I put those frames in my mouth, as if sucking tarnish off a
mirror. I'm talking to you, and at the same time I'm having
an extraordinarily vivid memory of going into that temple in
Honduras in 1956.

What's the last thing you remember in 1956?
I was crawling deeper and deeper into the temple, like that
blue spite worm boring into my foot. There was no light any
more, but I kept going. My fingers kept brushing metal. The
Mayans must have left a few trinkets behind. The metal had
something on its surface, though, a thin layer of something
spongy like mold. And I was starting to feel a change in my

consciousness. Of course, I'm exhausted, and torn up, and I probably have a zoo of infections in my blood. But it wasn't just that. I'm no beatnik, but I've smoked opium and hashish and sewing machine oil before, and maybe that's the best way to explain what it felt like when it started, except it also didn't feel like that in the least. It started to become so intense that I wasn't even sure whether I was still moving or whether I'd stopped somewhere.

So right now I'm in the temple. It's been a few minutes since I first felt something gritty in my lungs. I'm talking to you, and at the same time I'm having this extraordinarily vivid dream of sitting in some shithole of an apartment in Virginia in 1959. "Were I able to consider directly all that happens or appears to me at the present time," Leibniz says, "I should be able to see all that will happen to me or that will ever appear to me. This future will not fail me, and will surely appear to me even if all that which is outside of me were destroyed, save only that God and myself were left."

I think I'm in both years at once. Or maybe neither. It's as if, every time I ingest the fungus, that's a different entrance to the same place. The place where I am now.

There must be things you know in 1959 that you didn't know in 1956.
Yes. I know the fungus I found in the temple is an argyrophage, just like the medium of cinema. An organism that feeds on silver. I know it gives you knowledge that you couldn't have attained by any other means. Memories of events you weren't present for. Surveillance tapes of people's thoughts. That's why it's a spy's supreme fantasy, and it's what makes my memoir possible.

I also know that ten days after my airship crash, I woke up . . . or I will wake up . . . Let's use the present tense: I wake up in a sick bed in Wilson's embassy/brothel, just like Colby Droulhiole once did. I have no recollection of how I got there. Absolutely no recollection of how I got out of the temple, or how I evaded its inhabitants, or how I avoided the Pozkitos, or how I found my way to San Esteban. The conclusion I reach is that I must have done it all unconsciously. My intuition took control. The fungus made me capable of a kind of expert tactical sleepwalking, free from pain and fatigue and the cognitive bottleneck of conscious deliberation.

Wilson is anxious to know whether my employer, the firm of Letterblair, Handsom and Lowe, will compensate me reasonably for the injuries I have received in the course of performing my duties as a notary agent. He also asks whether I ever found Poyais O'Donnell, who still hasn't been seen in San Esteban. He is too tactful even to allude to the fact that several months ago I disappeared with Colby Droulhiole in the middle of the night, smashing a window as I left.

Reyna put all my belongings in a drawer when she undressed me. Among them is a fragment of silver armor, caked in living fungus, that I must have brought with me from the temple. So I have a sample.

The problem is that, when I wake up in that sick bed, I've forgotten the vision I'm having right now. I've forgotten everything I've learned from this mingling between 1956 and 1959. Otherwise all the decisions I make in the intervening years would be different.

Do you know who I am?
"If all that which is outside of me were destroyed, save only that God and myself were left . . ." I went into the temple and now I'm talking to somebody. Jeepers creepers, are you . . .
Are you one of the Pozkito gods?

No.
Just kidding! I know you're not. I don't believe in them. When Whelt went into the temple, he inhaled the spores from the fungus growing on the silver armor, he had a psychotropic experience, and he thought he'd dropped in on some deities.

He was always so proud of his rationalism, but the first time in his life he encountered something he couldn't immediately explain, he just lunged for the supernatural.

Thank you. I wanted to get a sense of your subjective condition. That will help prevent any misunderstandings between us. This is the first time in several days you've been so lucid and I'm very keen to make the most of it.
What the hell do you mean, lucid?

I'll ask you again: do you know where you are, Mr. Zonulet? Try to concentrate. Can you see this desk? Can you see that door? Can you see yourself in that mirror?
This isn't the desk I have in my apartment.

You're not in your apartment. You're in a psychiatric observation room in Camp Detrick in Maryland.
The mirror. That's a Fourth Wall, isn't it? It's one way. There are people behind it, watching us?

I want you to listen to me carefully. You are a research liaison working with Apex Chemical on behalf of the Office of Scientific Intelligence. Three weeks ago you removed a vial of Halorite 1219 without authorization from one of the laboratories here at Camp Detrick. We don't know what you were planning on doing with it. The vial broke inside your briefcase, and when you opened the briefcase you inhaled a huge dose of the drug.
Halorite 1219 is a fire retardant.

No, Mr. Zonulet, Halorite 1219 is not a fire retardant, it is a powerful experimental drug. And since you inhaled it you have been in a state of hallucinatory catatonia.
I'm with the Directorate of Operations, not OSI. I've never even been to Camp Detrick.

*Try to concentrate on what you see in this room. Try to con-
centrate on me and my voice. I'm your doctor. This is reality.
Everything is a fantasy. There is no temple. You've never been
to Honduras. None of these characters you've invented are real.*
Oh, I get it. This is an interrogation. Listen, buddy, I've read
the manual too. I know what you're doing. "The 'confusion
technique' is designed not only to obliterate the familiar but
to replace it with the weird."

*Throughout your account of the last twenty years there are
assertions both major and minor which stand in demonstrable
contradiction to the facts of history.*
You're talking to a veteran of OSS and CIA about "the facts
of history"? Come on. You may as well hang it up. This isn't
going to work.

*Actually, we are still very hopeful that your condition will
improve. We are considering a number of treatments. There's
a new procedure called the unilateral gradatorectomy. It's produced excellent results at other institutions in cases similar to
your own. It might be that you need only a straightforward surgery and afterward you will see the world clearly again. That
would be worth any side effects, wouldn't it?*
Now, say I did believe you were a Pozkito god. I'd conclude
you were trying to send me out of your temple screaming and
raving. But I think I know what's really happening. Yes, the
Halorite 1219 is the likely culprit here—that much we can
agree on. The fire retardant did something to the fungus on
the film. It queered the chemistry. If you looked at the spores
under a microscope you'd probably see they were all fucked
up like Hiroshima babies. That's why I'm having bad dreams
this time.

Please sit down, Mr. Zonulet.
Who's on the other side of that mirror? Who's watching me?
Hello in there!

Put down the chair. If you don't put it down immediately I will call for the guards to restrain you.
You'd better get out of the way. This is going to be all about the swing.

You've been in rooms like this before. You must know the Fourth Wall is unbreakable.
No harm in trying.

Put down the chair. Put it down. Hey, send someone in here! Send someone in before he—

The glass shatters.

Phibbs looks down and sees the pair of eyeglasses on the carpeted floor of the office, one lens crunched under his shoe. "Oh, I'm sorry about that, sir. Did Mr. Barry leave these behind?"

"He did," says Elias Coehorn Sr. His previous visitor, E. W. Barry, is the president of the Atlantic National Bank, and today, September 3rd, 1938, it has fallen to Coehorn to decide whether that institution should survive. During their interview just now, Barry did so much agonized fidgeting with the glasses in his lap that he bent them at the hinges. When he was getting ready to leave he put them back on, but as he rose from his chair they slipped off his head. Instead of stooping down to pick them up, he just wavered for a moment and then backed out of the room. If Coehorn read his defeated expression correctly, this was because Barry had come to feel that in the prevailing psychic atmosphere it was impossible for him to do anything whatsoever without first asking Coehorn for permission, and since he couldn't bring himself to ask permission to pick up his glasses, he had no choice but to leave them behind.

Now Phibbs deposits them in a wastepaper basket. "Are there any other matters to which you'd like me to attend in consequence of the meeting, sir?"

For a few minutes Coehorn gives detailed instructions. He has known for months, of course, that the Atlantic National Bank is rotten through its heartwood; most likely he knew before Barry did. The man had come here to beg him to save the tree. In fact, all he achieved was to alert Coehorn that this is the last possible moment to give the tree a gentle push. Thus he can determine the angle of its fall. Afterward he says, "What have you got for me?," referring to the document wallet under Phibbs's arm.

"Three items. First, this month's report from the inquisitors."

"Anything in it?"

"Nothing to speak of, no."

Coehorn has long since given up taking personal meetings with the Christian "visionaries" who offer their gifts to his Missionary Foundation. For years he harbored such high hopes for them, but in fact they have always been frauds, every single one of them, including those endorsed by pastors and deacons. Although his small team of trained inquisitors still conduct scientific interviews with the more plausible candidates in the tri-state area, even that has become a redundant measure. For Coehorn himself has now been blessed with the direct revelation that so many others only counterfeited.

When he was a young man, certain Bible passages already hummed on the page like telegraph wires bringing him a personal message—for example, the reassurance that if you pay your tithe to the church the Lord will "open to you the windows of heaven and pour out all the blessings you need" (Malachi 3:10), because the Lord too is economically rational. When Coehorn was still brewing pard liquor in Hershey, the Lord knew that his "tithe" would one day comprise one of the largest missionary foundations in the world and a program of church renovations across the United States. But evidently Coehorn's work is not yet done, because the Lord still has instructions for him. He doesn't hear them articulated in words, but in a concrete sense of mission that arrives from outside himself. Though there is no voice, the non-voice has its own timbre and he shudders with the holiness of it.

Outside the windows, a warm gray haze is draped over the tops of the nearby skyscrapers, which seen from this height have the disordered, jostling quality of shanties in a slum. "Next?" he says.

"The latest report on Master Whelt, sir."

Jervis Whelt. Twenty years old. A resident of Hollywood, Los Angeles. Elias Coehorn Sr.'s only son by blood. An error twice over.

The first error was the misallocation of seed. When Coehorn raped Arnold Spindler's wife, the woman herself was of no importance. Like a speaker in tongues, she was only a conduit for a word sent down from above, in this case a word of penalty. Coehorn was interfering with Spindler's property just as Spindler had interfered with Coehorn's, and he never bothered to look Spindler's wife in the face when he did it, any more than he met the eye of Elias Jr.'s pet dog when he broke its neck to punish the boy for persistent blasphemy. The rape was a performance for Spindler's benefit, nothing more. That the banal fact of anatomical conjunction might have substantive results would never have crossed Coehorn's mind. How absurd it now seems that he should have given his seed to his own wife Ada almost a dozen times in the course of their marriage without any procreative yield, and it only took one quite incidental jettison to put a child in Spindler's. Then again, it must be remembered that Spindler's wife was Jewish too, and a Jewess's loins will gorge on sperm like a bat sucking up nectar.

In 1918, Coehorn didn't yet realize that Ada had never actually borne him an heir. Here is the second error. The rape should never have taken place. Had he known at the time that Spindler's trespass inside her was not, as Ada so convincingly pleaded with all her theatrical training, a first instance there in the dressing room after the rehearsal, but in fact a regularity stretching back at least seven years—had he known, a hundred times worse, that Spindler had placed a cuckoo in his nest—then Coehorn would never have taken such a lenient measure as merely to rape Spindler's wife in front of him while he struggled and howled. Not until years later did he recognize his "son" as an interloper, and so not until then did he visit a more appropriate punishment on Spindler. He should never have been merciful in the first place. (Now, as Barry's broken glasses lie in his wastebasket like a carpal bone spat out after the devouring of a fresh kill, he knows he has not made that error since and never will again.)

The symmetry of Coehorn impregnating Spindler's wife just as

Spindler had already impregnated Coehorn's was on every level an accident. Whelt was a misbegetting based on a misallocation based on a misapprehension.

And yet the boy lives and Coehorn lives in him.

He knew nothing of Whelt's existence until four years ago, when the discovery was made in the following roundabout fashion. After Spindler's widow, residing by that time in La Jolla, California, died of breast cancer, agents from the Eastern Aggregate Good Conduct Division were sent to burglarize her house as a precaution. They removed any papers they could find whose absence would not be too conspicuous to her executors. No new information could be permitted to come to light that might complicate the job of the actor who had been posing as Arnold Spindler since the sabotage of Spindler's airship in 1929. Spindler had been exhaustively researched, of course. Through the plenitude of his Good Conduct Division dossier, which ran to thousands of pages, the man was more fully realized in death than most ordinary men are even in life. But it was still possible that some inconvenient new detail might scuttle out of the widow's house. What if it turned out that according to medical records, say, Spindler had once been told by his doctor that he was badly allergic to salicornia, and some very diligent reporter noticed that this stood in mysterious contradiction to the boxes of sea beans that were delivered to the kitchens of his Bel Air mansion every week of the summer? So the agents searched the widow's house overnight. And among the documents they removed was one suggesting that in 1919, about nine months after Coehorn raped her, she had signed over a male newborn to an orphanage in Hollywood.

Phibbs located the boy. And the instant Coehorn set eyes on a photograph of Jervis Whelt, he knew he was looking at a son. A genetic son, not like Elias Jr., whose face, when a belated puberty at last sieved some determinate features from the mush of his boyhood, was blatantly recognizable as an iteration of Spindler's. (Although Spindler, thank goodness, did not have a characteristic Jewish nose or hair, otherwise the situation would have been obvious to any onlooker.)

So the convention would be to say that Whelt is Coehorn's only son by blood. But there are other bloods. Name is blood. Faith is blood. Money is blood. The majority of Coehorn's legacy will be accomplishments of mind and spirit, not of animal fluids hand delivered. To privilege the latter above all else is ape-minded and profane, and he believes that, in the future, few among the American gentry will bother to conceive their own children. That Elias Jr. wasn't made in Coehorn's image is not in itself reason enough to disinherit him. After all, New York wasn't originally made in Coehorn's image either. He imposed his image on it and now he precedes the city's founders in importance if not in tenure.

Yet Ada's adulterine, raised since birth as a Coehorn, has thrown away that great gift, keeping only the gilt wrapping. As surely as he is a Spindler in his face, he is a Spindler in his character, which has drooped toward the fancy, the painted, the decadent, just like any theatrical. Elias Jr. is now twenty-six and Coehorn is more disgusted by him every year. Whereas Jervis Whelt, by all accounts, delights in hard work and self-improvement. He is obsessed with motion pictures, yes, and not much of a Christian, but that's because he had the misfortune to grow up a mile south of Sunset Boulevard.

While the cuckoo wastes Coehorn's money and joyrides his name, the bastard is kept ignorant of his origins. To this extent the Coehorn inheritance is confused. But soon it must be settled for good. He built Eastern Aggregate to perdure beyond a mortal lifetime. Rome fell when the empire ceased to expand, but this empire must expand forever. There are other empires—not just Rockefeller and Mellon and Ford, the usual idiots, but darker empires, secret empires—and when they press up against his borders, his borders must press back harder.

He needs a successor.

Either he must extend his twenty-six-year investment in the child who came out of his late wife, who is known by society as his son, who even now could perhaps be trained into a worthy heir if he were taken away from the city and confined for a number of years in a strict corrective setting; or he must upturn the whole business and summon a young Angeleno to the throne, acknowledging the slip-slop of patrimony for all to gawk over.

He flips through the report. There has been no change in Whelt's circumstances. He's still teaching evening classes about motion pictures at the Hancock Park Technical High School. In each of the classes an agent from the Good Conduct Division has been placed undercover as a student, although those agents have been told nothing about Whelt except that he is a person of interest to the company. Coehorn understands that, in Hollywood, people don't expect to advance by enterprise and virtue, they expect to be "noticed" or "discovered," to be raised from the dust to sit with the kings. No doubt Whelt has the sense to resist this fantasy, and yet funnily enough it describes just what will happen if Coehorn chooses him over Elias Jr.

His most recent instructions from on high have alerted him that he mustn't prevaricate any longer. "The Lord rewarded me according to my righteousness" (Psalms 18:20), because the Lord, like capitalism, is concerned with the proper allocation of resources and opportunities. The parable of the prodigal son might seem superficially relevant here, and likewise the Deuteronomic law of the inheritance of the firstborn, but in truth neither has any direct application in this case. Coehorn has become convinced that he must take his model from Solomon, not the famous story about the disputed baby but his general method. The Lord wants him to find some means of testing one almost-son against the other almost-son. This competition, whatever it is, will need to take place somewhere far from New York or Los Angeles, so that each of them will start on equal footing and nobody else will interfere until it is over.

He looks up. "You said there was a third item."

Phibbs puts the last file down on the desk. "I wasn't quite sure whether this warranted your attention, sir, but it is a rather singular occurrence. Here is an image we received by wirephoto from La Ceiba in Spanish Honduras. As you know, your foundation operates a mission station near a small town in the northeast called San Esteban. Three days ago a pair of French archaeologists arrived at this mission station requesting water and medical aid. After this was provided, they reported that deep in the jungle, near one of the tributaries of the Río Patuca, about fifty miles inland from the

Caribbean Sea, they had been astonished to come across . . . I'm extremely sorry, sir, but there appears to be something in your ear." From the leather instrument pocket sewn into the interior of his suit jacket, Phibbs takes a tiny pair of tweezers. "If I may . . . ?"

He leans over and plucks me out of Coehorn's ear. Before he can drop me into the wastepaper basket next to the glasses, his employer raises a hand. "I want to see what it was." So instead Phibbs places me on the desk with the care of a jeweler presenting a gemstone, and indeed my blue cuticle stands out with a sapphirine glint against the somber tones of the office as I lie there wriggling on the blotter.

"Have you ever seen one of these before?" Coehorn says.

"Not to my recollection."

"How the blazes did it get in my ear?"

For once Phibbs has no answer.

"Better kill it before you throw it away. Might get out again."

As fast as I can I try to squirm away from the tweezers, but the distance to the edge of the desk is fifty times the length of my body. Holding me over the wastepaper basket by my midsection, Phibbs increases the pressure on the tweezers just enough to—

When I woke up I was face down on my typewriter. My mouth was dry, my body drenched in sweat.

"You're awake. Good timing. I've just finished your manuscript."

I looked up. Meredith Vansaska sat in the arm chair by the window, a stack of typewritten pages on her lap.

PART FOUR

I saw the populous sea, saw dawn and dusk, saw the multitudes of the Americas, saw a silvery spider-web at the center of a black pyramid . . .

(From "The Aleph" by Jorge Luis Borges, trans. Andrew Hurley)

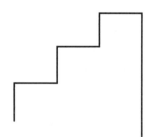

IN CUBA THEY BELIEVED THAT IF YOU HAD A FEVER YOU SHOULD ROLL some fingernail clippings into a cigarette and drop the cigarette at a crossroads without looking left or right. Whoever picked it up would also take your fever from you. Seeing Vansaska, I felt like I must have smoked her cigarette. The last time I'd seen her, three years ago in her bungalow in Silver Lake, she'd been soggy and abject, a charity case. Now we'd changed places. How she had looked to me back then, that was probably just how I looked to her today, whereas she'd recovered all of her considerable poise. She wore a gray wool suit, cut very slim, perhaps not untainted by recent French notions, with nylon tape at the seams and glass buttons in a wishbone pattern down the front of the jacket.

"How many brothers did Frieda have?" she said.

"What?"

"In one place you say she has two brothers, in another place you say she has three. Did you make a mistake or did she?"

I thought about it. "Well, fuck me. She contradicted herself. Odd thing to contradict yourself about."

"Has it ever crossed your mind that she might not have been who she said she was? That she might have been some kind of plant?"

"Not for a second. Not until now."

"Could somebody have staged that murder film just to make you think you'd lost your mind?"

I was serving a life sentence in the prison of "all the available evidence," with no hope of release by any means other than terminal hepatocellular dysfunction. I hadn't left Springfield, Virginia, in months. I was comprehensively defeated. Why should my opponents bother to launch such an elaborate psychological-warfare operation against me? It was a long way to go to discompose a guy who was already pretty discomposed.

But several times in my career at the agency I had gone even further to achieve even pettier aims. I thought of the hallucination from which I'd just surfaced. The interrogation, the Fourth Wall, the story about an OSI research liaison with delusions. Perhaps it hadn't been so malign after all. Perhaps it was more like a dream with a message, urging me to keep faith in my own sanity.

Frieda had claimed that McKellar sent her to me. I recalled Winch saying, "College girls aren't as innocent as they used to be." At the time, I'd taken it for an oblique acknowledgment of the favor he'd done me, sending over a pretty twenty-year-old to help me polish the family silver. If that was the case, then surely he must have been complicit in the scheme. My former best friend, my former closest ally against Branch 9, had betrayed me.

But another possibility, I now realized, was that he was trying to warn me not to trust her.

And a third possibility was that he genuinely had no foreknowledge of her existence, his joke had been nothing but a pleasantry, and her mention of his name had been another lie. I tried to recall his exact intonation, but Vansaska interrupted: "I ought to sock you, by the way." She gestured down at the manuscript. "You knew everything. And when you came to see me in Silver Lake you wouldn't even throw me a fucking scrap. No matter how much it would have meant to me."

I shrugged. "I couldn't. I'm sorry. And I didn't know everything. I still don't."

"You know a hell of a lot about me and my life. You got almost all of it right. And I'm supposed to believe this was because a fungus made you see things?"

"Do you have a better explanation?"

"Not to hand. I hope you admire my dedication, reading every damn page of this. Where did you learn to write this way? A guy whose apartment looks how this apartment looks, you don't expect him to be secretly addicted to ornamentation. What would Bev have said about all these frills? Don't you realize simile is a form of paranoia? Proposing a connection between two things because you, and only you, can make out some hidden correspondence in the manner of their operation? Also, it must be as long as *Moby-Dick* already, and you're not even close to finishing the story."

"It is not as long as *Moby-Dick*."

"You introduce this person Phibbs at the beginning and we're expected to remember who he is about ten thousand pages later?" She groaned. "I'm a reporter with a very retentive memory, and I read it in one sitting, and I still had to flip back and check. That's just one example of many. I hope the hardcover will have an index."

"The only other person who was ever supposed to read this—"

"—is the junior from the Office of Security who will have to go through your things after you die. Sure. But I don't believe this book is just a curse on anyone who disturbs your tomb. It's obvious you've taken some pride in it. Deep down I bet you hope it gets discovered—leaked—published—lauded in *The New York Times*."

I got up and went into the kitchen, where I poured a glass of water, drank it straight down, and poured another one to bring back with me. "How d'you get in here?"

"You left your door unlocked."

"That was you in the Bel Air," I said. "Parked there most of the week."

"Yes."

"What were you watching me for?"

"I was told you'd been put out to pasture," Vansaska said. "I found that hard to believe. I thought it might be a cover. I was going to watch you long enough to verify to my satisfaction the truth of your depressing life here—no offense. So I saw you had a routine, but when you stopped leaving your apartment I became a little concerned."

"Why should you care if this is a cover?"

"I needed to decide whether I could trust you. If you were still enmeshed in your agency, I probably couldn't."

"And what do you need to trust me with?"

"You know you were talking in your sleep?" Vansaska said. "I thought if you talked in your sleep they didn't let you become a spy."

"I wasn't asleep. I was just somewhere else."

"Even in your sleep you sound full of yourself."

"What do you need to trust me with?"

Vansaska produced a sheet of paper from her jacket and handed it to me. Unfolding it, I saw that it was a photostat of an agency memorandum marked "S-E-C-R-E-T." "Who gave this to you?" I said.

She told me, but I'm not going to write the name down here.

July 3rd, 1958

MEMORANDUM FOR: Deputy Director of Intelligence

SUBJECT: Summary of REMOTER's movements since 1935

1. In 1935 Dr. Sidney Bridewall, a Cambridge University ethnologist, encountered REMOTER at the temple site during an expedition to Honduras. REMOTER coerced Bridewall into arranging his passage to the United States, with the logistical support of Poyais O'Donnell, a fixer operating in San Esteban and Tegucigalpa.

2. According to O'Donnell, REMOTER took up residence in Red Hook, Brooklyn. Apart from that, nothing is known about REMOTER's activities in the interim period before Branch 9 first made contact with him in 1953. As a sweetener during negotiations with United Fruit, Branch 9 installed REMOTER in a residential suite at the Waldorf-Astoria Hotel in Manhattan.

3. In the aftermath of the events in northeastern Honduras in late 1957, REMOTER was found to have quit the Waldorf-Astoria. All subsequent efforts to establish his whereabouts have been unsuccessful. Analysts at Branch 9 believe he is likely to have returned to Honduras, but no word of him has reached our stations there.

"Who is REMOTER?" Vansaska said.

"That's what you came here to ask me?"

"I hoped you might know."

I shook my head. Because of my latest excursion with the fungus, there were things I knew now that I hadn't known a day earlier, a vast supplementary chronicle of events at the temple between 1956 and 1959. I felt as if my temporal lobes were running red hot with the effort to house it all, and I was looking forward to getting some of it down on paper simply to relieve the pressure. But that code name still brought nothing useful to mind. "Sorry you wasted a trip. Your source couldn't tell you?"

"No. You write in here that Tapscott mentioned REMOTER when you questioned him in Havana."

"Yeah, but all he knew was the name, same as you. Then McKellar found out a little more, but not enough."

Vansaska sighed. "Have you got anything to eat? I skipped lunch waiting for you outside the doors of perception."

"Well, I had a bit of trouble finding the latch," I said. "I have cornflakes, but I think the milk's sour. Some lemons. Maybe a little anchovy paste."

"Can we go out and eat, then?"

"They probably already know you're here talking to me, but even so, I'm not going out with you in public for no good reason." However, I was hungry myself. "I'll drive over and get carry-out from the diner. What do you want?"

"What do you usually get?"

"The hamburger."

"Is it good?"

"It's terrible."

She shrugged. "Fine."

As I was leaving, she said, "Why do you get so much mail?"

"I don't. I just gave up opening it. So it piles up."

"Shall I go through it for you? Zonulet, even when I'm at my lowest, I still open my mail."

"The last girl who did my clerical work gave her notice a little abruptly. So, sure, I guess I could use a temp."

Outside, the sky was violet over Springfield. These were the hours before dinner when all the boys and girls came out, on foot or on bicycles, never stopping to play but always in motion, aswirl around the wide leafy streets, yipping and voracious, so you felt they might swarm and devour any grown-up who hadn't had the good sense to lock himself indoors. Nevertheless, I survived my mission to the diner, and, back at the apartment, I hadn't even shut the door behind me before Vansaska shoved some paper in my face. "Look at this!"

Dropping the bag of food on the side table, I obeyed. First I examined the envelopes, of which there were two. The larger envelope had American stamps and was addressed to my apartment in Springfield, and the smaller envelope had Honduran stamps and was addressed to the offices of Letterblair, Handsom and Lowe in New York. In other words, the letter had been sent on to me by the forwarding service at the address I used when I was undercover.

Then I examined the contents of the inner envelope. There was a letter and a card. The letter was from Wilson.

April 15th, 1959

Manager's Office
Le Sphinx
San Esteban
Honduras

Esteemed chum,

I'll begin by explaining the address at the head of this letter. You remember I told you that when I first arrived in San Esteban, Tussmann was running the American consulate here and he needed a man who spoke good English so I took a job. Then when he died I stepped into his shoes. I was the first to admit the situation wasn't quite official but the Department of State wouldn't answer any of my letters. Well, the November before last, I finally had the opportunity to make enquiries in person, because there happened to be a number of chaps from your foreign service making a staging post of our little town. (From what I gathered there had been some sort of brouhaha in the jungle relating to an Indian ruin, rather a lot of dead, these Americans busy tidying up afterward, but that's by the by.) You'll never guess what they told me. There isn't, and never has been, an American consulate in San Esteban. So venerable Tussmann was operating it on spec, as it were, just like me. What an enterprising fellow! His reasons must remain an enigma, but perhaps he wanted a fresh start, as so many of us have at one time or another, and he had some very particular ideas about what that fresh start should entail. At any rate, once the veil of ignorance had been pierced, I felt I could no longer in good conscience introduce myself as the American consul. So I am now merely the proprietor of an establishment we've christened Le Sphinx, after the place in Paris. Quite an appropriate narrowing of purview, in a sense, because wasn't it Tocqueville who once said, "In America, a diplomacy of courtesans has not yet . . ."

That's as much as I seem to have of it just now but no doubt you can finish it off yourself.

Now, the purpose of this missive is to enclose the enclosed. The last time I saw Poyais O'Donnell, who these days is in San Esteban at least half the time, I asked him, just out of friendly curiosity, if he'd ever seen any sort of windfall from that business with the Irish inheritance, because I assumed it must all have been resolved by now, but he didn't know what I was talking about, and had never heard of you. So even after all this time you still haven't caught up with the blighter! Of course, it may very well be that the matter is closed, but in case on the contrary you remain in tireless pursuit like Culhwch after Trwyth (to put it in fittingly Celtic terms), I thought I'd draw your attention to an occasion at which Mr. O'Donnell can hardly fail to appear. I don't know much about the lady except that her clan is bally rich. No doubt there will be rumors that he is marrying her for her money. Well, what of it? My own father was always quite open about his motives in that quarter, even in front of guests, and I felt it perfused our household with a bracing atmosphere of straightforwardness and pragmatism. For that matter

Putting Wilson's letter aside, I turned to the card.

GENERAL AND SEÑORA JUAN GONZALEZ
REQUEST THE HONOR OF YOUR PRESENCE
AT THE MARRIAGE OF THEIR DAUGHTER
JOSEFA CANDIDA
TO
MR. POYAIS O'DONNELL
ON SATURDAY THE FIRST OF JULY
AT TWELVE O'CLOCK
AT THE LOS DOLORES CHURCH
IN THE CITY OF TEGUCIGALPA

Meredith Vansaska here.

It's after midnight, Zonulet is snoring, and I am writing this by hand on the back of his typescript. He has already put down so much of my history in here that I may as well cut out the middleman.

I was unpacking the carry-out bag on his kitchen table while he read the invitation. He still has a bullish physique, but since I last saw him there has been an alteration, or at least a modulation, in the way he holds himself: he is watchful still, in his face and in his posture, for you can never take that out of a man with his experience, but now it is a watchfulness that scans without expectation a foggy blank horizon, a watchfulness resigned to nothing much to watch for and even less to do about it. I almost wish I could have been here when he really thought he might have murdered that girl, if only because I might have got a look at his old hectic self. "That wedding is the day after tomorrow," I said. "If we go to Tegucigalpa, we can find Poyais O'Donnell, and he can tell us who REMOTER is. This could break the whole thing open, finally."

"In '56, after I got that tip from Tapscott, I spent three weeks in San Esteban waiting around for O'Donnell to arrive. He never did. I felt like a fool. You really think I'm going to go chasing after him again?"

(I still have, as I mentioned to Zonulet, a retentive memory, but nevertheless this must be understood as a reconstruction. I am not going to pretend, like him, that I deal in transcripts.)

"He'll be at that church," I said. "Most likely he's already in Tegucigalpa. Listen, according to your masterwork it was Poyais O'Donnell who supplied the extras for *Hearts in Darkness* in '38, and also the laborers for Eastern Aggregate, except he tried to sell the same natives to both sides. He's been involved in all this from the beginning. There probably aren't a lot of people alive who can identify REMOTER. And most of those people work for the CIA, and even if they don't, we don't know their names. But we know O'Donnell's name, and we know exactly where he'll be this weekend. Don't you want to interview him?"

Zonulet came over to the table. "Not if it means going all the way to Honduras."

"Three years ago, you sat on my bed and told me you'd take me to the tropics any time I wanted."

"That was before the tribunal. If I leave the country while the proceedings are still under way, they'll tell me I've forfeited all kinds of rights. They'll have my ass when I get back. That's just what they want."

"Are you sure about that?"

"Why wouldn't I be?" Instead of meeting my eye he took a bite of his hamburger.

I took a bite of mine. I must have grimaced. "This is ungodly."

"This is better than usual. Why don't you just go down there on your own?"

"I need your help. You've been to Tegucigalpa before. I don't even speak Spanish."

Neither of us was being entirely frank. I don't need his help. I can go and find O'Donnell on my own. Yes, it will run more smoothly if he comes with me. But that is not why I want him to. I want him to come with me because if I can get him out of this apartment, out of that warehouse, I believe I will have done a good thing.

Two objections might be raised here, both of them appeals to symmetry.

When he invited me to go to the jungle, I said no. So why should he say yes?

When he had the opportunity to help me, he did not. So why should I help him?

You might say he was trying to help me when he invited me to go to the jungle. And I will not dispute that he meant well. But he was asking a woman in the deepest trench of her depression to overcome, spontaneously, capriciously, an inner obstacle so fundamental that it stood not as a counterargument but as an axiom that preceded all arguments. "No. No. I cannot go to the jungle just now."

That invitation was not useful. What would have been useful, very useful indeed—and I know that he understood this because he says so in the typescript I am presently defacing—would have been to tell me something I didn't already know about *Hearts in Darkness*. That story was, and is, the sole nutrient on which my body seems capable of feeding. It is only due to the progress I have made on that story over the past few months that I now feel stronger than I have in many years.

That is what I mean when I say he had the opportunity to help me and did not. So, again, why should I help him?

Perhaps because it is important, sometimes, to show there is another way of doing things.

However, if I've conceded that back in Silver Lake in '56 I could not possibly have been persuaded to overcome my emotional block (to use a phrase that reminds me of a time when I could afford an analyst), then why should I expect Zonulet to be any more obliging now?

As I say: when we discussed it over hamburgers, I was not being honest about my reasons for asking him, and he was not being honest about his reasons for declining.

I said, "You don't want to go back to Honduras."

He did not answer.

I said, "In the letter, your friend Wilson says something happened at the temple the year before last."

He did not answer.

I said, "What happened at the temple? And what did you have to do with it?"

ℰ

Meinong had never been shot in the face before.

Later, what he would remember most vividly was not the impact or the pain—because he'd experienced those before, when he was almost killed under artillery bombardment at Weidesheim—but rather the extraordinarily disconcerting sensation of blood pouring into his mouth, out of the exit wound in the back of his head, and down the back of his neck. He lay helpless on the ground but he never lost consciousness, so he could hear the tumult as I ran off in the direction of the temple.

Right away he understood there were two paths he could take. In principle his authority here was guaranteed by wealth, but in practice, like all authority, it functioned in basically mythic terms. Now that the camp had witnessed him felled, he could either lie for weeks in the infirmary hut, a mere invalid praying for a minimum of sepsis and disfigurement; or he could rise like an immortal, speak in a voice louder than the report of that bullet, foreclose all doubt in the extremity of his response.

For some time now he had been enclosing the New York camp in his grasp. Ever since Trimble came to him in the forest and proposed a partnership.

That afternoon, eight months ago, he was out for a stroll. Far overhead, masking the breaks in the canopy, moths were making an immense migration in tattered black vortices and billows. Once again, his mind was on the question of how much longer to stay at the temple. Even now, an expedition might very well be on its way here from the United States. He had meant to intercept Colby Droulhiole just as he'd intercepted Walter Pennebaker a decade earlier. But he had failed, because he hadn't counted on the preternatural facility with which the boy moved through the jungle. Meinong's prey had escaped without ever knowing he was being pursued. So the seal on the outpost was broken. There were many other obstacles between here and Hollywood, of course, but if Droulhiole had even made it as far as San Esteban, then news of the Americans at the temple would at last have reached the outside world, and after that it was only a matter of time before Meinong's sanctuary was overrun.

Not that he needed it so badly any more. By now, Western capitalism would have moved on to some new crisis, the Jews would have wrung every last drop of sympathy from whatever exaggerated version of their hardships they had confected among themselves, and only the most intransigent political nostalgists would still be interested in prosecuting the misdemeanors of another era. Of all that he was confident. Even so, the revelation of the state of affairs here at the temple would be sure to attract a good deal of international publicity, and just to be safe he would prefer to slip away beforehand. Perhaps it was time to return to the Fatherland at last. Some new papers were all that would be required.

"Hey." A hiss from the trees.

Meinong turned, and Leland Trimble stepped out into the open.

He wore cotton socks and cotton underpants, with a pocked and scarified face and torso, long matted hair but not much of a beard. "Do you remember me?" he said. "If you don't, I won't take it personal. I was going out right when you were coming in."

Naturally, Meinong did recall Trimble's banishment, which had sent both camps into convulsions only days after he had first arrived here. Later, it would occur to him that this timing was one of the reasons why Trimble had chosen him as a confederate: Meinong had less acquaintance with Trimble, and therefore less hatred of him, than any other adult at the temple. Even Coehorn, who had opposed Trimble's expulsion at the time, had gradually soaked up the consensus opinion, and now talked as if he'd been wary of Trimble long before anyone else.

"I'm quite surprised to see you, Mr. Trimble," Meinong said. "I believe the general assumption was that you had gone a long way away from here."

"No, I decided to stick around." He didn't seem to be able to make continuous eye contact, but instead just flicked his gaze at Meinong every so often, like fingertips testing a hot stovetop.

"For ten years?"

"Would you believe it?" Smiling, Trimble nodded down at himself. "All that time and my suit still ain't back from the cleaners." In his right hand he held a bundle of rayon, which he now presented to Meinong. "Take a look at that, Mr. Meinong."

It was a large sum of Eastern Aggregate scrip. "You wish to buy something from me?" said Meinong, puzzled.

"No."

"Ah—perhaps you wish me to buy something on your behalf?"

"Snip snap, you got it in two," Trimble said. "Yeah, I want you to buy something. I want you to buy the temple." He smiled. "I'd do it myself, but I got a real peachy reunion planned with the old gang, and I don't like to be precocious. When Chick Bullock came back to one-night-only at the Lollipop for the first time in four years, you didn't see him working the coat check the evening before, if you see my meaning."

Meinong did not. Regardless, Trimble made his proposal. He claimed to have access to an unlimited source of Eastern Aggregate scrip, supplementary to, but indistinguishable from, the fixed quantity that had circulated around both camps over the years. Never in his conversation with Meinong did he acknowledge outright that almost everybody at the temple wished him dead, but plainly he was aware that he couldn't operate there in person. So he wanted to go into partnership with Meinong.

The current economic situation at the temple was the reverse of what it had been at the time of Trimble's departure. Back in 1946, the *Hearts in Darkness* camp was still in a long depression, whereas the Eastern Aggregate camp was in a condition of exuberant prosperity that could be traced all the way back to the punitive schedule of ransom payments they'd extracted in return for the release of the two men caught trying to steal ammonia from Coehorn's ice-making machine. In the multivalent amnesty that flowered from Trimble's exile, however, all debts were canceled, while trade between the two camps was liberalized and Eastern Aggregate scrip dollars gained in value after the Angelenos came to accept them as legal tender.

Over the ensuing period—as a year so prodigiously dry that the whole jungle seemed to brown at the edges passed into one as prodigiously wet—the economic standings of the camps swapped over yet again. After his descent into the temple, Whelt released from their obligations all of the *Hearts in Darkness* crew members who weren't involved in the manufacture of silver nitrate film. Since he was now more or less the sole contributor to the progress of the movie, it no longer made any difference to him whether the others were fed and clothed, so he willingly abdicated the last of his authority over his camp. Under Burlingame's unhindered leadership—which turned out to be surpassingly astute, conscientious, and decisive— the Angelenos thrived; whereas the New Yorkers still had Coehorn, more complacent than ever. Before long, the generous, even charitable terms of exchange that Burlingame offered were all that was keeping the Eastern Aggregate camp from famine. The tribe held together, but, within it, Coehorn was now an object of toleration at best, contempt at worst.

So Trimble's plan was sound. If you had the funds, you could establish as far-reaching and discreet an influence over the camp and its chief as the Rothschilds had over Great Britain and its prime ministers.

"How will you know I'm not just keeping the scrip for myself?" Meinong said.

"I'll be vigilating," Trimble said. "You won't see me, but you can be sure I'll be vigilating."

For the moment, Meinong decided, he would put aside his return to Germany.

The night after that unexpected meeting in the forest, he spoke to Coehorn, the two of them alone together in the presidential cabin, their faces lit by just one measly tallow candle. Meinong suggested a mutually beneficial arrangement. He told Coehorn he could subsidize him with enough scrip for the princeling to buy back his old majesty. In exchange, Coehorn would just have to follow a few instructions.

Meinong had anticipated that Coehorn might need some persuasion. When a man depends on an allowance well into adulthood, as Coehorn had, and then at last gains his own estate, as Coehorn had, he often makes some solemn pledge to himself along the lines of "From now on I shall be my own master and I shall answer to nobody." But the forty-four-year-old Elias Coehorn Jr. barely let Meinong finish before he agreed to the lease of himself.

After the payments began, the next stage was easy enough. Coehorn, for all his haughtiness, was really a submissive personality. At first, Meinong allowed Coehorn to show no more than tiny, automatic signs of deference to his benefactor when they interacted in public. But then, as if Coehorn were his partner in a waltz, Meinong began to make changes to the step, never tugging or prodding but only pulling away to let Coehorn bend a little further, fall a little further, so gradually that for a while even Coehorn himself didn't notice that he'd started to behave quite differently toward Meinong . . . until there came a point when it was obvious to everybody at the camp that the German was leading the dance, even if they didn't have any idea why that should be the case. As soon as Coehorn became conscious of what had happened, he rushed to correct it, and became ostentatiously rude to Meinong. But he didn't fool anyone. Meinong was in charge now.

This wasn't at all what Trimble had intended eight months ago. Meinong was supposed to be a mere go-between in this arrangement, not an *éminence grise* in his own right. Well, bad luck for Trimble.

Still, Meinong wasn't enough of an egotist to insist that, once his power over the camp was established, it must also be recognized, so for the foreseeable future he would allow Coehorn to retain the formality of his position, to sprinkle that scrip around, to play the munificent lord, to buy back a hollow prestige with false tokens of an imaginary currency, to undermine the only thing he'd ever put his name on that was of any use to anyone. But these dejected people yearned to take orders from a man they respected so that once again they could respect themselves. And it was to Meinong's advantage that he was an outsider, since they could see he was not infected by their madness. In the long run, they would turn willingly to him.

Except my 9mm round had just cut the long run short, because he now had to ensure that it didn't puncture his accomplishments like it had punctured his body. Also, deeper in him, underneath these calculations, the shock he felt in the immediate aftermath was already giving way to fury, and this fury demanded flesh on its altar. There was no option but to act.

"Help me up!" he gurgled. Many of the onlookers were off chasing me, but the others encircled him where he lay.

"You'd better not move, Mr. Meinong," said Mac Parke, Coehorn's former athletics trainer, who kneeled over him, trying to help. The shifts in power at the camp over the years had occasioned many proofs of Parke's primary virtue: an ardent, selfless, and lifelong fidelity toward more or less any man-shaped object that happened to be occupying his visual field at that particular time.

"I tell you to help me to my feet."

"You're bleeding pretty bad . . ."

"Staunch it, then!"

His vision spangling at the edges, Meinong was lifted up to lean against Parke while a second-generation girl pressed wads of kapok fluff against his wounds. To his astonishment, he could make out the American pilot—that was how he thought of me, because he didn't know my name—ascending the side of the temple on the rope-suspended platform. That confirmed his resolve. If I somehow survived long enough to announce that everything Meinong had told these Americans about the world war was a self-serving lie and that Meinong was very possibly a "war criminal" (that oxymoronic modern notion), it would be all the more important that by that point Meinong had already reinforced his position. He wasn't sure yet what kind of camp he would run, given the chance. Back in Germany, he had found the Third Reich's obsession with control to be rather dreary and airless in practice. However, a young man staying for a week at a grand old mansion with a troop of snooty butlers may think to himself, "This is absurd, I would never want to be master of such a house," but later on in life, if he finds he actually has the opportunity . . .

"What on earth is going on?" That was Coehorn, approaching in his embroidered sisal dressing gown.

"The ashu . . ." Meinong had to try once more to form the word intelligibly. "The assassin is still on the loose. Kindly escort Mr. Coehorn to hish cabin and keep him there." When he swallowed he could feel tooth fragments lodged under his tongue. A wave of nausea rose through him, but he kept his head up. What he felt from his wounds was not so much pain as a sort of panic of the flesh. The pain would come soon, he knew.

"No, I'm out of bed now, I may as well stay and watch," said Coehorn. "Why are you talking like that? What happened to your face?"

"Mr. Coehorn, we all know that your own comfort and shuf . . . safety is of no concern to you when the welfare of your community is at stake." Meinong puffed a jet of blood from his open mouth. "But I'm afraid we cannot allow you to put yourself in harm'sh way. You are too important."

"Don't be absurd, Meinong. I'll go where I like."

Here, ahead of schedule, was the first test. True power operated on a primordial and wordless level. It was on this level that Coehorn had been superseded, and on this level that these people all knew it. Would they nevertheless rally around this preening failure, just because he was still technically in command?

Once again Meinong gave the order, in the most unchallengeable tone he could manage. "Take Mr. Coehorn to his cabin. And keep him there."

The order was obeyed.

ෙ

I spent the first half of 1957 in Trujillo, mold gardening.

(This is Zonulet again, by the way. Even if I wanted to respond to Vansaska's unauthorized marginalia, I couldn't, her handwriting being so indecipherable that it might as well be in code.)

I didn't give a roasted rat's ass any more about the Branch 9 training camp, because I understood now that the fungus was a thousand times more important. It was going to transform the whole field of intelligence and probably win the Cold War. Before that, however, it was going to pay some dividends for McKellar and me. I had no intention of taking the fungus to my superiors at the agency, because I knew they'd try to steal it from me. Instead, McKellar and I would use it to win a series of victories that would make our ascension to director and deputy director rapid and unopposable. Except, lately, I was starting to wonder whether that wasn't a little unimaginative, whether in fact it wouldn't be better to use the fungus to start a kind of entrepreneurial breakaway organization of our own, still protecting the interests of the United States from within the executive branch but unoppressed by the old bureaucracy.

After I woke up in Wilson's sick bed, I found myself bloated with knowledge. I couldn't remember how I'd got from the temple to San Esteban, but I could remember a fantastic quantity of other things that had little or nothing to do with me, running from the night Elias Coehorn Jr. was marched out of the octopus-wrestling match in 1938, through the first eighteen years of the two camps, right up to the present day—not just scenes and conversations and documents but even the thoughts of the people involved, often with a great deal more clarity than I remembered my own rum-sodden life. The whole strange story of the American settlements at the temple— not the strangest I'd heard in my fourteen years in the intelligence services, but certainly stranger than most—was available to me, like a surveillance dossier the size of the Library of Congress. The fungus, when I inhaled its spores inside that stone duct, had brought me to the aleph, the point from which all other points are visible. Each lie that Trimble had told me was now amended with the full truth. No, I didn't have recollective access to every individual for every minute of every day—the clairvoyance was partial, according to principles I hadn't yet discerned—but I had nearly everything of consequence.

Consequence, relatively speaking. The campers and their follies didn't actually matter to me, except in the sense that they had brought me to this apotheosis. But if you could turn the fungal snooperscope upon the agitators in Cuba, or upon the Kremlin, or upon the Branch 9 offices in Foggy Bottom, and obtain the same haul of detail, that would be something. Tradecraft as we knew it would be mostly obsolete. Sometimes I couldn't help imagining what would happen if, for instance, the Stasi got hold of this stuff: gigantic underground typing pools full of agents huffing the spores out of respirator masks like addicts in an opium den, everything recorded, everything cross-referenced. But that vision didn't worry me too much, because once my allies and I put the argyrophage to use it would only be a matter of time before all of the Eastern Bloc intelligence services gave up out of sheer despair.

The only trouble was, before that could happen, I had to work out how to farm the fucking thing.

Since I couldn't risk sending a sample to Fort Detrick for analysis, I'd settled for examining the mold under a microscope, which was enough to satisfy me that it bore at least a basic resemblance to the canonical Deuteromycota illustrated in the textbooks I had obtained on laboratory microbiology. From a logistical perspective it would have been easier to run my subsequent experiments in the United States, but since I wanted an authentic Honduran climate, I rented a barn on the outskirts of Trujillo. To approximate the *terroir* of the temple, I arranged for the delivery of two hundred tons of limestone bricks, five hundred pounds of silver tableware, and three hundred pounds of animal bones. (Languishing on a shelf in a conference room in the American embassy in Havana, there was a Zhou Dynasty ritual bronze that Herbert G. Squiers, the diplomat and sinophile, had brought with him from Peking after he was appointed minister to Cuba in 1902. Ever since I had learned its provenance I had thought of it as my emergency fund. Discreetly I removed the bronze from the embassy and sold it through an antiquities dealer in New York in order to pay the expenses that my operating budget from the agency couldn't cover.)

With the help of Pavo and four other hired hands, I constructed a limestone passage, littered with silver and bone. Then, as a starter colony, I planted the stub of moldy armor I'd brought back with me. According to the textbooks, all fungi needed sources of carbon and nitrogen, but given that the temple didn't even offer the guano or dead wood that might nourish a cave toadstool, I figured there had to be some loopholes in that statute.

And yet this fungus that needed so little nevertheless seemed to need something I wasn't giving it. Weeks passed and it just refused to spread. Every day I put on a surgical mask and crawled into the passage to look for progress, but I never found a solitary hypha outcurled, even after I tried out four different configurations of the simulated temple, even after I resorted to artificial measures, glazing the silver with Czapek solution and dispersing the spores with a damp ponyhair brush. I recalled my widowed aunt in her basement apartment in Hell's Kitchen, battling obsessively against the black mold in her walls, killed in the end not by the "bad air," as she always feared, but by an incendiary malfunction of the "anti-mold heater" she bought from a catalog. What would she have thought of me, primping, coaxing, begging on my knees? Meanwhile, in Cuba, Batista's furious efforts to burn El Movimiento out of the hills were making about as much progress as my aunt ever did against her own insurgency, but I was gracing the Havana station with only token appearances.

One tyrannously humid day in July, I saw the date on my newspaper and it struck me that I had now spent almost six months with the fungus, longer than the whole airship operation had lasted, with nothing whatsoever to show for it. Ever since San Esteban, passing time seemed to be my main activity. Of course, what had changed was that I now understood, viscerally, how it felt to measure out eighteen pointless years in gallons of neck sweat. And I had not revised the judgment I made when I first set eyes on the settlers at the temple, which was that their heroic psychosis deserved more respect than any milksop sanity.

Bravo to them. But would I have endured it myself? Christ, no. Did their example mollify my extreme disinclination to spend even a single minute longer in stasis than I absolutely had to? Christ, no.

I refused to waste any more time. If I couldn't cultivate the fungus myself, I would have to harvest it from the source. I would have to go back to the temple.

But I hadn't made a very congenial impression on my previous visit there. And I wasn't willing to stake everything on a negotiation with Coehorn or Whelt or Burlingame. Somebody like Trimble could be relied upon to pursue his self-interest at least semi-rationally, but not those cultists.

I would have to take that festering silver armor by force.

Which meant armed men, enough to hold off dozens of people at gunpoint so I could remove it without hindrance. That was a far more drastic measure than I wanted to take—I was not a desperado like Jawbone Atwater—but there was simply no alternative. The fungus trumped everything. However, I couldn't just hand out rifles to Pavo and his friends. Not only would the stick-up be uncomfortably close to Branch 9 turf, but the getaway would involve transporting several hundred pounds of silver through at least fifty miles of jungle. The operation had to be efficient and well resourced if I wasn't going to risk a jumblefuck worse than my airship crash. Unfortunately, I'd already spent my Zhou Dynasty cauldron windfall, so the looting of one relic couldn't underwrite the looting of several more.

I needed investment. And I would have to go to New York to get it.

ഉ⊘

"Do you know what the old crowd is saying about you? They're saying you must have gone loco, absolutely loco, if you've stayed out here all this time where no white man ought to live. For pity's sakes, old pal, you've had your fun. Why don't you just come home?"

(Coutts's sister's fiancé to Coutts, from the original shooting script of Hearts in Darkness)

ഉ⊘

If the first half of the American occupation of the temple involved a general refusal to acknowledge the passage of time, as if those eight years were just a week stretched out very thin, the second half was the rupture, when time broke upon the two camps.

The occupiers got so old they couldn't ignore it any more. By 1957, even the most junior member of the original expeditions—Eastern Aggregate kitchen boy Merv Chavin, who had arrived as a teenager—was thirty-five and almost bald. And the most senior, Kingdom Pictures carpenter Dick Schwalbe, who even in 1938 had been anticipating his retirement, had actually managed to die of old age. He was the only one so far to have won that distinction. But he was far from the only one to have died. Because the jungle, which for so long had been merciful, seemed to have exhausted its patience.

There were singularities. One man shot himself through the eye socket while adjusting his bow and arrow. One man got so drunk on moonshine he drowned in a two-inch puddle. One woman slipped on the second-to-bottom step of the temple during a rainstorm and broke her neck. One man was knocked over by a galloping tapir and a broken tree branch impaled him through the rectum. One girl was bitten on the elbow by her pet porcupine and died of the infection.

Other causes were more routine. Disease, foremost. The language of medicine here was "sick," "hot," "thirsty," "rotten," and so forth, nothing as scholastic as "dysentery" or even "fever," because words like that implied associations of symptoms, semi-regular, semi-inferable, when on the contrary each failing body seemed to ring up its catastrophes like a slot machine. Common enough, also, were complications of childbirth and complications of surgery, the stings of scorpions and the fangs of jaguars.

But the stock was replenished. During those first eight years, there had been fewer than a dozen births. Some women found they stopped ovulating when there wasn't enough to eat. For the rest, the withdrawal method was so prevalent at the temple that Irma once remarked, to general agreement, "If I get jism on my tummy one more goddamn time my poor cervix is going to feel like it has no choice but to set up camp out there." After all, nobody wanted to come home storked from an overseas job.

Upon Trimble's exile, however, the atmosphere of liberation was so intoxicating that several children were conceived that same night. And from then on a new impatience was felt among the common-law husbands and wives of the two camps, with the result that, starting around 1947, Coehorn was often heard to complain that any previous hardships they might have endured were as nothing compared to the interminable screaming of what sounded like ten thousand babies.

Where the first generation had never been more than grudging halfway adapters, the second was a genuinely new tribe, with Colby Droulhiole as its founder. They spoke in American accents and they had all been taught a sort of eschatology in which they would one day return with their parents to Hollywood or New York. But they belonged to the rain forest and to the temple. And the geometry of the latter—its steps underfoot or its rise overhead, depending on where they grew up—was so primal to them that any talk of disassembly or reassembly struck them as abstract, almost paradoxical.

Yet if you talked to the older kids in the Kingdom Pictures camp, you would find they believed at least as devoutly as their parents that the movie must be made. Of course, they had never seen a movie, but they had all played make-believe and drawn pictures, and they knew that a grand analogue of these activities called *Hearts in Darkness* was the central imperative of human life. "Are we making the movie right now?" children would sometimes ask, trying to understand. "No, not yet!" their elders would reply. Not until everything was finally ready, and the actors and actresses could stand in front of the cameras to say their lines.

What threw these metaphysics into confusion, however, was that Mr. Whelt, the director of *Hearts in Darkness*, seemed to have just the opposite answer.

Between 1946 and 1958, Whelt filmed about twelve hours a day, every day. He used the last working 35mm camera at the site, which was a lopsided cannibal jalopy fixed up with spare parts from all the other rusted cameras, and adapted with a harness so it could be hauled from place to place by its operator, which gave the impression, since you almost never saw them apart, that the camera was now a prosthetic extension of Whelt's body, or that Whelt was an extension of the camera's, or that they had hybridized into a sort of centaur on five spindly legs. At the end of each day his arm was so worn out from cranking that it couldn't lift a fork to his mouth. Since he wasn't using lights or microphones, the only support he required from the *Hearts in Darkness* crew involved the film stock, before and after it was cranked through the camera: mile after mile had to be cooked up from wood pulp, tapir cartilage, rock salt, ureal ammonia, and silver filings, while the exposed reels had to be transferred to labeled clay canisters for storage. With the autonomy of a newsreel stringer, Whelt roved around both camps, shooting whatever he came across, patient and seemingly indiscriminate. He never intervened in the scene, unless he felt that somebody was acting, which he absolutely didn't want. No acting, no script, no props, no costumes. Just that vagrant man-camera drinking up the business of the day. And yet, if he was asked what he was shooting, he would say he was shooting *Hearts in Darkness.*

The first time Whelt went down to the New York camp to film was in 1946, two days after Trimble was ousted. The membrane between the two camps had never seemed so thin, and he was admitted with goodwill and curiosity. Only once Coehorn noticed him was he chased away. But he just kept coming back, day after day, to scrump with his lens from the margins of the settlement. In that period, when you looked at Coehorn, the first thing you thought about was how stridently he had come to Trimble's defense on that historic day, so his authority was already beginning the slide that would accelerate later when the camp's economy failed. His instructions were still followed, but each time he demanded that Whelt should be thrown out and his camera should be confiscated, it took a little longer before anyone actually put a gentle hand on the director's shoulder. Soon, Whelt was being given at least an hour's grace before he was made to leave, and the camera was never profaned. In the end, Coehorn gave up; the only proviso he could still maintain was that he should never have to encounter Whelt personally. To the New Yorkers it felt pretty screwy that they had among them not just one of the enemy but the leader of the enemy, like a dream where somebody famous turns up in the most illogical context. But they knew that even the Angelenos were mystified about what Whelt was now trying to accomplish—and it did seem very much as if he wasn't there in any recognized capacity, as if he wasn't, in fact, the same man they remembered, but a newcomer, innocent of the old squabbles, no affiliation save his indefinable project—so they half-ignored him like a cat or a ghost.

Eleven years on, it felt perfectly normal. Which meant Whelt was in a fine position to observe the changes in the Eastern Aggregate camp after Meinong took power.

It wasn't as if the German swept aside a bicameral legislature. The camp had always been an autocracy. But this new autocracy wasn't Coehorn's autocracy, which had been vague and capricious and self-absorbed, thus liberal by sheer neglect, not so much an iron fist in a velvet glove as an iron fist lost between the cushions of a velvet couch. Nor was it Trimble's autocracy, which most of the time had been targeted and intimate and unannounced, a secret police force attached to no state, so that you could share a nightly gourd of pineapple beer with your best friend and never have any idea he was compromised, desperate, following orders, until one morning you saw that he'd betrayed you to the *Pozkito Enquirer*.

No, Meinong was staging an old-fashioned honest-to-goodness kit-and-caboodle dictatorship.

Whelt's camera saw: squads of men performing army drills, climbing trees and throwing spears and wrestling in the mud.

Whelt's camera saw: a mother regarding her toddler's supper longingly after her own food ration was withheld because for the third time in a row she hadn't met her foraging quota.

Whelt's camera saw: Meinong giving a speech about the Angelenos to the assembled camp (minus Coehorn, who was still in indefinite protective custody).

Whelt's camera saw: a woman abasing herself in tearful public apology after she admitted to spreading a malevolent untruth about how some of the Eastern Aggregate scrip in circulation looked different from some of the other scrip.

Whelt's camera saw: a man being punished by caning after he was caught making love to another man's wife out in the forest.

Whelt's camera saw: three of Meinong's lieutenants approaching, stern looks on their faces, closer and closer until their chests blacked out the shot.

⚏

On October 4, 1957, I took an elevator to an upper floor of Eastern Aggregate's Pine Street tower for a meeting about an expedition to the jungle, exactly as Elias Coehorn Jr. had nineteen years earlier. Nothing had changed, not even the walleyed elevator operator, whom I recognized from my fungal cinematograph though we'd never physically met. In the old days, an Eastern Aggregate executive desiring psychological dominance in a meeting with an outside party could instruct the receptionists in the lobby to show his guest to the "express elevator," which looked just like the others but made such a rapid and jerky ascent that the guest would stumble out seasick. Naturally, the idea had originated with the company's redoubtable founder. I asked the operator whether it was still in use. "No," he told me, a little surprised that I knew about it, "they got rid of that a few years back." That was to be expected. An entire company as an extension of the personality of its founder, who, "in ordering the whole," like Leibniz's God, "has had regard to every part, so that it is a mirror of him"—that old style was in decline or reform. Today, business was supposed to look more like the United Fruit Company: rationalized, modularized, with no faces to speak of, just a colony reproducing itself with gray flannel spores. With Elias Coehorn Sr. gone, Eastern Aggregate was adapting to the times.

Yet Phibbs, like the elevator operator, had held out. And Coehorn's spirit would preside in this building for as long as Phibbs was still here—not only because of the echoic mannerisms with which the former Good Conduct Division agent paid tribute to his employer of so many years, but also because of a fundamental quality they had in common—the sense that his refinement was an exquisite polish on a very rough ore, that he was as comfortable as any Brahmin in his starched cuffs but it would be no novelty or perturbation for him to find them stiffened instead with dried blood.

"I'm certainly eager to find out the purpose of this latest visit, Mr. Zonulet," he said when I was seated across from his thirty-acre desk and his secretary had closed the door behind her. It was almost a year and a half since I'd come to look at the scrip. "Is there some further assistance our company can provide the State Department?"

"I'm going to be straight with you, Mr. Phibbs. Nineteen years ago your boss sent his son to Honduras to bring back a temple. He never came back. You must know at least that much. You may know a lot more. After all, somebody made sure that word didn't spread, and maybe that was your secret service here. But what counts is that the younger Elias is still in the jungle. And I don't think you can afford to leave him there any longer."

"This is quite unexpected," Phibbs said, although he didn't show the most microscopic sign of surprise in his tone or his body language—perhaps because he'd already guessed my purposes, but more likely, I thought, because this was a guy with such discipline over his involuntary reactions that he scheduled his belches a week in advance.

"The world still doesn't know any temple is there," I said. "It's a regular Shambhala. To the north and the east there are mountains and to the south and the west there are Indians running around the rain forest with guns. So up until now, no prying eyes. But that's going to change. Do you know anything about artificial satellites?"

"I'm afraid not."

"The Jet Propulsion Laboratory is a matter of months from launching one of their doohickeys into orbit around the earth. I have friends in that business so if I want to find out the latest all I have to do is make a long-distance call to California. Soon there'll be so many up there it'll look like rush hour on Lexington. Maybe the first one won't have a camera on it. Maybe even the second one won't have a camera on it. But after that? Come on. You know where I work. You can imagine the anticipation. So we'll have these satellites up there, transmitting pictures to us just like television. But we can't just park them up over Russia. That's not how they work. They keep going round and round. Over the oceans. Over the continents. Over Honduras. And even if nobody gives a damn what the Honduran jungle looks like to the birds, somebody is going to look at those pictures. We've got a lot of people in government just trying to pass the time. And they're going to find out the temple is there. I don't just mean my outfit. I mean the world is going to find out. And there aren't enough Indians with guns to keep the door shut after that. So there will be a lot of inquisitive people at the temple. And before long the front page of *The New York Times* will be reporting that in 1938 Elias Coehorn Sr. sent his son, and about fifty other Eastern Aggregate contract employees, out into the jungle, and they didn't come back, and he kept quiet about it, and he didn't fetch them home, and indeed he may have impeded any efforts to fetch them home, and golly, you won't believe this, but they're still out there, in an awfully strange condition. Now, is that your preference? I don't think it is. That doesn't sound to me like the Eastern Aggregate style. This temple thing has to be wrapped up one way or another, and I think you'd rather it was wrapped up with a minimum of embarrassment and a minimum of untidiness. That means stopping the party before the cameras roll from the firmament. Understand?"

"I believe I follow you, yes," said Phibbs evenly.

"So we send an expedition out there. Well trained, well armed. You pay for it. I lead it. Will it be official Eastern Aggregate business? That's up to you. Will it be official State Department or Central Intelligence Agency business? Not at the time, no. But afterward I expect to find myself in a position to make any retrospective endorsements that might prove necessary." I lit a cigarette. "Sure, you could just send an expedition of your own. You could leave me out of it. But right now there are only two guys outside Honduras who have ever been to the Eastern Aggregate camp. One of them is me. The other one is a kid who grew up there, and nobody except me knows where that kid is now. If you go out there without us, you're astray in a gloomy wood, as an old buddy of mine used to say. Bring me and the kid, and you know where to go and who to see once you get there."

"If you'll permit me the question, Mr. Zonulet, what would be your own incentive to steward such a venture? I assume you wouldn't be drawing a salary."

"Simple: there's something at the temple I want. The Americans living there are in the way of my getting it. And when I say I want it, I say that in my capacity as a servant of our government and our nation. I have the future of every free society in mind."

"I see." Phibbs paused, not actually for thought, it seemed to me, because he already knew what he was going to say, but as a courtesy, signaling to his guest that in principle he found this conversation important enough to be worth pausing over. As with all his courtesies, its absolute hollowness was part of its grandeur. "I understand that you believe the venture you propose would be to the benefit of the Eastern Aggregate Company, and for that reason I must give you my deepest thanks for bringing it to my attention. However, I regret to say that we don't see eye to eye on every one of your premises. The vision you present of a globe photographed from every angle by these remarkable stringless kites—no doubt such a thing will come to pass. One day. But if I'm correct, no country on earth has so far succeeded in launching a single such electronic satellite into orbit?"

"Both the White House and the Kremlin have stated the intention—"

"Our current war is a war of bluff," Phibbs said. "Naturally, intentions of all kinds will be stated."

"Like I said, it's a matter of months. A year at the most."

"With the greatest respect, you are far from the first visitor to sit in my office and tell me about a technological advance that will supposedly be critical to the future of this company. I am reminded of a proverb that Mr. Coehorn sometimes liked to use in analogous situations. 'Don't burn the milkmaid until you see the third tit.' Have you ever come across the phrase yourself?"

In the atmosphere of this office the word "tit" exploded like a neutron bomb, just as Phibbs must have intended. It made the remark definitive. There would be no point in arguing. "No, I never have."

"It refers to the old folk belief, still not quite lapsed during Mr. Coehorn's boyhood in Hershey, that witches possess a supernumerary nipple. I think it can best be elucidated as a combination of two more common proverbs: 'I'll believe it when I see it' and 'Let sleeping dogs lie.'"

"Right."

Another pause. "Is there anything else I can do for you, Mr. Zonulet?"

As I took the elevator back down after my failed sales pitch, I realized that Phibbs had never even admitted outright to knowing anything about any Americans in the jungle. Meanwhile, I'd laid out my own position in prodigal detail. That asymmetry was inherent to the situation, of course, and I'd expected it from the start, but I still couldn't help feeling as if I'd shamed my own training. Phibbs was truly a professional. I imagined him coming into Ada Coehorn's dressing room with a pistol when she was naked on the chaise longue with Arnold Spindler all those years ago, and how terrifying that must have been.

Outside, it was one of those blue fall afternoons like a cool windowpane against your forehead, the perfect curative for all those months in the tropics, but I was in no mood to appreciate it. If Eastern Aggregate wouldn't back me, who would? Kingdom Pictures no longer existed. Maybe a year or two earlier I could have gone back to Cuba to raise the money myself by brokering a few deals. There had always been opportunities, but I had rarely bothered, because dollars and pesos were so trivial to me compared to the more arcane currencies in which I preferred to traffic. However, I'd been neglecting my contacts there—and Batista's clumsiness was starting to breed a measure of anxiety and circumspection among those who had the most to lose, even though you only needed to take a calm look at the situation to see the rebels didn't have a hope in hell of reaching Havana—so I couldn't be sure I was still adequately placed to make those quick profits as an insider-outsider.

Until I could fund this mission, the fungus on the armor at the temple would just be waiting there pricelessly like sunken treasure; and I was in a worse position than I'd been in the day before, because I didn't know what steps Phibbs might now take. I cursed Branch 9 for diverting McKellar to Jakarta. Together we could have cracked this. I decided to go to a bar to think it over. Just a couple of drinks would help.

Seventeen hours later, I was woken by the telephone in my hotel room on Seventh Avenue. Deep in the Ebano Lagoon—beneath the dark water shackled by algae and fronds, beneath the trickle of effluent from the pumps of my lumber barge, beneath the rotting corpses of fish and fowl, beneath the spite-worm eggs quickening in the flatulent mulch, beneath the bottom-feeders and the parasites upon the bottom-feeders and the parasites upon those parasites—deep beneath all of that, in the most fetid zone in the world, creation might have found a place for an invertebrate as dismal as I felt at that moment.

Lying on the other pillow was a set of false teeth. I didn't recognize them. Maybe one day, I thought as I reached for the handset, they would package the scrying mold along with your Alka-Seltzer, so you could find out what had happened to you the previous night.

"Mr. Zonulet? This is John Phibbs. Good morning to you."

I was sure I hadn't mentioned to him where I was staying. "Hi. Yes." I could barely speak.

"As you will already have guessed, I'm calling to eat my words."

He seemed to assume I would know what he was talking about. I wasn't about to admit that I'd only just woken up. "Oh. Yes."

"Events have proven me wrong, and they have not tarried a moment in doing so."

"Right. Yes." With a titanic effort of will I hauled myself out of bed, and, carrying the telephone cradle with me, walked naked to the door.

"Today's news has prompted me to a reconsideration of sorts. May I prevail upon you to return to my office for another discussion? This afternoon, perhaps?"

"Okay. Yes."

I opened the door. As I'd hoped, my complimentary copy of *The New York Times* lay on the threshold. "SOVIET FIRES SATELLITE INTO SPACE," read the headline. "IT IS CIRCLING THE GLOBE AT 18,000 M.P.H.; SPHERE TRACKED IN 4 CROSSINGS OVER U.S."

Greetings from picturesque San Esteban.

I will quote from Zonulet's manuscript, because it describes me well enough, to say that during the period of my life I call the Pinch, "a connection or a logic seemed absent, grievously absent, absent like something stolen." I think Zonulet feels the same way about the events of the last few years, and that is why he could be persuaded to come with me to Honduras.

In this case if the absent logic has a name it may be REMOTER. In 1935 REMOTER left the temple in Honduras, which had been lost to the world for centuries, and set sail for Red Hook, Brooklyn. Three years later, Elias Coehorn Sr., the skyscraper khan of New York, made the decision to send two expeditions back to that same temple, one under his own name, the other under the name of Arnold Spindler, a dead man living on as an impostrous puppet, in order to test their two sons against each other. I do not believe the timing can be a coincidence. Somehow REMOTER must have precipitated all this.

If Poyais O'Donnell could explain to us who REMOTER is and what agenda he or she has been pursuing—well, this manuscript is an accounting, and even though it is too late now for Zonulet to avert the ruin of his enterprise, it would still mean something to him to fill out some of the vast blank spaces in the ledger.

I may as well carry on from where I left off (even if that is a nicety obsolete in these pages). Zonulet and I talked for hours at his kitchen table. I wanted him to admit what he has been hiding from me but he never did. I could not ask him outright because to do so would have felt like an act of aggression. There was nothing flirtatious in our talk, and yet this long, serious, difficult conversation was conducive to what followed because, as if the two of us were working a great crosscut saw together, it synchronized us physically, not only in the rhythm of our work but also in our exhaustion as the night drew on. We fell into bed together, as they say. There, we were not tired, and Zonulet belied his account of himself as a hospice case, even if he did take a very long time to recover afterward.

When I passed him a cigarette, he said, "I'll go to Tegucigalpa with you as long as we can get back here by Monday."

"Aha. The honey trap has sprung."

"Hey, no joke. I've been waiting for a chance with you since 1938."

"What a nice thing to say." I knew it wasn't true.

But he said, "I mean it. You ever think maybe this was all my plan, not yours?"

"All what?"

"The last twenty years. Maybe it was all leading up to tonight."

"The expeditions? The temple?"

He yawned. "Branch 9. Everything. And here you are. Worked out perfectly."

"My God. So when I plotted the connections between everything that's happened and in those connections I made out a grand conspiracy . . . a powerful and mysterious intent . . . a sort of kraken moving beneath the waters . . ."

"You know how far I'll go for a nice piece of tail." He turned over. After that he was asleep so fast I had to reach over and take the cigarette out of his hand. The sheet had fallen off him, and before I pulled it up over his shoulders, I saw for the first time that he has a scar on his left side from what must have been a very bad wound.

The next morning we drove to Washington National Airport. Ahead of us in line at the Pan Am counter were two unshaven men whose conversation returned so continually to the refrain "The important thing is to know when to cut your losses and get out" that I felt almost personally defrauded when they bought round-trip tickets to Mexico City instead of the more dramatic one-way tickets they had led me to anticipate. Our turn came and we booked our own passage to Tegucigalpa via Miami.

No need to worry: I do not intend to begin a travelogue. This is not *Life* magazine and I am not getting paid five cents a word for my evocations. (You would think Zonulet was getting paid ten.) I will only note that the Plaza Dolores in Tegucigalpa seems like a lovely place to get married, with its fudge carts and its russet pigeons and its lazy fragrant air on which confetti might drift for miles to seed other weddings in other houses. Which makes it a special pity that Señorita Josefa Candida Gonzalez was cheated out of her ceremony. No, we did not find Poyais O'Donnell in San Esteban, because Poyais O'Donnell did not attend his own wedding.

Arriving in the early evening, we checked into connecting rooms in a hotel near the church. Zonulet discovered that although the concierge had dealt with O'Donnell in the past, he did not know where he might be staying this time. So Zonulet slipped him a bill to call around his counterparts at all the other hotels, but none of them had seen O'Donnell either. As a fallback, the concierge gave us directions to the villa of General Gonzalez, O'Donnell's fiancée's father, only a few blocks to the north. Watching Zonulet, I could see he had already recovered some of his old springiness. He was buying information in a tropical climate. He was home.

As we approached the house, I drew Zonulet's attention to a beautiful young woman on one of the upstairs balconies. She stood there weeping, both hands on the rail as she looked out over the rooftops as if demanding some sort of explanation from the dusk. We rang the bell. A maid answered. I do not speak Spanish but I knew Zonulet was telling her that we were in town for our friend O'Donnell's wedding and wanted to inquire about his whereabouts.

The maid's tone was grave. Zonulet's tone was at first incredulous and then angry. He asked several more questions.

I said, "What's going on?"

Zonulet stamped his foot. "God-fucking-damnit!"

"What?"

"She says the wedding's off! O'Donnell's in San Esteban! He has a nasty case of hemorrhagic fever and they don't know if he'll live. Josefa up there"—the girl on the balcony—"wants to go there to be with him, but her father won't allow it in case she catches it too. That's their story." He backed a few steps away from the door and started shouting up at the balcony.

"What are you doing?"

"I'm asking her where the prick's hiding. I'm asking her what they've really done with him. Hemorrhagic fever my ass!"

"She looks awfully sad. Maybe you'd better not—"

But the fiancée, at first too taken aback to speak, was now screaming back down at Zonulet, her voice raw from crying and ablaze with fury. Zonulet replied with undiminished conviction. I tugged on Zonulet's arm but the exchange continued until Josefa darted indoors. I thought perhaps Zonulet had heroically routed the tearful young bride, until she returned to the balcony with crystal sherry glasses fanned in each hand and started hurling them down at us one by one. At that point Zonulet was finally willing to leave.

As we walked back to the hotel I said, "How do we get to San Esteban?"

"Oh, no. Not a chance. I might've squired you as far as Tegucigalpa against my better judgment, but I'm sure as hell not going all the way to San Esteban. O'Donnell's made an asshole out of me for the last time. I'm not even sure any more that he really exists. Nobody's ever seen him."

"But the concierge and the maid and the girl . . ."

"To hell with them," he said. "O'Donnell might as well be a fucking leprechaun."

"And your friend Wilson . . ."

"What kind of a name is Poyais, anyway?"

"I suppose it's Irish or something. Listen, we're already in Honduras. We know where O'Donnell is and we know he isn't going anywhere if he's sick in bed. We're so close to REMOTER. We'd be fools to turn back now. Imagine saying to Bev, 'Well, I went all the way out to Sheepshead Bay, but it turned out my source was in Brighton Beach, so I gave up and came home.'"

"Don't try to hoke me with nostalgia," Zonulet growled.

Perhaps the important thing is, indeed, to know when to cut your losses and get out. No doubt tidy people can make a tidy severance. But without my losses I am not sure what would be left of my life. I am not one of those tidy people, and neither is Zonulet. As far as he is concerned, until it is too late to turn back, you have not really set out.

He never announced a change of mind. When we got back to the hotel, he simply marched up to the concierge and started asking him about buses to Catacamas.

We left the next morning. I had been led to understand that when you take a bus south of the border there are chickens under every arm, there are chickens on every lap, there are chickens in the aisles, there are chickens on the roof, the driver and conductor are perhaps also chickens. But there were no chickens at all on this bus, which jounced for 150 miles over what I very naively took for bad roads.

About those roads I was mistaken too. I now know that in fact they were not bad roads. In relative terms they were wonderful roads. Only later, after nightfall, did I find out what bad roads are, when we hired a truck to take us from Catacamas to San Esteban.

We arrived around three in the morning. There had been no rain yet as we drove but it started with such abruptness and such profusion the instant I had one foot out of the truck that it was like that practical joke where somebody has balanced a pail of water on top of a door. As our driver Iván, stretched out in the truck to sleep, we rushed across the street to Le Sphinx. Zonulet gave a bailiff's knock.

After a short time the door was opened by a man in a dressing gown whom I took to be Wilson. He shook Zonulet's hand with some emotion. "It's marvelous to see you here, and I'm not surprised in the least," he said. "Come inside."

We followed him into the hall, and I introduced myself. Outside the dogs were barking at the thunder. "What do you mean, you're not surprised?" Zonulet said.

"My father used to say that in his day there was no such thing as a 'business acquaintance.' If one had fair dealings with a fellow then one called him one's friend. I can see you're a man of my father's school. Was it business that brought you together with Mr. O'Donnell? Yes, and in passing at that. But has that prevented you from coming here to pay your respects at his funeral? No, it has not. I call that sockingly admirable. I'd like to make you an honorary Englishman, ha ha! No offense to your own country, of course, but—"

"O'Donnell's dead?"

"You didn't know? But I assumed that was why you were here."

"We came here to talk to him," Zonulet said.

"So the question of the Irish inheritance still hasn't been settled? Well, I dare say now it never will be. I'm bally sorry to tell you the fever made off with him this afternoon. I've already been up half the night comforting the ladies. It's been a great blow to us all. You remember I used to call O'Donnell a pillar of our little community. So dependable, so forthcoming, always there just when you needed him . . ."

"I want to see the body."

"We interred him right away, out of regard for hygiene, but we'll be holding a proper service tomorrow."

Zonulet grabbed Wilson by the shawl collar of his dressing gown. "There is no O'Donnell, is there? You've all been in on it this whole time! Tell me the truth or I swear to God I'll knock your head off, you fucking limey pimp!"

"I can assure you I bore the pall myself!" Wilson protested. "So to speak."

Zonulet let him go. "Where? Where is he buried?"

"In the southerly graveyard."

Zonulet went back out into the rain. "Sorry about . . . ," I said, tailing off into a hand gesture.

"Oh, it's quite all right," Wilson said. "I know grief can positively knock a man for six. Do you suppose he's off to lay a wreath on the grave?"

I supposed he was off to do a lot more than that.

I asked to borrow an umbrella. Returning with it, Wilson said, "You must remind me to show you our lending library later."

When I got to the truck Zonulet was already haggling with Iván about an overtime bonus. I followed them to the graveyard. Along with two hurricane lamps they carried the two shovels Iván kept in the truck for rockslides on the road. Cacti grew amid the graves. At first I told myself I would watch them dig, since if I was to be complicit in the defilement of a fresh grave some obscure principle of moral integrity seemed to demand that I should at least invest myself fully in the enterprise. I stood there in the downpour hoping that lightning would strike neither my umbrella nor the shovels. It was a gothic scene. But after about a half hour of digging they had made so little apparent progress that I asked Zonulet how long he thought it would take. He told me four or five hours. I did not want to get Wilson out of bed again so I went back to the truck and slept in the front seat.

Later—a few hours ago as I write—I was wakened by the sunrise. For the first time I saw San Esteban in daylight, and for the first time it struck me with real force that I was at the threshold of the jungle, which for so many years had been to me as perhaps the afterlife is to others: I had kept the faith that this ineffable region would solve all mysteries, mend all voids, and yet so far I had rejected any offer of passage there. A few children were already out of doors, guinea pigs scurrying at their feet, and they stared at me as I found my way back to the graveyard. Iván was resting but Zonulet was still digging. When he looked up at me from the deep hole his eyes goggled brightly from a balaclava of mud. Zonulet claims that because of his liver he is not far from the afterlife himself, and yet seeing him then I could tell he would have gone down without fear into Hades and scattered the dead from his path to drag O'Donnell back up to the surface. Remember, we did not even know for certain that O'Donnell could have told us anything of use about REMOTER. But Zonulet's heart was set. I had myself to blame for that.

"We're already close!" Zonulet said. "I can feel it. The *sepulture-ros* did a rush job."

He was right. About a dozen more turns of the shovel and it struck wood.

Iván got up and helped Zonulet scrape the rest of the soil from the lid of the coffin.

"Open up, please, Mr. O'Donnell!" Zonulet shouted giddily. "Open up or we'll have to break down the door!"

Together, they pried off the lid with their shovels.

The coffin was empty.

☙

About the cruelty and injustice that the New Yorkers were now suffering under Meinong's rule, Burlingame felt sadness: deep, genuine, abiding sadness. Any decent person would have. But about Meinong himself, Burlingame felt sadness too, and this sadness was not so much humanitarian as professional or aesthetic: it was the sense that Meinong had debased his own abilities. She had met the German several times before his elevation and she had found him well mannered, intelligent, humorous, cultured. And now he was conducting his dictatorship like a much stupider person.

For the last eleven years—ever since Whelt's abdication—she had run the Kingdom Pictures camp, and she had run it pretty well. She worked hard. But did she seek to observe every last thing that was going on? Did she seek to regulate every little subdepartment of life? No, of course not. Perhaps her old self, a prig and a swot and a virgin, would have assumed that such a tight nervous grip was necessary for control. Today she knew better.

Her education in power could not be separated from her education in sex. Sex in particular, not love. At best, her experience of love had given her some useful insight into the effects it had on other people. But love could not be used as an analogy or manual for anything else. It was only itself, untranslatable and incommensurate. Sex, on the other hand, had shone its light all around. From the day she was born until the day she met Gracie, she had felt unwelcome in the world. You weren't invited; you quite obviously don't belong here; if you must hang around, for goodness' sake try not to get in the way. But all that had changed. Now she knew she wasn't at the edge of the world, but rather at its center, or at least a few rosy inches from its center when she pressed herself against Gracie in bed. The world yielded to her touch now, disclosed every secret of its workings. Take; take all that you want; take more, actually, just in case your stomach is bigger than your eyes. From those dissolving hours came the strength and the serenity that made her such a good chieftain. She wasn't feared (except by some of the children), but she was respected, even revered at times, and everything she wanted done—everything that mattered—was done. Whereas Meinong seemed to think you had to be clenched and rigid at all times. How like a man. Labored and tedious, unironic and unerotic: that was his idea of power. His transformation had been the reverse of her own.

So her people had food, shelter, clothing (all of which had found their own styles over the years, distinct on each side; the Hollywood camp was regarded as the more modernist of the two). They had box traps and shaving horses, puppet theaters and chess sets, crutches and dentures. They had as much comfort and security as could possibly be expected on these island steps. And yet there was still one respect in which she sometimes felt she was failing them.

"You know next year it will be twenty years?" Burlingame said.

She lay there with Gracie's head on her chest. Their bed had no springs, of course, but their mattress, woven from sisal leaf and packed with kapok fluff, was cushiony enough. Outside the cabin, the camp went about the business of the afternoon. More and more often lately she'd found herself coming back here with Gracie to make love after lunch, as if the season had blown in some aphrodisiac pollen from the jungle. From here, when she raised her own head an inch, she had an interesting angle on Gracie's nose. This nose was Burlingame's heathen idol, the fetish of her cult. It was a horrendous shape—on any other face, it would have been grotesquely bulbous—and yet somehow in this particular context it didn't just leave Gracie's good looks undiminished, but in fact was the capstone of the entire setup, uniting all her features into a perfect whole. You didn't have to be in love with Gracie to think so. Burlingame was certain that, if they had lived to see it, Aristotle and da Vinci would have gone to their graves obsessed with the mystery of how this nose could be so beautiful.

"Twenty years," Gracie said. "We better start planning the anniversary ball."

Burlingame smiled. "That's not what I meant. I thought of it just now and it reminded me of something Apinews said a long time ago. This was when we'd been here about a year, I think, which already seemed rather absurd. Someone, I don't remember who, said, 'Do you think you'll ever, ever get used to these mosquitoes?' And he said, 'Oh, sure—'"

"Please don't try to do an accent," Gracie said.

Burlingame gave her a flick on the ear. "He said, 'Oh, sure. No problem. I'll get used to them eventually. Just give me about twenty years.' And we all had a great laugh about that, of course. The thought of still being out here in twenty years. But it isn't a joke any longer. Twenty years. The shooting schedule was two weeks."

"If the movie had finished up in two weeks, we never would've met." Gracie squeezed her hand.

"I know that."

"And even say we had, someplace else, we would have had to hide."

Although Burlingame had never met Gracie's first lover, she felt that the tragedy of Emmeline in the Texas madhouse had become a part of her own history. So she was proud that she had led by example here: seeing their new boss canoodling quite openly with another woman had helped the Hollywood settlers toward an outlook that was tolerant even by the standards of that town. Today, no high position was required to immunize you from reproof over your living arrangements: there was, for instance, Floyd Noisom and Wally Charters (Burlingame found them a charming couple); Emil Berg, Vinton Miehle, and Janet Jones (Burlingame anticipated hurt feelings in the long run but didn't see anything wrong with the venture in the meantime); even Wayne Dutch and his raccoon "Mrs. Dutch" (frankly Burlingame did feel this was beyond the pale but let he who is without sin, etc.). "For my own part I don't regret a thing," she said. "But not everyone here has been as happy as we have. There are some people who might have been better off at home."

"Well, maybe they ought to go home, then."

"But you know no one here would ever think of leaving. Not unless someone told them to. And the only person who could tell them to, and then expect to see it happen—"

"—is you."

"Yes."

"Are you going to?" Gracie said. "Tell everybody to run off home to Hollywood?"

"I sometimes wonder if I should."

"But we're still making the movie. Every man, woman, and child here, even the littlest, they all want to see the movie finished come hell or high water. We didn't put in twenty years just to give up now."

Burlingame did not dispute that. Never had she permitted an interruption to the steady manufacture of nitrate film—no matter that Whelt and his camera gorged themselves on such quantities that it was a continual burden on the camp, no matter that when asked he would elucidate his scriptless enterprise in only the most gnostic terms. She hadn't come to the jungle to make *Hearts in Darkness,* but everyone else in this camp had. If there is one thing that's forbidden even to an empress, she thought, it is to question the very existence of the empire. Though she might very well have doubts, it wasn't her place to lead a sort of civic suicide.

Nevertheless, she did wonder: how was it possible that nobody had ever deserted either of the camps in the nineteen years they'd been here? Loyalty and steadfastness were excellent virtues, but in this case couldn't they be regarded as a form of insanity? Some of these people had left families behind. If she ever did get back to Cambridge, with such a paltry amount of serious anthropological or archaeological work in hand, it would almost certainly jeopardize the chances of other undergraduates getting permission from the faculty to take trips like this in the future.

But Gracie was right. The film did have to be finished.

Gracie shifted atop her, probably just to ease her limbs, but something in the friction made Burlingame's breath catch. Her hand slid down toward Gracie's hip bone. They made eye contact for a moment, and then Gracie started kissing around her nipple. Burlingame sighed happily.

There was a knock at the door of the cabin.

"Not now, please!" Burlingame called out.

Rick Halloran's voice: "I really am sorry to disturb you, Miss Burlingame, but it's important."

Gracie was now kissing her way down Burlingame's stomach, saunteringly, touristically, as if she had no particular object in mind but was curious to find out what might lie in this direction. "How important?" Burlingame said. Did she seek to regulate every little subdepartment of life? Less than ever.

"Meinong's guys have taken Mr. Whelt."

In thirty seconds Burlingame was up, dressed, and conferring with Halloran outside the cabin. "What do you mean 'taken'?"

"You know that they've been keeping Coehorn locked up 'for his own protection'?"

"Yes."

"Well, now they've slung Whelt in there with him. He was down in the other camp shooting as usual, then three of Meinong's guys took his camera and hustled him off."

"Had he done anything to provoke them?"

"We don't know."

Whelt's mere presence in the Eastern Aggregate camp might once have been regarded as a provocation. As the years passed it had become routine. But Burlingame could well believe that now Meinong was in charge he might contrive fresh umbrage. And, yes, if he felt like it, he would have been entirely within his rights to turf Whelt out of the camp. This, though, was quite different.

"Rick, I'd like you to go down there. Find out if they have some sort of grievance or if this is just a kidnapping. Make it clear we won't stand for it. And by all means carry a weapon. Not obtrusively. But visibly."

Burlingame would have liked to go herself, but it would give the wrong impression to Meinong if he could bring her scurrying down the steps every time he transgressed. So instead she waited, anxious.

By the time Halloran returned, the news had spread through the camp, and he had a large audience for his report. "They say he's under arrest."

"On what grounds?" The last time the New Yorkers had "arrested" anyone was in 1942, after they caught the two men Whelt sent to steal ammonia from their ice-making machine.

"They say he's been trespassing. They say he's been asked to leave, but he's carried on shooting, which he hasn't any right to do. They say they suspect him of spying."

"On what?"

"Private conversations. Manufacturing techniques."

"Oh, for goodness' sake!" Burlingame said. "In other words, he's done absolutely nothing wrong."

"He's going to be put on trial."

"I see. What's their price?"

"I asked them that and they pretended to be offended."

Most likely, Meinong thought a *coup de main* would impress his little populace, unite them behind him once relations between the two camps turned to feud; and if that got out of hand, so much the better for him. Most likely, he thought he would have the advantage in any confrontation. Burlingame had seen his soldiers drilling. Of course, Meinong was an ex-soldier himself, and she didn't like to resort to stereotypes but the Germans had started one war this century already. He hadn't even been here from the beginning, and he thought he had the right to spoil years of peace.

"What now?" said Gracie.

"We shall give them one night to come to their senses. Then, tomorrow, if they haven't let him go, we shall go down there in force and fetch him ourselves." She was aware of the gravity of the order. Not once in two decades had the long squabble over the temple actually broken out into violence. And perhaps she was playing into Meinong's hands. But he had Whelt. This was not a time to quail. "We don't want a fight," she said—even though (she was surprised to realize this) the thought of leading a charge did hold some appeal, as a sort of culmination . . . A vision passed through her mind of Gracie unstrapping her battered armor and dressing her wounds, like Achilles beside Patroclus . . . Nevertheless, she repeated, "We don't want a fight. But if they must have one then we shall supply it."

∾

Recent developments have at last proven the futility and misguidedness of Whelt's position. Everyone now understands that Coehorn was right all along. Even Whelt himself can't deny the facts. But the man-boy will not give up gracefully. Instead, in his humiliation, he lashes out, snarling, spitting, animalistic—putrid breath—also hunchbacked, come to think of it—maybe even facially disfigured, for some reason? Coehorn, on the other hand, stands calm and statesmanlike, declining to gloat or to punish.

This fantasy, for Elias Coehorn Jr., had long since taken on the definitive quality of recorded history. Which made it extremely vexing that almost the opposite was now taking place.

When Meinong's enforcers brought Whelt into the protective-custody hut, he greeted Coehorn civilly and without emotion, as if they were just a couple of strangers in a train carriage, even though this was the first time the two of them had come face-to-face since 1938. Coehorn, by contrast, burst out that he would not share a hut with this criminal. But he was ignored by the enforcers, and as he heard the thunk of the door being barred on the other side, his anger at this new indignity led to a broader mental review of Whelt's behavior over the last nineteen years—so that within five minutes he was regarding him with a gaze of such oxyacetylene heat it was astonishing that Whelt didn't seem to notice it at all, and within ten minutes his fingers were curling and quivering with an urge to throttle and snap, and within fifteen minutes his rage had reached an intensity so high that he couldn't have held himself back one heartbeat longer—if Whelt hadn't spoken at exactly that moment.

"I'd like to go back to filming," he said. "I expect you'd like to get out of here too. I think it might be easier if we cooperate."

"No!" Coehorn roared. "I will not cooperate! I will not cooperate with you!"

"You've been shut in here for ten months. Have you tried to escape?"

"Ten months? Don't be absurd." Coehorn hadn't been keeping count of the days—he was not a secretary—but he knew it couldn't be anything under five or six years. Lately he had been pleased to recognize in himself the maturity and wisdom of a man about to enter his fifties.

"It's October 1957," Whelt said. "That makes ten months. I don't think Meinong's ever planning to let you out. But if we cooperate then maybe between us we can get somewhere."

"Oh, there's that word again! 'Cooperate'! My God, how it sickens me to hear you say that. If you had been willing to cooperate all those years ago then none of this would ever have happened!"

"Actually, Mr. Coehorn, that's wrong for two reasons. The first is that I was ready to cooperate back then if you would've just let us shoot the movie, but you wouldn't wait two weeks so we could put the temple back toge—"

Coehorn hurled himself at Whelt.

After languishing for so long in the hut, Coehorn's physique no longer showed much evidence of the impressive rigor and athleticism that had definitely characterized his entire life prior to this confinement. Which explained why he didn't manage to seize Whelt, force him to the ground, and knock the impertinence out of him forever with a hail of precise blows. Instead, this became another fantasy that turned against him: he gave Whelt a single wild open-handed clip on the ear before he felt something yank inside his upper back and he toppled over howling.

Whelt helped Coehorn to his bed. They didn't speak. Later, Meinong's enforcers brought in two plates of food, and they both ate. They didn't speak. The whole muggy night passed. They still didn't speak.

But the curiosity was like an ulcer on Coehorn's tongue, and at last, the next morning, he said, "What was the second reason?"

"Huh?"

"You said there were two reasons why we couldn't have sorted things out sensibly back then. What was the other one, as you see it?"

"I think even before you took the temple apart, it was too late," Whelt said. "I think even before either of us set foot in Honduras, it was too late. We were already in the temple's gravity. The diagram works backward in time as well as forward."

"What on earth are you talking about?" By dignifying Whelt with this conferral Coehorn felt as if he were treasoning himself. And yet it had occurred to him while he tried to fall asleep that Meinong might have jammed the two of them in here precisely in the hope that one of them would murder the other and afterward he would be rid of them both without taking any blame. If that was the case, Coehorn was at least spiting his plans. More and more, he regretted letting the others bully Trimble out of the camp. His old adviser would certainly have warned him off before he indentured himself to Meinong for that dubious scrip.

His back still ached. Morning sunlight shone through the high window slits, casting subsident pale rectangles on the opposite wall. The longer Coehorn went without setting eyes on the jungle, the more it withdrew like dying grass from his reality. Sometimes he imagined the hut on a Park Avenue corner, or nestled in the grounds at Braeswood, and those old recollected surroundings seemed far more solid to him. But even then he couldn't dream the temple out of existence. Always it was there in his visions, the behemoth wedge, in place of the Waldorf-Astoria or his father's mansion.

"Are you aware that in 1946 I went inside the temple and I met the Pozkito gods and I found out the truth from them?" Whelt said.

"If you're asking me, did we receive the news that you went crazy? Yes, we did."

"You must also be aware that for the last eleven years I've been making a different kind of film. I've been trying to counteract the diagram."

"And who or what is the diagram?"

"That's just my own name for it." Whelt crouched down to draw on the dirt floor with his finger. "'In any successful story, the action must intensify in a series of five or six regular increments, reach its highest level before giving way to a thrilling interval of weightlessness or flight, and then return safely to the status quo.' I thought the Whelt Rule was a formula for making movies, and I thought I'd come up with it myself. But really it was just instructions for drawing the diagram. The Pozkito gods must have put it into me somehow."

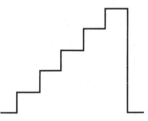

"That's a picture of the temple," Coehorn said.

"No. It's the diagram. The temple and the diagram look alike because the temple is the diagram built in stone." Whelt rubbed out the drawing and started another by tracing a single line.

"This is the river."

"What river?" Coehorn said.

"Any river. Every river. Now, imagine a man starts traveling along the river. This is his path. He wants to get all the way to the source."

"What is he going to find there?"

"He doesn't know," Whelt said. "Maybe he thinks truth. Or paradise. Or oblivion. Or the missing half of himself. Whatever it is, he just knows he wants to find it. But before he can get there, the river claims him. There he is, falling into it."

"He dies?"

"Maybe. But first he loses his mind."

"Like you," Coehorn said.

"Like all of us. Surely you recognize the pattern. It doesn't have to be a man and it doesn't even have to be a river but this is how it goes. Later, another man hears about the first man. And right away he gets an irresistible urge. He has to set off next to the first man's trail. Find out for himself what's at the end of the river. He knows it'll be tough but thinks he'll get all the way there because he won't let the same thing happen to him that happened to the other guy. He'll stay further away from the river, because he's not following in the other guy's footsteps, he's just writing the other guy's story. His journey isn't a journey, it's 'about' a journey. That gives him a margin of separation. So he thinks he's safe.

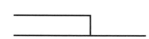

"But it doesn't work. The river claims this second man even sooner than it claimed the first.

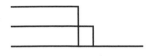

"Then a third man hears about it. He decides to make a movie about the second man's story about the first man's expedition. So he's two degrees of separation from the river. But the river claims him faster still.

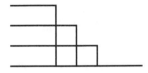

"A fourth man comes along," Whelt said. "Let's say he's writing a diary about the third man making a movie of the second man's story about the first man's expedition. Three degrees of separation. But the river will get him in hardly any time at all. Whatever's at the source of the river, he'll be lucky to get anywhere near it.

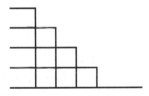

"And then maybe a fifth man writes a novel about the fourth man writing a diary about the third man making a movie of the second man's story about the first man's expedition. Maybe he doesn't even leave his house to do it. But all the same he's screwed from the very beginning. And so on. Do you understand?"

"I wish you'd stop speaking figuratively."

"I have to speak figuratively because the diagram is a figure."

"You seem to be saying this kind of misfortune is inevitable."

"We made it inevitable when we built the diagram," Whelt said.

"When you did, that is—when you took half of the temple away. Intact, the temple was just a palace for the gods. But when we gave it this new shape, we turned it into something else. A shape with power, like a sigil. Did you ever talk to Burlingame about the Pozkito cosmogony? The Pozkitos don't believe the gods created the world, they only believe they designed the Platonic forms, or they calibrated the laws of physics, or they invented the rules of the game, or something along those lines. That's what this is. The shape ripples out across the world. Backward in time and forward. It influences events, makes them more likely to bend into this pattern. That's what the Pozkito gods wanted. That's what we did for them. We all fell into the river here. We all went insane. We made the shape with our lives, and at the same time we made the shape with the temple. That was like a transmitter and a power supply for the diagram, and we stayed here all these years and kept broadcasting. Again and again, all over the world, people will feel compelled to set off down the river, and then other people will set off after those people, and so on, and when they lose their minds, as they all will, that's like a sacrifice on the gods' altar. There are probably incidences of this that, when we left, hadn't happened, but now, because we're here, it has become the case that they happened before we left . . . Some of it's hard to explain. But you see now why we'll never leave the temple. We're closer to the diagram than anybody, so it holds us tighter than anybody. We can't overcome it. We can't make any other shape with ourselves. I thought I could weaken it if I made a new kind of a movie. A movie that smashes the Whelt Rule to pieces. A movie that just is. With people who just are. No center, no subject. No beginning, no end. But I don't think it's been working."

Coehorn raised an eyebrow. "Right. And I suppose you're about to tell me that if we mess with this 'diagram' by—oh, I don't know—reassembling the temple, we'll all be magically liberated from our folly?"

"Yes. And if we disassembled the rest of it, just the same. Either way, the temple wouldn't be the right shape to make the diagram any longer. It would just be a pile of stone again. The broadcast would end, so to speak. But I know neither of those things will ever happen. My people wouldn't allow the disassembly and your people wouldn't allow the reassembly. We won't come to our senses until the diagram is gone. And we can't get rid of the diagram until we come to our senses. That's the bind."

Recent developments have at last proven the futility and misguidedness of Whelt's position. Everyone now understands that Coehorn was right all along. Why? Because Whelt has turned out to be even more demented than everybody feared. Just look at his fingers, dirty from scrawling nonsense on the ground.

Coehorn might have found it agreeable to believe that. But too much of Whelt's account felt plausible to him. He was thinking of that morning in 1938, in his father's office, right after he'd watched the octopus try to drown the wrestler in the tank at the Bering Strait Railroad Association headquarters, when Phibbs had passed him the wooden model of the temple and it had broken in half in his hands. At the time he hadn't realized it, but surely, yes, he was "already in the temple's gravity." The flimsy prop had the mass of a basalt star.

What, after all, was the alternative? That he had meekly obeyed his father's order to come to Honduras. That he had invested himself in such arbitrary make-work. That he had, more or less voluntarily, set himself on the course that ended here, down in this humiliating ditch. That the octopus and the wrestler—a couple of freaks too stubborn to give up a meaningless clinch, before an audience too passive to intervene—wasn't just the best analogy for the bloodshed that Meinong probably aimed to provoke between the two former leaders in this hut, but also for every pointless day of the last nineteen years.

There had to be a more favorable, less nauseating account of his behavior. And Trimble's cabbalism wasn't really so hard to believe. Of the grand interventions his father made in the world, almost all were invisible to almost everybody. And Eastern Aggregate's most senior accountants had long since passed beyond human mathematics. He had grown up understanding that. So he could believe that in that same darkness other corporations might operate.

The two halves of the balsa-wood model spinning in his mind, he considered Whelt's claim that the objective was not to win the temple but to win *against* the temple. He looked at Whelt. "What if there was another way?"

෨

When Meinong woke in the dark from a traceless dream, he found that his fingers had already closed tight around the handle of the machete. Someone was in the cabin with him. He wasn't sure where but he had sensed it even in sleep: an impurity in the night. "Who's there?" he said.

"It's Trimble."

Meinong held his breath, listening for the almost imperceptible screak of a bow and arrow held in tension. He heard nothing. The machete Meinong slept beside was the last remaining usable metal blade in the camp. If Trimble did have a bow but hadn't yet drawn it, Meinong would have time to throw the machete before he loosed an arrow.

However, he didn't know if Trimble's benefactor had brought him any other weapons. Conceivably the American pilot might even have been irresponsible enough to entrust him with a gun.

"I have a machete, Mr. Trimble," he said. "You'd better not come any closer."

At this stage, a man with a gun would most likely have alluded to that advantage. But Trimble said, "I didn't come here to mix it up, Mr. Meinong. You know that ain't my modus o."

"Why did you come here?" Now that Meinong's eyes were resolving the darkness a little better, he could see that Trimble was leaning casually against the opposite wall of the cabin, both hands propped behind him.

"We had a deal," Trimble said.

"Yes. And that deal was premised on a supply of scrip. There has been no more scrip since the American pilot was shot down. So the deal is kaput." These days his diction was only faintly affected by the hole in his face that had never quite closed up.

"You wouldn't be running this place if it weren't for me."

"That is true. I am, of course, grateful for your help."

"Gratitude's a jingle in the hand, not a jingle in the mouth. That's what Tommy Gagliano used to say."

"I am unfamiliar with the idiom. But you no longer have anything to offer me, Mr. Trimble. So I consider our association concluded. I ask you to leave my quarters." With deliberate motions he pushed his sheet aside and swung his feet onto the ground.

"But I do got something. I knew gratitude wouldn't come into it so I made sure I got something you'll just pop your cork for."

"And what is that?"

As best Meinong could follow, Trimble had some photographs of a woman called Emmeline Sapp, a former lover of Gracie Calix, who for more than twenty years had been immured in a mental asylum in Texas. The photographs gave evidence of electroshock treatments and abuse by the orderlies. Accompanying them was a letter from the director of the asylum stating that under certain conditions he would be willing to approve Miss Sapp's discharge.

"I assume the American pilot brought you these materials," Meinong said.

"That's right."

"Who was he, may I ask?"

"Just an old pal of mine."

"Show these materials to Gracie Calix and put her in your power. Put Calix in your power and the ground beneath Burlingame falls away. That is your idea?"

"Right again. And with Burlingame out of the running, those steps are as good as yours. You're the mayor of the whole city. Uptown and downtown. Seems to me those pictures ought to be worth a lot to you, Mr. Meinong."

"Assuming they are real, what do you want in exchange?"

"We'll be partners again. But this time everybody knows about it. Tomorrow at noon you make an announcement. Throw me a welcome-home party. 'Here's my good buddy Trimble, come back to help me out. You better treat him nice or you'll get it from me pretty hard.'"

Meinong smiled. "I'm afraid that is quite impossible."

"That's my price and I'm the only one selling. Take it or leave it."

"Where are these photographs now?"

"Oh, they're stashed out in the jungle. But you'll never find them. And even if I had the inclination I couldn't tell you where to look. I know how to get there, sure, but it ain't a case of 'Turn left at the kapok tree,' if you catch my drift."

Once Meinong was on his feet, Trimble was only three long paces away. Very fast, Meinong moved across the cabin, grabbed him by the wrist, and pinned his left hand to the mud-pile wall. He swung the machete. The angle of the blade took off the top joint of Trimble's index finger, two joints of each of the next two fingers, and nearly all of his little finger. With a soft drumroll, as if of impatience, the nubs fell to the ground.

Trimble didn't make even the faintest sound, but he gave a slow buck of the head, mouth gaping, eyes bulging. Then he slid down the wall, part squat and part collapse, to grab for his severed fingers, frantically, as if he were afraid somebody else might get them first.

Meinong tore a strip of fabric from his sheet. When he tried to take Trimble's injured hand, the other man flinched away. "Keep still, please," Meinong said. "I'm going to bandage you so you don't bleed to death. You must hold the hand higher than your heart." He tied the bandage tight. As instructed, Trimble kept the hand up in the air, which made Meinong smile. *"Heil Hitler,"* he replied. "Now you are going to take me to the extortion materials. If you do not, I will cut off the rest of your fingers. And after that your ears and nose and genitalia and so forth." Trimble looked at him, breathing hard, rageful but defeated, an expression to savor.

Meinong draped his sheet over Trimble's head in case they met anybody on their way through the camp; none of his subordinates would have the temerity to ask who was in the ghost costume.

With a hand on Trimble's upper arm he guided him to the edge of the forest. Then he pulled off the sheet and poked him in the small of the back with the tip of the machete. "I will walk behind you. If you try to run I will cut you down."

"It's dark. Can't we wait til morning?"

"No delays. You've lived out in the jungle for eleven years. You can find your way." But Trimble had only taken a few steps forward when a precaution occurred to Meinong. "Wait." He gathered three sticks from the ground, tore three long leaves from a palm, stripped the leaves down to their midribs, and used the midribs to lash a stick to each of Trimble's feet and the third to his head. The point was to make him as clumsy as possible. Meinong was going to have to follow wherever Trimble led, even though he didn't know what sort of infrastructure Trimble might have in place out there. He recalled the case of a clever Armia Krajowa girl who managed to walk an *Untersturmführer* right into the trip wire of a spring gun during a raid on a safe house. So these prosthetic augmentations to Trimble's height and shoe size would make it difficult for the American to duck under or step over any of his own traps.

"I can't walk with these on," Trimble complained.

"Yes, you can. Proceed, please."

"I'm still bleeding."

"I wish to remind you that when your 'old pal' shot me in the face I did not scream for my nursemaid."

Like two brave boys in a fairy tale they trekked through the dark woods, except that this jungle had to be regarded as a crazed and degenerate mutation of the Grimms' noble *Deutscher Wald*, suitable for the disposal of only the most low-grade characters in the most low-grade stories. Meinong did his best to keep his bearings so that he could find his way back to the temple alone if he killed Trimble.

"What did your 'old pal' tell you of the current world situation?" Meinong asked.

"He told me the Yankees won the World Series five years in a row."

After that they didn't speak for a while. At their slow pace it was most of an hour before Trimble stopped, although they had reached no perceptible landmark, and said, "All right, we're here."

"I see nothing."

"I buried the pictures in front of this tree. You can't tell in the dark but the tree looks like Marie Dressler. That's why I picked it."

Feeling around with his foot, Meinong found there was indeed a bump in the earth. "Very well. Dig them up."

"But . . ."

Meinong raised the machete. "Dig." Trimble's shoulders slumped. He got down on his knees and started scraping the ground away with his intact hand. Meinong found it a pathetic sight, and, furthermore, maddeningly inefficient. "Stop that," he said. "Get up. Come over here." He made Trimble stand with his back against a trumpet tree, then reallocated a couple of the palm leaf midribs from his head to tie his wrists together behind its slim trunk.

"This tree's full of ants! I can already feel them!"

After giving Trimble's wrists a tug to make sure they were secure, Meinong went to look for a trowel. The jungle was a dank cellar beneath the early dawn, only a little light washing down through the grate of the canopy. Before long he came across a tree trunk on the ground, its insides mostly eaten away by termites. Pushing down with his heel, he snapped off a broad curve of thick bark, and a second for when the first one broke. When he got back, he found Trimble writhing against the trumpet tree, trying to rub the ants off himself just like a dog. Setting the machete aside, Meinong knelt down and began to delve for Trimble's cache with a two-handed grip on his bark scoop.

"How deep did you bury these items?" he asked when his arms had begun to tire.

"Pretty deep," Trimble said.

"Was that necessary?"

"Can't take any chances out here."

Meinong detected a change in the feel of the soil. It had a mild endogenous warmth. He ran his fingers through it, puzzled. Actually, the soil wasn't just warm, it was thrumming. Shifting. The soil was alive.

The soil exploded.

Meinong was knocked on his back by a geyser of spots and snarl. A claw opened his throat. Fangs ribboned his forehead. The jaguar pressed down on him, hot and ecstatic. It baked his face in its breath, drooled in his eyes, and in return the splash of his own carotid blood overpainted the beast's own mottle.

He tried to roll out from under it but it had him pinned down on the ground like foolscap on a blotter. Instead he stretched out his left arm, groping for the machete. He saw that where the exhumed jaguar's eyes should have been there were only voids. As it gnashed a chunk out of his shoulder, his fingers closed tight around the machete's handle.

With the last strength he would ever have he hauled the machete in an arc overhead. It found meat, and the jaguar squealed. For a few seconds it ran in place on him, small half-absented jerks of its feet as if it were asleep and dreaming of a chase. Then it slumped sideways, and the machete fell from Meinong's hand. The whole struggle had taken only a few seconds.

"You lucky bastard," Trimble said behind him. "That was a fluke, you know that? A real slop shot. She should've had you for breakfast. She was strong as a subway train, considering she wasn't even fully grown. I found her maybe two years back when she was a baby. All alone in the forest. So I adopted her. I took her peepers out with a stick so she'd always rely on her loving foster daddy. Brought her up, fed her anything I didn't like to eat myself. I knew one day she'd come in useful. Then about a day and a half ago, I knocked her on the head and I tied her up so she couldn't eat. And right before I came to see you, I knocked her on the head again, untied her, buried her with her face in an armadillo nest so she'd have a little air but she couldn't dig herself out. By the time you got here she must've been hungry. Hungry and a little exacerbated about the situation."

Meinong tried to respond but found he couldn't speak. The dead jaguar, like a companionable house pet, still had its heavy tail draped over his thigh. As he lay there he felt no pain, just cold, and his well-intentioned heart was flushing more and more of his blood out of his body. The sensation was quite different from when he'd gargled that bullet: this was no emergency, there were no further measures to be taken. He wondered whether Trimble had ever really had those photographs of Emmeline Sapp in his possession; probably not.

"Now I just have to get free. Shouldn't take too long. Then, if you don't mind too much, I'll saw off your head and I'll take it back to camp and I'll . . ."

But then Trimble tailed off as three figures materialized soundlessly out of the trees.

To Meinong they looked just like the men who had shot dead the Erlösungfeld farmers during his pursuit through the jungle eleven years ago: Indians in khaki field trousers carrying bolt-action rifles. One of them had a crude sailorly tattoo on his bicep, showing off pouty lips and naked breasts and a pert bottom, except these parts did not belong to a human female but rather to some sort of anthropomorphic banana dressed in ruffled sleeves and an oversized bowl-like hat. "Good morning, fellas!" Trimble said, his voice not so confident now. "I can guess what you're wondering, and it's a doozy of a story." Two of the soldiers moved past Meinong, out of his diminishing field of vision, while the fruit-wench Indian kept his rifle trained on Trimble. There was some activity around the trumpet tree. "Thanks a million, my arms were sore as hell, and these ants!" Trimble said. "Listen, fellas, I think my bandage needs changing, so how about we—hey, fellas—now, if you'll just—hey—*hey*!" And the last thing Meinong heard before his consciousness trickled away forever was Trimble shouting as the three men dragged him off through the forest.

☙

"We were hoping to rescue you both from Herr Meinong," Burlingame said, "but I'm not sure that we can if he isn't here."

When Whelt and Coehorn emerged from the protective-custody hut, they found Burlingame's army milling around in a state of mild frustration and embarrassment. This morning around twenty of the Angelenos had armed themselves with bows and spears, hurrayed at a tremendously rousing St. Crispin's Day–type speech from Burlingame, and marched down to the New York camp to liberate the prisoners by force. But now there was nothing for them to do, and they were conscious of people staring.

"Well, it's very nice of you to go to the trouble all the same," said Coehorn in a rare access of good manners, the feud between the camps forgotten for the time being.

The suggestion that Meinong might have fled in terror at the Angelenos' approach had been tested for seaworthiness and regretfully discarded as untenable. As far as anyone could tell, he was simply truant. Of course, there were still plenty of men and women here who took orders from Meinong, but his unexplained absence must have interrupted the trance of their flunkeyism: as recently as last night it had seemed pivotal that Whelt and Coehorn should remain locked up, but today they found themselves unable to articulate the reasons why. As usual, Mac Parke could be everlastingly loyal to something only so long as it was dangled in front of his face. Having met so little resistance, the disappointed Angelenos asked one another: are we absolutely sure there isn't anything here that we can rescue from anyone?

But now more and more New Yorkers were mixing into the crowd in front of the protective-custody hut, and when Whelt noticed how they were looking at Burlingame, he realized that even if her war party had found itself redundant in one area, it had accomplished something quite unprecedented in another: barring a stupendous reassertion by Meinong, from this day forward the Englishwoman might have open to her the leadership of both of the camps at the temple.

"I almost feel I should apologize that we didn't come sooner," Burlingame told Coehorn. "I know you've been in there for a terribly long time."

"I certainly have. I felt every moment of the last seven years of captivity."

"Seven years?" Burlingame began. "But it was only—" and then, apparently thinking better of it, shut her mouth.

"I hope you recognize this as a historic occasion. Indeed, I can't help wishing our old friend Trimble were here with his reporter's notebook so he could immortalize in rough-hewn tabloid prose—" But when Coehorn saw Burlingame's expression it was his turn to tail off. "Anyway, the point is, Whelt and I have made an agreement about what to do with the temple."

"An agreement?" said Burlingame, astonished.

"Yes. We've come to a perfect understanding. Perhaps he'd better be the one to explain—he knows all the technical details."

In fact, the understanding was not quite perfect, because Whelt had kept one thing back from Coehorn. Eleven years ago, the gods inside the temple had, as a mere footnote, explained that Whelt was really Elias Coehorn Sr.'s son and that Elias Coehorn Jr. was really Arnold Spindler's son. Whelt had chosen not to reveal this to his stepbrother (a long and oblique "step," but he could think of no better word for the relation) because he feared the resultant emotional complications might prevent Coehorn from thinking calmly. Now, however, as the sun rose over what might be his last day as the director of *Hearts in Darkness*, he thought back to his very first. The mansion in Bel Air, dark and spooky and mazed from floor to ceiling with tatters of airship canvas, had been nothing more than a sound stage; its occupant, mellifluous and reeking and alop in the face, nothing more than an actor; the whole production mounted by Elias Coehorn Sr. to obliterate the reputation of a dead man while simultaneously preserving his occasional usefulness as an undead puppet. Or at least that was part of it; but it also seemed possible that, even as early as 1929, he might have dreamed of river damp in his vicuña-wool socks—that, unconsciously, he might have felt the temple's pull, might have seen madness in his future (because nobody was immune), and might have decided to expurge that madness from himself, to dump it somewhere far away like a few tons of coal spoil from one of Eastern Aggregate's mines, to use the false Spindler as a sin eater or Gadarene swine absorbing the madness on his behalf.

If so, Whelt's father had shown a farsightedness that Whelt himself hadn't matched. He had spent most of his first three decades compiling axioms for life, axioms that were supposed to be rational and self-sufficient, but he now believed that if you examined those schematics with a magnifying glass you would find nothing but the diagram, repeated over and over again in different transpositions. And later, with his scriptless film, he had attempted to break free, but wasn't the anarchy of that project just as reverent an offering to the temple as his original master plan? He had never told the story; the story had always told him. And he knew he still hadn't escaped it, because when he thought about what movie he wanted to make next, the idea that always came to him first was a movie about the shooting of a movie, not necessarily in the jungle but maybe in the salt flats or at the bottom of the ocean . . . Until the diagram was neutralized he couldn't know what movie he might want to make once free of its influence.

"We ought to talk about it in private," Whelt said. The three of them went back inside the protective-custody hut, despite Coehorn briefly insisting that he would sooner die than cross its threshold again.

". . . So we won't come to our senses until the diagram is gone," Whelt concluded, after repeating to Burlingame the explanation he'd given to Coehorn. "And we can't get rid of the diagram until we come to our senses. We'll never agree to disassemble the temple or reassemble it in its original form. But there is a way to give it a new shape, and this was Mr. Coehorn's suggestion. Imagine the two halves of the temple; now, turn one half upside down, and slide it across so it fits over the top of the other half. The two sets of steps lock together just like a zipper. You have a square cuboid two hundred feet high and two hundred feet wide and four hundred feet long. That's what we will construct." With a gesture to the open door of the hut he took in the felsenmeer of limestone that still defined the layout of the Eastern Aggregate camp, rocks on which the New Yorkers had run aground, the mess of their own unfinishing accommodated like geography. "Nobody gets what they want, meaning nobody has to let the other side win. The temple still can't be shipped to New York and the movie still can't be shot. Because of that, there shouldn't be any objections. And when the temple is cubed, when it's not in its current shape any more, the power of the diagram will be broken and we will no longer feel compelled to stay here. Until my discussion with Mr. Coehorn it never would have occurred to me to venture anything so perverse. But I think it's our only escape. And I think you're the only one who can persuade everybody. Nobody but you is so respected in both camps."

"I'm respected in both camps," said Coehorn.

"No, you aren't," said Burlingame.

"With Meinong missing, it's the perfect time," said Whelt. "A few days from now we could be free."

Burlingame didn't answer right away. Whelt watched her dispassionately, knowing he'd done all he could, which was not very much. Whatever she decided, it wouldn't be because of the strength of an argument. That was never the reason. When he was younger he'd put such faith in arguments, the logical deployment of the relevant facts of the case, as if those could be isolated without difficulty. You wade chest deep through a swamp without end and every so often you peel off whatever happens to be clinging to you and you call those the relevant facts.

Burlingame nodded. "We'll start today," she said.

When the soldiers brought Trimble into Atwater's quarters for his audience with the colonel, the room was so shadowy that he could make out only part of the figure on the bed, corpulent, bald-headed, smelling of slow death. The figure lifted a bowl to splash cool water on a face that was golden in the half-light, with puffy lips glistening as they formed the words "I expected someone like you" in a voice like malaria and nightmares. Trimble was too shaken to respond.

Then Colonel Atwater came in. "Ah, I see you've met my wife," he said. The figure on the bed mumbled something Trimble couldn't hear. "She thought you'd come to give her a lymphatic drainage massage. No, honey, this is the prisoner. The man from Tegucigalpa's been delayed a day or so." More mumbling. "Yes, he'll be Honduran. But he has a qualification. I'm sure his methods are sound." The colonel turned to Trimble. "Don't be alarmed. My wife's just going through a few, best way to say it, temporary metabolic side effects from a medicine called—tell me the name again, honey?"

"Theorozole," said Atwater's wife.

"What is it? Theoro . . ."

"Theorozole!" she repeated.

"It's for migraines."

"It's for sexual and emotional frigidity," slurred Atwater's wife. "They wanted to warm me up. I guess it worked."

"Our family doctor prescribed it. All aboveboard."

"It's untested. He has a college buddy at Apex Chemical who gave it to him in a pill bottle with no label."

"That's enough, honey." Turning back to his prisoner, the colonel waved at a camp chair. "Take a seat, Mr. Trimble."

Trimble sat down and his two escorts took up position behind him. For the last eighteen hours, since his abduction from the jungle at daybreak, he had been held under guard in a tent. And on the way there, a great easing of curiosity about the third camp in the forest, which he'd always been too cautious to come near. This one didn't have any rigid cabins like the camps at the temple, just khaki tents, though some of those were as large as marquees and all of them looked as if they could bear up in a storm. Also there were latrines, generators, lamps, radios, cookstoves, chainsaws, mosquito nets, and various other modern conveniences in good working order. He guessed about half of the soldiers at the camp were Pozkitos, but many others had lighter or darker skin, and he had noticed a few white officers who could have been American. The whole place had the atmosphere of bona fide military discipline that Meinong had never quite managed to bolt into place at the New York camp before his timely demise.

It had not been Trimble's intention to shed fingers last night. Certainly he'd expected Meinong to threaten him with violence if he didn't lead him to the (notional) extortion materials. But he hadn't planned on Meinong paying out some of that violence as an advance deposit.

Nor had he planned on being taken captive before he could make the most of his victory. Now Meinong was just a buffet for the forest and maybe nobody would ever know about it.

"I hope my boys have been giving you proper care for your injury," said Colonel Atwater. He was a packet of sinews, not much more than five feet tall, with thinning gray hair, and he spoke without variation in pitch or rhythm. "As you can see, I have some idea of what it's like to lose a part of your body you depend upon." He gestured at the black patch he wore over his right eye. "Souvenir of my army days."

"He beat a man to death in a beer hall in Stuttgart and that's what he got for his trouble," slurred his wife, splashing some more water over her head.

"We've been wanting to talk to you for a long while," Colonel Atwater said. "My boys made visual contact a few times, enough to be pretty sure you were the one picking up those airdrops in the forest. But they never could catch up with you, and they never could catch up with any of those airdrops, either—until that last one. We'd already fired on the airship and we saw the pilot jettison the weight not far from here. After we found the crate we opened it up and we found some"—he lifted the manila file—"best way to say it, puzzling photographs and a puzzling letter."

"For my husband those pictures were better than a nude cabaret," said Mrs. Atwater. "Close-ups of burns and welts on pale skin. A woman with dead eyes like you could do anything to her and she wouldn't complain. I'm surprised he didn't take them into the latrine with him."

Her husband looked pained. "Honey, I wish you . . ." He turned back to Trimble. "I'm posted overseas for so long sometimes that it's nice for us both when I can bring her out here for a little while."

"Since the Theorozole warmed me up he doesn't dare leave me unattended back in Washington. We've been married for twenty-four years and I know everything he's done and I'll tell anybody who asks."

"Now, honey—"

"Make him give me a massage."

"I told you, honey, he's not the masseur. He probably doesn't have a qualification." Colonel Atwater turned back to Trimble. "Do you have a qualification?" He didn't wait for an answer. "This letter says that under certain circumstances a woman named Emmeline Sapp could be allowed to leave a mental institution in Texas, where the conditions are not very, best way to say it, modern, judging from these photographs. Now, why was this material in the airdrop? Was there material like this in every airdrop? Who was responsible for these airdrops?"

"Give me back what's in that file and I'll tell you everything you want to know," Trimble said.

"I think you may have, best way to say it, misconstrued the nature of this conversation, Mr. Trimble. I work for the State Department—"

"He works for the Central Intelligence Agency," said Mrs. Atwater. "You'd better spill. He may talk like a furniture salesman but the only thing that gives him pleasure is causing pain. I bet he's jealous of whoever got to take those fingers off you."

"I don't think anything like that will be necessary," said the colonel.

"Oh, but he sure hopes it will be necessary," said his wife. "He prays to God, Santa Claus, and Eisenhower it will be necessary."

"Like I told you," Trimble said. "Let me have the file and I'll sing the whole songbook."

"Hold him," Colonel Atwater told one of the soldiers behind Trimble, who clamped down on Trimble's upper arms. Then he gave Trimble a punch in the gut hard enough to turn shit into diamonds. Trimble bowed his head, retching, until Atwater pushed his chin back up and walloped him twice across the face.

"Don't make me watch this again," said Mrs. Atwater. "Not if you're going to go all the way."

Trimble's cheekbone felt like it might be broken. "I'll tell you all about Emmeline Sapp for nothing," he said, in a voice as slushy as Mrs. Atwater's, "and then after that we can make a deal for the real hot cockles."

"What's a hot cockle, honey?" said the colonel. His wife mumbled something. "Me neither." He turned back to his interrogatee. "No deals, Mr. Trimble." He wound up for another punch.

"Sir?" An officer had come into the tent.

Atwater dropped his fist. "Just a moment," he said to Trimble, almost apologetically. He went over to confer with the officer in an undertone, and Trimble was surprised to make out a word that sounded a lot like "Burlingame." Mrs. Atwater and the metal frame of her camp bed groaned in chorus as she turned onto her side. Outside, Trimble could hear music playing from a tinny speaker, maybe some Honduran dance hall number.

"What's the Central Intelligence Agency?" he said. "Is that like Hoover's bureau?"

"No, a much better invention," said Mrs. Atwater, "because it exports so many of our assholes to other countries."

At last, Atwater came back to where Trimble sat bleeding from the mouth. "Our guy at the temple—"

"You've got a guy at the temple?" Trimble said. "An American?"

"Sure. We recruited him a long time ago. He keeps us up to date with what's going on over there." Trimble felt sick with indignation that somebody at the temple had the kind of secret you could display in the window at Tiffany's and he'd never heard about it. "We just got an urgent report from him. They're talking about putting it back together. Do you know anything about that?"

"You mean Whelt won?"

"No. For some reason they've decided to put it back together the wrong way. They're going to stack it up like a pallet of bricks. On Burlingame's initiative. This is what I'm told."

"He works for the CIA but he takes orders from the United Fruit Company," said Mrs. Atwater. "He was sent to take over this camp from the natives. They only train guerrillas to pay the electric bill. Really they're here to make sure nobody meddles with the temple. He doesn't know why. It tortures him that he doesn't know why. But back in Washington we get big hampers of mangoes and pineapples sent to the house."

"Actually, I'm just here as a, best way to say it, neutral observer," said Atwater, "and I can tell you that the United States has no policy of intervention in this region. All the same, there are good reasons why the temple ought to be kept how it is."

"I can help you with that," said Trimble. He understood how power flowed and pooled and cascaded over the temple steps, so it was no surprise to him that, with Meinong gone, Burlingame was bossier than ever. But he wasn't sure why she would give such a screwy order. "You just got to give me back what's in that file."

He explained that he only had to show the pictures and the letter to Gracie Calix, Burlingame's moll, and Calix would do anything he asked. And if Calix threatened to leave her lover over this pallet-of-bricks idea, Burlingame would drop it like a poisonous snake. You couldn't get to Burlingame by Trimble's usual method, a friendly exchange of favors. She was too much of a bluenose. But you could get to her through Calix, because, as Trimble saw it, Calix was like the magical Crown of Shambhala that the Imperator wore to battle evil on (the mention of the company had brought it straight back to him) the old *United Fruit Company Radio Hour.* Take it off and Burlingame would transform back into a frightened little nobody.

"But if I give you this file and let you go," Colonel Atwater said, "what's to stop you from just hightailing it?"

"Because you still got something I want," Trimble said.

"And what's that?"

"I want a job with your Central Intelligence Agency. I think it would suit me pretty fine."

Colonel Atwater took a cigar from a box on his desk, lit it, and puffed a couple of times. "You want a job."

"That's right."

Atwater raised his eyebrows, as if to say, stranger things have happened. "All right, it's a deal. I'll give you this file. Heck, I'll throw in a first-aid kit and a few cans of pork loaf. And if you can get Burlingame's sexual companion to talk her out of interfering with the temple, you have my word that afterward you will have a job waiting for you with the Central Intelligence Agency of the United States. Entry level, of course. But people move up fast." Trimble got to his feet and they shook on it like two men who hadn't just been on opposite ends of a beating. "I'd better warn you that if you can't manage it, I will probably have no option but to send my boys to, best way to say it, supervise things there for a while."

"One time he came back whistling from a mission like that," said Mrs. Atwater, "and he sat down with a pocketknife to get a stone out of the sole of his boot, but when it fell out, it wasn't a stone, it was a tooth. Another time I actually saw pictures. The convent in Bangassou. Some men have mistresses . . ."

"The men and women at the temple are American citizens and their safety is paramount. Good to meet you, Mr. Trimble."

"Tell him to give me a massage before he leaves. I can't wait any longer. My neck is full of fluid. These damned pills. It's impossible for words to describe what is necessary to those who do not know what Theorozole means."

"Honey, he doesn't have the fingers for it."

"I'd rather feel his bleeding nubs on my back than smell the reek of your socket the next time you take off your eye patch to get into bed with me."

"My socket emitted an odor only in the first few weeks after the injury and even then just intermittently," Colonel Atwater assured Trimble. His wife mumbled something. "That's hurtful, honey."

⌒⌒

November 5th, 1957

The Lovelinch Institute
3350 Sheldon Avenue
Dallas, TX
United States

My love,

    I never thought I'd write you another letter. The first time was the day I met Trimble & the last time was the day before Trimble left the camp. Now he's back & I'm writing you again. It figures I'd say because you're the opposite of him, he's you with a minus sign in front, Trimble walking this earth would be grounds to condemn the whole property like one of those plague houses in Galveston if you weren't walking it too to make up for him. So maybe before I even knew how bad he was I was already trying to set your blessing against his curse. But that's why it spins my eyes in my head to think of you tangled up with that man. I swear it shouldn't be possible, it doesn't make a lick of sense, I mean metaphysically speaking, him & you shouldn't be able to touch any more than noon can share a porch with night. But he found you. I don't know how but he found you.

    He was a shadow out of the rain when I was foraging.

Missing fingers, busted face. Both recent by the looks of it. I
don't know who did that to him but whoever it was I'd like to
shake his hand.

He showed me the pictures of you & when I saw them

Twenty years but I still recognize every part of you
like the sound of a voice. Do you know color pictures look
[illegible] now than they used to, I guess they came up
with a way to put in more colors. Well I wish they hadn't.
All those bruises. All those scalds. Too many colors. No
mercy in what those colors tell. Have they been doing that
to you these twenty years Emmy. All this time you've been
burning in hell. I swear I never knew you had it as bad as
that, I heard stories about some of those places, but I figured
your folks, my kin, they may not have half a heart between
them but they wouldn't let anything like that happen to their
Emmy. But it's my fault as much as it's theirs. I know that.

You're still so beautiful Emmy. More than in my memory
even.

All this time & I still don't like to talk to you about Joan.
It's not because I think you'll be jealous, I'm not such a fool
as that, not quite. It just feels like a discourtesy to both of
you. I do love her, I'll tell you that straight out. In bed one
night she asked if I loved her more than I loved you, but
I think only her tongue was still awake because she was
snoring before I'd pronounced a word on the matter & the
next day she said she didn't remember asking. But I lay there
thinking on it. Well what do you love the most, the air you
breathe or the lungs you were given to breath it with.

She might do it, that's the trouble. If I went to Joan & said
to her what Trimble asked me to say, that she's got to hang
up the cubing or I'll leave her, then she might do it, I really
think so. If she even heard that he had me in a fix, & there
was no way around it because this fix reaches all the way up
to Texas, she might go ahead & hang up the cubing without
my even asking. She's that good to me.

Oh Emmy I haven't even told you what the cubing is, I

haven't told you anything that's been going on, & there's so much to tell. Mr. Meinong's gone & we still haven't any idea what became of him except his machete was gone too, so he must have had some business in the forest, unless somebody went in his cabin & took them both but not the credit afterward. It was lucky for the New York folks that Joan was down there the next morning because they were so used to Mr. Meinong telling them what to do they needed reminding to breathe I'd say. Not to mention Mr. Coehorn out of his jail cell & acting like a gentleman, that might have been the biggest shock of all ha ha.

But we didn't have the leisure to get accustomed to it all because right away Joan & Mr. Coehorn & Mr. Whelt were telling us about the cubing. Joan reckons the cubing is the only way we can all get right in the head & I guess she's right because just hearing about it I felt righter in the head & we hadn't even started yet. Now everybody's pitching in. We're going to put the temple together again but together according to our own fancy this time & nobody else's. Joan's set on it & all hell couldn't stop her now.

All hell couldn't but one lady could, & that's your unfaithful correspondent. She's got one weakness & it's me & I never asked to be her weakness but I am. Eleven years back Trimble tried to bend me to his purposes & for a while I let him & I learned that nothing you do for that man is harmless, even the small things are evil, & the big things, they're the destruction of us all. When he wanted me to say Mr. Aldobrand had misused me I saw things clearly for the first time & I didn't do it & I'm glad I didn't. I don't know why he wants to stop the cubing now but I'm not going to help him. I'm going to call his bluff. You understand don't you Emmy.

But that means he won't spring you. If I say no to him it'll be like I had a chance to spring you right in front of me, easy, & I didn't take it. All this time I've lived with you on my conscience but after that. No. It doesn't bear contemplating. So I'll have to spring you myself.

I'll get you out Emmy, I'll do it with a shotgun if I have to. I'll come back to Texas & I'll find you & I'll get you out. I'm just sorry it took me so long. I ought to be grateful to Trimble I suppose, it sounds like a bad joke but first of all if he hadn't shown me those pictures I wouldn't have seen for myself the arrears I was in, & second he proved it isn't ever too late to come back & make good on your promises. It isn't crazy to wait all those years, or maybe it is crazy but crazy's better than giving up. I should have come for you with Lyndon's 12-gauge the same night they put you in, but I was just a raw little girl then, I didn't know how to do the least thing for myself. Now I've lived out here all this time & seen what a body can do if she only sets her mind to it.

It'll hurt Joan something [illegible]. I know it will & I'm sorry for that too. But she's too strong for the hurt to last. She was a sapling when I met her but now she's a kapok tree. I don't want to say goodbye to her face in case I change my mind. I'll leave her a note but I won't put Trimble's name in it. I don't want to set her thinking he might could fetch me back for her if she does what he says. One day I'll see her again & I'll explain. I'll tell her I was just trying to be as gutsy once as she is all the time.

I'll see you soon Emmy. Yours forever. Feels like we've been here forever already but don't you worry forever still isn't up so I'm still yours.

And like they say that's all she wrote.

Gracie

Vansaska here, yet again.

This morning Zonulet almost throttled Wilson after it turned out that O'Donnell's coffin was empty. I will not go into detail, because the events were along much the same lines as last night, when Zonulet almost throttled Wilson after it turned out that O'Donnell had died of hemorrhagic fever, except this time they were of a rather greater intensity and I had to go to rather greater lengths to talk Zonulet down. Wilson seemed sheepish, not because he admits any involvement in O'Donnell's continuing incorporeality—he does not, and I believe him—but only because a host of his breeding will always feel personally responsible if one of his guests should happen to find himself inconvenienced during his stay by a head cold or a forgotten shaving kit or an uncontrollable urge to commit a reckless murder in front of a number of witnesses.

Afterward, I thought we had better leave, and Zonulet agreed, but Wilson would not allow it. Instead, we all sat down in the drawing room of Le Sphinx and his housekeeper, Reyna, poured us all glasses of horchata, which looks like milk and tastes like chocolate. "I believe I may have grasped the situation at last," Wilson said. "I would not for a moment accuse you of dishonesty. But there may come a time in even the most upright fellow's life when, like King Cymbeline's daughter Imogen masquerading as a pageboy, he must 'disguise that, which, to appear itself, must not yet be, but by self-danger.' (Admittedly not the Bard's most tripsome lines.)"

"Would you start that again from the beginning?" said Zonulet.

"I think he's suggesting you're a woman dressed up as a man," I said.

"No—" said Wilson, although he did pause to give Zonulet a brief searching look, "no, I'm not suggesting that. I'm only suggesting that when I observed the agonies of grief with which you met the news of O'Donnell's passing I immediately twigged that you could not be who you say you are."

Zonulet met my eyes. I shrugged back at him, meaning: is there any use in keeping that ragged old cover story going after everything that's happened? "You've got me dead to rights, Wilson," Zonulet said. "I'm not a notary agent."

"I knew it!" said Wilson, shaking his fist in triumph.

"I am, or was, a case officer at the Central Intelligence Agency. A spy. I first came to San Esteban because I believed O'Donnell would know something about a secret training camp in the jungle. I am here now for similar but more complex reasons."

"Oh . . . ," said Wilson, crestfallen. "I was almost certain you were going to say you and O'Donnell were long-lost brothers. Exactly like in *Cymbeline*. 'You call'd me brother, when I was but your sister,' or brother again in this case, 'I you brothers,' but just one of them, 'when we were so indeed.'"

"But I'm not Irish."

"Separated at birth, I thought. That would have been bally exciting and Shakespearean. Anyway . . . it doesn't matter, of course," Wilson went on, trying to put a brave face on what was obviously a pretty significant disappointment. "Please go ahead."

"'In 1935,'" I said, "'Dr. Sidney Bridewall, a Cambridge University ethnologist, encountered REMOTER at the temple site during an expedition to Honduras.'" I could recite from memory the memorandum to the deputy director of intelligence because I had reread it so many times. "'REMOTER coerced Bridewall into arranging his passage to the United States, with the logistical support of Poyais O'Donnell, a fixer operating in San Esteban and Tegucigalpa.'"

"Who is this REMOTER?" said Wilson.

"That's just what we're trying to find out."

"Nineteen thirty-five was long before my time. That would have been under the Tussmann regime. But Reyna might well know something. She's Victoria, I'm just Gladstone." He spoke to the housekeeper in Spanish, and she replied, nodding. "She says she does recall the gentleman from Cambridge." Wilson asked her another question; this time, Reyna seemed hesitant, so Wilson encouraged her, and she gave a shy reply. Wilson thanked her, but then turned back to us with a smile of apology. "No use, I'm afraid. The local superstitions are always picturesque but just occasionally obstructive. She said—"

"It's all right, I speak Spanish," said Zonulet.

"I don't," I said. "What exactly did she say?"

Wilson continued: "She said that, on his return from the depths of the jungle, Dr. Bridewall brought with him *un espíritu*—a spirit— that he'd found at the end of the river. I've never heard of such a thing happening before. The river traders give offerings to the angry spirits of the rapids, but in my understanding those are more or less confined to their own parishes."

When I was in Puerto Penasco with my then husband in 1942, my stomach couldn't get used to the food, and each of my vomitings was preceded by a slow lifting sensation that was easy to mistake for a sort of giddiness or weightlessness brought on by love and lei-sure. I was in such stupid good spirits that it was not until the third or fourth time that I learned to stop enjoying that feeling. As I sat there listening to Wilson, I said to myself, you had better be quite sure that you are not mistaking for the thrill of revelation a shiver down your spine that is really only the rigor of some old decay inside you. You had better not welcome madness like the renewal of a gift. "Ask her about this spirit," I said.

Wilson gamely asked Reyna another question. "She says she doesn't know much more about the spirit," he reported, "she only knows that relations between Dr. Bridewall and the spirit were rather fraught, whereas after O'Donnell came on the scene, things were more businesslike."

And it was at this stage that it finally occurred to Wilson that between 1932 and 1939, Tussmann had kept a diary. "After he died I had every intention of mining his chronicle for pointers about the job but somehow I never quite got round to sitting down with it."

April 2nd
Dr. Bridewall, the English ethnologist, back from forest. Ran into him at Gonzales's. Looked about as sick and tired as any white man will when he gets back from being out there for too long. And he was drunk. But something queer in his eyes too.

"How was your expedition?" I said. Bridewall didn't answer question. Just said, "Everything I learned in church is a bloody lie. Everything I learned at school is a bloody lie. It's all a lie so you might as well just fuck for the rest of your life. There's noth-ing else worth doing. When I get back to England all I want to do is fuck. I'm going to tell everyone it's all right to fuck all the

time. And then I'll just fuck and fuck and fuck." Wouldn't say any more. Told him if he wanted spiritual counsel he could try the Coehorn Missionary Foundation station.

Yet again, French Bulldog Club of America Annual Hard Cover Treasury for 1934 is nowhere to be seen in mail delivery. Now three months late—the limit.

April 3rd

Last night, after I wrote here, Bridewall woke up P and me banging on consulate door. I went downstairs. By then he was even more fried. Could hardly understand him. "Please," he said, "you have to help me. It's waiting on the edge of the forest. It won't let me leave here until I find a way to get it to America." "Get what to America?" "I can't tell you. You won't understand." "If you refuse to tell me what you're talking about, I can't very well help you." "No," he said, "I don't suppose you can. I don't suppose anyone can." As he went away I shouted after him, "Have you asked O'Donnell about whatever it is? He can manage almost anything."

Thought about whether to write letter of complaint to French Bulldog Club of America or to postmaster general in Tegucigalpa. Who at fault? In the end decided to write to both. Got pretty worked up in letters.

April 4th

Late afternoon, ran into Bridewall at Gonzales's again. "It's in O'Donnell's storehouse on the riverbank," he said to me, as if I knew what he was talking about. "It's going to live there until O'Donnell can build a box big enough for it to travel in. Then he'll put the box on a truck and drive it to Trujillo and put it on a boat." Thought to myself, could Bridewall be smuggler of some kind? Or dealer in exotic animals? Doesn't seem type. Asked, "Did you have to pay O'Donnell for all this?" "O'Donnell will be rewarded for his work," he said. "But not by me."

Asked him to explain himself—hopeless. "When it leaves

here on that truck, it won't need me any more," he said. "It will release me. I'll be a free man again. But I'll never be able to forget what I've been through. I'll wish until the day I die that I'd never found that bloody temple." "What temple?" I said. "You mean some native shrine by the river?" As ever, Bridewall incapable of giving straight answer. "The next time an explorer comes through here, you must send them away," he said. "Don't let them go into the forest. Tell them there's nothing to find in the northeast. Better to just stay at home and fuck. Fuck and fuck and fuck. Nothing else means anything."

Afterward played poker. On way home went by O'Donnell's storehouse to have a look. Windows were covered and door was locked. Back at consulate, happened to mention letters of complaint to P. She told me Annual Treasury arrived weeks ago and she just shelved it with the others. Too late to retrieve letters of complaint from mail.

April 5th

Spent whole afternoon in drawing room reading French Bulldog Club of America Annual Hard Cover Treasury for 1934. Best number yet in my opinion, although pleasure inevitably tainted by embarrassment about letters. Have never longed for French bulldog so much. Must ask O'Donnell again if importation really still impossible next time I see him at Gonzales's—in which case will not mention Bridewall affair despite curiosity, don't want him to feel like I'm breathing down his neck about every little thing that happens in town.

But what is in that storeroom? What could be "living there"? What the hell did Bridewall bring out of the forest?

That was the last reference to Bridewall we could find in the crinkled pages of the diary.

"Very puzzling," said Wilson. "Very puzzling indeed. Tussmann never once mentioned anything to me about an interest in French bulldogs!" He chuckled. "I'm joking, of course. I realize that the other aspect, not the French bulldogs, is the pertinent one."

"I prefer his style to yours," I said to Zonulet. "Less flowery. More direct. If you wrote like this, your memoir would only take about an hour to read."

Later we sat in the shade at a table outside a cantina (not Gonzales's but a rival) eating fried fish and plantains. A stray cat nuzzled me with what seemed like great affection until I realized it just wanted me to itch a crusty purple sore inside its ear, but since I had already got so much out of the relationship I did not feel I could refuse without exposing myself as flighty and selfish.

"Bridewall went inside the temple and inhaled the spores and saw visions just like me," Zonulet said.

"So what did he bring back from the jungle?"

"Maybe nothing. Or maybe a stone idol he thought was talking to him, like a Babylonian. Come on. You can't seriously think . . ."

Once again, I recited the agency memo, substituting only one of the words. "'In 1935 Dr. Sidney Bridewall encountered a Mayan god at the temple site during an expedition to Honduras. The god coerced Bridewall into arranging his passage to the United States, with the logistical support of Poyais O'Donnell.' The ship arrives in New York, and the god asks somebody, who is the most powerful man in this region? The god is told Elias Coehorn Sr., founder-chairman of Eastern Aggregate. Soon afterward, Coehorn Sr. comes to believe he's receiving direct instructions from the Lord himself. REMOTER has infiltrated his mind somehow. In 1938, he obligingly sends two expeditions to Honduras, timed to arrive at the same time. He thinks he's testing his sons against each other to see which one will inherit his empire. He doesn't realize that he's been manipulated by REMOTER into arranging for the creation of the diagram."

"Oh, sure, the diagram," said Zonulet. "*A Secret Philosophy of the Whole of Things, Geometrically Demonstrated.* Working title for a book Leibniz was afraid to finish."

I had learned many of these details about Coehorn Sr. from reading the freshest pages of Zonulet's manuscript. Which made my exertions as an investigative reporter seem almost like a waste of time. But really they were not a waste of time. Because for so many years they were all I had. "At first Coehorn doesn't expect the test to last more than a few weeks, but even after years have gone by he refuses to step in," I continued. "And meanwhile Phibbs and the Eastern Aggregate Good Conduct Division—and maybe other divisions and subsidiaries we don't even know about—are making sure that anybody who asks 'Whatever happened to my cousin who got a job on a movie called *Hearts in Darkness*?' can't get any answers. Remember, the exact location of the temple was never made public. We know Adela Thoisy's family hired a search party to go into the jungle. But they never came back. There were probably others looking. But it must have been hard to get any publicity after the war started, and in the end I guess they gave up hope, or at least they ran out of avenues to pursue. Next: 'According to O'Donnell, the Mayan god took up residence in Red Hook, Brooklyn. Apart from that, nothing is known about the Mayan god's activities in the interim period before Branch 9 first made contact with him in 1953. As a sweetener during negotiations with United Fruit, Branch 9 installed the Mayan god in a residential suite at the Waldorf-Astoria in Manhattan.' "

"Which is where this story passes from the merely cockamamie into night-blooming dementia praecox," Zonulet said. "You think Branch 9 and United Fruit held a summit in New York with a . . . shit, I can't even bring myself to say it."

"A god." I threw the head of my fish on the ground for the cat to clean. "Why not?"

"What would the god get out of it?"

"The CIA signs on as a partner in the Pozkito training camp. Keeps it running at full strength. Makes sure the jungle is always lousy with guerrillas. So no outsiders can ever get close enough to the half temple to disrupt the diagram it's become."

"I wish I'd never let you in on the diagram. So the gods got their night watchmen. What about the secular parties to this deal?"

"Why do primitive people pray to gods?" I said.

"I don't know . . . Rain? Good harvests?"

"You're on the right track. From around 1954, United Fruit's banana plantations in and around Honduras were immune to white sigatoka and nobody could understand why. Who arranged that for them? Who has power over something like that?"

Zonulet shook his head. "If only Bev Pomutz were here to put a decisive end to this snipe hunt."

"You said United Fruit can go to the State Department any time they like and engage the CIA to do some troubleshooting in Central America. So they say to Branch 9, 'We have a problem and we think you could help us solve it.'"

"And Branch 9 say, 'Sure, we've had lots of experience bargaining with gods. I'm sure we can get this leaf blight taken care of.'"

"The CIA is full of veterans from the OSS. They went all over the world during the war. Mount Ararat and the Caroline Islands and the South Pole and who knows where else. They must have come across a few things."

"Vansaska, you are hallucinating by proxy. The only reason anybody ever mentioned gods or spirits is because the argyrophage inside the temple makes people see things—"

"Some of which are authentically clairvoyant. Your competing fungus-related theory is the sober and sensible alternative?"

Zonulet did not know what to say to that.

He had hardly slept since Tegucigalpa so after we paid for our lunch we went up to the room that had been made up for us at Le Sphinx. It was bare of decoration, but in the top drawer of the dresser I found a few things that might have been stashed inside upon the departure of a former occupant: the brass handle, engraved with arabesques, of a feather fan with no feathers attached; the skull of a small horned animal I could not identify, as polished as the brass was dull; and a celluloid cigarette case painted with cherry blossoms and, on one side, the words "THE BLACK SHIPS." The latter did not make sense to me until I remembered it was the title of an old Hollywood melodrama about the Convention of Kanagawa. This was the sort of trinket that might have been handed out at a studio party; perhaps it had been carried from Hollywood to San Esteban in the pocket of one of the *Hearts in Darkness* crew. I put everything back in the drawer. Then, a few minutes after I sat down to begin the account of the day's events that I am now attempting to finish—

and this is the last time I intend to deface Zonulet's manuscript—I noticed he was lying on the canopy bed with his eyes wide open and an expression on his face like a naked person regarding very cold water.

"Aren't you tired?"

"Every time I fall sleep—every time since I licked the fungus off the film I brought home from the warehouse—I have that dream again. Where the interrogator's telling me I'm just an OSI research liaison at Apex Chemical and it's time for my unilateral gradatorectomy."

There are few sights that arouse in me a greater sympathy than the exhausted unable to sleep. I took off my shoes and lay down behind him, my arm across his chest. I thought it might help. But then he turned over, or I turned him over, I am not sure which, and before long we were making love again, quietly, because even in a whorehouse I did not like to be heard through the walls. Since this morning he had washed only his face at a basin and I found grave dirt in his chest hair and between his toes. The less charitable side of me said that if there was to be anything like romance between us the only grounds could be that each of us was chronically unfit for the company of anyone else. But perhaps there are no finer grounds than that.

Afterward, as we lay side by side, the poor guy probably thought he was safe.

"What exactly are you looking for in that warehouse?" I said. "You think there's something in Whelt's footage that will confirm what you told the tribunal. Prove to them that your story is true. Prove to them that you were 'acting in the best interests of [your] country.' But I don't understand what that could possibly be."

"Let me sleep," he muttered. "I've got a beautiful dreamless sleep coming on. I can feel it."

"Are you looking for anything at all?"

"Why the hell would I spend every day in that goddamn warehouse if I wasn't looking for something?"

"When you went out for hamburgers, and you let me go through your mail . . . I looked in your desk, too. I found an official letter.

From the sounds of it, if you are willing to sign a two-page statement, the CIA will cancel your tribunal. You'll be discharged with a full pension. The whole thing will be over. You won't have to live in Springfield any more. But you've been refusing to sign."

Zonulet didn't meet my eye. "You ransacked my desk?"

"Nobody is keeping you in that warehouse but you. You talk about it like you're chained up in a dungeon but you've committed yourself voluntarily. You must know that nothing you find there is going to be of any use. And nobody's forcing you to subject yourself to fifty thousand hours of footage. But you're insisting on it. You're so damn stubborn. That must be why Branch 9 tried to hoax you into thinking you might have gone crazy and murdered that girl. They don't want this tribunal to drag on any longer. They don't want you going through that evidence. All they want is for you to drop the whole thing and walk away."

"That statement they want me to sign is a lie. If you read it you'd think nothing happened worth remembering. I'm going to tell the tribunal the truth."

"Classified proceedings in a closed courtroom. You'll be telling the truth to a handful of people who already know and don't especially care. And in any case, the tribunal will never begin because you'll never make it through all the evidence. You're not doing it for the tribunal. You don't need the tribunal. You've already sentenced yourself. This is a penance, isn't it?"

For the flight to Tegucigalpa I brought with me Zonulet's old Scribner's edition of Leibniz. Zonulet brings the old Saxon up so often that I thought if I read it I might get a little insight into his thinking. I found a passage underlined in which Leibniz says that "every mind is like a world apart, independent of every other created thing, expressing the infinite, expressing the universe. So every mind is as eternal and absolute as the universe itself." To Leibniz I suppose that was a description of the glory of the soul. To me, at least in certain moods, it is a description of a hell to which we are all condemned. I promise I did not scheme in advance to ambush Zonulet when he was at his most vulnerable—postcoital, dog tired, fanned by a breeze on which every scent was reminiscent of a former life—but I felt I might never have a better chance to persuade him to confide in me. And yet before he could say anything more, I found, quite without warning, that I was the one who was sobbing.

"What's wrong, sweetheart?" he said.

"Will we ever be free of it?" I said. "Will we ever be free of the temple?"

ͼͻ

I don't believe Vansaska's story about REMOTER. But I do believe that a god could be borne unseen over the hills like an emperor in a palanquin, because two years ago I may have seen it happen, not with a god of the Mayans but with a god of Manhattan . . .

That day I looked down on the jungle through the window of a railroad car. For many years the car had plied the Caracas–Valencia line at the pleasure of the Venezuelan oil baron Julio Méndez, but it was now suspended on steel cables between two Sikorsky S-56 cargo helicopters as they flew south toward the temple. Even though the fulsome use of onyx, mother of pearl, tortoiseshell celluloid, and other such materials by Méndez's decorators gave the entire car a sort of congelated or membranous atmosphere, it was certainly cushier than riding up in the helicopters with the Good Conduct Division (or, for that matter, in a thermal airship). However, the car had been partitioned into two sections, and I knew it wasn't just for the benefit of the three passengers in the fore section—myself, Phibbs, and Colby Droulhiole—that these first-class accommodations had been specially imported from Caracas to Trujillo.

"What's the other cabin for?" I said to Phibbs. We were about 250 feet above the ground, moving at about 150 knots, and the wind buffeted us like a baby in a stork's sling, but it wasn't any worse than a ship at sea.

Phibbs's reply cannot be adequately transcribed. Though polite, it was an answer so evasive it transcended human language.

"Is it to bring back the Coehorn boy?"

Once again, Phibbs demurred.

I rose from my couch and walked over to the wooden partition.

"Can I take a look?" But before I could reach for the handle, Phibbs had inserted himself between me and the door, shaking his head apologetically.

So far, I had only one theory about what it was that Phibbs didn't want me to see in the aft section of the railroad car. But the theory was almost too preposterous to entertain.

Although I wasn't airsick, I took an airsickness mint from a bowl on the sideboard, and went over to join Colby Droulhiole. This was his third time flying, and his worship of the window was as fervent as ever, which didn't surprise me—to be capable of drawing a map like the one he'd drawn for me, a kid had to have a mind built for the top-down view. He would have been an asset to the 2nd Photo Tech Squadron, or, no doubt, to the Soviet satellite photography program that in a roundabout fashion had made his presence here possible. His other two flights had been in four-seater planes from Tegucigalpa to the Isla de Pinos (nineteen months ago) and from the Isla de Pinos back down to Trujillo (three days ago). In the fishing village I'd left behind a bewildered and bewasted boy; when I returned to fetch him, I found him healthy, strong, a good swimmer, fluent in Spanish, in love with a fisherman's daughter, but still, on some fundamental level, paralyzed by confusion, as if he would never, ever get over the shock of seeing the world beyond the temple.

"How are you holding up, kid?" I said. "Are you looking forward to seeing your old friends? Probably your mother?" I knew that the gutty drone of the helicopters' approach would already have reached the temple, a subliminal anxiety until it crossed the threshold of consciousness as an uncanny, unidentifiable sound, a fear without object, like madness. "They'll all be proud of you. You did what they sent you to do. You got word back to America. But keep in mind that right now you're working for me. You know this turf better than any of us. We'll need your assistance."

Instead of answering, Droulhiole just pointed out the window at something. From a mile away, it wasn't much more than a moth hole in a sweater; but as the helicopters ate up the green distance, I realized I was looking at a sizable gap in the canopy.

This gap, it transpired, had been made by a team of loggers with chainsaws who had trekked into the forest a few weeks previously in order to clear a landing zone for us, far enough from the temple that their work wouldn't be noticed, close enough that we wouldn't have far to go on foot ourselves. In this respect, as in every other, Phibbs's preparations had been extraordinarily thorough. The two helicopters lowered our railroad car gently to the ground and then landed on either side. For a moment I hoped Phibbs might leave the car first so I would have a chance to try the door of the partition, but of course he waited until Droulhiole and I were out before stepping down himself.

I knew that Eastern Aggregate had suspended the Good Conduct Division's recruitment during the war, and afterward, when corporate goon squads had become an anachronism, dissolved it entirely. Sure enough, most of the twenty men who came out of the helicopters were at least as old as I was—lots of scars, lots of displaced cartilage, but in pretty fine form nevertheless, because calisthenics and clean living were both strictly compulsory in the division.

I also knew, however, that the guy who climbed into Colby Droulhiole's bedroom in San Esteban was too young to have earned his stripes in the twenties and thirties, which meant that Eastern Aggregate hadn't entirely forsaken what you might call the business of practical solutions. Sure enough, a few of the men were younger, leaner, frostier in the eyes.

Scarlet petals, blown by the rotors from the orchids that bloomed in the treetops, were still fluttering down around us. I noticed that the steam-bath air didn't seem to affect Phibbs at all, and for Droulhiole it must have felt like home. Machetes and carbines were handed out—the latter only as deterrents against anybody with a bow and arrow—followed by powdered sulfur so we could dust our clothes against insects. The windows of the aft section of the railroad car were occluded by silk drapes, and when Phibbs wasn't looking, I stretched on tiptoes to press my ear against the glass. I heard a thrum like a generator running, which hadn't been audible in flight.

We set off. And for what happened next, while our party was hacking through the jungle toward the temple, there was nobody but me to blame.

From the day I met Colby Droulhiole, he had seemed so guile-less, so pliant, that I just never stopped to worry he might cross me. Also, I was distracted, thinking about what was to come. Later, the helicopters were going to make a series of round trips to Trujillo, to transport, first, all surviving members of the 1938 Eastern Aggre-gate expedition; second, any items I wished to collect from the site on behalf of the United States government; and, third, once they'd supervised all that, the returning Good Conduct Division squad. In a matter of days, the silver armor would be back in Washington. I would have all the fungus I needed. From then on, I wouldn't just visit the aleph from time to time—I would live in the aleph. Omni-scient, I would be ready to correct the destinies of 1. myself, 2. the agency, 3. the nation, and perhaps 4. the world. On the question of 5. the inhabitants of the temple, I felt I was merely hastening the inevi-table. Sooner or later, they would be discovered, no matter what I did.

That was what was going through my mind when Droulhiole suddenly took off running into the trees.

I went after him, with three of the division men at my back. But he was too quick. The forest swallowed him up. We never had a chance.

〰

"I'm glad you're here, Mr. Trimble, because I've been wanting to talk to you. We had a deal. I gave you that file relating to the lady in the mental institution in Dallas, and you were going to use it—

"Let me finish, please. You were going to use the file to, best way to say it, torpedo this initiative of Burlingame's to stack the temple up, but our guy there says there's been no cessation of activity in that—

"Please let me finish, Mr. Trimble. If you keep on interrupting, well, you remember how our conversation got off to a, best way to say it, uncivil start last time, and I don't want to be uncivil to you again. As I was saying—

"I'm sorry I had to do that, but you've got to learn to let a guy finish the point he's trying to—

"You are testing my patience, Mr. Trimble.

"And who the heck is Colby Droulhiole?

"A little while ago I sent out a patrol to see if they could find out anything more about those helicopters we heard to the northeast. Are you sure this kid didn't just come across my boys and mistake them for somebody else?

"So if this kid had to hightail it all the way to the temple with his report, and then you had to hightail it here, does that mean that by now these men might be—?

"What was Burlingame's reaction?

"And you heard all this yourself?

"I see. You've got yourself quite a skill there, Mr. Trimble. Tends to be just the deaf-and-dumb category who are good at that, especially from a distance. Well, you have my thanks. Like I told you, I sent out a patrol, but they aren't back yet and all this is news to me.

"That's exactly what I'm going to do. The intentions of this faction are still, best way to say it, dubious, and I have a responsibility to ensure the safety of the men and women at the temple. Brace up. We'll move out right away.

"With all due respect, I don't care whether or not it's your 'slice of pie.' I want you with me. You know the temple and the people there a lot better than I do.

"Do you—

"Do you want to—

"Like I told you, Mr. Trimble, you've really got to learn to let a guy finish. As I was saying: do you want to come along to the temple on your own two feet, or do you want me to put a hook through this and drag you behind me?"

☙

"We've just got to make ourselves scarce," said Coehorn. "Leave them to hash it out between themselves. After all, that's what they did with us."

Burlingame stood beside him at the very top of the temple, both of them looking down at the clearing. On each side, armed men were visible at the tree line; on their right were the soldiers from the Pozkito training camp, some native and some foreign, dressed in khaki fatigues, recognizable to anyone who'd had the hairy experience of spying a patrol through the trees when foraging too far to the southwest; on their left, the newcomers from Eastern Aggregate, all Caucasian, dressed in safari suits. The two parties stood glaring at each other across the two hundred feet of the New York camp, or at least glaring in each other's direction, because even though dozens of limestone blocks had now been shifted in preparation for the cubing of the temple, there weren't many clear lines of sight between the huts and lean-tos. This spangle of unfamiliar eyes, scores of them looking in, made the day feel dreamlike to the temple's denizens (not least to Irma, who over the years had offered a number of extravagant pledges to the Catholic God of her youth "if just once more in my life He sent me a man in uniform—but, good grief," she'd exclaimed earlier today, "I daren't even imagine what He must expect in return for all this"). In recent times, the question of why nobody from the outside world ever turned up to relieve the two camps had, on the whole, ceased to be asked—it no longer seemed to hold much force or relevance—but now the outside world had arrived in a flood. Above, the huge noon blue was paled by a haze so exquisitely thin and even that it could have been a single drop of rain spread across the entire sky.

Burlingame shook her head. "We're not leaving."

"If they start shooting, and we're in the middle, it'll be like the Owl's Head Pier massacre."

"We're not leaving."

Coehorn looked at her. Until the last few days they'd scarcely ever spoken, but they were finding, like so many others, that having lived in such close adjacency for so long was almost as good as having known each other for all that time. "Joan, I know it's been a tumultuous week, but you must take a good hard look at things."

"I have."

In fact, Burlingame's thinking had never been so lucid. Gracie was gone, and she had left a note that professed love and regret but gave no real explanation for her departure. Perhaps one would normally expect to find oneself a bit distracted by this mystifying and incredible event, a bit overcome by this inversion of everything that had seemed most dependable and congruent in life. The heart could sometimes yaw the head. But in practice that was not the case. This catastrophe was like an acid, the strongest acid in the universe, effortlessly reducing all that it touched to nothing but a scummy black residue, which was the true form of most things, Burlingame now understood. After the acid flowed through, however, there were still a few solid remnants, undamaged, shining cleaner than ever after their rinse. And one of those was the temple, which the men and women here had possessed for nineteen years, and possessed still, with Burlingame as their undisputed leader. They had not gone through everything they had gone through just so they could relinquish their self-determination to thugs with rifles. Nothing was more important than that they held firm. She was almost relieved by Gracie's departure, because without that annihilating caustic wash she might not have had such a perfect and untarnished comprehension of their circumstances.

Less than an hour earlier, Colby Droulhiole had come running into the camp. Burlingame had always joined in with the optimism when people discussed his return from America, but she hadn't honestly expected ever to see the boy again. The original logic of his dispatch—that he was innocent of longing for civilized comforts and therefore would not be diverted from his mission by them—had not struck her as very robust. But now here he was, back in the arms of his bawling mother, after more than eighteen months away. And he had urgent news, which included an explanation for that throb in the distance unlike any airplane remembered from the old days. By now the Eastern Aggregate Company had become a mere abstraction, a mere ancestry, like a dead empire honored only in toponymy and legalese, but today, at last, here were the actual masters of the New York camp, in stern formation, as if they'd come not to rescue but to resubjugate their colony. As soon as word spread, most people had what seemed to Burlingame the correct instinct: they took up bows and spears, calling to mind either (if they were New Yorkers)

the training that Meinong had given them or (if they were Angelenos) the spirit of the valiant rescue mission that never quite happened. They didn't expect to fight but they were determined to man
their borders. Only later, when the arrival of the Eastern Aggregate
men was quite soon followed by the arrival of the guerrillas opposite, was there talk of quitting the field entirely.

"We'll fight if we have to," Burlingame said. "This is our temple.
Why would we have stayed here for two decades if we were just
going to give it up as soon as a few bullies came along?"

"We don't have to give it up for good. We just have to get out of
the way. Where's Whelt? He'd tell you the same."

"He's down there filming."

Coehorn shaded his eyes to look for Whelt. "Oh. I thought he
might have kicked that habit after his epiphany about the diagram
but I suppose this is too much for him to ignore." He stiffened, seeing something else. "My God, that's Phibbs! My father's assistant!
It's really him! Just the sight makes me feel queasy!" Two babies
were wailing from opposite corners of the New York camp, each filling the other's silences, as if debating which of them was in the most
unendurable torment. Up the steps came Rick Halloran, carrying the
megaphone. Coehorn thanked him. "I asked Rick to bring this up
to us as soon as he found it. You've got to make an announcement."

Burlingame reflexively accepted the megaphone, but she did not
raise it. "There's no need. Everyone already knows we won't budge."

"We will budge. We must budge. Tell everybody to scatter. Please.
You were the only one who could make everyone listen about the
cubing and you're probably the only one who can make everyone
listen now. Joan, for God's sake, can't you see what an apocalyptic
juncture we have reached when I am the one who's here in front of
you arguing the case for pragmatism?"

Burlingame was thinking of eleven years ago, when she had stood
high on these steps with the megaphone in her hand and called for
Trimble's censure. She had saved the temple from him, and that
night love had touched her for the first time. Now love had wisped
away, had perhaps been a sort of trick all along, but the temple was

as solid as ever, and once again it was time to save it, to shoulder the responsibility of defending everything they had worked for. "We'll fight if we have to," she repeated.

Coehorn sighed in exasperation. "All right. If you won't do it, I will. Let's see if they'll listen to me."

He grabbed for the megaphone. Burlingame, suddenly furious, swung it at him like a weapon, so he had to jerk his head back. "Get your hands off it! You don't deserve to say a word to my camps! All you have ever been is a filthy, lazy, greedy—"

But she was interrupted by the shooting.

༄

Ever since my first sight of them across the clearing, I was braced for the first shot, and when it finally came I was down on my belly before I even knew I'd heard it. During the standoff, each of the two squads had sent scouts edging along the tree line around the clearing, trying to gain some ground on their counterparts. Then the scouts must have met somewhere around the midpoint. And just one reckless bullet was like a lit match to a reel of nitrate film. By the time I'd wriggled behind a kapok trunk, the shots were coming in a fusillade from both directions.

I raised my carbine and leaned out an inch from behind my cover, ready to return fire. But I couldn't find a target because most of the guerrillas were still on the other side of the clearing. Shooting at them would mean shooting right across the New York camp. Which was out of the question.

And yet that was exactly what everybody else was doing.

Before it started, there had been a few dozen men and women and children standing out in the open. Some had hunting bows and now they were returning fire as best they could. The rest were rushing into their huts to shelter behind walls of mud and wood and thatch that even in triplicate wouldn't have stopped a .308 round. My fungal clairvoyance, even more than my actual visit here, had supplied me with an eidetic blueprint of the camp, but that had been rendered out of date by the removal of the numbered limestone blocks that might previously have offered some real defense.

I saw one archer get hit in the chest while she had her bow drawn, and as she collapsed to the ground her cane arrow soared into the air like an essence loosed from the body at the moment of death. For the time being the Angelenos up on the steps were safe, but both squads could be expected to send flanking parties to circle around the ruin, and from then on the battlefield would include at least its lower levels. "Stop shooting!" I shouted. "Stop fucking shooting!" But nobody was listening.

I looked around for Phibbs. He'd advanced into the clearing and was now firing from behind a cabin. I dropped my rifle and sprinted toward him, keeping my head low.

"Phibbs!" I pounded on his shoulder. "Tell them to stop!"

"I'm sorry, Mr. Zonulet"—he fired—"but the Eastern Aggregate Company must protect its assets."

Indeed. We all had our missions. I was prepared, if necessary, to spill blood to get my hands on that armor inside the temple. But I was not prepared to spill innocent blood, American blood, not so much of it, not in this witless shambles. I took out my pistol, held it to the back of Phibbs's head, cocked it so he'd hear the click through his skull bone. "Tell your men to stop firing and fall back, or I'll kill you right here."

Phibbs gurgled and slumped over. My hip stung.

I hadn't pulled the trigger. A rifle bullet had cored his Adam's apple, grazing my side on the way out. I'd been preempted. He was dead.

Before dropping prone again, I took a hurried look around. A year earlier, when I'd first set eyes on the outpost in daylight, I'd felt respect for the supralogical tenacity with which these émigrés had devoted themselves to their cause, but now it revealed itself to me as sheer cultic folly. I saw an arrow cut down a man in fatigues and heard a whoop of triumph afterward. But there was nothing to whoop for. At the start, the archers defending the camp had been little more than bystanders yearning to be acknowledged, but by

this point they'd been honored with full participation in the proceedings, meaning the soldiers were actually firing right at them
instead of just letting them catch a few stray rounds. I didn't know
how many others might already lie bleeding inside the perforated
huts. The crossfire was only getting more intense. And with nobody
to call off the carnage, the Good Conduct Division would keep at it,
like the fingers still twitching on Phibbs's left hand.

But then I caught sight of Jawbone Atwater, moving along the
foot of the temple, no more than sixty feet away.

I shouldn't have taken off running. But maybe I sensed something, a tunnel of good luck, a negative cyclone, a transect of time
and space where the bullets wouldn't be, like the line you can draw
through the absences in a stack of classified files. Madness, really.
No better than these templars. But I did run, and I did not get shot.
Instead, I tackled Atwater from the side, hard enough that his rifle
flew from his hands as he sprawled to the dirt.

I kneeled on top of him, pointing my Browning between his eye
and his eye patch. "Zonulet?" he said. "What the hell are you doing
here?" We hadn't seen each other in almost a decade.

With my free hand I found his holster, pulled out his sidearm,
and tossed it behind me. "Order your men to stop firing and fall
back. You'd goddamned better do as I tell you because the last guy
who said no to me is dead." A little misleading but technically true.

"Who are you working for nowadays? These guys in bush jack-
ets?"

There was an explosion on the other side of the temple. "Christ,
you're using grenades?" I said. "Do you know how many civilians
live up on those steps?" But I knew it was no use warning Atwater
about casualties. Quite the opposite. For Atwater, pits full of corpses
were like silos full of grain, a harvest that secured the future. He
lived for casualties. So instead I jammed the barrel of my pistol into
his good eye, not quite hard enough to pop his cornea. "End this or
I will restore your symmetry, you fucking rabid dwarf."

Something landed behind me. I glanced back and saw a human
hand, singed at the wrist. At that moment I felt something enter my

body. I looked down. Atwater had pushed a combat knife into my flank, right up to the hilt. Seven inches, give or take.

While I was contemplating this surprise, he jerked his head out from under my gun, then threw off my weight. I collapsed sideways. He got up, stamped on my wrist so I let go of my pistol, picked it up, and aimed it down at me. "I've known you a long time, Zonulet, and, believe me, I will take no pleasure in this, best way to say it—"

A man-sized object flattened him.

Not a man-sized object, in fact, but an actual man. An actual man had fallen out of the sky, a brown-skinned soldier with a spear through him. And Atwater wasn't actually flattened, but he was on the ground, under the actual man, and neither of them was moving. I looked at the severed hand again, and then up at the temple, but from this angle, against the glare of the sun, I couldn't make out anything going on at the top. "Miracles always conform to the general order," wrote Leibniz in the *Metaphysics,* "even though they cannot be foreseen by the reasoning of any created mind."

The knife inside me felt white-hot and effervescent. I didn't pull it out, because that would only uncork my heart blood. Instead, I began crawling toward the tree line. I wasn't thinking about my safety, I was only thinking that there was one last possibility of ending this—a remote possibility, a ludicrous possibility, but it was all I had left. Nearby I could hear a woman screaming. She was dying or her child was dying, it could have been either one.

A year earlier, on a come-down from the argyrophage, I'd tap-danced my way from the interior of the temple to the threshold of Wilson's consulate without ever quite waking up. Now, by force of will, I tried to enter the same state, just for a little while. It wasn't easy. The universe orbited my body and my body orbited the knife. With every motion I was making the injury worse, cranking the edge around in my guts. It wasn't exactly a yogic situation. But I knew that in principle I was capable of turning over command to the instincts I'd honed for twenty years instead of my mewling and distractible consciousness, of becoming the shark in the depths instead of the "confused murmurings of innumerable waves" on the surface.

And as I squirmed through the alleys between the cabins, I did enter a vigorous kind of trance, where I no longer had to force every action or cringe at every stimulus.

Only when I reached the shade of the forest did I lose momentum, because my trance was profaned by a conscious thought. Plainly the wisest thing for me to do, now that I had a few big trees between me and the firefight, was to rest here, cradle my wound, wait for one of the Good Conduct Division men to come along and help me.

But I hadn't observed any exodus from the temple. Therefore those imbeciles were still there, stubborn unto death. None of this was part of the plan. They weren't meant to be dying. There wasn't meant to be a fight. We weren't meant to have seen our expedition mirrored across the clearing when we arrived at the temple, just like the bad timing that had started all this twenty years ago. I had to regain some sort of control over events. So I hauled myself to my feet and submerged myself in the trance again so I could carry on into the jungle, following the route we'd cleared with machetes this morning.

Nature was so rapacious out here that when I arrived at the other clearing I half-expected to find the railroad car and the cargo helicopters already rusted, overgrown, converted into microhabitats. But in fact I scared off only a single topazine hummingbird from the car as I staggered inside. All that movement had torn up the seal around the knife, and by now blood had saturated my shirt on that side. For a moment my legs went weak and, groping at the sideboard for support, I scattered the airsickness mints across the parquet floor. Almost there now.

I tried the door of the wooden partition, but it was locked, of course. Pressing my ear to it once again, I could still hear that thrum, as of a generator. I had so little strength left. Once, twice, three times I banged on the door with my fist. Each strike, in some obscurely Newtonian fashion, made a shattering impact on my own body but little to none on the door.

"Mr. Coehorn?" I shouted, leaning against it. "Are you in there?"

Elias Coehorn Sr. would now be eighty-six years old. His passing had never been announced, but the tradition of privacy and composure and remove at the highest levels of the Eastern Aggregate Company might have rejected even a death notice as undesirable publicity. Even if he was still alive and compos mentis, it was utterly absurd to imagine the old emperor sweating in the tropics with the rest of us. The world came to Elias Coehorn Sr. (when permitted), not the other way around; that was how it had been for decades.

And yet, ever since Colby Droulhiole and I had rendezvoused with Phibbs at the airfield outside Trujillo, it had been obvious Phibbs was keeping something from me. The operation had some kind of shadow annex, a major surplus of activity and materiel, all of which had converged, by zero hour, on the curtained half of the railroad car. Was it possible that Elias Coehorn Sr. might have come here in person to collect his wayward son? That he might recline just a few feet away within an electric womb of air conditioners and dehumidifiers and life-support machinery?

"Mr. Coehorn, if you're there . . . A gunfight has broken out at the temple site. A lot of people are dead already, including Phibbs. I don't know where your son is, but the longer this goes on, the worse his chances." What a tragedy for Coehorn Jr., I thought, if he came so close to the reckoning with his father that he had deserved for so long, but never actually got it. "Somebody needs to tell the Good Conduct Division guys to retreat, but they only take orders from the executives. Mr. Coehorn, if you're listening . . . Is there anything you can do? Is there anything . . ."

I passed out.

∽

What Trimble knew about the Owl's Head Pier massacre that very few other people did—because back in 1937 he'd been told he'd be force-fed his own "greasy nuts" if so much as a hint of it got into the *Mirror*—was that it was the cops who had tricked the heads of two rival crime syndicates into arriving simultaneously that night, retinued, twitchy, each expecting to negotiate the purchase of a small ex-navy submarine from a Turkish arms dealer. By a wild exchange of tommy-gun fire, the population of mobsters in New York City was duly reduced. But so was the population of black-tie revelers who happened to be streaming onto the pier after an engine fire aboard the *Golden Goblin* had resulted in the emergency termination of their pleasure cruise. Which was why the cops were afterward a mite bashful about their gambit.

These events were the inspiration for Trimble's latest prank. They came straight to mind as he spied on Colby Droulhiole warning Burlingame that the Eastern Aggregate party was bearing down on the temple. If he could pass the news on to Atwater fast enough, then Atwater would arrive in full force before these newcomers had a chance to get themselves properly established at the site. The subsequent dispute was unlikely to stop at raised voices. And maybe, just as an incidental matter, a few of Trimble's auld acquaintances would finally collect what was coming to them.

He hadn't planned to watch it happen. If the temple was in range of his opera glasses, then Trimble would be in range of a bullet. Better to stroll over the next day and see what was left of the camps. He had assumed that Atwater would be grateful for the tip-off—and he was grateful, sure, but not *that* grateful, not overflowing with the "What can I possibly do to repay you?" type of gratitude—a little discourteous, actually, in the sense that he forced Trimble to come along at gunpoint, which was not convenient for Trimble at all. So on the march through the jungle, Trimble was looking for any opportunity to escape. And after the shooting started, he was looking even harder. The trouble was, Atwater had given his soldiers an order: "If you see him try to run, don't even bother telling him to stop. Just put him down like a dog."

But then Atwater ordered five men to climb to the top of the temple so they could snipe at the enemy from above and call down observations in the whistle code they used to communicate in the jungle. And Trimble volunteered to go with them.

No, he hadn't wanted to come along today; but now that he was here, the chance to watch from the best seats in the house as, one after another, his onetime pals felt the consequences of treating him so shabbily—that was just too good to pass up. There was a hell of a lot of shooting, but although the first few shots had made his breath catch and his hands tremble and his ears ring, the noise didn't bother him any more. It was the music of his prank coming off perfectly.

The five men—two Pozkitos and three younger Guyanans—rushed the steps. Trimble scrambled to keep up. Many of the Angelenos had gone down to join the fight on the ground, but others were still among their cabins, so the soldiers wheeled around as they moved up the temple, covering every direction with their battle rifles, firing at anyone who even reached for a bow or a spear. They climbed so fast they were at the top of the steps before any real defense could be organized. A nice testimonial for Atwater's training camp.

Burlingame stood alone on the upper terrace, the megaphone at her feet.

To the soldiers, she was only an unarmed woman, so they motioned at her to move aside. But Burlingame just stared at Trimble, unmoving. Wheezing from the ascent, he watched a series of expressions pass across her face: shock, to start with, which was understandable, because they hadn't seen each other for eleven years, and this was the first time she was finding out that he'd never quit the neighborhood; then some sort of understanding, using her trusty old feminine intuition—"You had a hand in all this, didn't you?" she said. "You wanted this," and he grinned back at her; succeeded by a further understanding, which seemed almost too much for her to bear, like all of a sudden she could feel something big and furry and six-legged moving inside her—"Gracie . . . ," she said, although by now one of the Guyanans was forcing her down to the ground, "Gracie wouldn't have left like that unless you had something to do with—"; and last of all an expression that made it clear she was not going to be a good sport about this, an expression, to tell the truth, that gave Trimble the chills like no expression ever had in a lifetime of playing pranks. Fortunately for him, she was on her knees, powerless.

Except the soldiers no longer looked quite as composed. Trimble, turning, saw that a lot of Angelenos were now approaching up the steps, at least twenty, enough that even with a rifle you couldn't be absolutely sure of firing fast enough to drop them all before they tore you to shreds, which was just what they seemed ready to do. "You got the queen, fellas," he warned, "and now the ants are after you." He expected the soldiers to shoot into the mob to scare them off.

Instead, one of them took a hand grenade from his belt and unpinned it and tossed it down the steps.

While it was still rolling, Rick Halloran jumped on top of it.

Most of the others probably wouldn't have known a pineapple grenade from an actual pineapple. But Halloran had served in Europe during the Great War after lying about his age. Trimble remembered that biographical detail just as the first assistant director erupted into gobbets.

For just a moment, the mob faltered in astonishment. But then they came pelting up the stairs even faster. They were spattered with Halloran's blood, and they had their mouths open like they were shouting, but after the blast Trimble couldn't hear anything. He moved behind the soldiers for protection. But there was something frantic in their motions now as they fired shot after shot. They were starting to get rattled. So was Trimble.

Then a thrown spear hit one of the soldiers in the shoulder and spun him around so hard that he pirouetted off the edge of the temple.

Burlingame, unattended, brained another one with the megaphone, and he dropped his rifle. She looked like she was going to come for Trimble next, and there was nowhere for him to run.

Down the entire length of the steps ran the wooden haulage ramp, constructed by Rusk in '39 and used daily ever since. Trimble threw himself onto the ramp as if it were the Bowery Slide at Coney Island.

He went down headfirst, straight past the mob—fast—already too fast—and not only too fast but too askew, because he was slipping diagonally toward the edge and in a few more seconds he'd fly off the side of the temple. So he jerked himself in the other direction, but he overcompensated, and came rolling off the ramp right about where the grenade had minced Halloran.

He'd succeeded in looping around behind the mob. But some of them had turned around and raised their spears, and he wasn't sure he could pick himself up and take off running before he was harpooned. Beside him, he saw a crack in the steps, a foot wide. The grenade had blasted straight through the limestone. He flopped sideways into the crack.

After that he was sliding again. The temple must have been more of a badger's den than they'd ever realized, because this chute wasn't anywhere near the one where Calix had found the silver armor and Whelt had "met the gods," but it was taking him deep inside the ruin. When his hip smashed into a wall, and he hoped he might have reached the bottom, it was actually just a dogleg, and he went tumbling in the other direction, now in total darkness. He tried to slow himself but the limestone was too smooth under his palms. If the haulage ramp had been like the Bowery Slide at Coney Island, this was more like the Down & Out Tube that was famous for making kids cry.

At last, the slope evened out, and he came to rest, only a little bruised. Cursing the Mayans, he gasped for breath. But what filled his lungs was fuzzier than air. He got a taste in his mouth like soil and truck exhaust. And then he could see again, but not with his eyes.

The first thing he sees is his own death from a heart attack, in a few minutes' time, because a human nervous system cannot stand this for long. His body stiffens, his skin turns blue, his sperm die like dogs in a locked basement. In this humid air he froths down to a skeleton in less than three weeks. He lies undiscovered until, about a year later, the temple's disassembly is completed at last, and the workers make no distinction between these young bones and those of a dozen Mayans who have rested here all along.

Trimble sees all this, and it's such a pity. Such a waste. He couldn't have picked a worse time to die. Because he has what he's always wanted. He sees everything.

He sees everything that has ever happened on this site and everything that ever will happen. He sees construction halt for almost a year after the architect, having been accused of conspiring with the enemies of Lord Kak Tiliw Chan Chaak, is tortured to death, and no qualified replacement can be found. He sees an airplane flying overhead, dowsing the forest with concentrated beams of light to trace the outlines of the small city that once surrounded the temple. He sees Professor Sidney Bridewall bursting into song from sheer joy after he first sets eyes on the ruin. He sees an eight-foot salamander with an upset stomach vomiting up half-digested chunks of a commensurately monstrous caterpillar. He sees a documentary maker talking to her husband back in Lisbon, promising him they will be able to pay back all the money she's borrowed, even though in her heart she has lost faith that the doomed *Hearts in Darkness* shoot is anything more than a myth.

And of course he sees everything that happened in the two camps. He sees things he didn't know about even when he was at the apex of his power, even when it seemed like a person couldn't murmur a word into their pillow at night without him finding out about it. He sees scoops, hot cockles, a thousand front pages for the *Pozkito Enquirer* that slipped by him. He wants to kick himself when he sees all that.

Yet he is happy, too, happier than he's ever been, because he knows so much. He sees New York too, everything he was ever curious about there, every sin, venal and mortal, of every "extremely private person," every secret that ever made someone say to themselves, "Thank God this will go to the grave with me." He sees Arnold Spindler's affair with Ada Coehorn, and Elias Coehorn Sr.'s rape of Arnold Spindler's wife, and the two sons, the bastard and the cuckoo. If only he could have put this stuff in the gossip column of the *Evening Mirror*. What a story.

But for the first time Trimble realizes that maybe deep down he never cared all that much about ink on paper, at least not for its own sake—that maybe newspapers were only a useful racket for opening doors, cozying up to sources, rewarding the cooperative and punishing the rest, so you could find out more, know more, know what others didn't, which is all that matters in the end, even more than getting even. He may have only a couple more minutes to live, but it's not a pity after all, it's not a waste, because somehow it's time enough for all the gossip in the universe, now and forever. He's in paradise.

☙

I don't want to write any more. But Vansaska is forcing me. She says it would be an ugly place to stop, both for my subjects—arrested in their "thrilling interval of weightlessness or flight"—and for myself. She says it's my sense of that day as the end of the story, the end of the world, that has made me turn away from the future. But it really was the end, in at least three respects. Great steel shutters came slamming down, with me on one side and the temple on the other.

First: the fungus won't take me any further. When I sat at my desk and licked that strip of silvered cellulose, I saw everything that took place between my first visit to the temple and my second. But beyond the second, very little. I don't know what happened to those people after November 1957. The film melts inside a jammed projector.

Second: on the most mundane level, the temple became unreachable. In my present state of health a long trek through the jungle would be a death march, and regrettably I didn't bring an airship home with me from the agency the way some guys hang on to their service pistols when they retire. Furthermore, I can pull no strings from a distance. Once, I dreamed of tinkering in the fates of sovereign nations, but now even a couple acres of clearing in the middle of nowhere is vastly beyond my powers. Compared to the old Zonulet, I'm a quintuple amputee—hands, feet, and dick—and I knew it the instant I woke up in that hospital bed in Panama. The clean sheets and white walls and hushed conferral were a mortification to my senses because they told me it was over.

About a week had gone by since I lost consciousness in the railroad car. I never learned who found me there and saved my life, but I assume it must have been one of the surviving Good Conduct Division men. Meanwhile, somebody in Atwater's camp climbed a tree with an antenna so they could radio a report of the battle to the CIA station in Tegucigalpa. That report was passed on to Washington, where it caused quite some consternation. Choppers were dispatched from Howard Air Force Base at the southern end of the Canal Zone, and that night I was evacuated.

The cleanup operation snowballed until it was at least twice the size of *Hearts in Darkness,* with coordination courtesy of Branch 9 and supplies courtesy of the State Department. Atwater's camp was razed. The corpses at the temple were zipped up into rubberized canvas bags. The rushes of the movie were doused with Halorite 1219 and sent back to Virginia. But at the time I didn't know any of this, because although I begged the nurses to bring me a telephone so I could call up somebody, anybody, who might be able to tell me what had happened, they'd been instructed to keep me isolated. I couldn't even crawl out of bed because my stitches hurt too much. That was the beginning of my afterlife.

Those were the first two reasons to regard that day in November as a definitive end. And the third, I explained to Vansaska, was that it would be a moral obscenity if I were ever to set foot at the site again. "They died because of me and I'd be walking on their graves. It would be an insult to them to go back there."

"They didn't die because of you," she said.

"They did. I wanted that armor so much I brought twenty men with guns to the temple and I didn't care what it might lead to." She tried to reply and I held up a hand to stop her. "Last year I sat in my apartment and I listened to the radio while Cuba fell to Castro. Cuba. My Cuba. Do you know what that felt like? That made a mockery of everything I ever worked for. That was real hara-kiri material. You could listen to a hundred guys' life stories in a row and you wouldn't hear a dereliction as shameful as that. But it was nothing—absolutely nothing—compared to how I fucked up at the temple."

"You never wanted anyone to die. Trimble did. It wouldn't have happened without him. He was always the one pushing, pushing, pushing, until it all went over the edge. That's perfectly clear from your 'memoir.' "

"But I'm to blame for Trimble too," I said. "I supported him at the end. I kept him strong. I brought him those pictures. It all comes back to me."

"You tried to stop it."

"And I couldn't. Because I'd created a situation that nobody could stop. Vansaska, I know you're trying to be nice to me, but it doesn't make me feel any better, all right? You can argue the technicalities all you like, but if you read in the paper about some other guy who did what I did and you didn't happen to know this guy personally you'd think he was the scum of the earth. Those people died because of me. Any putz could see I can never, ever go back."

And yet we were talking about going back.

Lately, the Pozkito hinterlands had undergone a series of convulsions. At the beginning of 1958, United Fruit's banana plantations in Central America suffered the most apocalyptic outbreak of white sigatoka the industry had ever seen. Tens of millions of banana plants were lost to a contagion that made their leaves crumble like cinders (more gray than white, really). To make up for the shortfall in revenues, the company was forced to sell off most of the uncultivated land it had bought cheap in Honduras in anticipation of rising demand in the United States. The major buyer was the logging tycoon Wilfredo Nazar, a close ally of the deposed former president Juan Manuel Gálvez. Nazar, finally able to consolidate his holdings in the forests of the northeast, embarked on the construction of the industrial railroad from the cordilleras to the Río Patuca that had been his ambition ever since, as a boy, he read of this plenteous but "untraversable," and therefore unexploited, territory. He hired hundreds of workers to prepare the route (a few of them, most likely, veterans of the guerrilla-training camp). At long last, and without ceremony, the other half of the temple was disassembled.

But Nazar's monumental project, which began at such a remarkable pace, was no less expeditious in its collapse. In less than a year he was found to have badly overextended himself. He couldn't pay any more wages. Tools were set down, and workers returned from the jungle with tales of mismanagement and disease and ancient, cursed, unfellable trees. Others did not return, but chose to stay and plant crops on acreage that Nazar had paid them to clear. The fiasco had still been on the inside pages of the newspapers when Vansaska and I arrived in Tegucigalpa. Nazar was claiming his own accountants had lied to him. His accountants were claiming that he sometimes scourged them with a bullwhip when they brought him bad news.

Regardless, the upshot was that when you disembarked from the boat that had borne you up the relevant tributary of the Río Patuca toward the concrete dam beneath the hills, it was now possible to hire a mule from a farmer and ride the rest of the way to the temple site over something resembling a track, without serious fear of ambush from the Pozkitos who were no longer training mercenaries nearby. The neighborhood had really changed.

We were sitting, once again, outside the cantina with the pussy pussycat when Vansaska said, "I want to go to the temple. We've come so far. Why not?"

I told her exactly why not. I warmed up with the practical reasons: decrepitude on my part, inexperience on hers, better men than you and I have not returned alive, etc. The trouble was that Nazar's frontiersmen had eased the situation. After that I moved on fleetly to the judicial reasons: how would it look to the tribunal if I not only fled the state of Virginia but actually returned to the scene of the crime? The trouble was that Vansaska knew I didn't really care about the tribunal any more. So I climaxed with the moral reasons. That was a pretty unfamiliar field for me, a field in which I could only be regarded as an amateur, as if I'd taken up the piano late in life. But the moral reasons did the trick.

"I don't agree with you," she said. "But it's not my place to overrule you. I just hope you remember when it was the other way around. When you were trying to convince me to take the cure. Go to the jungle, breathe the air, drink the water, get a new lease on life. But I was too low to listen."

"I remember."

It was time to leave San Esteban. Although I felt such fond nostalgia for all the happy days I'd passed in this wonderful burg that I practically wept to tear myself away from the place, our business here was concluded. We were walking back to Le Sphinx to say our goodbyes to Wilson when Vansaska said, "If you don't believe in the Mayan gods, then you don't believe in the diagram."

"No."

"You don't believe the diagram was the trap. The trap that caught Whelt, Coehorn, you, me, everybody. That kept hold of all of us for years."

"I shouldn't be on that list," I said. "I never even heard of the place until '56." I had got myself into one of those cycles where every time you wipe the sweat from your eyes it just makes them sting worse.

"Yes, you did. In '38. At that meeting in Bev's office, remember? Trimble was there too. And over the next eighteen years you made it as far down as Havana. The right bearing, and only a few hundred miles to go."

"Listen here—"

Vansaska waved me off. "All right, all right. So you weren't consciously aware of the temple until '56. You weren't consciously moving closer to it. But after '56 you were as enthralled as the rest of us. Why? Why did it have that power? Why were we so compliant? The temple brought us nothing but madness. Why didn't we try to escape? There was nothing stopping us. If the diagram wasn't bending our wills toward the temple, why did we make so little effort to get away from it?"

"Maybe madness was just what we wanted," I said. "We'd been hankering for it all our lives and the temple gave it to us and we loved it for that." I stopped walking. Vansaska overshot me by a few paces before she stopped too and turned back. We were observed by a woman who was bleeding turtles dry for cooking by stringing them up from nails hammered into the timber of an unfinished frame house; they swung in the breeze like the leaders of some thwarted reptilian coup.

"What is it?" Vansaska said.

As I spoke, I had come to a realization, one that was unwelcome but unavoidable. In the ranking of potential trespasses, failures, and negligences that still lay in my future, a new disfavorite had asserted itself. If I was to be quartered like a regicide by my obligations, one horse had pulled decisively ahead. I sighed. "You've got to see it, sweetheart. After everything that's happened, you've got to see it. It's not there any more, but I think if you stand in the right place you'll see it all the same. We'll go. I'll take you."

"A few minutes ago you were talking like it would be a crime to go back there."

"Yes. It will be. For me. A dirty crime. But I'm not going to make you go home without seeing the temple just so I can tell myself I'm keeping clean. I won't be as selfish as that."

So we went up the river.

Hiring a diesel boat was like hiring a truck, meaning we got both the vessel and a local skipper who knew the route better than I did. We set off northeast with enough fuel and provisions for a round trip to the temple site, which I estimated would take ten to twelve days. I felt no excitement about heading back into the jungle, but Vansaska was seeing it all for the first time: the villages that sloped amphibiously into the shallows where most of the fishing and washing and playing was done; flashes of color among the houses, a printed calico dress or a spectacular heap of cashew apples or a Coca-Cola emblem torn from an old carton and pasted up on a wall; the traffic on this great boulevard, canoes and alligators and tucuxi dolphins and sometimes horses forced to swim from bank to bank; later, no villages, just abandoned grass huts and clay ovens, or once in a while a prospector's cottage snarled up in rusting barbed wire; and later no huts, just white-faced monkeys swinging from tree to tree as they followed the boat, and flamingoes squatting over their nests, and toads the size of boxing gloves; and trees almost slipping off the bank like a crowd pressed up to the edge of a subway platform.

"So how do you like the jungle?" I asked on the morning of the second day. Vansaska glared at me because she knew I was making fun of her: for about the first ninety minutes of the voyage she had been an eager tourist, pointing out every novelty on the shore, scribbling notes in her diary, but quite soon her spirits had wilted, and since then she had almost entirely narrowed her purview to the fragile microclimatic intersection of her sun hat, her hand fan, and her mosquito net. Last night, at the camp we'd pitched, she'd been kept awake past dawn by noises in the trees.

"I do not like it as much as perhaps I thought I was going to like it," she answered me primly.

Twice on the banks I saw blocks of limestone, one propping up a jetty, the other diverting a waterfall, and I knew where they'd come from because under their coats of moss I could make out not only carvings but also, the second time, what I thought was a painted serial number. From the Mayan cities to Nazar's railway, from Erlösungfeld to San Esteban, all human attacks on the jungle would eventually falter, and the wounds would eventually heal; but sometimes the shrapnel still itched under the skin.

After six days we came to the last navigable stretch of the tributary before the dam kinked its course. We tied up the boat and disembarked. These days the dam was leaky, and the basin Whelt had mined for rock salt was now a swamp, but a few spars of the *Hearts in Darkness* steamer could still be seen poking up out of the brown water. Vansaska stood staring at them for several minutes before we continued. From then on, her vigor was restored. She was tired and filthy and sunburned and bug-ravished and she had an irritation in her left armpit that was almost certainly fungal, but it might as well have been her wedding day.

Our skipper made enquiries with the farmer we found tending plots of maize and cassava nearby. As advertised, a mule was available; and, without much interest, as if it were a busy afternoon at the rental counter and he was quoting me the standard terms, the farmer pointed at my watch, which he wanted not as a deposit but as a day rate. I was ready to haggle but Vansaska was simply too impatient. "We'll walk," she said.

"I don't know if that's a good idea."

"I'll carry you myself if I have to."

We left our skipper drinking cacao with the farmer and set off east into the forest. Apparently the track ran directly to the temple site, unlike the circuitous routes of the past, and it proved to be generous enough in width that no machete was necessary to rip open a corridor (although, because it had been cleared with axes and saws, not bulldozers, you had to watch your footing if you didn't want to trip on a tree stump or a snake burrow). Back toward the dam, the undergrowth had been a crisper and more radiant green, but here it seemed wet and bruised and aromatic as if it had been ground into the earth by an enormous pestle.

"After all this is over I want to go live in a place where I'll never see another tree again in my life," I said. "Some sort of tundra. Not a desert—you might think you're safe at first, but you never know when you're going to run into an oasis."

But Vansaska had another subject to bring up. "You still don't know if Elias Coehorn Sr. was in the other half of that railroad car."

"No."

"What if it was empty all along?"

"They wouldn't have taken the trouble to install it just to leave it empty."

"You were going to bring back the armor," she said. "What if Phibbs was going to bring something back too? Back to New York. Apart from Coehorn Jr."

"Like what?"

"United Fruit got a lot of use out of the Mayan god they parleyed with in New York. There were more of those gods inside the temple. What if Eastern Aggregate thought they could—"

"No more theories," I said.

"What if they thought they could go to the temple and bring back another one of the—"

"I said no more theories! It's too late for more theories."

After that we didn't speak for a while. But then, over the sifting and popping and nagging and burping of the forest, we heard the sound of a jazz band.

Vansaska looked at me. We picked up our pace until we were practically running along the track, and I forgot I was weak. I almost believed we would emerge into the clearing and find the two expeditions just arriving for the first time, the temple and its claimants reborn like the world after Ragnarök, because the eternity they spent there could never come to a definite end . . .

What we saw instead was even stranger.

There were thirteen of them in the clearing. Eight from the Hollywood camp, five from the New York camp. Meeting somebody in real life who you already know from your hallucinations—sure, that's nice enough, but it is nowhere near as exciting as meeting somebody in real life who you already know from the movies. During the six months I spent mold gardening in Trujillo, I generally avoided the town's only movie house because of the lice in the seats, but one night I got so bored I decided to brave it. When I bought my ticket I learned that rather than the scheduled *Showdown at Abilene*, which hadn't arrived from the distributor, they were showing a twenty-two-year-old print of a Kingdom Pictures comedy called *Fat Chance*. One entire reel was missing, and the rest looked like something a pack of dogs had chewed on, but it was nonetheless a pretty good picture, especially the supporting performances from George Aldobrand and Adela Thoisy, both still on the cusp of stardom in 1935. I'd always liked them both. And now here they were in front of me.

They each wore an animal skin of a different kind. Aldobrand's was a loincloth of banded fur, whereas Thoisy's was the same Revillon Frères mink she'd kept with her ever since she left Hollywood, draped across the shoulders of a tattery sisal dress that was older than the loincloth but not as old as the stole. Even now, it was startling to see Aldobrand's ruined face, the mask of gnarled, waxy scar tissue, collapsed cheeks and no upper lip and not much of a nose. But it was not as startling as the look in the eyes of these survivors, Aldobrand and Thoisy and the four-piece band (with gourd drums and a deer-femur flute and an old dented trumpet and a singer clicking her fingers) and all the others here. The look was bright and cheerful and camera ready.

"Greetings!" said Aldobrand in the Americanized accent he used onscreen. "Who might you two be?"

Another actor stepped forward, whom I recognized but couldn't quite name, which made me wonder if the memories I'd assimilated from the fungus were finally beginning to blur like any other memories. Perhaps writing it all down here, sending it off to the archives, has hastened that. "My name's Coutts!" the actor said. "This is my sister Marla, she's come with this fellow to fetch me home, but I can tell you I'm not going anywhere! New York's a real yawner compared to the tropics!"

"What is he talking about?" Vansaska whispered to me.

"Don't you remember *Hearts in Darkness*?" I whispered back. "The movie Whelt was supposed to make?"

"I've got to get my silly old brother back to New York so he can give me away at my wedding!" said Thoisy. "There's a tradition in our family that it has to be the brother who gives away the bride, otherwise the marriage won't last six months!"

"Where were you when they cleared a path to the river and took the temple apart?" I said.

"Yes, we played a few games of hide-and-seek with those locals!" said the actor playing Coutts. "There were some pretty close calls, believe me! Not easy running a nightspot in the jungle, you know! But when they left, we all just came back and carried on! The good times never stop around here!"

The rest of us had fled outward through the layers of adaptation and aboutness, telling a story about a story about a story, thinking it would keep us safe from the pull of the river. But these people had gone in the opposite direction. They had barricaded themselves inside the original story, bricking up the Fourth Wall along with all the doors and all the windows.

"The next round of cocktails is on its way!" said Thoisy. "In the meantime, won't you join us for a trot?"

Vansaska and I exchanged a glance. In the circumstances it would have felt perverse, even spiteful, to turn the invitation down. "What's the fashionable dance here?" she said.

"The Half Doodle, of course!"

"I haven't danced the Half Doodle in twenty years," Vansaska told me. "But I think I remember it."

So we put down our hats and I took her in my arms and we danced, cheek to clammy cheek, where the temple had once stood. Our shoes dragged a little in the grass, but the ground beneath was perfectly flat, as if all along the real purpose of the temple had been to level out an eventual dance floor. "I'm glad we came here," Vansaska said.

"So am I."

"We had to. So it could be over. Really over. So we could be free. We're free now. Can you feel it? I really think we're finally free."

"Yes," I said. "I feel it. We're finally free of the temple."

The band played on, discordant but in fine rhythm. My feet still remembered the Half Doodle, the steps I must have learned in some Broadway nightclub from some girl I'd just met, so long ago.

Up and across and up and across and up and across—and all the way back down . . .

Up and across and up and across and up and across—and all the way back down . . .

ACKNOWLEDGMENTS

For their comments on the first draft, thank you to Allison Devereux, Ben Eastham, Courtney Maum, Edmund Gordon, Jonathan McAloon, J. W. McCormack, Kiloran Campbell, Onur Teymur, and Spencer Matheson. For hospitality and inspiration, thank you to Beatrice Monti della Corte and everyone at Santa Maddalena; Alex Gerson, Matteo Zevi, and everyone on the Land Art Road Trip; and the Literature team at the British Council. For all their hard work on my behalf, thank you, as always, to Jane Finigan, Juliet Mahoney, Felicity Rubinstein, and everyone at Lutyens & Rubinstein; David Forrer and everyone at Inkwell; Drummond Moir and everyone at Sceptre; and Gary Fisketjon and everyone at Knopf.

A NOTE ABOUT THE AUTHOR

Ned Beauman was born in 1985 and studied philosophy at the University of Cambridge. In 2013 he was included on *Granta*'s list of the twenty Best British Novelists Under 40, and his work has been translated into more than ten languages. He lives in London.

A NOTE ABOUT THE TYPE

ITC Slimbach is the work of California calligrapher and type designer Robert Slimbach. Inspired in part by German fonts and Hermann Zapf, Slimbach created a "contemporary text font with a progressive look," combining clean serif shapes with the warmth of calligraphic forms.

Typeset by Scribe, Philadelphia, Pennsylvania

Printed and bound by Berryville Graphics,
Berryville, Virginia

Designed by Betty Lew